ROCKS, LOGS
and
CONCRETE BLOCKS

AJ LENNOX

Zeta Publishing

Ocala, FL

Zeta Publishing, Inc
3850 SE 58th Ave
Ocala, FL 34480
www.zetapublishing.com

This is a work of fiction. All of the characters, names, incidents, organizations, and dialogue in this novel are either the products of the author's imagination or are used fictitiously.

Ordering Information:
Quantity sales. Special discounts are available on quantity purchases by corporations, associations, and others. For details, contact the publisher at the address above.
Orders by U.S. trade bookstores and wholesalers. Please contact Zeta Publishing: Tel: (352) 694-2553; Fax: (352) 694-1791 or visit www. zetapublishing.com

Rev. Date: Jan 2018

ISBN: 978-1-947191-58-7 (sc)
ISBN: 978-1-947191-59-4 (e)

Library of Congress: 2017964632
Printed in the United States of America

Table of Contents

Foreword

"Rocks, Logs and Concrete Blocks" presented in fictional form, is factual; basically biographical, containing requisite changes of proper names and some locations, in the interest of protecting the innocence and/or guilt of persons living and/or deceased. The period encompassing the late 1800's through 1940 has been reconstructed from documents and oral family history related by individuals having personal memories of events.

Beginning with 1941 material is derived from the author's own experiences and memory. Some more painful elements have been purposely omitted; however, all events herein described occurred in the life of "Ariel" as they are set forth; not masked in political correctness or politeness.

We as humans encounter numerous rocks, logs and concrete blocks in our lives; some positive and others negative. While it is impossible to avoid all such encounters, we always have choices as to response.

That Ariel's parents both had mental problems is undisputed: one a diagnosed, committed, conditionally released manic depressive of that era (n/k/a bi-polar); and one undiagnosed, but plainly evidencing both paranoia and schizophrenia.

It was into this environment an only child was born; largely isolated from peers, dearly loved and cherished by one parent, possibly dear to, but consistently criticized by the other. An interesting, challenging and puzzling childhood environment at best. Any timidly posed question went, for the most part, unanswered. Could, or even should, she find answers. Did any exist?

Rocks, all around us on open ground and pathways, sometimes teach us to walk more carefully and watch where we are going, rather than wildly run unheedingly. We skip flat ones across ponds and lakes; pretty ones discovered are sometimes saved; larger pieces may become garden paths, walls, border pathways, encircle flower beds or construct landscape features; possibilities are endless. Some we stumble over, fall onto, inadvertently drop on our feet, or are even thrown, out of idle boredom, amusement, or even in anger.

Logs may lie prone on forest floors, their branches flattened, needles or leaves dry; eventually succumbing to moss and new growth, becoming soil as they decay. Trees hewn to logs become firewood and sources of heat and cooking; are sawn and planed for lumber; cut in lengths they serve well in building mountain trails and steps, controlling erosion; purposely placed to stabilize hillside landscaping; support building projects, form cabin walls and lakeside docks. Logs may also impede our travels, block paths and lead to stumbling and falls; climbing over them can pose possible sources of injury before opening our way to a new course or viewpoint.

Concrete blocks purchased in small or large quantities, chosen, hauled and stacked, become projects from foundations to borders to barriers or avenues of access. At times stacks of those blocks require moving from place to place as plans are initiated; halted, amended, new structures take form, renovations and new projects are undertaken. Raised vegetable and flower beds are built and still more uses found. These, too, are sometimes stumbled over or dropped on feet, occasionally inflicting bumps, bruises, cuts and scratches. As years pass, and blocks are moved to new locations, they unfailingly increase in weight, becoming far heavier than they were initially.

Psychological rocks, logs and concrete blocks are also encountered in favorable form to build, support and enhance lives; or negatively in forms of denigration, blame, disparagement, fault-finding, and long-term criticism. Resultant emotional scars are not always clearly identifiable as those gained from the physical encounters.

Ariel's story begins decades before her arrival, chronicles her forebears' immigration, their building of new lives in America, economic hurdles encountered, wars; also addressing mental and physical rocks, logs and concrete blocks. Long-hidden secrets are probed, some truths discovered.

A Funereal Reflection

Standing quietly beside the tastefully plain brushed metallic coffin situated in Grendahl's Funeral Home for viewing, Ariel carefully scrutinized the elderly female form reposing on the light green satin. Hair carefully arranged, a touch of color placed on cheeks and silent lips, body garbed in a new green dress and adorned with matching necklace and green earrings. No hint of respiration was detected. Edythe might possibly have been content with arrangements made for her final presentation, although fault certainly could and would have been found. Nothing Ariel knew of had ever truly pleased the lady in 90-plus years.

Arriving the previous day, she had stopped briefly at the cemetery business office to confirm arrangements, provide the appropriate green garments purchased specifically for this occasion, along with details for the graveside service folder. Everything from wearing apparel to wall color to kitchen counters and bath mats and towels had always been green, ostensibly to enhance the highly vaunted once-red hair color long since faded to a drab dull pinkish-gray. Edythe's final resting place had been arranged for years earlier when Dad had passed away.

Ariel's three adult children were also to be in attendance for the burial of their maternal grandmother. Jillian and Ryan planned to travel together, with Annie having tersely indicated she had a separate travel plan. Ariel envied Tom's decision to stay home, and primarily his freedom to do just that. As the 'sole survivor' Ariel had little choice but to at least try to appear somewhat the dutiful daughter. No way could she pretend devotion or overwhelming grief. Just smile, accept the politely phrased condolences, express thanks to the attendees while inquiring as to their wellbeing and keep smiling; always stand tall, back and shoulders straight and smile.

She remained beside the casket for several minutes, quietly re-confirming there was absolutely not the remotest hint of possible respiration. Edythe Agnes Johnson Pedersen was indeed quite deceased.

The lifelong dread, ill-defined fear, nameless sense of foreboding in Edythe's presence, the apprehension and trepidation that had permeated her very being from earliest memory began to wane ever so slightly. A tentative sense of freedom tickled at the edges of her consciousness. The first two decades of her life in a household consisting of one certified manic-depressive (n/k/a bi-polar disorder) adult, and the other exhibiting clearly paranoid-schizophrenic behavior had been a challenge at best. Only a faded much-folded, black photocopy served to document her alleged birth to the couple.

Scanning the room for her son and daughters, she caught sight of her younger daughter and went to greet Annie, who stoically accepted a brief hug before claiming the need to look for her siblings. Watching her younger daughter's back, Ariel mused a bit as to what the sentiments might be when she, herself, passed. Would this daughter also feel relief, or might she be just a wee bit sad? Time would tell. Besides, it really would not matter at all.

Estrangement from her middle child had occurred at Ariel's desperate escape from the 20-year marriage to Roger, her first husband. Her efforts to keep the children out of that conflict had been in vain. The initial separation was anything but pleasant and the divorce proceedings required nearly three years to finalize. Annie had sided with and fully supported her father throughout the lengthy proceedings, despite all Ariel's efforts to avoid involving her and her siblings. Roger had painted Ariel as an unfit mother, insane, alcoholic; a truly inadequate individual in every possible manner. Annie had believed every word, stuck by Roger and made very clear she had no regard whatever for her mother. She had carried Roger's wild tales to Edythe, also convincing her that Ariel was still unfit, not just as a wife and mother, but as a human being. That was not at all surprising, having been her opinion for decades; new evidence only enhanced her firmly-held negative assessment of her daughter.

In truth, Ariel had fled after enduring years of belittlement, constant criticism, and denigration, mental and emotional abuse along with numerous death threats. He had carefully avoided making direct threats where any witness might be present. Physical abuse was also carried out privately as most is. No witnesses and no documentation.

His final threat had been of Ariel's commitment to a mental institution and permanent prohibition of contact with her children. Court-ordered commitment of Ariel's father by Edythe had been accomplished just a few months after their 1934 marriage. Even though somewhat aware that 1935 tactics might not work well in 1978, Roger knew the threat would not only wound Ariel deeply, but further undermine what little self-confidence she might still possess. He knew that would further enforce her ever-present sense of inadequacy and worthlessness as a person. That he had put her down and criticized virtually her every thought, word and deed throughout their marriage was of no consequence whatever. All Ariel's attempts to maintain positive relationships with her children had been countered by her husband, successfully to greater and/or lesser degrees. Annie cut off contact, not responding or acknowledging any of Ariel's calls, invitations, cards or gifts. Many tears were shed over this rejection and only served to heighten Ariel's life-long sense of guilt and utter inadequacy.

Ariel had utterly failed in all attempts to please Edythe, and then Roger; each seizing eagerly on opportunities to point out her inadequacies and faults. Criticism and blame was what she had heard consistently and accepted as only her due.

Determined to shake off the gloomy cloud of past memories, fears and negativity that lurked and permeated her very being in Edythe's sphere, Ariel turned toward those quietly entering the parlor. She greeted each with a sincere smile, indicated the guest book, gave each a copy of the remembrance folder and remained at the door as they slowly passed by the open casket.

Several of Edythe's old neighbors, church friends and acquaintances had come, solemnly greeted Ariel and expressed their condolences. They were of a rapidly dwindling generation. Many of these people she had known from early childhood and it truly was nice to see them again. The minister made an obvious point of introducing himself; as though this was a first meeting. Ariel had met with him in his office for more than an hour the previous afternoon regarding the service details. His remarks then and now centered on what a splendidly marvelous, totally wonderful, caring and loving person Edythe had been; the very kindest, most generous and absolutely best up-standing Christian woman ever to walk the earth. Ariel had kept silent maintaining a rather tight smile, trusting he would take that as evidence she agreed with everything he said.

She had never known the individual he so glowingly described. She rather suspected her Dad also had been unacquainted with that saintly personage especially in later years. Ariel was thankful that he had passed nearly twenty years prior and did not now have to sit through all the accolades. But, on second thought, perhaps he had been able to forget major portions of the past and have forged a more generous mind set. A physical distance of some 300-plus miles from Edythe had been beneficial for Ariel, to be sure.

The graveside procedure was blessedly brief. Following another dissertation on Edythe's beneficence, splendid upstanding Christianity and sterling character, the preacher finally delivered a dour and somber benediction. He then gave Ariel a cold, limp handshake and quickly departed with a dark and disapproving look directed her way.

Old acquaintances shared a few memories, offered their condolences and left to resume their Saturday schedules. None seemed to have anything significant to share relative to the decedent, which didn't even occur to Ariel until hours later when she was well on the road back home. These men and women were allegedly Edythe's close friends, some of the younger women having been described by Edythe as the 'daughter(s) she never had'. This observation probably should have been thought-provoking, but only brought a soft giggle.

Over the years numerous younger women had temporarily filled that 'daughter' role, each in time falling from grace at various intervals as they pursued higher education goals, careers and their personal lives. Other interests, marriage, children and relocations occupied the time each had previously spent listening to Edythe's dissertations, complaints about Ariel, church, the government and her endless list of medical problems, real or imaginary.

Ariel invited her three children to share lunch before journeying to their respective homes. Annie declined and quickly departed. Jillian and Ryan joined her, enjoying lunch and catch-up conversation. They had a few good memories of their grandmother; Ariel not so much, actually none. Grandpa Pedersen was remembered with great affection by all as they shared some of his pithy statements, good memories of conversations and stories of his early travels.

SECTION I
Questions

Open that Black Trunk?
Maybe Not
(what about the cedar chest and old leather cases?)

Months later Ariel stood in the basement storage room of her home facing the circa1925 black steamer trunk bearing gold-stamped letters *"EAJ"*, and contemplated its fate. That object, together with the ornate dark cedar chest and two leather strap-bound cases had been major negative elements for decades. Not just an elephant or two in the room, but an entire herd. The trunk itself had always just been there, big, black, ominous, more than slightly mysterious. Ariel's strong temptation was to just call any listed antiques' dealer and have it hauled away – unopened. She was even willing to pay someone to take it; sell whatever they could and keep the proceeds. Just eliminate that thing from her life. She and Tom had carted it, unopened, to each place they lived for over twenty years. Ariel wanted absolutely nothing that had been Edythe's.

Some contents could be of interest to her children and grandchildren, however, and perhaps they would seriously question her decision in future years. It was also possible some documents relating to her Dad's family might be stored there. Those she definitely wanted … if any such still existed. Edythe had zealously destroyed most everything Pedersen-related and particularly any items her husband had valued. She did the same with anything Ariel wanted to keep, including better clothing items purchased with berry-picking and babysitting earnings. Those had routinely disappeared while Ariel was at school, never to be seen again or mentioned; quickly shipped off to various worthy far-flung church missions. After all Ariel had another skirt, blouse, dress, whatever; and sometimes even two or three others. Children in other countries and climes could use those nicer items far better. It had always seemed just a trifle strange that none of Edythe's personal property was ever subject to sudden shipment to far off lands.

Along with the trunk were two vintage suitcases stuffed with books and papers Edythe had carefully guarded for decades; what those might contain was unknown. Tom and Ariel had moved them along with the cedar chest and trunk so many times over the years, repeatedly assuring Edythe that all was quite safe, nothing had been removed or destroyed and all was secure, available whenever she wished.

Now she was dead and buried; no need of the contents. Had she stored some deep dark secret there? Could there possibly be some clues or even answers to the myriad jumbled questions Ariel had silently pondered for years? Might something be found here that could shed light on why she had been consistently isolated from other children her age, not allowed to play as other did; possibly why she had consistently felt monstrous suffocating waves of guilt over things she didn't even know about? She knew there were old documents, and perhaps bits of family history that might shed some light on what, who, or why Edythe, and also her father always seemed so unlike other adults, neighbors, church members and the few school-mates' parents she had been permitted to meet.

Edythe had consistently placed extreme emphasis on keeping the most mundane activities secret, lest the neighbors see. See what? That she went to school, fed the chickens, or played at the creek and caught trout? What was the big deal? Were there any answers, clues? Or should she just chalk all that up to wishful thinking, childhood misunderstandings, unfulfilled hopes, dreams; simply ignore the past completely and get on with living.

Her present life with Tom was really quite pleasant and relatively uncomplicated. They were conversant, quite compatible, had a comfortable home, both worked at jobs they enjoyed, spent weekends at the lake boating and entertaining friends; she sang in the church choir and served on committees. He adored Ariel and wasn't shy about showing how much he loved her. Why should she even think of stirring up who-only-knew what by digging into old stuff.

Still, the question of what to do with that trunk, the chest and cases remained. Would any of her children want them or any of the contents? Perhaps a grandchild had some interest, and would actually value them. Painfully recalling her own feelings of betrayal at Edythe's frequent destruction of her things there was no real choice. Open and sort. She owed her own children that opportunity of deciding for themselves at least, if not grandchildren. This was not merely a matter of left-over long-term guilt imposed by Edythe, but an obligation to those who might see these items as part of their history and thus of some value.

The heavy lid raised, revealing first the covered tray; lingering scent of long-past perfumes and faded moth crystals wafted up. Unsnapping straps and lifting the cloth-covered cardboard, she found doilies, crocheted runners and embroidered serviettes together with tiny crystal salt servers and silver spoons, rarely used and then only for very special guests. Below was yet another tray with more table linens, larger crocheted pieces. Putting it to the side there staring up at here was the white crochet-covered, black beady-eyed dog lying atop a somewhat dingy, well-worn chenille bedspread also used only on extremely special occasions. She had never really liked the little dog, quite wary of it when very young, but also a bit sorry he was forced to spend so much time locked up in that trunk. It hadn't seemed at all fair in her child's mind; and somehow still didn't.

From earliest childhood, the possibility of guests of any sort sharing even the simplest bite of food or drink had required a total upheaval and major house-cleaning. No one ever just popped in for a cup of coffee or casual lunch, much less to share supper. Company for dinner required thorough scrubbing of all vertical and horizontal surfaces. Cupboards and countertops were scoured; all dishes, pots and pans washed and replaced. Curtains were washed, starched, ironed; windows cleaned inside and out; the linoleum floors scrubbed with cold water and fine steel wool, waxed and polished to a high gloss. All varnished wood surfaces received still more coats of dark polish and endless buffing. The good china, crystal and table service were washed and polished; table linens also re-washed, starched and ironed. At minimum two of the largest hens, good layers or not, were dispatched in lieu of a fatted calf. Any guest for a meal was a major event; but largely limited to the current preacher or a foreign missionary on furlough.

Having sorted table linens, doilies and miscellaneous drawn-work items, she divided the fabric pieces fairly equally into each of the three lidded plastic storage bins. Those would definitely be given to her children to do with precisely as they pleased. Ariel had no wish to keep any of the items, or even have to see them again. No pleasant memories were evoked by any, only that all-too-familiar fear, sense of dread and guilt. Fear of somehow inadvertently blundering, speaking without specific instruction, or in some unknown manner causing embarrassment to Edythe had been with her from infancy. Guilt had been imposed from earliest memory and grown year by year.

The lower levels of the trunk held her father's leather document folder and it was quite full. Could this worn leather pouch contain any clues, let alone answers, to any of the unanswered conundrums? Dusty folded documents, faded newspaper clippings, 1920's road maps bound and covered in faux leather; old school books, bank statements and canceled checks, and even pocket watches, together with a few costume jewelry items comprised the remainder. That sorting all this was to be quite a task became crystal clear. Pandora's Box had been breached.

With Richard E. L. Pedersen's well-worn black leather folder opened, crinkly papers spread out and flattened a bit, Ariel began tracing her father's background with documents dating from the mid-1800's.

Pedersen: Maywood

Richard was born in January of 1905 in the small city of Red Wing, Minnesota, along the Mississippi River and lived there with his parents and brother his first five years. Papa worked steadily as a skilled carpenter and cabinet maker, busy building new homes and commercial structures in the growing community. Mama Alma was quite busy with two small boys, cooking, cleaning, baking, keeping a garden and canning food for winter use, tending chickens and selling eggs, doing laundry by hand on a washboard in galvanized tubs; ironing with the flatirons heated on the wood-burning stove top. Both Swedish emigrants, they were living the American Dream and building for the future in this first decade of the 20th Century.

Alma had been born in Minneapolis, but raised in Sweden with her sister Frieda, both returning to America as teenagers in the late 1880's, quickly finding work as domestics cooking, cleaning and child care in private homes. Their mother had died in childbirth and father took the girls to his family in Sweden for care and schooling. He then resumed seafaring. Little is known about his life beyond a few cherished jewelry items apparently brought to his daughters from various Asian ports. Well educated, pretty young ladies skilled in household tasks did not remain single for long.

Edd Pedersen emigrated from Sweden in the 1880's along with the many thousands of Northern Europeans fleeing depressed economies in search of good jobs and a better life. He was a skilled woodworker; however, precious little work was then available in any of the Scandinavian countries. America was a different matter; people pressed westward, towns and cities sprang, land was available for farming. New farms meant new housing, barns, and silos, with need for cabinetry and furnishings as well as structures. New towns built on the prairies needed housing and commercial buildings. Work was plentiful in America. Many of these immigrants headed for the Upper mid-West, and Edd set out for Duluth, Minnesota. He met Alma and her sister Frieda, Gust Lundsten and the Erickson's – all having hailed from the same regions in the old country. Soon Edd married Alma; Gust and Frieda were wed, and each couple set out to establish new homes in this new country of great opportunity. Gust purchased farm land near Foley, north of Minneapolis, where they settled, soon welcoming twin daughters Anna and Esther, and then a son Leonard.

Edd and Alma traveled south to Red Wing along the Mississippi River with every hope and expectation of raising a family, enjoying a long, prosperous and pleasant life. They found a nice house with a barn for the horse and buggy, a fenced yard for chickens, some flower beds and good garden patch. Edd was soon earning good wages in the building trade; Alma busy turning the house into their home. Life was very good and they looked forward to raising a family in this new land.

That was not to be immediately, however. Baby girls born to Alma and Edd did not survive infancy. Such was quite common at the time, and the infant girls were laid to rest in the local cemetery. First Harold and then Richard Edward arrived in 1903 and 1905; both strong, healthy boys who thrived. The Pedersens were a lovely little family embracing the future.

Street cars were the usual mode of public transportation in most cities and towns at the time along with horse-drawn carriages, buggies and wagons for freight drayage. There was an abundance of work for skilled tradesmen and Edd did not lack in any way both opportunity and ability; working long hours doing well. His little family prospered. As usual for the era, he boarded the trolley early each morning with toolbox and lunch pail for a long day of labor-intensive work. Power tools were still far in the future, and workers carried their own large toolboxes with them.

Coming home one evening in 1910, Edd stepped off the trolley only to see a wildly out of control team and buggy rushing headlong toward him. A frantic woman pulled vainly at the reins, her feet braced against the dashboard of the carriage, leaning as far back as possible struggling to pull the horses to a stop. A small child clung to her skirts and the carriage seat. She had no chance whatever of controlling the frothing creatures.

Without a thought Edd dropped tool box and lunch pail, dashed into the street, and plunging into the mayhem managed to grab the bridle and get between the wild-eyed animals. 6 feet, 3 inches tall, and just over 200 pounds, he successfully pulled both horses' heads down. Despite flailing legs and thrashing hoofs he brought all to a tumultuous, entangled halt. A terrified young mother and child were spared, but not so Edd. He lay trampled and lifeless in the street. His beloved Alma now widowed; sons Harold, 7, and Richard, 5, fatherless.

Edd was laid to rest beside his tiny daughters in a Red Wing Cemetery. Alma Pedersen now faced the future alone with two young sons and the question of how and where to raise them.

With a sister and brother-in-law settled on their farm north of Minneapolis Alma deemed that to be a good location for her to begin over again as a widow and raise her boys. There she would have family support for Harold and Richard as well as herself. Anna, Esther and their younger brother Leonard were close in ages to her boys. Gust's brother Ted, his wife Mattie and son Ted, Jr., also farmed nearby. Moving closer to her sister Frieda and Gust Lundsten was the most sensible thing to do.

Stalwart and resolute, she sold their lovely little house, also horse and buggy, cow and chickens. Sadly she packed away her hopes and dreams of what had been quite reasonable expectations for her future with Edd and their sons. She boarded the train with her sons, starting over again, with greater responsibilities. From Minneapolis to Sweden, back to Minneapolis, Duluth, then to Red Wing and now to Maywood; it was quite a journey for a still-young woman. She had no clue there what lay ahead, but pragmatically faced this new phase of her life.

Gust and Ted Lundsten, Sr., had located a little house and barn situated on ten acres at the Maywood crossroads available at a reasonable price. The property was located about five miles east of Foley, the County Seat. Alma found this property to be an un-painted, un-plumbed and un-wired mid 1800's saltbox house, a barn, chicken coop, pig pen and enclosure, vegetable garden, small orchard and pasture occupying the SE ten-acre corner at the crossroads.

A one-room school, with requisite outhouses and play field occupied the SW corner, where songbirds nested in the cupola. Across the dirt road to the Northwest stood a tidy little white church with an almost-too-tall bell-tower steeple and narrow peaked windows. Well-trimmed shrubs flanked the entry. Fat Jerseys and Guernseys grazed in lush pasture on the NE corner then; and where for decades their progeny followed suit. This was a quiet peaceful rural area sparsely populated by Scandinavian farmers, predominantly Swedish, a smattering of Norwegians, an occasional German or Danish family. Farms were generally in the 80 to 200-acre range, with cattle, horses, pigs, small orchards, pastures and grain crops. Vegetable gardens and fruit trees, together with the chickens and eggs, pork and beef also from the farms, fed families and also served as supplemental income sources.

Young widows did not generally purchase real property in their own names in 1910; they were expected to either return to their family homes or re-marry and continue with childbearing and housekeeping. Alma's only family in the United States was her sister and brother-in-law; and a quickly arranged marriage was most definitely not something she would even consider. She and her sons would survive on their own.

Departure from that generally accepted 'norm' did not deter Alma in the least; she snapped up the 10 acres immediately. The purchase included a cow, a few pigs, chickens and remnants of farm equipment along with the house and outbuildings. An excellent well and hand-pump in the yard, with cistern under the house and small pump in the kitchen provided cool, clear water for both humans and animals.

The little house was thoroughly scrubbed, household furnishings fetched by horse and wagon from the Foley rail station, and they settled in. With her boys enrolled in the public school and church Sunday school, she quickly set about planting vegetables and tending to the animals and assorted fruit trees. A start of her favorite soft pink cabbage rose took root by the back porch and thrived on weekly applications of the rich Fels-Naptha laundry soap wash and rinse water.

Edd's Woodmen's insurance had enabled her to pay his final expenses, sell their Red Wing house, move and buy this little farm. However, she needed to find sufficient income to support herself and her boys. Education in Sweden had prepared her for being a wife and mother not to independently support herself and a family in America.

She spoke English well, but had no specific training, American degrees or certification or any sort. Lacking any documented American or English educational background, even grade school teaching was not an option, nor was the nursing field. She was neither trained, nor was there any hospital facility nearby. Country doctors did not hire nurses; and nearest hospitals were in Minneapolis and St. Paul. Reaching the Cities meant a long journey by buggy or train from

Foley and no public transportation existed in farm country. Automobiles were rare. Alma neither owned such nor knew how they functioned. Even had such been available, how would her young boys manage if she was working miles away in the Cities.

How to make a go of it on 10 acres was answered by opening a small corner store in the front parlor space of her little house. Farm product and tools she knew. Her little parlor market was soon stocked with grocery staples, chicken feed, vegetable seed packets and garden tools together with basic dry goods. She arranged with the local creamery to be a collection point for milk and eggs produced on local farms. Availability of closer, more local collection saved considerable time for neighboring farmers not having to travel by horse and wagon into town so often. Dairy products were brought to her store daily from surrounding farms, kept cool in the cellar, and then transported to town by the creamery, again by horse and wagon, for processing and rail shipment. Motorized transport for general farm use was still years down the road.

New retail grocery products were being regularly introduced in the early 1900's and so Jell-O™ was quickly added to her inventory. When a pair of elderly spinsters purchased a box she was careful to show them the directions printed on the back of the container that were specific for this new product.

"Humph", was the immediate response, "we have been making puddings since long before you were born." With that, the sisters gathered their purchases and abruptly departed. Early next morning one was back, storming through the door, Jell-O™ box in hand. Without any greeting she spouted, "We boiled that stuff all afternoon and it never did set up". They were accustomed to bringing a rennet pudding product to a rolling boil, at which time it would begin to set; directions were unnecessary – everyone just knew. Alma quietly refunded the purchase price of the offending Jell-O™, gently suggesting the lady might keep the box for reference if she wished to read the directions at some future time.

In spite of occasional glitches the Maywood corner store succeeded quite well. Richard and Harold spent those growing-up years between 1910 and about 1922/23 rather pleasantly at the little farm and store in Maywood helping their mother, attending school, Sunday School and spending time with cousins Esther, Anna, Leonard and Ted, Jr. They finished 8th grade and passed their State Boards with top marks. Cousin Ted suffered from childhood diabetes for which there was no treatment at the time, and he died shortly before graduating eighth grade.

A favorite farm critter was a big muscular tuxedo cat that had wandered in and soon took to following Richard faithfully. A history book account of the black Revolutionary War hero Attux had a major impact on Richard. When the bold black and white cat came on the scene, quickly exhibiting excellent hunting skills, Attux was the only logical name choice. His very favorite kitty game was to perch on a high point in the barn loft on full alert for dislodged rodents while Richard pitched hay down for the cows. Once spotted, a mouse was quickly dispatched, its body placed off to the side, joining a tidy row of such creatures having mistaken his barn for a good home. Only when no more could be found hiding in the hay would one decedent be selected and carried down from the loft to a sunny patch of grass for leisurely dining. Richard was left to dispose of the less worthy specimens.

During those years Alma's little store prospered and she was able to accumulate sufficient cash money to enroll her sons in the Dunwoody Institute for training in carpentry and cabinet making. Both were to follow in the footsteps of father and grandfather, who were schooled in Sweden. In addition to their Dunwoody studies they also learned a good deal from the books brought from Sweden, and utilizing contents of the inherited toolboxes. Their formal courses included engineering, physics, math, drafting, and hands-on construction in a two-year technical training course and apprenticeships.

While studying in Minneapolis they boarded with widowed friend of Alma's and helped her with maintenance projects. Only moving picture houses were air conditioned in that era, so hot humid summer nights found the brothers at the "Nickel Movies" sleeping in theater seats. In winter they earned extra money chopping wood and shoveling snow. Upon completion of studies at Dunwoody their skills were put to immediate use. Young, strong, willing and well-skilled carpenters had no problem finding good jobs in the bustling boom times of the 1920's. The Minneapolis/St. Paul metro area was growing quite rapidly, residential development spreading out onto the prairies, and there were good jobs in construction as well as fine cabinetry. They had good friends, family ties with Aunts, Uncles, Cousins and life was pretty good for them and their mother. It was not too long however, before adventure beyond the Mid-west called these two Swedish lads. California and the Great West beckoned.

Another element in this decision to leave Minnesota was the advent of Prohibition; the Roaring 20's with rum-running routes, bank robberies and assorted gangsters. Booze was transported from Canada by enterprising folks along the heavily forested but sparsely populated upper U.S./Canadian boarder. Additionally the infamous Chicago gangster, John Dillinger, was known to have a North Woods hideout. The two Pedersen boys were tall, dark, good-looking and resembled Dillinger sufficiently to run the risk of being shot before anyone might bother to determine their identities. Lawmen and private citizens alike were out gunning for that bad guy as well as other assorted lawbreakers. Putting some mileage between themselves and wanted persons seemed a judicious move. West they went.

An Indian motorcycle with sidecar provided transport. Their mother was doing well on the little farm, even closing her country store as both cars and roads improved, with greater reliability and availability. Trucks now picked up dairy products directly from farms. She also indicated the distinct possibility she might wed a local widowed farmer, a stolid Swedish gentleman by name of Carlson. His eldest son and wife had assumed running his much larger farm and were living there. He felt it was time to move on, and apparently so did Alma. She had raised her sons, provided their secondary education, succeeded in business and now she could enjoy life with a good companion. With their mother well cared for, healthy, active and establishing a new life the brothers felt quite confident in pursuing an adventure of their own. So Alma Pedersen became Alma Carlson; and the couple enjoyed several years together before his passing.

Harold and Richard worked their way across the country, stopping at road construction sites along the way to earn travel money. Strong farm lads who could easily manage the teams of horses used to pull scrapers and wagons were in high demand. New roads and highways had begun crisscrossing the United States meeting the ever-growing need. Once in California they readily found woodworking employment and kept riding motorcycles. Wooden horse-drawn hearses being retrofitted on Model T frames definitely required skilled woodworking. The San Francisco/Oakland area was growing, new housing and commercial buildings were going up; reconstruction following the 1906 earthquake and fires continued and further stimulated growth. The economy was booming.

A motorcycle accident one morning on a city street severed an artery in his leg, and nearly ended Richard's life. A gas and electric company worker was on scene in moments, applied a tourniquet, performed initial bandaging; and used his truck for emergency transport to hospital. A lucky coincidence that the trained PG&E repairman was on that particular street at just that time? Perhaps… or one of those Angel-wing moments?

When their mother was once more widowed, the brothers returned to Minnesota, purchased a Dodge Touring Car and brought her to California. The late 1920's were a splendid time for all of them, and several albums were filled with black and white photos of travels and their California home.

Alma Hanson Pedersen Carlson passed away in about 1930 shortly after returning to Maywood.

The Pedersen brothers remained in Minnesota following their mother's death, living on and working the little Maywood farm. They also did carpentry work in The Cities until construction projects slowed to nearly nothing as a result of the October 1929 stock market crash. All was not gloom and doom, however and they did a fairly good job of eking out a living despite the emerging Depression. They spent good times with cousins Leonard, Esther and Anna, all piling onto their motorcycles or into Leonard's car for short road trips, enjoying lake-side picnics, squirrel and rabbit hunting, music and theater productions at the Anoka Rum River amphitheater—good memorable family times. Their lives were all changing as well.

Esther married John Strombeck who had a farm close by, so the social group increased as all enjoyed each other's company. When a baby boy was welcomed into their home the Strombecks spent less time socializing with siblings and cousins. Anna married Ernest Eckholm; a fine man who agreed to join in farming with his father-in-law Gust Lundsten, and his help was definitely needed. This arrangement also allowed Anna to remain and assist her mother Frieda. Automation had definitely not come to farms and country houses. Many hands and strong backs were needed to keep things going. The young Eckholm family grew to include a daughter and three sons.

Cousin Leonard Lundsten had not taken to farming at all and once Anna and Ernest wed, he headed to The Cities to work in machine and equipment manufacture. Richard and Harold were rather on their own regardless of always being welcome in the family homes, including Aunt Mattie and Uncle Ted's. Their son Teddy had died of childhood diabetes. Esther and John also lost their son at an early age following a routine tonsillectomy. Both young boys had succumbed to medical situations not treatable at the time.

The little Maywood farming community did not escape the worldwide political and social upheaval during these years. The surviving cousins had all grown up, completed schooling, and moved on with their lives, coping with disappointments along with savoring better elements of family and friends. Leonard, Harold and Richard were still single. Only two years apart in age the brothers had always been very close and worked well together. They were excellent company for each other, interspersing conversation and jokes with dry humor and Swedish phrases. Their motorcycles provided transportation, often each with a date riding tandem and picnic baskets secured. There wasn't much cash money, but life was not all that bad on the little Maywood farm.

Johnson: Deerwood

Another packet of newspaper clippings, hand-written letters, notes and a few documents revealed the other major element involved in Ariel's search through the black trunk. Edythe Alfhild Johnson was born in August of 1903 on a beautiful farm bordered by three small lakes near Deerwood, Minnesota, the sixth of Alfred N. and Hilma Johnson's eight children. She was soon joined by sister Bertha, and baby brother Alfred, named for their father.

The eldest daughter Gerda only attended school through 4th grade as younger siblings arrived and her help was needed at home. A faded photograph showed her as a young girl standing with her parents and four younger siblings, holding Edythe, the new baby. Olga and Judith completed eighth grade at the country school, did their State Boards and left home for high school in nearby Crosby, boarding with town families. They learned to type, take shorthand, and quickly found secretarial positions in Minneapolis, returning to the farm for occasional visits. The older boys finished eighth grade and their State Board exams before returning to full time farming. Inability to continue their education presented little difficulty in working the farm, nor adversely impacted their military service with the outbreak of the Great War. Both Robert and Arthur served in France in the trenches and were gassed. At the War's end and discharge Arthur settled in nearby Milaca making use of his military training in truck maintenance. He opened a gas station and auto repair business, married and raised his family. Robert suffered more lingering effects of the War, now most likely known as PTSD along with residual lung damage from mustard gas. He eventually bought a little farm and married a widow, Minnie, who loved houseplants and raised six-toed cats. In their later years Bob and Minnie worked nights cleaning Deerwood retail establishments, including a favored tavern, generally finishing there just before the arrival of breakfast patrons.

During those early 20ᵗʰ century years Edythe and her siblings walked to the one-room school, crossing between two of the lakes in warmer weather via a low-lying narrow strip of land on which layers of logs had been placed to form a road. The washboard road kept horses and wagons as well as children from sinking into muddy ground, shortening the distance to school, church and town. The firmer and better traveled county road made those trips significantly longer. Once ice was set on the lakes those distances were shortened even more.

Schoolboys hauled and split wood for the one-room school's heating stove; girls drew fresh water from the well, swept, dusted and tidied the little structure before classes. Teachers boarded with one of the area families whose children attended. After school hours and weekends were busy with farm and household chores. In addition to care and feeding of animals, there was firewood to cut, split, stack and supply the cook and heating stoves, ashes to remove at home as well; barns to clean and straw to be replaced in stalls. Chickens had to be fed, their coops cleaned and eggs gathered. Used chicken coop straw was hauled to the garden plot; stove ashes used for the outhouse as well as the manure pile behind the barn. There were ample tasks awaiting children of all ages.

Animal waste and used hay from both barn and chicken coops was plowed into the soil before spring planting. Composting and recycling were not subjects studied in a classroom, or researched in any manner, but practiced simply as a normal part of daily life. Seldom did anything on a farm constitute garbage or trash. Canning jars were saved and re-used; vegetable and flower seeds dried and saved each year; seedlings planted to replace trees felled for lumber or stove-wood.

Girls helped with the ever-present laundry; scrub-boards in tubs of hot soapy water, hand wringing garments, rinsing in more tubs and hanging out to dry on clothes lines strung in the back yard. Ironing was another task requiring hours of standing at the ironing board by a wood stove on which the sadirons were heated, picked up by curved spring-clamp wooden handles. Washing was done one day and ironing the next. Baking bread also required a full day in the kitchen and hands young and old, to provide loaves, rolls, cakes and cookies for the family.

For reasons never explained, and held a closely-guarded family secret, Edythe was kept out of school for at least one full year during upper grades, which she sorely resented. Upon returning to the one-room school she completed the available studies, aced her State Boards and entertained high hopes of high school and even college.

A professional studio eighth grade graduation photograph shows her in a white lace-trimmed dress, hair beautifully done up with a large ribbon and holding a bouquet of roses; a very pretty young lady, albeit somber, unsmiling in studio photos and even snap shots.

Papa objected strongly to more formal education for Edythe. Two of his daughters had made use of their high school studies, already left the farm for jobs in the Cities, and there were still young children at home to care for. For reasons also kept secret, he wanted Edythe to remain on the farm; perhaps so he could keep an eye on her there. Another question.

Over the years a sizeable amount of surrounding acreage had been added to the farm and put into production. More crops and produce translated into more work, far too much for one now middle-age couple to handle alone. They had emigrated from Sweden, each in their early 20's, worked in Duluth and Minneapolis/St. Paul before meeting, marrying and buying the farm in Deerwood. Years of effort and eight living children later, they were no longer young, and both a bit weary. Alfred felt quite strongly that Edythe should remain on the farm to help her mother and elder sister, Gerda.

There were vegetable gardens and orchard, chickens and eggs, canning of winter food supplies, laundry and ironing, sewing the family's clothing, to say nothing of all the cleaning and cooking. Hilma was a tiny woman and hard worker, diligent in the care and keeping of her large family. For years she had trekked to town on foot and later by wagon with butter and eggs for sale, purchasing staple items to carry home. The years and miles had taken their toll on her health and strength, as had the numerous pregnancies and births. Gerda had followed the pattern of the day for eldest daughters, despite her hopes and dreams, and remained her mother's helper. They both would certainly welcome Edythe's help and Papa thought that quite appropriate. Emphatically Edythe did not agree. She had precious little interest in housework, then, or ever after.

High school attendance for farm kids required several miles' travel each day or boarding with a town family. Boys could travel by horseback, but that took labor off the farm – of both boy and horse. Consequently many attended school only through 8th grade.

A girl's attendance required boarding with a town family in exchange for household help and child care. Costs to the students' families were involved in all instances. Somehow Edythe found a town family home meeting Papa's standards, overcame his objections and attended high school in town for three years earning high marks as usual. He was well aware of Edythe's high intelligence and burning desire for continuing education; however, she was a girl and there were many lingering constraints in that era. It most assuredly was a father's duty to protect his daughters, and for whatever reason, especially this one.

He had not been as concerned about Olga or Judith, working and supporting themselves in large cities. Olga quickly found good employment and soon married, becoming her husband's responsibility in Papa's estimation. Judith had even moved to Chicago for a good job and it was there she met and married David Johnson, recently arrived from Sweden. Knowing both these girls were settled appropriately was comfortable. Bertha was younger and still safely at home, along with Fred, the baby. For reasons never revealed, he had serious concerns over Edythe. One more question without answer.

In 1924 Papa learned that Swedish Hospital in Minneapolis accepted young ladies with just three years of high school for their three-year nurse-training program. Course study, hands-on training together with room, board and a small stipend were included. Students performed regular shifts of floor-duty as part of their training course, learning tasks under supervision. He promptly enrolled her, and before long Edythe was through with high school classes, off the farm and on her way to Minneapolis for training at Swedish Hospital to be a registered nurse. That not being her choice was not addressed.

The black steamer trunk was purchased, engraved with her initials and packed for Edythe's move to the Cities. That trunk contained her personal belongings, moved from the farm to the nurses training dormitory, accompanied her from that point on, and now reposed in Ariel's basement.

As usual Edythe excelled at her studies, and graduated with honors in 1927. While she would have much preferred to finish high school and go on to college that was not to be. Accepting her future in nursing, she embraced each new experience and opportunity, soon taking on private duty assignments which now would be categorized as critical care duty. Nurses in that era however, did not have the level of responsibility, expertise or knowledge of today. Private duty nurses basically monitored one post-operative or critically ill patient per shift, summoning physicians for any needed treatment or procedures. Regular floor nurses did ward rounds; administered prescribed medications checked on numerous patients each shift, and charted any noted changes in condition for doctors' review. Long before the era of private rooms for patients, most were assigned to multi-bed wards, or two to four-bed rooms.

Private rooms were for the affluent who required actual hospitalization rather than treatment in their private residences with live-in nursing care. Only select duty assignments were in private rooms. Edythe's aspirations did not include a lifetime of bedpans, taking and charting of vital signs and changing bed linens doing floor duty in wards.

Then, as now, not every hospitalized patient successfully recovers, recuperates sufficiently and is discharged to home and family. Even in the later 1920's and beyond, mortality rates were considerable. Infections developing from surgical procedures, injuries and general disease posed far greater threats in that pre-antibiotic era. Edythe worked many nights, particularly with private duty patients, frequently being the nurse designated to contact and meet with various mortuary representatives when patients succumbed.

The family-owned, large and highly regarded mortuary firm in Minneapolis frequently responded to Swedish Hospital. The family was quite wealthy and socially prominent. The eldest son, and presumed heir to the business, had received his university degrees, made his European tour, and then set about working through all phases of the business in preparation for his leadership role. In the late 1920's he represented the family firm in dealing with hospitals, and in particular, Swedish. Upon notification of a passing, it most frequently was he who handled documentation, preparation and transport for services and burial. He was also a very handsome young man for whom several local debutantes had set their caps. Hospital nurses were definitely not in the same social strata; however, that was not a total deterrent to his social pursuits, or those of young nurses. He most assuredly enjoyed the company of pretty young women. That those pretty young women at Swedish Hospital were also trained nurses and some fairly available was available was a benefit for a benefit for a handsome young man.

Her night shift and private duty scheduling provided Edythe numerous opportunities to meet and converse at length with this eligible and highly sought after bachelor. She apparently made good use of those opportunities and became quite convinced there was a possibility of her marrying into this wealthy and prominent family. What a dream come true that would be. She had lost all hope of continuing her education and most reluctantly settled for nurse training; off the farm, yes, but hardly the life she wanted and had hoped for. Marriage into one of the area's most prominent families was truly a lofty and golden hopeful goal.

She dreamed of becoming his wife; could it truly happen…if only. Entry into wealth and Society would indeed be a dream comes true for Edythe.

Night after night in her starkly unadorned room she envisioned her wonderfully glittering future as his wife; mistress of the mansion; hostess at social events for charities; elegant dinner parties.

She saw herself exquisitely gowned in shimmering green to accent her carefully coiffed auburn tresses, alighting gracefully from the sleek limo, and on the arm of her handsome husband, gliding up a marble staircase for yet another splendid evening at the symphony. All eyes on her; photos in the next morning's society pages.

Another scenario found her seated in a powerful cherry-red roadster with leather upholstery and dark walnut instrument panel, green chiffon scarf floating in the wind, as her handsome undertaker husband skillfully maneuvered the sleek vehicle along lakeside lanes to her old hillside farm home. There her parents and siblings would eagerly await her arrival in wide-eyed awe.

More than just late night meetings, he had gifted her with several rather costly and quite personal items, a delightfully beautiful crystal atomized fragrance on one occasion; a splendid silk scarf and several lace hankies on others. He specifically sought her out when summoned to the hospital, even when the call originated from a different floor or department. Did he view this relationship as a serious budding romance with deeply-held mutual and lasting affection, or merely a most pleasant, but largely insignificant dalliance with an attractive, intelligent and available young nurse? The answer to that question also remains forever unknown.

One evening he made another special point of seeking her out just after her shift, just before she checked in at the nurses' residence. They could again spend a bit of private time together. Not at all unusual, as this was a somewhat frequent occurrence, Edythe eagerly made her way to their meeting site. He carried a beautifully-wrapped package and appeared just slightly ill at ease as he handed it to her. It was not a holiday, her birthday or other special occasion. Her quizzical expression evoked no explanation, just a hesitant smile and slight shuffling of feet. Upon opening, she found another very personal gift, an expensive dressing table tray and set of grooming items. This most definitely was not a casual, trifling gift. Edythe's hopes rose at this seeming indication of the relationship escalating.

His somewhat halting and slightly embarrassed explanation however, cruelly dashed all Edythe's dreams of being this man's bride. His engagement was being announced, not to her, but to the wealthy, prestigious eastern university alumnae daughter of another prominent Twin Cities family. This was to be not only a socially proper and acceptable marriage but the merger of strong, longtime family associations and business interests. He was sorry if she had somehow misunderstood their relationship. Edythe fled in tears, clutching the beautifully boxed gift tightly to her breast.

The announcement, complete with studio photo of the appropriately-chosen young lady, graced the next day's Tribune society page. Edythe's fondest hopes and dreams were reduced to ashes. She cherished the dressing table ensemble all her life, along with the atomizer perfume bottle, silk scarf and fine lace handkerchiefs. The dressing table ensemble constituted the center-piece of her dresser, only relegated to the trunk with the other keepsake gifts when dementia totally triumphed and she was moved to a secure care center.

Ariel was grown and married with children of her own before she had any concept as to the depth of meaning embodied in those highly treasured objects. These carefully preserved gifts had always seemed the most important things in Edythe's life, far more valued than anything Richard had ever given her. Clues in old penciled notes found in that black trunk had filled out some detail in the veiled hints and subtle remarks of prior years.

Could her own experiences as a young nurse, having her dreams so thoroughly dashed explained in part the way she treated Ariel; down-playing anything positive and finding only fault with whatever she did, wanted or said. Could it have been an attempt to save her daughter from wanting too much from life, striving too hard for dreams and having those cruelly smashed? Certainly a possibility, or evidence of a mental aberration. Edythe's life had been quite interesting as she sought to take advantage of opportunities, hoping to move up in society.

Ariel also wondered if Edythe's experiences had also influenced her insistence that Ariel show more interest in the rather non-descript son of a wealthy couple who attended the same church during her teens. This fellow was rather socially inept, pleasant enough in a less than exciting or very interesting manner, and seemed to find Ariel quite similar. While they were not totally averse to spending some limited time together, neither was overly enthusiastic about their mothers' plans. To comply with those mutual wishes they rode horses a few times, she dined with him at the family table occasionally, and that was about it. They never went anywhere together in any sort of date.

Years later Ariel came upon a photo of him with his bride in the local paper society section and was thankful to have successfully avoided any potential relationship. Neither party appeared very happy in the photo despite the elegant setting.

Edythe also fretted for decades about alleged gaffes made in her attempts to present as an exceedingly proper, well-educated, socially appropriate and available young woman. These perceived blunders were recalled, recounted and stewed over for decades, still worrying as to negativity this or that person may have perceived at whatever long-past time. In most instances, the people about whom she worried and fretted so seriously were long dead and gone. Still Edythe wondered, fussed and fluttered.

One such incident, and seemingly a favorite, occurred during the 1920's, still troubled Edythe into her 70's before dementia finally silenced it. One Sunday evening she and another nurse attended the Minneapolis Swedish Covenant Church vesper service. This particular girl was from a more socially prominent family and Edythe wanted her to be favorably impressed. Horror of horrors, the organist played the classical Moonlight Sonata theme as an offertory.

Consternation as to her friend's potential reaction was due to the theme melody being used in a popular song of the day, heard frequently on the radio. Edythe had no knowledge of its quite proper classical origin, knowing only the current radio airings and recordings. She was utterly aghast that a "popular" tune had been played in her church. She never forgot her mortification of that evening, retelling and worrying about it well into elder years.

Was her friend concerned or upset? More to the point, if even noticed did she care? Probably not, as the popular treatment was arranged from the well-known classical piece that would have been commonly known. That was just one of many minor incidents that constituted major catastrophes in Edythe's mind. She cherished each of those, along with perceived slights, repeatedly bringing them out to review and fret over also for decades. She fretted about casual comments made by co-workers, acquaintances, relatives or just about anyone with whom she had ever come in contact, questioning what they might *'really, truly'* have meant. Each and every simple conversational comment by anyone absolutely had to be covering some devious, ulterior motive or hidden agenda. Of that Edythe remained absolutely certain to her dying day.

Decades later when Ariel was married and had her own children Edythe frequently brought up something she had allegedly said in grade school and query the actual, but hidden, true meaning of that alleged comment at great length. Clearly Edythe had spent a good deal of time dwelling on whatever had/had not been said by Ariel, and what any such comment might possibly have *really* meant. Ariel learned fairly early in life to be very careful in mentioning or commenting on anything at all. The most casual remark would absolutely come back to haunt months, years or even decades later.

Edythe's hospital nursing career at Swedish in Minneapolis continued; interrupted briefly by employment at a tuberculosis treatment facility in Sandstone, Minnesota. Patients contracting this highly contagious disease during that time were placed in somewhat isolated clinics or small hospitals, treated mainly with fresh air, monitored exercise and nourishing foods. No antibiotics existed and thousands of people died from TB annually, all over the world. The Sandstone facility was founded and run by a doctor who had met Edythe at Swedish a few years earlier, and later offered her employment. She was able to leave Minneapolis for a change of scene, returning to Swedish in the early 1930's. There she resumed regular floor duty and special private duty cases, a full-fledged registered nurse, class of 1927 and now with the additional specialized clinical experience.

Edythe also developed a very strong attraction and deep romantic feelings for this doctor despite his being married to his former office nurse, and father of at least three sons. Some Swedish Hospital nursing students and graduates of her acquaintance had succeeded in finding husbands among medical students, residency doctors, hospital administrators and on occasion, patients. As yet Edythe had not, and her hopes for a permanent relationship with the socially prominent mortician had been quashed.

Decades later she managed to have that very Sandstone physician visit at her Washington State home for a luncheon. He was in the Puget Sound area for a medical society speaking engagement. Ariel and Jillian had been summoned for the occasion. She doubted he spoke two dozen words while at Edythe's home or during the drive back to his hotel. He barely thanked Ariel for the ride, and never acknowledged Jillian's existence. A most uncommunicative individual; Ariel never understood the strong attraction and longings Edythe had frequently expressed over many years, especially not after meeting the person. The greener grass always being on the other side of the fence thing perhaps, or the strong attraction possibly initiated and fueled by that very reticence? Who is to say, or speculate, certainly never to know.

Lives Converge

Late October 1929 saw global financial structures collapse. Investors were hard hit. Paper fortunes crumbled into dust. Not only were many millionaires suddenly paupers, worldwide stock market crashes disastrous for business and industry moguls, but the situation soon became critical for nearly every citizen of the land regardless of their prior economic status. The super-rich, as always, were barely impacted. Not being super-rich by any stretch, Richard Pedersen and Edythe Johnson were not exempted.

The Depression hit larger cities and major industries harder and far more rapidly than rural areas and farming communities. Farmers still raised animals and crops, were able to sell some farm produce on occasion. Dairy products and meat sold—albeit at far lower prices than had previously been commanded. They lacked income from farm product sales, but did manage to feed their families. Many farms were foreclosed on when bank loans could not be repaid. As the 1930's progressed, families moved in together on free and clear farms, pooling slim financial resources and sharing work.

City dwellers were far more dependent on regular salaries and wages; many of which shrank or simply ceased. Fathers tried to sell apples and pencils on street corners; mothers took in available sewing, laundry and ironing. Establishment of the Civilian Conservation Corps provided young men with vital jobs, wages, hope and also built roads, bridges, monuments and parks across America. Another World War loomed on the horizon the latter part of the 1930's and the American population as a whole wanted no part whatever of another armed conflict in Europe. The Great War had been more than enough for the majority; that War that was to end all Wars.

Construction in the Minneapolis/St. Paul area nose-dived with the Crash of 1929. Richard and Harold picked up occasional carpenter jobs, built some furniture and farmed. Harold suffered a compound leg fracture requiring a long recuperative period that did not help his mental state. Richard also suffered motorcycle-related injuries and was unable to ride for a time. Once back on bikes, they sped along country roads between The Cities and Maywood occasionally hunting squirrels and rabbits for stew.

The economic depression of the 1930's also fostered personal depression in many people; Harold was no exception. He was single, batching it with his younger brother at the Maywood farm with cash-paying work sporadic at best. Despite any number of girlfriends over the years, he had found no one special with whom to share his life. The economy throughout the country had tanked and around the globe---only to get worse, much worse. The woodworking trade was not exempted. Even if he had met that special girl he could not afford marriage in the depressed economic state.

Harold had struggled with mental depression most of his life and that worsened with their mother's death, shortly after her second husband passed. He and Richard were back living on the small farm of childhood, eking out their living with whatever work was available. Life was not all that wonderful, but certainly far better than what many people were coping with in those years. His financial assets consisted of the little farm he shared with Richard, a motorcycle and tools of the trade in which there was precious little work. Depression, both personal and economic, overwhelmed and crushed him.

Harold took his own life at the amphitheater on the westerly bank of the Rum River in Anoka, Minnesota. Richard was the one to find him and carry his brother's body up the flight of steep steps where they had spent so many pleasant afternoons and evenings enjoying varieties of entertainment at concerts, readings and plays with picnic baskets, good friends and dates.

Interring Harold beside their mother, Richard remained on the little farm, alone, completely on his own at 30 in an ever-worsening economy.

Ariel visited that Anoka amphitheater site decades later descending carefully from street level with her cousin Gayle. She found it a peaceful site alongside gently rippling waters of the Rum River, just below an old dam. Mossy vestiges of stone structures blended into the encroaching trees. Wood ducks fed and swam about in the river, then darted into their tree-hole nesting spots, calling out to each other as they flew. Birds sang as a soft breeze rustled through leafy branches; a virtually overwhelming experience.

Hours later over glasses of chilled wine she was able to share somewhat with her cousin how deeply moving it had been to walk along the shore and climb those steep moss-covered steps. For Gayle it was simply a pleasantly weathered overgrown local venue from a long-past era. For Ariel it was putting a real physical site on a horribly painful event in her Dad's life, especially treading the very steps he had climbed carrying his brother's body.

Though only five years old at the time, Richard vividly remembered the events surrounding their father's death, mother's grief; the enormous loss and resulting upheaval of their lives. Now his mother and brother were also dead. The economy had tanked, work that could serve to distract and keep his mind occupied was scarce. He tended the animals and crops, sold some eggs, produce and potatoes on occasion, managing to at least have food on the table. His motorcycle provided transportation around the local area and to Minneapolis when work was available there to earn a few cash dollars. There was a little work, and lunch, to be had helping local farmers. And so it was on one particular day enroute to a carpentry job in Minneapolis that another incident permanently altered the course of his life.

Richard was traveling down Nicolette Avenue when a chauffer-driven Pierce Arrow and a Lincoln town car each moved to change lanes—toward each other. Caught between these behemoths, Richard and his cycle definitely came out on the short end. He was transported, unconscious and critically injured, to Swedish Hospital for emergency treatment and surgical procedures. Post-operative, he remained comatose for well over two weeks, with a very uncertain prognosis, closely monitored by special duty nurses.

And so it was that Edythe Johnson was the nurse on duty the day a tenuously semi-conscious Richard Pedersen emerged from that lengthy coma, cautiously questioning his location and status. His only memory was of riding to a job site. Gradually the reality of his grave injuries became only too clear.

Slowly he regained a degree of physical healing, a bit more strength each day and even some bits and pieces of memory. He continued to heal physically, and building strength; however there was a long way to go before he could even consider returning to the Maywood farm able to care for both himself and it. Physical rehabilitation facilities as such did not exist in that day. Gravely ill or critically injured patients remained hospitalized for far longer periods then and when discharged were generally cared for by family or hired nursing staff in the home. Richard had no family able to provide necessary care, and he certainly could not afford to hire a caregiver to live in a little farmhouse out in the country. And, at least of equal concern…such an arrangement would simply not be socially acceptable; nurses of the era were predominantly female. Despite a specific nurse's professionalism, training and/or intent, living alone with, and caring for, a bachelor in his little farm home was totally out of any question. It simply was not done.

Edythe however, had family living on the fine farm at Deerwood, sister Gerda, brother Robert and parents in residence. There was plenty of room, good food, fresh air, fields and walking paths available, her siblings to assist and provide appropriate chaperonage. Proper young ladies of that day simply did not drag bachelors home for extended visits, no matter how battered and bruised. Anything of the sort fell far outside any acceptable behavior, for either party.

However, the Johnson farm family was quite a different matter, well within acceptable parameters. And so arrangements were made for his recuperation and rehabilitation. Richard was discharged from hospital, transported and installed in a downstairs room in the Johnson family farmhouse.

As his recuperation continued, he gradually regained most of his former good physical health and strength.

He took advantage of opportunities to increase his physical activities as strength returned, incrementally joining Edythe's father and brother Bob in the farm work. His own little Maywood farm had been closed up by Uncle Gust and his cousins; animals distributed among them for care and keeping.

As they worked together, Edythe's father and brother came to appreciate and truly like this Pedersen. He was a straight-up fellow of good solid Swedish background, a willing hand with tasks, and had a great sense of humor, once they caught on to the dryness and learned to watch his eyes twinkle. All in all, they liked him. Alfred came to think very highly of this fellow Edythe had dragged home and strongly favored his becoming a permanent member of the family. For whatever reason Papa still held considerable concerns as to Edythe's future.

Fast forward to November 24, 1934, where in the little Swedish Covenant Church, Maywood, Richard Edward Lennox Pedersen and Edythe Agnes Johnson were married by the Rev. Carl W. Johnson. Edythe had turned 31 in August; Richard was a year younger. A few relatives and friends from both families were in attendance for the simple ceremony. Following a coffee and cookies reception, the new Mr. and Mrs. Richard Pedersen crossed the Maywood intersection to their home – the 10-acre farm and little saltbox house where he had spent his childhood and youth.

It remained a rather simple domicile. Richard had done maintenance work throughout the years, made improvements and always kept it scrupulously clean. Their mother had trained both sons well in cooking, cleaning, canning and laundry chores in addition to raising animals and crops and putting them through Dunwoody Institute. Gas-powered washing machine and rinse tubs stood at one end of the back porch with copper boilers ready for weekly laundry chores. Clotheslines were strung in the porch as well as outdoors. The house was not wired so numerous kerosene lamps and lanterns were filled, chimneys cleaned and wicks trimmed. The house also lacked plumbing; a path through lilacs and rose bushes led to the outhouse. A little hand pump at the sink brought water from the cistern, with a deep well and large pump in the yard. Containers of water were kept close at hand to prime each of the pumps.

Freshly washed and starched curtains hung at the windows, new rag rugs at the sink and doors, parlor floors scrubbed white and lace doilies under kerosene lamps on small polished tables. Wood boxes in kitchen and parlor were filled, a low fire in the cook stove and coffee pot ready to start in the morning. A lace-covered round table, horse-hair settee and carved high-back chairs completed the parlor; bright new oilcloth graced the wooden kitchen table. Two plain wooden chairs had newly sewn colorful cotton cushions. Cooking utensils and dishes on open kitchen shelves near the sink, pump and priming pitcher to raise water from the cistern, and telephone on the wall completed the scene. Small, somewhat rustic, but a quite comfortable little house. Cozy bedrooms were tucked under the eaves upstairs, well supplied with warm quilts against late November's ever-lowering temperatures.

And so the newly-weds were home. Richard was no longer alone here, day after day; Edythe no longer an *"old maid"*.

Winters are harsh in Minnesota and the one of 1934-35 was no exception. Snow piled up, clouds loomed dark and gray; paths needed to be shoveled out each morning to barn and chicken coop. Chickens had to be fed and coops cleaned, eggs gathered, under-floor barn and coop rat traps checked and re-set, cow fed, watered and milked, cats fed, new hay put down in stalls, milk separated and stored, wood split, wood boxes filled, and stove ashes removed, lamps refilled and chimneys cleaned. Laundry was a weekly matter to address, drying clothes on the porch lines, followed by a day of ironing with flatirons heated on the stovetop. A major portion of any winter day was taken up with tasks required just to survive. No sitting comfortably in recliners watching television in that era.

Traveling the few miles into Foley required additional shoveling to get the old Dodge touring car out of the barn, heat and replace the drained engine oil, heat radiator water, adjust spark and magneto, before hand-cranking the engine in hopes of it turning over and starting. Warm coats, gloves and lap robes were totally necessary for winter driving before there were fully adjustable and automatic temperature/climate control options for vehicles. Life was not easy, even for newly-weds. Not exactly the stuff of pulp fiction honeymoon tales.

So, as of November 1934, she was his wife and daily companion for the remainder of his life. Richard had rescued her from much-dreaded spinsterhood status. Her Papa Johnson relaxed a bit about this daughter and breathed more easily.

As winter wore on Richard suffered more and more from depression. Years later he shared with Ariel his feelings of considerable obligation to Edythe who certainly had provided him with experienced nursing care both in hospital and at her family's farm. That care and the generosity of the Johnson family had been major factors in his recovery from the near-fatal motorcycle accident.

During his recuperation he had also learned something of how concerned Edythe's father was about her future as a single woman making her own way in the world. That she and Richard should marry seemed to him a highly logical and reasonable step. They were of similar Swedish backgrounds, both diligent and skilled workers with good prospects for the future, particularly when the economy improved. And Alfred Johnson was certain that improvement would come, having lived through hard times in Sweden, and turn-of-the-century depressions here in America. Times would change and things would improve. He strongly favored this union. Papa's concerns eased. And in actuality, he truly liked this Richard fellow his daughter had managed to snag; 'an all-round good man'.

As his depression deepened along with winter, Richard spent much time sleeping, but still faithfully accomplishing all the necessary farm chores. At alternate times, he was animated; out-going, and eager to go to town where he purchased items on credit they really could not afford and probably didn't actually need. Cash money was tight. Edythe's fears about her husband and their future grew.

The longer daylight hours, melting of snow, greening of fields greatly improved Richard's outlook. Summer farm work of planting, tending and harvesting kept both Edythe and Richard well occupied most of 1935. In recent decades those periods of seasonal depression have been linked to decreased exposure to light, with many sufferers seeking appropriate treatment. Scandinavians and other far-northerly persons historically experience more sensitivity than others to this lack of natural light during winter months. Additionally, Richard did have a naturally occurring tendency toward despondency that was aggravated by winter gloom, heavy snowfalls, rain, and windstorms. February was consistently his worst month.

Edythe remained highly concerned about Richard's bouts of depression that alternated with the periods of quite energetic activity. She consulted the local general practitioner in Foley, and with considerable ease had him diagnosed as being manic-depressive, now termed bi-polar. Enlisting a few of Richard's relatives, primarily the Carlson step-siblings, she petitioned the county court for his committal to the Stillwater Insane Asylum for an indeterminate period. No medications existed in that era to mitigate and control this condition. When the limited treatment possibilities were considered, Edythe readily consented to electro-shock procedures.

Richard had not posed the slightest indication of danger to himself or anyone else at any time. That Harold had taken his own life became a major factor in the court ruling, bolstered by Edythe's testimony and written statements she had obtained from others and submitted.

Throughout the remainder of Richard's life, he suffered varying degrees of depression during much of January and February every year, brightening with longer daylight hours and springtime.

In her early teens, Ariel realized she had inherited this tendency toward winter sadness and specifically sought activities to counter it, spending as much time as possible outdoors despite inclement weather. Outdoors was consistently more pleasant, the daylight of course, but primarily distance from Edythe's ever-present negativity. Even weak daylight outdoors was more cheerful than being inside with Edythe's constant fault-finding which focused on virtually everything and everyone.

Having committed her husband to an insane asylum, Edythe left the little farm for a time, and worked at selling magazines and sewing notions door-to-door. How she traveled and where she may have lived during that time was never mentioned, nor was any clue located in materials found in the trunk. A small account book contained only recorded expenditures for a period during that year; 3-cents for needles, 5-cents for a spool of thread, 20-cents given to church, etc. The only thing ever said was that she had to go to work and it was terribly difficult; no details were shared She did, however frequently complain about how many troubles she had encountered throughout her life from childhood on, consistently stressing how misunderstood, disappointed and ignored she had been.

After he had been confined for over a year and endured electro shock treatments at the Stillwater Asylum, Edythe again petitioned the county court and succeeded in having her husband released. Richard was released by court order into her care, custody and control for the remainder of his life.

Farm life at Maywood resumed.

The Carlson family had warmly welcomed Edythe into the community and their extended family. They had also fully supported her committing Richard to Stillwater. The extended family all lived and farmed in the area; most attended the same Maywood Covenant Church. No matter how geographically close, visits between Carlsons and the little Pedersen farm were infrequent, somewhat restricted to seasonal crop and livestock considerations. Edythe made no secret of her reluctance for much social interaction with them, or with anyone else for that matter. Only the preacher and his immediate family were deemed worthy of her attention.

It was the mid-1950's before Richard shared any of this with Ariel who was then a teenager. Edythe had never mentioned his having been committed to Stillwater, and not even the slightest hint as to her having the primary role in that action. Ariel had often wondered at her comments about perhaps having "to do something about Richard". Those had made no sense whatever at the time.

After receiving some background from Richard's extended family and finally from him, the lack of social interactions and strange family dynamics became clearer. She finally understood why his consistent, seemingly automatic response to whatever Edythe said was, "yes, Pet". He had quickly learned while at Stillwater the way to survive with any degree of peace was to agree with whatever the staff, and now Edythe, said or told him to do. He just agreed, went along with whatever was wanted, not disputing. "Yes, Pet" was his unchanging response quietly spoken with a fleeting twitch of smile and a twinkle in his eye. For years it had seemed quite odd, but after learning some of the background and rationale, Ariel enjoyed it immensely.

Edythe apparently never tumbled to his mildly sarcastic tone of agreeability. She retained her thoroughly relished position of authority and control. The mind, however, can only be controlled if willingly yielded, which he had not done, keeping thoughts and opinions to himself.

Growing up, Ariel greatly valued her Dad's intelligence, insights, and their quiet conversations out of Edythe's hearing.

Somewhat more normal life resumed in 1936, with Richard tending the farm, taking on carpenter work as available, but frequently working for area farmers, sometimes at only 50-cents a day and lunch. He sold the little farm's eggs, cream, potatoes, and occasionally other produce, for mere pennies.

Times were tough in the country. With vegetables from the garden, fruit trees, chickens and a cow or two, people had food on their tables and canned supplies for winter. Cash money was something else.

Household refrigeration was still limited to more urban areas, and with no household wiring such was not a consideration even had Richard been able to afford the appliance. Ice was available in blocks delivered from Foley for placement in the old icebox. This service was largely limited to a few weeks in summer, with the root cellar used for cooling on a regular basis and freezing foods in winter.

Ariel salvaged and regularly used her Grandmother Pedersen's ice pick, valuing its history and also the faded advertising print: *"The Foley Ice Co. Phone 157"*. It worked beautifully to open new super-security packaging. A much-used slogan was also faintly visible: *"if we please you tell others. If we don't, tell us"*. Marketing changed precious little in a century.

Section II

Early Years - Another Change

Spring of 1938 brought a major change in life on the little farm. Ariel arrived April 28th at that same Swedish Hospital in Minneapolis. A somewhat freakish late snowstorm of blizzard proportions also made its appearance in northern Minnesota and adjacent states. Was that storm a harbinger of her future?

A couple weeks later an extremely proud and pleased Richard Pedersen carefully piloted the venerable Dodge touring car home to the Maywood farm and settled his little family into his childhood house. He always claimed apple blossoms had never been more beautiful and fragrant than they were that spring. Richard continued working the little farm and picking up any available outside farm or carpentry work he could find as the country began a slow financial comeback.

One hot and humid early summer afternoon a neighboring Norwegian farm wife unexpectedly called on Edythe without any invitation; simply stepping onto the porch and knocking at the door. She wanted to see Richard's new baby, meet his wife and just chat a bit before continuing on home from town. Edythe was caught completely off guard. No one just stopped by at her house without at least prior notice if not a rarely-granted specific invitation.

In any Scandinavian household a visitor is always, but always, served "coffee", actually any form of refreshment always referenced as coffee, and the more the better. Edythe had cookies and other baked goods, of course, but what to drink? It was too warm for coffee; and clearly freshly chipped ice and a glass of well water would not do. Having eliminated any other choice, Edythe resorted, just short of complete panic, to a jar of canned raspberry juice from the root cellar…this from the previous summer crop. She poured the juice into glasses, added a little of the precious chipped ice and served.

At first sip, this neighbor smiled broadly, licked her lips appreciatively and commented, *"ja, you haf vin, dat is gut."* Edythe was mortified. Wine? Oh no, that could not be; not in her house. She was absolutely dead set against alcoholic beverages of any sort whatever being consumed anywhere, by anyone at any time, and especially not in her house. This guest thought she had served wine – a totally incredible horror. If anyone at her church ever found out she would never live it down.

In actuality not a single soul ever knew unless she told them, nor would any have cared one wit. However this dreadful and horrible gaffe troubled Edythe for decades. Even into her late 70's it was recalled, mulled and stewed about with great consternation over the grievous sin committed, however inadvertently. Edythe never recognized the humor.

Richard and Ariel however (once it was known years later), found the entire matter highly amusing. At any reference they were very careful to avoid eye contact, lest even a single smile or chuckle escape, adding yet another layer of guilt to be harbored and nourished.

Life on the little Maywood farm was quiet, with Richard tending the animals, orchard, the garden plot and working at any available carpentry. Ariel grew, learned to walk and talk; took great delight in playing with the barn cats, picking daisies and being outdoors with her Dad. Edythe had household tasks and her church involvement to occupy her time, recounting of minor procedural errors at the Ladies' Aid Society, and dwelling on various physical complaints.

Ariel amused herself outdoors whenever possible, playing with kittens, digging in her sand box and making mud pies waiting for Dad to come home from work, or up from the pasture. She loved playing in puddles following summer showers, much to Edythe's dismay. When rain puddles dried, she used a little bucket to scoop water from the roadside ditch to refill them.

One specific memory of those early times stayed with Ariel throughout her life during dreams in which the recalled event took place at her then-current age. She saw herself in a narrow ravine; the sense of dread and unidentified fear at the back of her head lessening slightly as her feet touched ground and she began to walk. The dream-path was just wide enough for her to follow a rivulet from which small green frogs jumped to continue sunning themselves where she wouldn't step on them. Soft warm mud squished between her toes.

Sunlight filtered through tall, slender trees and warmed her face. The farther she walked in the tiny stream the happier she became. The ever-present fear lessened slightly with each forward step. She never knew the source or identity; it was just part of her like her arms and legs. In those dreams she saw Dad reaching down with strong arms picking her out of the ravine and holding her up in the warm sunshine. He smelled of hard work, fresh-cut hay, warm milk, and safety.

In the actual childhood scenario, once Bessie had been milked, the cream can was placed in the wagon with Ariel standing holding on to it firmly, and Dad pulled them to the barn. A faded snapshot confirmed cream can and Ariel in the little wagon with Bessie following.

In her 50's Ariel visited the old Maywood farmhouse and at last that sharp visual and clear early memory became not only obvious, but quite logical. Even into her adult years it had haunted her, but never made any sense.

Her '*ravine*' was the roadside ditch; tall skinny '*trees*' were marsh reeds, and the '*stream*' a trickle of run-off from the country road. Little green frogs still inhabited the ditch, just as they had decades earlier. That ditch was a great way for Edythe to ensure little Ariel could go down to the pasture where Richard milked the cow. The ditch was straight and deep; she couldn't climb up onto the road, or stray off anywhere. Moving away from Edythe and closer to her Dad explained the lessening of tiny Ariel's fear.

As a young adult, she knew all too well the source of that ever-present fear was none other than Edythe. Exactly why that should be was never entirely clear, but she finally realized Edythe definitely suffered from mental difficulties, if not specific diagnosed illnesses.

Ariel's own daughters experienced similar fear and the prevailing general sense of dread on the one occasion she had agreed to their staying overnight at Edythe's house. Her Dad was still living and Ariel knew he would be quick to comfort them as he had her during childhood should they waken in fear at night. Neither little girl had wanted to say anything to Grandpa about being afraid during the night or even to Ariel in the morning. Their subsequent nightmares lasted for weeks. Despite all Ariel's efforts, neither was ever able to identify a cause for their terror; no strange noises, calls of wild animals, sirens, thumps, bumps or anything identifiable. They were simply afraid, dreadfully afraid. Ariel knew all too well what they meant; she had never been able to identify a cause, either, except Edythe. When Edythe was anywhere near, so was the unidentified, pervading fear.

Anoka

While the world and national economies were slowly emerging from the Depression, largely due to numerous governmental programs in the United States, the CCC and other economic stimuli, farming areas still struggled. Minneapolis and St. Paul businesses and industries were recovering at a slow and steady, but better pace. Not so for farmers with small acreages. As agricultural practices developed and equipment improved it became increasingly clear the 80 to 120-acre farms were too small to support families. Diversification of crops required considerably more land, and 10 acres was actually never intended to be profitable and capable of supporting a family. No, that was never going to work. It hadn't been feasible in 1910, and certainly not some three decades later. Something had to change.

Despite all efforts, cash money remained in short supply the winter of 1939, so when Ralph Boberg had new houses ready for interior finish work in Minneapolis, he contacted Richard with an offer of steady employment. Richard moved Bessie, pigs and chickens to his cousin's farm where they would be well cared for and closed up the Maywood house for winter. The little family took up temporary residence in an Anoka motor court. It was not luxurious by any means, but he was not about to leave Edythe and Ariel alone on the little farm during a Minnesota winter. Since the house was not plumbed, there were no concerns about frozen pipes. Also, the nearby relatives all had quite enough to do on their own farm places, without having to worry about Edythe and a baby.

The motor court cabin consisted of one room, a sink, table and two chairs, wood-burning stove, a double bed, occasional chair and an old wooden rocker, a single light bulb over the stove and sink, with another hanging down in the center of the room. Rag rugs were placed at each of the doors; another at the sink, on the bare wood floor. A path from the back door led to the woodpile and outhouse.

Edythe surely must have deplored her situation; stuck in a dingy tourist cabin with a small child, in a strange town to endure cold winter months. She spent much of her time keeping fire in the stove, reading, doing hand laundry to dry on a small rack, and cooking simple evening meals. This definitely was not the life of her earlier hopes and dreams.

Ariel played on the floor with her wooden alphabet blocks, cloth books, Teddy Bear inherited from Cousin Dale, and tried to be as quiet as possible. Childish chatter was not encouraged. She did practice counting, using her blocks and lining them into rows; Dad liked to hear her count for him after work. She was bundled up in her warm coat and mittens when Dad shoveled snow, playing outdoors before they went inside again to get warm. After supper and washing up for bed, she cuddled in a blanket on his lap for a story. Evenings were short, with bedtime quite early. Ariel and Teddy Bear slept in a big leather suitcase that had been Harold's, wrapped snuggly in one of Aunt Gerda's old, but warm, down quilts.

One bright winter day Edythe bundled her up with coat, hat, sturdy shoes and mittens to go outdoors; and placed money and a note in one mitten. As specifically instructed, Ariel walked down the path through the high snow-banks to the sidewalk, turned at the walk and on to the little office and store on the corner. She had just stepped up onto the porch when the door opened and Ariel was lifted up and hugged by the owner.

"What is a wee thing like you doing out on a cold day like this? she asked, finally lowering Ariel to the floor and smiling warmly. Ariel just held out the mitten and waited; after all, she would soon be two years old…a big girl. "Oh my, it looks like your mother wants something, doesn't it," she said, unfolding and reading the note. "We can take care of this, but are you to carry all this yourself?" Ariel just nodded silently, and waited. Children did not chatter or demand attention in that era; Ariel was no exception.

Soon a sturdy brown paper bag was packed with a small loaf of bread and bottle of milk. Coins were placed in the mitten, Ariel's coat re-buttoned and hat tied securely under her chin. Mittens were put on, and Ariel felt the coins touching her fingers. She held the bag firmly, being careful not to squash the bread, and was guided down the steps to the sidewalk. The milk bottle was not very large, but ever so hard to hold onto in the stiff bag. The milk was important and to drop that would be very bad; the glass bottle would break, the milk spill, freeze and it would be her fault.

She knew what direction to walk; but, just which gap in the high snow-bank was the way to their cabin? Stepping ever so carefully to not slip on the ice and drop the milk, Ariel looked down each '*snow-tunnel*' and up to the tops of the high banks. She had walked to the little store with Dad, and even helped shovel some of the snow, but the tops were all way higher than her head now. What if she went to the wrong cabin? Then one path looked just a little more familiar, and it was the right one. Edythe opened the door, took the bag and hurried Ariel inside. She had not dropped anything, and the right coins were safe in her mitten. The winter adventure had been successful. Teddy Bear listened patiently to the tale.

When Dad came from work that evening and learned about her errand, he frowned at first, but then lifted Ariel up high and whispered in her ear how very proud he was of her. That experience helped initiate one of Ariel's life-long habits; of watching carefully where one is going, also looking back regularly to see what things look like from the other direction. It proved quite valuable in her adult experiences hiking in the Cascade Mountains and kayaking on new waters.

Richard and Harold had worked both commercial and residential construction in the 1920's with Ralph Boberg who operated his business out of Anoka, just north of the Cities. When the residential building trade dried up and recovery was slow, he finished up the Minneapolis houses, pulled up stakes, moved to Washington State. Soon he was building new housing on the Olympic Peninsula near Bremerton. Demand for residences was increasing there due to build-up at the Bremerton Naval Shipyards. War clouds were gathering during the latter 1930's, and despite nearly universal abhorrence of another major conflict, U. S. military involvement appeared imminent. By 1939-40 Europe was already suffering from German invasion, with England in dire fear of being invaded and overrun. Industries across the United States and Canada were quietly gearing up for expansion despite increasing Americans' isolationist direction following the Great War.

Relocating to Washington State presented both excellent opportunity and a concern. There was work available out West to be sure, but how to get there and finance relocation constituted a major problem. Cash money was required, and that was in very short supply. Working construction in Anoka and the Cities during winter had netted a small profit, but insufficient to allow for moving a family half-way across the country. Reliable transportation was a must, and only one need; the old touring car was definitely not up to that task.

Economics and Pending Conflict

In early 1940 Richard learned of a program initiated by the U.S. Navy to establish a new construction branch to build bases, military housing, storage facilities, whatever and wherever needed. Experienced carpenters, electricians, plumbers, draftsmen, general contractors were encouraged to apply. These were to be good steady jobs at good wages; but not necessarily in the continental United States. Initial projects were apt to be in far-flung locations.

Applicants were required to present at West Coast Naval bases with reliable transportation and their own living accommodations in addition to trade skills, tools and certifications. If they passed the somewhat cursory physical exams and were accepted, workers with/without families, with car/truck/housing would be loaded aboard battleships, transports or destroyers and shipped to existing or proposed base sites. Travel from Minnesota to Washington required cash money in addition to reliable transportation and portable housing.

That nothing much was happening in northern Minnesota was irrefutable fact. It would be several years before significant construction jobs resumed in the area. Then an errant major storm slipped north of the usual tornado alley track into northern Iowa and southern Minnesota, wreaking havoc. Damage to businesses and residences was severe.

What was certain tragedy for many served to provide Richard with sufficient funds to accomplish his relocation goal. Reconstruction work was available under Federal disaster funding, and paid not only good wages, but also daily subsistence for workers. Richard responded immediately and with good weather, was able to leave Edythe and Ariel at the Maywood farm to pursue this opportunity. His cousins and uncle were available to help her with the little farm.

Several weeks' work plus the subsistence money gave him a cash reserve unknown for years. To maximize net earnings, Richard slept in his old canvas tent and bedroll, cooking meals in the old cast iron pan and bathing in a nearby stream, as did many others. With cash money available, he purchased a more reliable Model "A" coupe that even had a heater. That was a true upgrade from the Dodge touring car and multiple lap robes. He could now provide for his family and even begin planning for their future. His spirits rose as he looked forward to this chance for a brighter future.

Two opportunities were readily available in Washington State. The new U.S. Navy construction division that would become the Seabees was one; and his friend Ralph Boberg was building houses as fast as he could on the Olympic Peninsula. He wanted and needed help. Richard could certainly frame structures and was highly skilled at finish work and cabinetry.

A house trailer was also purchased. Richard relished going west again and starting over in new territory whether that be with the U.S. Navy, new construction with his friend Ralph or something else entirely. He had also learned of an airplane company located in the Seattle area that was expanding from an existing Lake Union site and building a new manufacturing plant. Surely one of those three would provide a good job. He was more than eager to be off on this new adventure and better his little family's future.

However, late summer and fall were not a particularly sensible time to pull up stakes and begin a trek across the country with family and pulling a house trailer. Roads remained somewhat primitive in many areas, especially through the mountains where many routes were still under construction. There were the Rockies and then the Cascades to cross before reaching Puget Sound and Bremerton. It was a considerable distance and several years had elapsed since he and Harold had traveled West by motorcycle.

A move like this was a far different matter from just packing a kit-bag and hopping on motorcycles with his brother, working their way out to California, knowing home was still there, back in Minnesota.

Years before life had indeed been far simpler. Bed rolls, work clothes, fry pan, coffee pot and a very few utensils all wrapped in a tarp, some strong line and stakes had been about it. Leather jackets, sturdy boots, goggles, work trousers, leggings, shirts, some socks and underwear pretty much completed their kit. When they needed cash it had been simple to sign on to a highway construction job for a brief period. With good wages in hand providing pocket cash and full gas tanks, they just packed up and went on their way.

Going west would now mean leaving everything of his past as well as Edythe's, at least for the foreseeable future. Both extended families were in Minnesota, Wisconsin, and just north in Saskatchewan where Edythe's sister Judith and David Johnson were farming sections of wheat and raising their three children. Richard would be towing a very small, but weighty, house on wheels with a well-used Model "A" coupe.

The decision was reached. Richard and Edythe, now with their little daughter, would bid farewell to family and friends, close up the little farm, pack the house trailer and head west, much as early settlers had used covered wagons in opening the frontiers. Then in the 1930's masses of desperate farm families used whatever means available to flee the dust bowl and depression. So with transportation and temporary housing now available for use wherever they might settle, they decided to set out. Richard was sure to find work wherever they ended up, even temporarily.

Not yet three, Ariel was blissfully unaware of the numerous discussions, considerations, listing of plusses and minuses, questions, searches for answers and no doubt sleepless nights that constituted this process. Her travel recollections began with the spring of 1941; but she also clearly remembered the previous spring, in 1940 when she was only two years of age, prior to winter in the Anoka motor court cabin. That was when she had walked in the ditch to the pasture, played with kittens under apple trees, and held onto the cream can when Dad pulled the wagon up to the barn.

When she visited Maywood decades later as an adult so many questions were answered and childhood memories clarified.

Ariel's View of the Farm

Sometimes when Ariel sat in warm afternoon sun, with soft sand at her feet, it almost seemed she was back in Maywood on the farm, on the warm bare wooden back steps that 1940 spring. She recalled that as a mostly good time in her childhood, being outdoors, playing with barn cats, pulling weeds from the garden to feed chickens and scratching pigs' backs with a stick. She had loved being outside, especially spending time with Dad out in the pasture or in the barn while he milked Bessie, sending accurate 'shots' of supremely fresh milk into mouths of the waiting cats. Perhaps as thanks for their fresh milk, the cats quickly resumed sniffing out and eliminating any wayward mice seeking to invade their territory; nicely completing their kitty dinners.

She had helped a little to clean out stalls and put down new hay, not very well, but she was only slightly over two years old. Cousin Dale visited quite often with Aunt Bertha and Uncle Cle. Those were great times. Ariel and Dale played outdoors in the little orchard with the barn kitties and even little piglets. Dad and Cle talked and laughed while tackling various chores; Bertha listened to Edythe's litany of concerns and helped prepare dinner. Bertha always brought fancy cookies from her modern kitchen; and there was always a yummy meal with special dessert to be enjoyed before they started back to Minneapolis. Ariel and Dale picked great bunches of daisies and dandelions for Bertha to take home in an old fruit jar.

Ariel visited Dad's Aunt Frieda and Uncle Gust many times and loved being at their house. It was so happy, friendly and loving. There were more kitties, lots of cows, horses and pigs. Great Aunt Frieda let her help gather eggs and feed the chickens. Fresh milk and cookies always followed farm tasks. Except for Byron, her second cousins were older and went to school, much to Ariel's envy. She had no idea what school was, but definitely wanted to go there. She and Byron spent time in the barn trying to help feed animals, and playing out in the orchard. At big family dinners they often crawled under the round dining room table, sat on the claw feet; and poked their fingers into the ladies' open-toed shoes. Such fun.

Aunt Mattie's kitchen was another place Ariel loved to visit. Mattie's lap was so comfortable, and of course there were cookies and milk. One large cat lived in the house, only going outside occasionally to check out the barn and dispatch any errant rodents. He really liked to sleep under the cook stove, curled up in a tight ball; but woke up immediately when he heard Ariel's voice and wanted her undivided attention petting him and rubbing his ears.

Johnny and Esther Strombeck lived in a new, very modern house with electricity, running water, and … a flush toilet. That was a scary thing at first encounter and quite unlike the outhouse at the Maywood cross-roads farm. Esther also had a shiny white electric stove with a big oven and temperature settings. Despite such an elegant modern stove, her cookies were still yummy and fresh milk as cold from her electric refrigerator as from a cellar.

Leaving Minnesota

Spring of 1941 it was time to head west. Bessie again joined her barn and pasture-mates at Strombecks; chickens and pigs moved as well. Tools and farm equipment was distributed to relatives for use and safe-keeping, or serviced, tarped and stored in the barn. Household furnishings were sorted; some items into the trailer and some boxed up and moved to the attic or barn for the anticipated eventual return. When, or even if that might occur was unknown. Good-bye visits were made at the Church and throughout the community.

Gust and Frieda were somewhat in doubt as to Richard's plan to work so far from home and family; however, understood the need. They all realized it could be many years before good non-farm jobs might be available in the area. Frieda packed several tins with cookies for the journey and fussed much about taking little Ariel on such a long journey so far from home when she could just as well stay right here on their farm until Richard and Edythe settled some place.

Everything here was significantly different from what they had known in Sweden. Families had lived in the same places, farming the land and raising multi-generational families in homes built by their forebears. Adults cared for children until years passed and the younger then provided care for their elders. Sons and daughters married within the immediate communities, living and raising children in family homes on family farms. America was so different. Children left homes and family farms for wage and salary work in cities, at times far distant. Understanding of the economics was one thing, coping with emotions quite another. Now Richard was taking his little family to place totally unknown to them. When might they return? Or would they?

Ariel thanked her for cookies and great-uncle for letting her help in the barn, ride in the wagon with him to town, and buying penny-candies at the store. She loved sitting on the wagon seat beside him as the big brown plow horses clippity-clopped down the dirt road pulling wagon-loads of grain sacks and baskets of eggs. When she asked, he said he didn't know if there would be wagons and horses in the West, but assured her she could come ride with him any time she pleased. They would definitely go to town and get penny candies.

Many times over the years Dad regaled her with stories of uncle and his horses pulling cars out of the spring mud when despite having large powerful engines, big shiny motor cars couldn't move an inch no matter how their wheels churned and spun. Uncle Gust and his one-horse-power rescued Fords, Chevys, Packards, Cadillacs and Lincolns, pulling them from deep mud and depositing them safely on the paved road. The horses rather seemed to enjoy the whole process, swishing their tails, bobbing their heads so their manes fluffed in the wind. They were always ready for the carrot treats Gust kept in his pockets. Totally frustrated drivers readily conceded that 4, 6, or even 8+ cylinders were no match for spring thaw mud from which those sturdy beasts rescued them.

Gathering eggs at Auntie Frieda's was always such fun; the fat brown hens were friendly and Auntie never scolded Ariel, just helped her reach carefully under the soft warm feathers and gently pick out the eggs. She baked the best oatmeal cookies ever, and always had fresh cold milk to go with them.

Both Richard and Harold had spent weeks at Gust and Frieda's on occasions while recuperating from various motorcycle injuries. Waiting for one badly broken leg to heal, Harold had crafted a small table and two chairs for a little girl who was a somewhat distant relation and lived in Duluth. It was a beautiful set, made of black walnut, perfect for childhood tea parties with teddy bears and dolls. He remembered a delightful small child; however when the furniture was finished, discovered the little girl was quite grown up and no longer played with dolls or stuffed bears. The set was safely stored away and became Ariel's many years later.

It was decades later before Ariel understood how wrenching this move must have been for Gust and Frieda. Their son had moved to the Cities, and visited only occasionally. Their daughter Esther had married and moved to Johnny's farm several miles away. Daughter Anna, husband and children were still on the family farm; Mattie's farm was a few miles away. Gust and Frieda were not young and the help was not only welcome, but needed. Sister Alma, her husband Edd, and then second husband, and nephew Harold had all died; a brother and nephew were also deceased. Their family was shrinking. They had left Sweden decades earlier for better lives in America, fully expecting to remain a close-knit family in a fairly close community. That Swedish tradition had not held true in the vastness of America. Now Richard was taking his family so much farther west, also seeking to better his family.

Richard's Aunt Mattie was also a very special person in his life and saying good-bye to her was extremely difficult. Her son Teddy had been one of the cousins who played together and all went to school and Sunday school together. Harold, Richard, Leonard, Esther and Anna, and Ted had been so close. But Teddy had died of Childhood Diabetes at about 10, nephew Harold and her husband Ted, Gust's brother--also gone. Nephew Leonard lived in the Cities, and now Richard was leaving for the west. This was realistically the last time she would see him. Their conversation was mostly in Swedish; Ariel only understood bits and pieces as they reminisced about years gone by. Edythe did not join in the conversation, but remained silent, seated at the kitchen table handbag clutched on her lap.

Ariel silently stroked kitty's soft fur and stored away memory of this friendly farmhouse kitchen. Narrow windows sparkled behind cheery print curtains, shiny oilcloth covered the plain wooden table, pine flooring had been scrubbed nearly white with braided rugs at the sink, door, and by the big black wood-burning cook stove and full wood box. Freshly baked cookies graced a plain white platter, with more sealed in a tin for travel. No one left Aunt Mattie's without cookies. Kitty purred contentedly on Ariel's lap.

Then Aunt Mattie looked over at her, rose from the chair, moved kitty to the floor and picked Ariel up in strong sun-tanned arms. "Well, young lady, you are starting out on quite an adventure aren't you," she said, giving Ariel a big hug. "I think you need to take something along to help remember your Old Aunt Mattie" and walked to the cupboard. "Young ladies need to have breakfast juice if they are to grow strong, and you should have a pretty glass for that juice. So you pick out a glass to take out West for your breakfast juice." Ariel didn't know exactly what to do. The cupboard held so many glasses. She looked to her dad for help, but he just stood there, grinning broadly. Edythe sat looking out the window, still holding her handbag.

Ariel finally selected a small glass, a perfect size for juice; with tiny red stars all over it. It was so pretty; but, was ever so special; maybe she should not choose that one. Mattie smiled, hugged her again, handed her to Richard and began wrapping the precious juice glass in a soft worn table napkin. Then it was placed in a small paper bag and handed to her with instructions to "drink lots of good juice in that glass and remember your old Aunt Mattie". Ariel notice moisture teetering on the edges of Mattie's eye lashes.

Time came they really had to say 'good-bye' and start on the journey. Dad hugged Aunt Mattie really hard for a long time and even kissed her cheek. Ariel was totally surprised; she had never known him to hug anyone but her, and rarely had he kissed anyone that she knew of. Edythe shook Mattie's hand and thanked for the cookies. Ariel hugged, kissed and was again hugged and kissed in return before they finally climbed into the little coupe. With more "good-bye's, God Bless you", and waves, they were on their way. Edythe looked out the side window, handbag safely on her lap.

Ariel, an adult in her mid-50's, stood in her basement beside the trunk, fondly remembering that little glass, her great Aunt Mattie, cookies and soft purring kitty, knowing the precious glass with little red stars was safely tucked away in her own small trunk of memories. Would any of her now-grown children even want it? No matter, she valued it and had kept it safe all the years.

Northward to Canada

This move west might be temporary until they saved enough money and could afford to return to the little Maywood farm; or perhaps more permanent. Who only knew. Before crossing the Dakotas, Montana and Idaho to Washington, a stop in Saskatchewan at Aunt Judy and Uncle Dave's wheat ranch was totally in order.

It was slow going that mid-April of 1941. The Model "A" coupe pulled a much heavier 18' house trailer over roads, some paved, many graveled, and headed for the border. Dad knew of good camping spots along the way from his earlier years riding motorcycles, hunting and fishing with his brother Harold, and this was rather adventurous. However, even a few hundred miles required days, not hours, to accomplish.

Ariel sat on her oatmeal box that held all manner of apparently necessary documentation, birth certificates, property and tax records, his Dunwoody Institute diplomas, certificates, and other documents Dad would need when they arrived at the Naval Base in 'the West'. She could see out the windshield from her perch, which was perfectly fine with her. Sitting down on the seat she couldn't see the road at all and Edythe didn't like when she wriggled. Up on her oatmeal box was a good spot; she could hold onto Dad's sleeve and wriggle around a little now and then. It didn't seem to bother him like it did Edythe.

She still had no clue as to where this 'west' was. Dad assured her she would find it and there was an ocean with so much water it couldn't be measured. There would be so much sand she could dig all day and there would still be plenty more. Lakes she knew about, ditches and a few creeks, but what was an ocean? Dad just grinned, eyes twinkling, and said, "You'll see. It's really big and lots of fun." If Dad liked this ocean thing, Ariel knew she would, too.

Finally after miles and miles, they came to a stop at a sturdy gate across the road with signs in the middle. A small house on the right side of the road also had a sign in front of it. Not yet three, she couldn't read those, but they must be important because Dad lifted her from the oatmeal box on which she sat, opened it, and took out some papers. He carried those to the house and talked with a uniformed man who then came back to the road with Dad. They spoke for a while, and both pointed up the road past the gate. Edythe explained briefly that this man was the boarder guard, and needed to know who we were, where we were going and why.

Ariel heard him ask Dad if he could look inside the trailer. "Of course," and he eagerly opened the door. With a shy grin, the boarder guard then asked if it would be okay for his wife and son to also see this house trailer; it being the very first one to come through the area. They had seen magazine pictures, but never a real one. "Certainly, by all means," Dad replied, "by all means. Come on in and look around." Soon all were inside, peeking into the well-packed cupboards and tidy storage compartments. Dad was rather proud of this little mobile house; he had made several improvements to it, increasing storage without compromising the small living space. Scant attention was paid to the papers presented; talk was of travel, jobs in the west and road conditions. Outside Ariel played with their son and his dog, enjoying time to run around while the adults talked. For the most part, Edythe had stayed in the car, politely stepping out only briefly to meet the family members.

Soon it was time to get on toward Uncle Dave and Aunt Judy's place if they were to arrive before dark. The big gate was swung open and with many calls of 'good luck', and 'thank you', they were in Canada and headed north again.

Pony Cart Ride and School

It was only a few miles from the U.S./Canada border to the tiny town of Viceroy in Saskatchewan. Soon a familiar-looking road sign was spotted and Dad pulled off the main paved road onto a gravel road; then into a lane that seemed to extend forever.

"We're almost there," Dad said, and sure enough just over a little rise Ariel saw a house, huge barn, silo, a long row of smaller buildings, a few trees and bushes. She saw a lady running from the house waving her apron. Was that Aunt Judy? Sure enough and she was quickly joined by Cousin Shirley. Bill and Bob came from the barn, soon followed by Uncle Dave. A big brown dog emerged from under a lilac bush and several cats scurried about, looking a bit uncertain as to what they should do about this strange machine approaching. It wasn't a tractor, pick-up, wheat truck, combine, or anything else they had ever seen and they scampered to safety in the barn. That strange thing could be figured out later, or not.

There were hugs and kisses all around; Ariel was lifted up in strong arms, playfully passed from aunt, uncle and cousins and finally back to Dad. After the Model "A" and house trailer had been inspected, 'ooh'd and aah'd over, everyone gathered in the big farmhouse kitchen for coffee and fresh pastries. Next it was off to the barn to pet new kittens under the watchful eye of their mother and meet cows and horses. The barn at Maywood was just big enough for Bessie, the cats and hay storage in the loft. This barn was enormous. What fun it must be to live on this big farm and have so many people and animals around.

Edythe remained in the kitchen helping her sister prepare supper for this larger group. Dad helped Dave and the boys with evening chores of milking, feeding, watering the stock, cleaning stalls and putting down fresh straw. Soon everyone had washed up and all were seated around the large table for a good meal and more conversation. This had been a long day of farm work and travel. Before long Cousin Shirley helped Ariel brush her teeth, find her nightie, Teddy Bear and tuck into a bed. So much had happened that day, she quickly drifted off to sleep thinking how exciting and fun it all was.

Morning brought another new adventure. With chores done and breakfast eaten, it was time for school, and Ariel could go, too. Bill and Bob brought a small cart to the kitchen door. Shirley had combed Ariel's hair and helped her into a proper little dress for school. The pony stood patiently in his harness while everyone clambered onto the cart, each with a lunch pail—even Ariel. Bill took up the reins, again promising to drive carefully and watch Ariel. They didn't need to worry. She was not about to jump out or fall off this delightful little cart. It was much smaller than Uncle Gust's big wagon and easily pulled by just one pony, even with four kids riding. Off they went down the lane to the road and school. Ariel was thrilled; getting to go with the big kids and even to school. She still didn't really know what it was, but very eager to find out. This prospect of her very first day at school further whetted her enthusiasm to grow up, go to school every day, and learn what was in all those books. The teacher was ever so nice; let her look at so many things in the room and color on fresh white paper.

At lunch time everyone brought out the carefully wrapped sandwiches, pumped cold water from the well and sat on the grass under a big tree to eat. There were more pretty books to look at and pictures to draw after lunch.

Before she knew it, school was over, and she drifted off to sleep during the ride home, head resting on Shirley's lap.

All too soon it was time to say more 'good-bye's' and head west again. Everything was packed and neatly stowed into the trailer, hitch and chains connected and checked. With many more hugs, kisses, admonitions for safe travel and best wishes, Ariel resumed her perch on the oatmeal box in the Model "A", and Dad started down the lane. Edythe waved out the window and dabbed away tears as the farm and her family receded. There was no guarantee as to when, or even if, she might next see her sister.

This second border crossing farther west was soon passed. Canadian and U.S. guards both basically waved Richard and his little family on through, wishing everyone safe travel. Border guard questions centered on their having enjoyed their stay in Canada and welcoming them back to the U.S. After driving south for a bit, Dad turned the little car and house trailer West on a paved road. Now they were truly on their way. Ariel still wanted to know just what "the West" was and where, but thought it best to attempt patience a least for a while. How would she know when they were in the West? Dad would know; he had already been there at least three times.

Mountains

Miles passed slowly beneath car and trailer wheels on narrow strips of concrete that seemed to stretch endlessly toward the horizon. Fewer trees and even fewer farms came into view. There were miles and miles of land where it appeared no one lived, and very few animals of any sort were seen. Even birds didn't seem to live here. This was huge open country with very few cars or trucks. When another car did loom on the horizon and then come into view, drivers waved to each other as they passed. In late afternoons Dad looked for likely camp spots, wide enough to get off the highway and preferably with a stream for fresh water. He took caution to fill the gas tank in each small town, together with all water jugs and the reserve storage tank at every opportunity. This was less familiar territory now and he could not be assured of finding creeks or rivers easily. Travel by motorcycle with Harold had been faster and very little room required for camping.

Ariel enjoyed helping Dad set up camp each evening, filling her little pail with water from a stream and carrying it up to the trailer. Dad always said every little bit helped and encouraged her efforts. He unfolded the gas stove, brought out the big cast iron fry pan, and somehow always prepared a delicious meal. One evening she couldn't wait any longer and asked, "Where is 'the west' and when will we get there?" Dad grinned and tried to explain how far it was to the Pacific Ocean from Minnesota, and it would take a few more days yet. Oh.

He then brought out a large floppy black fabric-covered book that had colored lines all over the light green and gray fold-out pages. He said it was an atlas and it showed the roads, states, counties, lakes, rivers and mountains. He pointed to a spot on one of the bigger lines as the place they were, and then traced with his finger the lines that were roads they would take over the

Rocky Mountains, across a flatter area and then over the Cascade Mountains before reaching Bremerton in Washington state. Maps didn't make a lot of sense to Ariel, but it was reassuring that Dad knew where they were going and that he understood all those colored lines. There certainly wasn't much of anything where they were camping. Maybe tomorrow they would get to 'the West'.

Each day was much the same as they continued. Then, as the road narrowed and they began going up more hills, Ariel was given a new task. Dad very calmly said, "You keep an eye on this needle in the circle on the dashboard, and if it goes past the black line middle mark, where it is straight up, please tell me right away. Can you do that?"

Of course she could and what fun to be given something real to do. She soon learned this was more than a tiny bit important. They had driven up then slightly down several hills, each a little steeper than the other. The needle started moving; past first one line, and slowly creeping over to that middle mark. When she told Dad, he quickly found a place to pull off the highway and stop, carefully setting the hand brake and also blocking the trailer wheels. After opening the hood, he took a small pail of water from the trailer reserve tank, put it down in front of the car, held one hand over the radiator cap and waited; it was far too hot to touch. What was he doing, just waiting and holding his hand above the radiator every so often? This did not seem to be a good time for questions, so she waited.

She did need to go potty again, however, and there certainly were no bathrooms or outhouses to be seen; just trees, brush and tall dry grass with some new green shoots close to the ground. This had been true since leaving Maywood, and again Dad assured her those bushes also would do just fine. Now he used a stick to bounce branches and grass around and make noise before letting her go a few steps away from the car. There could be snakes here and he was not taking any chances. After all the noise of the car doors opening/closing, talking and more sticks stirring in the grass, Edythe ventured a little farther away, but also stayed fairly close to the road. That scenario was repeated innumerable times during the travel days.

Once the motor had cooled sufficiently, Dad loosened the radiator cap to let steam out. As he carefully poured in cool water the needle on the temperature gauge slowly moved back down.

As the road continued to go up hills more than down, stops for water became more frequent, and the reserve water tank was refilled every time a stream was nearby. Beautiful meadows were nestled between even higher hills, with buttercups popping into flower. Deer browsed on shrubs, nibbled flowers and frolicked in the new grass. Bigger animals were identified; elk in large herds, and even huge bison; all busy grazing, drinking from streams and pools; enjoying the warm spring weather. Occasionally brown bunnies hopped across the road in search of better grasses and flowers; Dad carefully slowed and steered around them. Coyotes and even a few wolves were spotted on hillsides and rocky ledges. The more hills they came to the meadows had more and bigger snow patches with fewer flowers. It was also a little colder outside when they stopped for water and to make camp at night. Some times there were tiny bits of ice on twig ends and skiffs of snow by the creek banks.

"Are we getting to the mountains soon?" Ariel queried. "We're in the mountains, the Rocky Mountains," Dad answered; "We're going even farther up in the mountains and will soon come to the Continental Divide." Oh my, now just what was that? She had not understood what mountains were; now they were in those somehow, and what was a continental divide? She had pelted Dad with questions all the way. Despite needing both hands for driving most of the way, and dealing with tire, engine, fuel, oil and water concerns, he had patiently answered each. Ariel was eager to learn and tried very hard to remember all he told her.

He reminded her of the fold-out pages he had showed her a few days before, and talked about the lines he had traced with his finger that were roads they would travel. Still intent upon the road, he pointed upward to the huge stone, tree, snow-covered heights rising skyward on each side of the highway. "The Rocky Mountains are so high, and they stretch so far—from far North in Canada all the way down South into Mexico—that it is difficult to see when we are going up higher and higher for miles and miles before we reach the top, and the continental divide. Snow-melt, streams and rivers on one side go East down the mountains we have just come up, eventually join the Mississippi River and on to the Gulf of Mexico." That river she knew about; the Minnesota River ran close to Cousin Dale's house in Minneapolis just before it joined the Mississippi. He then explained that water on the other side went west into streams and rivers that emptied into the Pacific Ocean. That was the ocean he said they would see, and it was fun. Obviously this was an important place.

Before long they climbed yet another steep hill and the needle slowly crept past that middle mark again. "We'll stop at the top" Dad said when she told him about it; and the road widened slightly as a sign came into view. "Here we are. This is the Continental Divide."

Dad set the brake, blocked the wheels. They looked at the sign, and let the engine cool before adding more water. There was even a tiny creek alongside the road with bits of ice along the edges; and Ariel's little tin pail was just the right size for scooping up clear cold water; some for drinking, more for the radiator and topping off the storage tank. Edythe rummaged about in the trailer to find the box camera, make sure it had film, and then snapshots were taken by the sign marking this important place. When developed, those would be placed in a big black book and marked with white ink as to date and place. Numbers on the sign also indicated how high this was, but they didn't mean much to Ariel.

Once back on the road, the little car didn't have to work quite so hard pulling the heavy trailer. There were still many hills, but more down than up, and Ariel's ears plugged up and then popped open over and over. Dad explained that as we traveled to higher and then lower elevations, pressure built up in our ear canals and then released as we talked or chewed gum, making the popping sound. Since we were traveling down faster than we had going up, elevation changed more rapidly, so ears 'popped' more often. Edythe didn't approve of gum, but decided it would be alright for an occasion like this. The temperature gauge needle stayed below the center mark more, and fewer water stops were needed.

There weren't so many meadows and not quite so much snow for several miles; streams became a little wider, and it was not as cold at night. Then the forest looked thicker with different kinds of trees. Fat furry little animals sat in the gravel and grass along the highway, nibbling at something only they could see, looking up questioningly. Dad said they were rock-chucks, or marmots; he thought they mostly dined on bugs, but wasn't certain about that. When he and Harold had gone to California on motorcycles and camped out, they had to tie their leather boots and jackets up high on tree branches so the marmots couldn't chew on them.

As an adult years later Ariel hiked in the Cascade Mountains and took similar precautions to protect her well-oiled boots and stuff-bags of food and clothing items, then securely zipping her alpine tent against these persistent furry creatures.

Mile after mile they slowly descended the western slopes of the Rockies, through lush forests and grassy meadows, following rushing streams that grew into foaming rivers. Here were deer, elk and some really odd-looking animals Dad called moose, which he thought somewhat larger than the ones in Northern Minnesota, although their ears and antlers looked very much the same. He also explained they had poor eyesight, were super strong as well as huge, and we most definitely did not want to hit one. A moose would easily destroy a car, especially a little Model "A" coupe. No bison seemed to live on this western side for some reason; at least none were spotted. Once a bear lumbered across the road, but it was still early in the season and many were still hibernating. That one did not seem to care much about cars or trailers; but, Dad was very careful to avoid him; he was big and quite intent on getting across the road.

The road followed alongside train tracks in several locations, and rivers as well, especially in canyons where it seemed all three were competing for the narrow space between high mountains. Occasionally there were small settlements also clinging to the river banks. Most of those consisted of just a few cabins and perhaps a little store with an assay sign. This was mining country and people had been prospecting and mining here for many years. Towns had some storefronts, mostly taverns. Dad told some fanciful tales of the early mining days in these towns and recounted some of what he and Harold had encountered going West in the 1920's. That sounded wonderful and Ariel wanted to hear more. Edythe soon put a stop to the stories, most of which she apparently deemed unsuitable.

They stopped one night in Kellogg, Idaho where Dad set up camp along the river. Ariel and Dad walked into town to the grocery store where several people greeted them and updated information on road construction projects they might encounter farther west.

From the sidewalk Ariel looked in shop windows at the displays of picks, shovels, and all sorts of tools Dad explained were for mining on claims up in the mountains. There were shops she recognized with bolts of cloth, sewing machines, groceries and drug stores. Walking farther down the street they came to shop windows with people in them. Pretty ladies with fancy hair, jewelry and make-up, wearing brightly-colored lace and ruffled dresses sat on chairs facing the street, waved and smiled at everyone who passed by.

Ariel's curiosity overcame the learned polite hesitancy and she pointed to the ladies, "what are they selling in that shop, Daddy?" He just coughed a bit, took her hand with more firmness, picked up their pace and didn't really answer her question. "Well, they don't sell cloth yardage, groceries or garden tools, and we won't say anything to your mother about the pretty dresses, ok? That can just be something we noticed and won't share." Ariel wondered what that was all about, but silently agreed to keep those windows, the beautiful ladies and their pretty dresses another secret she shared with Dad.

The next day would get them to Washington State, closer still to that mysterious west and the Navy Base, whatever it might be. Ariel fell asleep quickly after supper holding Teddy Bear and listening to the river.

Next morning was bright and sunny, even sunnier for Ariel because it was her birthday. She was finally three years old and today they were finally getting to the "West". Breakfast out of the way quickly, trailer and little coupe all hitched up, it was on the road and on down the mountain. The road went down, up, down and back up over and over; again more down than up.

Through the tall evergreens Ariel spotted something big and flat and shiny. "What's that over there?" she asked. "Lake Coeur d'Alene," answered Dad; "and that means we are getting very close to the Washington state border. It's less than twenty miles now until we cross the Spokane River and into Washington. And, we are arriving in Washington on your birthday. That's pretty special."

Ariel giggled and hugged herself with excitement. Birthdays didn't mean much to her yet; parties or presents were unknown, but they had finally arrived in the West the very day she was three years old; that was special. No comment from Edythe.

Still Farther West

That first night in Washington was spent under a big shady tree at the state line weigh station by the Spokane River. Fragrant little wood violets peppered the grass, along with buttercups and daisies. Edythe liked the flowers and wondered out loud if they would grow as well on the other side of the Cascade Mountains. They would soon find out. Dad brought out the book of folded map pages and traced the lines showing roads they would now travel in Washington, where they would cross a big river and then go over another long line of mountains.

Now decades later standing by the old black trunk in her basement and looking at that worn atlas, Ariel clearly recalled the day they had come to the Columbia River and looked down at it from the top of a palisade. She clearly recalled how concerned Dad had been about getting down that narrow twisting dirt trail that clung to the steep hillside.

Standing at the top Dad pointed to a small building at the river's edge and identified the flat thing floating in the river next to it as the ferry that would carry car and trailer across to the opposite side where there were tall poles in the water, and an uphill dirt road that disappeared into scrub brush. The road at the top of the palisade was also unpaved with only a thin layer of gravel over the graded dirt.

The house trailer outweighed the little coupe which had only mechanical brakes; trailer brakes didn't even exist. There were no guardrails. He had walked down part of the road and spent several quiet minutes just looking;

Ariel now realized he had probably spent much of that time praying for strength, wisdom, courage and protection for his little family. Motorcycles, even with side cars, had been one thing in the 1920's; traversing it with car and trailer quite another, especially given the limited braking capability and certainly no power steering.

When he came back up to the car, Dad picked Ariel up and held her very close, before placing her on the car seat, not her oatmeal box, and whispered in her ear, "I want you to sit all the way down on the seat, be very still and not say even one word unless you feel your bottom slip. If it does, you yell out right away." Then he had wrapped her arms and even her chubby little legs tightly around the gearshift lever. She was to hold that lever as hard as she could and not move. Edythe was on the passenger side, window rolled down so she could see the right edge of the road. Dad checked the connections one more time, unblocked the wheels, started the motor and gripped the steering wheel with both hands. His arm muscles flexed as they started down slowly and carefully. It was an anxious descent, seemingly hours long to Ariel hanging on to that gear shift with all her strength.

Finally reaching the ferry landing, Dad again set brakes, picked Ariel off the seat with a hug and kiss before placing her back on her oatmeal box perch. A happy smile spread across his face as he approached the man who jumped off the ferry to greet him. Ariel watched as they shook hands and then the fellow wrapped an arm around Dad's shoulders, and with a wide grin, almost shouted, "That was one hell of a driving job you did getting this heavy trailer down safely". Dad looked pretty happy, too.

Before long the car and trailer were on the flat platform, wheels blocked again, and with the ferry engine cranked up, they moved smoothly across the swift-flowing dark water.

The next part of the journey was through a prairie area that looked much like the Dakotas and Montana. It was dry and appeared almost barren with mostly dry dirt and rocks, only a few streams, trees and an occasional farm. The road here was also just dirt and gravel. Once up from the river it was fairly level so there weren't many water stops for the car. That was a good thing as streams were few, far between, and shallow at best, providing limited opportunities to refill the radiator or storage tanks.

Finally the Cascade Mountains appeared on the horizon and slowly looked bigger and clearer with beautiful snow gleaming in the sunlight. The Sunset Highway had been improved considerably since the mid-1920's, both Blewett and Snoqualmie Passes were now two-lane concrete roads with brightly painted yellow lines. Tall evergreen trees lined most of the way; streams and rivers were glimpsed through the forest. The highway was 'Main Street' for many small towns, and gradually more and more farms and orchards came into view. Ariel had played under the few apple trees at the Maywood farm, but here fruit trees in bloom covered acres of rolling hillsides. Farms were larger, too; with cows and horses grazing in fields of tall grass. This was much prettier than the dry rocky lands. Edythe seemed to relax a bit and smiled some, commenting on how good the air smelled.

Several times on this journey people had mentioned a new bridge that was being built over a big lake out there in the west, someplace near Seattle; but they didn't know precisely where, or if it was completed. Dad consulted his old maps and finally decided to just stay on Highway 10 until we came to Lake Washington and then figure out what to do; go around the lake or take another ferry across it. If that bridge was actually built and open to traffic it would be very easy. Time would tell. Finally he said the little town they went through was Issaquah, and that Lake Washington was only a few more miles west.

More and more traffic was headed west, cars, trucks, motorcycles and just about any sort of wheeled vehicle. There had not been very much traffic until now, mainly some trucks and a few cars; but this was almost like being in Minneapolis, and the road widened to four lanes. Seeing a high bridge ahead, Ariel asked if it was the new floating one. No, Dad explained, this bridge crossed a narrow portion of the lake from the Bellevue side onto Mercer Island. Edythe frowned, and worried they would be turned around and need to go back to get on a ferry if the new bridge was not open yet. Dad was his usual calm self, replying that since here had been no indication of Seattle traffic being diverted to a ferry landing, or south to Renton, the bridge most likely was completed and open.

And so it was. A line of little buildings that looked a bit like outhouses stretched across the lanes and Dad pulled into one on the far right where trucks seemed to go. Not an outhouse at all, but there was a little open window and a man wearing a uniform and cap. This was a toll bridge with fees based on size of vehicles and number of occupants. The toll taker asked where we were going, and recommended a route through the city to the Bremerton ferry dock. He took the toll money and wished everyone good luck and good travels.

Then down a short ramp where all the lanes merged back into two west/ two east, and onto that bridge, floating on Lake Washington. Ariel could see out both to the right and left; water on both sides, not very far below the car; boats sailing around on both sides. Edythe watched both the road and water closely, with a worried frown until the roadway rose again and disappeared into a huge dark hole - a tunnel.

Ariel was very excited about this new experience, knowing Dad would keep everyone safe no matter what it looked like at the moment. Inside that big dark hole car tail lights shone softly and Dad turned on headlights. Then she saw there was a line of yellowish lights high up on the ceiling. Quickly she could see quite well. Tunnels were fun she decided, giggling and clapping her hands. Edythe shushed her, "quiet; don't disturb." Out of the tunnel into full daylight a whole city spread out as far as she could see. Dad followed the route given him by the toll taker and before very long they came to another big lake.

No, this was not a lake, but part of Puget Sound and even farther west was the Pacific Ocean. The air smelled different, a breeze was blowing off the water, and big white birds floated gently above the waves, squawking at each other and swooping down to grab bits of food. "Those are Seagulls," Dad explained, "and they will eat just about anything that doesn't eat them first." Was there no end to this 'west' place and new things to see and learn about she wondered, but didn't ask.

Dad bought tickets for the ferry and they waited in a long line. It looked like the road just went down to the water and ended. Sensing her concern, Dad explained they were waiting for the ferry to come from the Bremerton side. All the cars and trucks would drive off, and then everyone going to Bremerton could get on. Lots of people just walked on and off, not riding in cars; but used the ramps and walkways connecting the upper deck of the ferry to the terminal.

It was warm and comfortable with her head resting on Dad's shoulder as they waited; Ariel drifted off to nap.

"Wake up; here comes the ferry," said Dad; Ariel blinked, and right there in front of her was the biggest boat ever. It was tall, wide, white, green…enormous. Ariel could see all the way through it from front to back, and it was packed full of vehicles … all sizes, shapes and colors. Way up on top in a little square building a tall man stood behind a huge wheel, his hands on what looked to her like short ends of shovel handles. He turned the wheel just a tiny bit right, then left, and watched closely as directions were signaled. Men scurried all about moving posts and chains as the huge craft bumped gently against pilings. Big ropes were thrown from the boat to fat posts and pulled tight. People started walking off, car engines were started, wheel blocks removed the front row vehicles and one by one cars and trucks moved up the ramp, through the terminal gates and out onto city streets.

Soon it was their turn to drive down that ramp and with a bump, bump, a few creeks and louder bump, both car and trailer were guided forward toward the far end of the boat. Was it the front end, or the back end? Dad explained that for them it was the front end so they could drive off that way straight ahead at the Bremerton dock. When people drove on to go to Seattle, it would be the back end. Oh. Ariel didn't quite understand, but she was certain Dad knew what he was talking about.

Bremerton, U.S. Navy, Pacific Ocean

The trailer made it easy to locate a spot to camp, fix supper and get a good night's sleep. Next morning all were up bright and early, everything stowed into place and headed for the U.S. Naval Base … the primary goal of this journey west from the little Maywood farm.

Entrance to the main gate was right in town, not far from the ferry landing. Huge gray ships were lined up along docks, all facing the open water. At the gate, Dad identified himself and his reason for being there. He had removed several important-looking papers from Ariel's oatmeal box seat and handed those to the guard. "Glad to see you," he responded in acknowledgment.

"You can park your car and housing unit over there on the right. The entrance you want is just down that row of buildings; the door marked 'construction' is about mid-way on the port side; that's left." Dad grinned and nodded. " Welcome, and good luck, sir." The cozy little house trailer was called a 'housing unit' and Dad called, 'Sir'. That was new and interesting. She remembered the 'housing unit' was one of the requirements for this new work, and a car to be transported by ship to a place called Pearl Harbor, Hawaii.

With the car and trailer parked, Dad turned to Ariel; gave her a little hug and kiss, smiling and eyes twinkling. Edythe was busily looking all around without much comment except that everything certainly was painted the same dull gray color. Ariel watched Dad walk between the rows of buildings, wave and then disappear trough the construction door. Would they get to go on the ocean on one of those giant boats? Oops, Dad said they were ships, not boats; something else to remember.

Before very long he reappeared and strode toward where Ariel and Edythe sat waiting, a broad grin on his face. "Well, that's moving right along," he said, settling behind the wheel. "We have time enough to go out and spend a few days playing on the beach before the final processing; so unless something strange shows up in the physical exam process, we could soon be on our way to Hawaii and a whole new adventure."

Ariel clapped and giggled; that sounded like lots of fun. Dad would have a good job building houses and all sorts of things. There would be other children to play with; and they would ride on a big ship on the ocean to get there.

With a wave to the guard who saluted, off they went up onto city streets, through town and even farther west to the ocean. Ariel puzzled a bit more over just what an ocean really was. Lakes large and small, streams and even wide rivers and what was called a 'sound' she had seen, but Dad said the ocean was so big they wouldn't even see land when they were sailing. That was far bigger than anything she could imagine. Dad kept driving for what seemed like hours and Ariel drifted off to sleep again, her head resting on his shoulder.

She popped awake to bumps on the road. They had turned off the paved road onto a narrow dirt track through thin brushy trees that were all bending toward them. That was strange; all the long branches were on one side of the trees, really short on the other, tree trunks leaned sideways, and there was just enough room for the trailer to get through. Just as she was about to ask, an open space appeared. Edythe gasped at the sight. Before them was a wide flat sandy beach and beyond that … water and more water that must go on forever. No land could be seen; just more and more water and white lines that rose up, went down, and came closer and closer, growing bigger and higher until they splashed all foamy against the sand, spread out and disappeared.

"Well, here we all are at last … the Pacific Ocean, and way out there is Hawaii," Dad declared. He found a good place to park and immediately set about making camp. Ariel hopped down to help. Edythe slowly got out, walked around the car, and holding her hand above her eyes, gazed out at the vast expanse of this huge and strange body of water. Waves never stopped, but kept forming on the horizon, building and falling back, rebuilding and crashing in foam onto the sand. Ariel ran about in the soft sand toward the water sending the large white squawking birds soaring into the sky. Oh, to fly like that, riding the winds and then dropping into the sea to bob about on the waves. She was totally enthralled. Now to get into that wonderful water.

Edythe roused a bit and called to Ariel, "stay out of that water with your clothes on. Come here and get your swim suit". Dad had their woolen suits and rubber beach shoes all out and ready. She could hardly wait, struggled into the itchy wool suit and the funny rubber shoes and scrambled out the trailer door to find her little shovel and pail. Dad caught up with her just as the sand changed from dry and soft to damp and hard, almost like a paved road. There were long wispy green stringy things scattered here and there that Dad called kelp or seaweed. They sure looked like giant skinny weeds with big shiny onions at the end.

She picked up some smooth white roundish things that looked a bit like small dishes, wondering what on earth they could be. "Seashells", said Dad, "and we might find some sand dollars, too." Sand dollars? What could those be? This ocean place was full of all sorts of new things, all the wonderful sand, huge logs up toward the high bank and bushes, shells and 'dollars'; and she hadn't even been in the water yet. Looking away from the water, she saw Edythe slowly walking toward them, still looking out at the water and shielding her eyes with a hat. The sunshine was bright and reflected off the water.

Continuing to where the waves splashed in foam on the sand, there were holes scattered about and water spurted out of some of them as Ariel stepped close to them. "Those are clam spouts." Dad explained, "and perhaps we can try digging some for supper". Another brand new thing … clams. He went on to describe how the clams live in the water in the sand; and when they sense pressure on the sand they quickly dig down deeper. That makes the little water spout, so if you want to dig up the clam you need to dig between the little water spout and the ocean, very quickly and deep. Clams were fast.

Finally they reached the foamy edge, soft wet sand and cool water swished between her toes, even with the rubber shoes. This was fun. Before long Ariel and Dad were wading out into the waves, splashing and laughing. She lost her balance and sat down just as a wave rolled in, over her legs and tummy, sending drops onto her face. She licked her lips … they tasted salty. Ocean was wonderful.

Edythe had almost joined the fun, but didn't go into the ocean deeper than her ankles. When Ariel waded farther up over her knees, the waves splashed all the way over her head. That was a little bit scary, but exciting and fun. Then Dad picked her up and carried her way out toward some of the bigger waves that splashed over both of them; those were really fun and Ariel could feel Dad being pushed a little. He held her safely and they bounced about as he jumped into the foam.

After splashing in the waves, Ariel went back to the wet sand and played with her shovel and little pail, digging holes, filling her pail, and turning the packed sand over to make sand castles with shells and pretty stones. Edythe sat nearby on a big smooth gray log reading a book. Dad walked down the beach for a long way; almost disappearing from sight; looking out over the ocean and then back toward his little family and the trailer. When he returned, he took a shovel and pail down to the water's edge and started digging. Ariel ran to see what he was doing, and found some long, fat shiny hard things in the pail. Were these clams? "Yes, indeed, and we will have them for dinner," said Dad, "these are razor clams. The white shells you found are from a different kind of clam; these are really yummy with a little butter". Was there no end of new things to see and learn about here in the West?

The next days were spent playing in the ocean and the sand, climbing on logs Dad said were driftwood, and falling asleep to the continuous muffled roar of waves. Waking in the morning the water would be in a different place on the beach than when she went to bed. Putting that question to Dad, he said the water levels were called tides; they came in and went out because the moon has gravity and so does the earth. The moon's gravity was what controlled how high and low the tides are. Still more new things to remember. Each day Dad walked along the beach, almost but never quite out of sight, so Ariel didn't worry about him. Edythe spent most of her time reading, or writing on a tablet, and always wore her hat.

One afternoon just before supper, she saw Dad and Edythe sitting together on one of the big driftwood logs near her, talking and watching the waves crash onto the beach. Dad put his arm around Edythe's shoulders and asked, "well, now that you have seen a bit of the ocean, what you think about getting out on it and sailing to Pearl Harbor?" The whole journey from Minnesota had been focused on getting to the Navy base, being accepted into the construction division, and crossing the ocean. Nothing really stood between Dad and the good paying job with the Navy; but he had yet to actually sign on. They had arrived at the Naval Base with the requisite vehicle, housing unit, tools, certifications, experience and good health. All his documentation was in order; everything ready to be loaded onto the deck of a Navy ship, lock, stock and barrel.

Edythe didn't answer right away, just gazed out over the beach and crashing breakers to the horizon. This was the first time in her life she had been more than a hundred miles from her childhood home. They had now traveled half-way across the country; to a seemingly endless ocean.

Rather softly, she finally stated, "It's even bigger than Lake Superior. Hawaii is hundreds, no, thousands of miles away across this ocean. I'm not going."

Dad's shoulders sagged just a little, but he hugged her, and said, "OK". With that simple acknowledgement his dream of a new and distant adventure was snuffed. Back to the ocean, he walked through the soft sand to the trailer and began fixing supper.

Next morning they had a quick breakfast, packed up the trailer and car, made sure they didn't leave any trash, headed back to the main road and Bremerton. At the Navy Base that same guard was on duty and welcomed them with a smile, and waved Dad over to the parking area. He retrieved the remaining papers from Ariel's oatmeal box seat, walked to that same construction building door and disappeared, briefly. Soon he was back with the sheets of paper and placed them in the oatmeal box. Ariel resumed her perch.

He turned the car and trailer toward the gate, with a somewhat wry smile and answering wave to the guard's salute, drove up the ramp to city streets and out of town to find a place for the night.

Point-No-Point, Renton, and Medina

They were not sailing to Hawaii. Dad contacted his friend Ralph Boberg who was quite pleased to learn that help was available. He had a number of houses started. Several were framed in and ready for the finishing work that was Dad's specialty. He also had acreage just outside the town at Point-No-Point where the trailer could be parked in a large grassy field overlooking the Strait of Juan de Fuca. Running water was available and a new, sturdy outhouse quickly built.

Mid-May 1941 and an absolutely beautiful spot. Daisies and buttercups bloomed in the field; blackberry vines bloomed along the steep bank above the water; song birds built nests in the trees; and seagulls squawked as they soared out over the waves, diving for food. What a marvelous place for a little girl to play. There was dirt to dig in; flowers to pick, little brown bunnies scampering about in the field and space to explore. A small cat appeared one day and quickly became Ariel's companion.

Dad was busy every day working on Mr. Boberg's new houses, and always had a smile and kiss for Ariel when he came home in the evening. Some days she went to work with him, carrying her peanut butter sandwich and apple in a little brown bag. She loved the smell of freshly cut boards, and just being with Dad. There were tools to find for him from the big wooden box, and bent nails to pick up from the ground. Ariel particularly hunted for the little round knock-outs from electrical outlet and light switch boxes. They looked almost like money so she put those in a separate coffee can. New houses being built were great fun. She also picked up scraps of wood and piled them for burning. At lunch time she and Dad sat on stacked lumber in the sunshine to eat their sandwiches. When Mr. Boberg saw the scrap wood pile and her cans of nails and 'coins', he gave her some real coins to put in her pocket. He said she was a very good worker and saved the carpenters a lot of time by cleaning up the job site. It was such fun to help.

Spring turned to summer and by mid-September the houses nearly finished and ready to sell. Edythe was not particularly happy living in the trailer out in the middle of a field. There really was not much for her to do; a bit of cooking and the little cleaning required did not take much time. Laundry was taken into town on Saturdays to a wash-a-teria and then hung out on lines at the trailer to dry. She could not get good reception on the little brown table radio for the church programs she liked. The evening news broadcast was on most evenings, but when recorded music and singing were played the radio was abruptly snapped off. While her husband worked all day and daughter played quite happily outdoors with the kitty or picked nails and scrap on a job site, Edythe was rather confined to the trailer with a few books and her writing tablet. It was time to re-pack, hitch up and move along to … somewhere.

Dad wanted to look into possibilities of work at the new plant in Renton being built by the Boeing Company to construct airplanes. He wasn't quite sure just where it was…somewhere in the town of Renton.

Once again there was a ferry ride and on the east side of Puget Sound, they traveled south of Seattle. A small sign along the highway indicated "the Boeing Co." with an arrow pointing to the right. The road consisted of a single set of dirt tracks through tall reeds and scrub brush, with no sign of any construction.

At last they came upon a man leaning on a shovel handle at the side of the road and Dad stopped to ask if he knew where this "Boeing" company was located. "You found it – right here," he replied, not offering any additional information. This did not look very promising as far as jobs of any sort were concerned

Dad thanked the fellow, found a place to turn around; back to the main road and on into Renton where Ralph Boberg and his son had purchased more lots on which to build more single-family houses. A job was waiting there; space located in a trailer park, under a big tree and beside a small creek. Ariel quickly found Asumi to play with; Edythe had other women to talk with and seemed a little happier.

Winter months in the Puget Sound area are rather dark, cloudy and rainy. Three people living in an 18-foot house trailer was not particularly easy for anyone. Dad worked during the weekdays and sometimes Saturdays as well; Asumi and Ariel played with toys and colored, at Asumi's when it rained and outdoors with kitty in clear weather. Asumi's Mom baked yummy Japanese cookies and didn't mind a bit when the girls giggled and laughed.

Edythe had located a church east of Bellevue that was much like the one at Maywood; Sundays found them all in regular attendance. Dad liked to stop at a small restaurant for a good chicken dinner on the way back to Renton, and Edythe rather grimly agreed to this frivolity. Two such dinners were ordered with an empty saucer for Ariel. Small portions of those dinners were shared with her; Dad ensuring she had a drumstick despite Edythe's frowns.

One Sunday in early December they were invited to the Minister's home for dinner. Everyone was seated, grace had been said, and dishes of hot, yummy food passed around; the Sunday Concert was playing on the radio. It was a very nice day and Ariel looked forward to playing outside with Benny and Marion after dinner. Suddenly the pretty music just stopped; not at the end of a selection, but right in the middle. A man's voice interrupted; identified himself as Lowell Thomas, and grimly spoke.

"It is my sad duty to announce that early this morning, December 7th, Hawaiian Islands time, the nation of Japan carried out an aerial attack on Pearl Harbor. Heavy casualties and loss of material have been incurred. All military personnel are ordered by President Franklin D. Roosevelt to report immediately to the nearest Military Base for assignment. All leaves are canceled. Additional details will be broadcast as those become available. We now return you to the regularly scheduled programming."

Conversation halted mid-sentence, dinner forgotten; the stunned silence interrupted only by the resumption of violins, cellos and slowly wind sections of the recorded orchestra. Even little Benny in his high chair was quiet. Ariel would remember that day all her life; sitting on three volumes of an encyclopedia, concerned about which utensil to use and proper placement of her lap napkin—that Sunday the whole world changed.

December 7, 1941 was described by the President as "the day that will live in infamy".

Finally the Minister softly spoke and offered "a prayer for all military personnel, the President, Congress, State and local officials, people caught up in the European War, Navy and Hawaiian residents, churches and congregations across the country, and the Japanese people whose leaders had initiated this attack. Amen."

Little by little conversation slowly returned, hesitantly, lest a further announcement be missed; portions of the now-cooled meal consumed. It was a somber dinner table. Marion, Benny and Ariel were soon dismissed from the table despite vegetables remaining on their plates, and ushered outdoors to play. No one was very hungry. The adults definitely wanted to discuss this dreadful new event without little ears listening.

Winter was an uneasy time with adjustments to war in the Pacific and fear that the mainland would also soon be under attack. Industries of all sorts increased production and companies hired just about anyone willing to work. Both Ariel's and Asumi's fathers worked long hours of overtime, with only Sundays off.

However, by spring 1942 fears of invasion had grown to an alarming degree and President Roosevelt, backed by Congress, ordered the internment of all persons, U.S. Citizens included, having Japanese heritage. Asumi's dad immediately quit his good manufacturing job, even though he and his wife as well as their parents were all U.S. citizens, born in Seattle. He hoped they might be safe with extended family in Montana, far away from any defense facilities or military bases. They packed what they could into their old sedan. He hoped to get them there before trucks would arrive to haul every one to internment camps.

Ariel and Asumi listened quietly as their dads discussed the war, possibilities of invasion and concerns for citizens of any Asian descent, not only Japanese.

Asumi gave her kitten to Ariel; traveling several hundred miles in a fully-packed car did not have space for a busy kitten. They managed to get away one day before the Army trucks arrived and loaded remaining Asian families for transport.

Fears mounted. At the church there was concern about Ariel and her family living in Renton. Several manufacturing plants were located there along with the expanded and still growing Boeing Aircraft Company. It was also a rail center with the Ports of Tacoma and Seattle close by. A large shipyard facility was located on Lake Washington at Kirkland, with the Sand Point Naval Air Base at the north end of the lake. Renton could definitely become a target area for any attack on the mainland.

A church member, Mr. Swanson readily offered a place in his apple orchard, and only wanted to know how soon this little family could get there; he wanted to have water and electricity in place for them.

Arrangements were made to move to Medina and packing began, again. Edythe was glad to leave Renton. While she had enjoyed one or two of her neighbors, she liked being closer to the church and people who thought more as she did. Those folks also liked some of the same religious programs she listened to on the little table radio. She had considered the other trailer park people more than slightly inferior and not quite acceptable.

Ariel really did not like having to say 'good-bye' to Asumi who had not wanted to go to Montana, but both were just little kids and not involved in decision-making. Ariel promised to take good care of kitty, and she did.

The orchard spot was beautiful and a large apple tree accommodated the trailer very nicely. Dad dug a big deep hole and built a sturdy new outhouse under a tree. That was followed by a platform on concrete pillars with four-foot walls and posts to hold a frame for a tarp roof. Many things could be stored in that tent-shed, making more living space in the trailer. Kitty adapted quickly to chasing butterflies and playing in buttercups, soon learning to leave bees alone.

Ariel had received a doll and doll buggy for Christmas, and she could keep those in the tent-shed as well. Each day the sun shone, she placed dolly and little blanket in the buggy and pushed them up and down the Medina/Hunts Point Road. One such afternoon huge raindrops started falling and she ran toward the orchard and trailer as fast as she could. Her toe caught on a seam of the roadway and she fell – hard onto the concrete. Ariel, buggy and doll were a jumbled mess. Skinned face could be explained by a bush, elbows and knees covered with stockings and long sleeves; but there was a deep cut on her wrist that bled onto the bent buggy. That was not something Ariel could hide and take care of herself; she had to tell Edythe. The wound was examined, probed, cleaned, medicated with the dreaded '*tincture of merthiolate*' and bandaged with clinical efficiency and a scolding. That evening Dad straightened the buggy framework and washed stains from the doll and little blanket. He re-attached dolly's broken toes using glue and wax, and hugged Ariel close, assuring her some hard falls and bruises were part of living and growing up. Edythe remained frowning and silent when he told Ariel about some of his motorcycle falls, omitting most details. That was comforting and reassuring.

After all, Dad survived lots of falls, even from motorcycles, and he was still here, strong and healthy. If he had survived all those, she would be just fine as well.

A girl living down the road occasionally came to play with Ariel in the orchard after her school was out. They had a great time romping bare-footed through the grass, picking flowers, and on occasions being stung by honey bees from Pete Swanson's hives. Both girls quickly learned to put a little swamp mud on the stings, and not tell her mother or Edythe about them. Getting the mud was fun, too, wading in the warm, shallow water to find the very best mud. They also learned to check swing seats for bees before sitting down.

Ariel liked going to Mr. Swanson's house because everyone there was so nice and, they had a little black dog that could stand up on his back legs and dance. He liked playing ball, too, and wanted Ariel to keep throwing it for him until he was all out of breath and settled at her feet holding the ball between his little paws. The Swanson kitchen was the friendliest place, and always smelled of homemade soups, freshly baked bread and cookies. These friendly people reminded Ariel of Uncles and Aunts and kitchens back home. Ariel often stayed there until Dad came to get her after work; he liked the Swanson kitchen, too. He enjoyed talking with Philip, Uncle Pete who raised bees, and their sister Hilda. Philip's daughter Ethel went to high school and didn't have much time for playing, but always took Ariel with her to collect eggs from the hen house and fill water buckets for the cows. This was Ariel's get-away place where everyone seemed to like her and no one scolded. She was always careful to behave – at Swansons and everywhere else, too, simply because she wanted to, and also wanted grown-ups to like her. She didn't run or jump about indoors, and truly didn't want to be a 'bratty kid'. Only Edythe seemed to constantly find things to criticize and scold her for. She often wondered why and stayed outdoors or at Swansons as much as possible. Philip Swanson let her go to the barn with him for milking, putting down fresh hay and petting the kitties.

The War continued; Dad worked long hours at a boat-works company building plywood P-T boats. Some things were in short supply at the stores, and everyone saved scrap metal to turn in for the War Effort. Even Ariel picked up any metal pieces she found on the roadside while pushing her doll buggy, and Dad took those to work, adding them to the shop collection. Everyone talked about the War and the young men in the community who had joined the Army or Navy. It all seemed very far away to Ariel and she truly didn't know what War really was; but, something bad.

Flowers bloomed in the orchard grass and buds appeared on the apple trees. Pete tended his bee hives, wearing a netted hat and long sleeved shirts. The hives were lined up on one side of the orchard and bees were very busy visiting flowers from fields and gardens as well as the blossoming orchard trees. Ariel watched out for them, receiving only a few stings while running barefoot in the grass. One day without looking, she plopped down on the seat of the swing Dad had hung from an apple tree branch. A bumble bee had chosen that spot to sun himself and was not pleased about being sat on. He just barely started to sting when she jumped up and brushed him away. It hurt, but she also hoped the bee would be OK, and so he was, quickly buzzing off to a flower, without even a backward glance.

Before anyone thought about it, April 28th and Ariel's 4th birthday arrived. They had been in Washington for a whole year already, and what a year it had been. Dad had found a good steady job, and they now lived in a beautiful orchard; but, still in the house trailer. It was definitely crowded living, even with the tent-shed for storage.

One late summer evening when Ariel and Dad were at Swansons getting eggs and milk, Philip told them about a Mrs. McGhee who wanted to go to Florida for the winter and was looking for someone to take care of her house and little dog. War fears had grown and she also wanted to get away from the Seattle area where there were factories, ship yards and airplane companies that could come under attack. Would Dad and Edythe be interested in doing that?

For Dad and Ariel that sounded absolutely lovely – a real house to live in at least for the winter. Edythe had a lot of questions and worries, but quickly realized that a summer house on Lake Washington would be a big improvement over the trailer, especially in the wet and colder months. Philip Swanson made the arrangements and the little Pedersen family prepared to move yet again. Ariel was really excited about this move; a real house with her own bedroom, and … a dog to play with and take for walks. Wow.

Kitty had opted to live in Mr. Swanson's barn where Ariel brought saucers of milk, visited and played with him.

Arrangements were quickly put in place. The Pedersens met with Mrs. McGhee who showed them the house, out buildings, and identified things they might need for winter. She trusted Philip Swanson implicitly and anyone he had recommended was certain to take good care of her property, especially little Toby.

She was particularly pleased that Ariel loved animals and would happily take Toby for walks each day, using his special leash. And so Mrs. McGhee departed by train to spend the winter, and perhaps longer, with her sister in Florida. No one knew how long this War would last, and just what might possibly happen on the West Coast. She did not want to be caught in a possible Japanese invasion for sure. Florida seemed a much safer place, and she was happy to be on her way, traveling across the entire country by train.

The house trailer was parked in a shed next to the garage, the Model A coupe in the garage, and with clothing, personal things and dishes moved, they were living in a real house after 18 long months. Ariel had a room … all to herself with a big comfortable bed and pretty wallpaper.

Toby's little basket was right by her bed. Sometimes he whimpered to crawl up and cuddle with Ariel, especially if there was a thunder storm; they both hid under the blankets. In Maywood thunderstorms were fun; she watched the lightning with Dad and laughed when thunder rolled. Here was different; there was a war and people said thunder sounded like bombs. She didn't know just what those were, but had to be something very bad.

It was so nice to have a little doggy friend. There hadn't ever been many children to play with, Peggy Johnson once in a while at Maywood; and then with Asumi at the Renton trailer park. Swanson's little dog was a dear and loved to play ball, have his ears rubbed and sit with her. There had been few non-critter friends in her life. Asumi's kitty had moved with her from Renton, but quickly settled into the Swanson barn. Now she had little Toby for a friend.

The wallpaper in her room was white with big green strawberry plants and plump red berries in an irregular pattern. During the day and when the light was on, it was ever so pretty; Ariel could almost taste the juicy berries. At night when shadows seemed to move across the walls and tree branches brushed against the house, those berries and leaves turned into faces, enemy Japanese faces, and she was very frightened. Not once had Ariel related the "Japanese enemy" talked about so much on the radio as related in any way to her friend Asumi in Renton. There was no connection whatever in her mind between Asumi's family and any enemy; they were her friends. She truly did not understand why they had to move to Montana to be safe. Safe from what? She had no idea then, and it would be several years before she understood any of it.

Ariel loved taking Toby for walks far down the road and back. At the house, he played in the lake with her and she talked to him about sailing on ships across the big ocean as they bounced and splashed in a partially sunken row boat on the sandy beach. Toby didn't like to swim and he yipped and yapped at Ariel when she waded out into deeper water. They had grand times in the water and on shore as Ariel dug holes, built little forts with branches and made up adventures.

One sunny afternoon they set out for a walk down the road past the store, golf course, many big houses set back from the road with vast lush green lawns and tree-lined drives. They walked and walked until they reached the end of the road where a tall gate was closed to the last driveway. Ariel could not read all the words, but "no" was quite clear and that gate was locked.

No matter; they would just turn around and go back. All was fine for a long way until rain started to fall, just lightly at first; then thunder rolled and huge drops pelted down … so hard they bounced on the concrete. Toby started running for home. Ariel kept up with him as long as she could, but her little legs didn't move as fast as Toby's; he pulled the leash out of her hand and raced down the road without her. She worried that Edythe wouldn't know what to do when Toby arrived alone, and she hurried as fast as possible, running until she was completely out of breath, walking a little and then running again, rain and tears all running down her face and soaking her dress. Edythe would be so unhappy that she had let go of Toby and got her clothes all wet and dirty, slipped in the mud and skinned her knees. This was not a good thing.

At last she spotted the little store through the downpour and then Mrs. McGhee's driveway. There was Toby on the steps, soaking wet with leash still hooked to his collar, looking up the drive.

He ran to Ariel just as Edythe stepped outside. "Well, there you are, finally. Where have you been? Toby came home long ago, and you weren't with him, why? We are responsible for him, you know. He isn't supposed to be just running all over by himself."

With gulping sobs Ariel tried to explain about the rain, thunder, and that Toby was scared and she couldn't hold on to him when he ran so fast. "Oh, well you dry him off with an old towel, hang up his leash, get him some fresh water and see there is food in his dish. Then you get out of those wet things and wash up. Your father will be home soon". She did as instructed; very glad Edythe had not grabbed her arm to make certain all was understood. Fingernails pressed into her inside upper arm always hurt and the red marks lasted for days. She didn't ever want Dad to see those and ask about them; fingernail marks could not be explained away by tree branch scratches. Dad was not apt to buy any such story.

82

Blackouts & Rationing

Ariel truly did not understand the War everyone talked about other than it was a bad thing. By then known as World War II, that was the topic of radio newscasts as well as the newspaper articles and photos. People continued to collect scrap metal to be melted down and made into other things for the war. Rationing of many items was instituted and shopping became a matter of counting ration tickets and not wasting anything. Gasoline was also rationed, so there were no Sunday afternoon drives just to see the area. Sugar, meat, and even eggs were in short supply and rationed. Dad worked swing shift at the boat yard and sometimes didn't come home until well after the day shift men arrived. Living in Mrs. McGhee's house, and with rationing placing limits on what could be purchased, along with the good wages Dad earned, money began to accumulate for building a house here in the west.

Edythe volunteered for what she said was a watch organization of some sort that was never identified and Ariel didn't understand at all. She brought out all her nurse uniforms, white hose and shoes; even the starched nurse hat with Swedish Hospital 1927 pins. Several evenings each week, after supper and with Dad working at the boat yard, she changed into her uniform and cape, took a shielded flashlight and set out to walk through the community. Ariel had been told only that it was necessary that she do that because of the War. Ariel was to stay inside the house. It was just one of the many changes in lives of adults and children due to wartime conditions. There were air raid warnings at night without any advance notice and everyone turned off all indoor and outdoor lights. Car headlights had covers that could be put over the lights and stuck out in front so that only a little bit of light shone straight down on the roadway. Sometimes Dad drove home in the middle of the night without any lights, just stars or a bit of moonlight, the window open so he could hear more clearly.

When the sirens sounded, and Edythe went out to walk on the streets, Ariel and Toby crouched in the darkened house by the big front window overlooking Lake Washington and peeked out through a narrow space at the bottom of the Venetian blinds. Little by little the city lights went out across the lake, becoming great blocks of blackness. Then the floating bridge went black, section by section until no lights reflected on the water and everything they saw out that window was dark. Only search lights stretching into the night sky from Sand Point Naval Air Base pierced the dark; sirens wailed on and on. It was a scary time for little girl and small dog. Many times they and Teddy Bear crawled into Harold's old leather suitcase and closed the lid over their heads. They felt safer there.

One day when Ariel was sent to the little store, the owner asked if she could help collect eggs for the war. Those would be gathered at the store and taken to the Sand Point Naval Air Base and made into powdered eggs for feeding soldiers and sailors. There really was something a little child could do for the war after all. She found a little basket and was soon walking up one road and down another, stopping at each house to ask if they could donate an egg or two for the war. Soon her basket had several eggs and she took those to the store, very carefully. Each day she took her little basket and gathered as many eggs as she could, delivering them all to the store unbroken.

On an afternoon when Toby was sleeping on the porch Ariel went exploring on her own, poking through the tall hedge just to see what was on the other side. She came face to face with a startled, confused man down on his knees pulling weeds, who blurted out, "Oh my, what have we here? Who are you? Where did you come from?" Ariel tried to explain that she lived in the house next door, but he said he didn't think so. That house belonged to Mrs. McGhee and she certainly didn't have any little girl … definitely not a rather grubby one with leaves and twigs in her untidy braids.

Gingerly taking her hand he led Ariel up to the back of a beautiful white and brick house to the kitchen door, where he told her to wait. She stood absolutely still wondering what she had done wrong. She just wanted to see the other side of the hedge; now she had and could go back the way she had come. But, she stood very still and waited for what seemed a very long time.

"My, my, and just who are you and where did you come from?" asked a tall beautiful lady with white hair and a wide warm smile. Ariel again explained that she lived next door in Mrs. McGhee's house, because she was visiting her sister in Florida. "Well, you simply must come in and stay for lunch. May I call your mother to be sure that is alright with her?" Ariel hesitated for a long moment before nodding and giving her the telephone number; R276, and the call was placed. Edythe hesitated and then agreed. Soon Ariel's face and hands had been washed, hair somewhat smoothed and she was seated at a small table in what Mrs. Fitzgerald called a 'morning room. Windows overlooked the enormous lawn and the lake. It was all so beautiful, indoors and out. Huge long-haired, gorgeous cats sat on colorful pillows in a window seat; the biggest and most beautiful animals. Ariel had never seen such wonderful kitties. They looked at her as though whatever she was should be properly removed from their presence… immediately. Ariel did not attempt petting them.

Lunch was delicious; tiny open-faced sandwiches and lemonade served by a smiling lady wearing a black dress and lacy white apron. Mrs. Fitzgerald spoke with Ariel on an adult level, asking about the westward journey and also about Toby. He had once chased her kitties, but had stayed away after they scratched his nose. Ariel giggled at that, and told about Toby breaking loose in the rain and running home by himself. Mrs. Fitzgerald chuckled and declared Toby to be a very bad little doggie for doing that, but she could understand.

With sandwich and juice consumed, and napkin neatly folded, Ariel thanked her and suggested she just pop back through the fence again. "Oh no, George will bring the machine around and see you safely back home" she said, and rang a little silver bell. The smiling lady appeared, took Mrs. Fitzgerald's message for George, and soon it was time to go. Ariel put the pretty pink napkin back into the silver ring and followed this beautiful lady … not to the kitchen, but to a side door that opened onto a covered porch, No longer in overalls, George was now wearing black trousers, white shirt and bow tie, a black jacket and a cap with a silver band around it. Ariel shook hands with Mrs. Fitzgerald and thanked her again for lunch before walking toward the front passenger door of the biggest, blackest, shiniest and longest car in the whole world. She was to ride in this beautiful car, the 'machine'? But George stood in her way and opened the back seat passenger door, helped her up a step and onto a plush bench seat before closing the door and going around to the driver's door.. There were little sparkly vases in silver brackets high on each side of the seat, and a glass window between the driver area and where she sat. George looked back to see that she was still safely seated before starting the engine. It hardly made any sound at all; not like the rattley little Ford coupe.

Up the long curved, tree-lined drive they went, to the main road, down to Mrs. McGhee's drive to the porch where little Toby waited. "I see you are taking good care of that little dog", said George; "Mrs. F will be happy to hear that. She likes him even if her cats don't." George opened the door and took Ariel's hand; she shook his and thanked him for the ride. Wow, what an experience; she could scarcely wait to tell Dad about it. Edythe just wanted to know if she had remembered her manners, washed her hands and thanked properly for lunch. She had. Edythe's frown softened slightly.

Patsy and Doug who lived in a small older cottage next door to Mrs. McGhee's were a little older than Ariel. Their parents both worked during the day, and sometimes they found Ariel playing with Toby down by the lake. Being inquisitive children it was not long before the three began opening shed and garage doors, crawling about under workbenches and opening old boxes. What treasures abounded…hammers and screw drivers, car parts, old appliances, broken furniture, books, and discarded fireplace tools. One splendid find was part of a discarded fireplace set, a steel rod with three sharp points at one end and big polished handle at the other. It was quite sturdy and long enough to stab a piece of wood to put on the fire. It was just right for the kids to stab and move downed tree branches. When Ariel's turn came she took careful aim at a piece of wood, gripped the handle, raised her arms high and drove one sharp point directly into her left foot. It stuck firmly in the top of her shoe, but didn't really hurt at first. She had never even thought of a dilemma like this; now what to do. She definitely didn't want Edythe to know. The neighbor kids took off for home.

Ariel yanked the point out of her foot and shoe, hopped into the garage and hid that fireplace tool under the work bench, then back out the door and shut it. Now what could she do about her shoe and ruined sock? He foot really hurt, and it was bleeding, too.

Toby had hidden from all the excitement, but came out when she called him, and they made their way down to the lake. Ariel struggled with the laces for some time before the shoe was loose enough to get her foot out. That did not look good at all; there was a nasty round hole in her sock…and on the top of her foot. Cold lake water eased the foot; she rinsed out the sock and put it on a branch to dry. Once cleaned, the shoe tongue was not so bad; the hole was not too big and she pushed the leather edges together as much as she could. Dad would be home later, and maybe he could fix it a little.

After supper Dad took her by the hand and they went out and sat on the front steps. "Now you tell me, little one, just what have you been up to that you are limping a bit?" and she whispered the afternoon's events in his ear. He went into the house very quietly and casually brought out a wet cloth, medicine bottle and bandage. Removing the abused shoe and sock, he declared the wound quite clean; she had done the right thing to soak her foot in the cool lake water. It didn't take him long to apply the medicine, small bandage and clean sock. Everything was much, much better.

Another afternoon she ventured into and began poking around in another shed, soon joined by her neighbor pals. They discovered an old dusty paint can. With a rusty screwdriver and hammer, the lid popped off revealing yellow oil. The can wrapper indicated white paint; what was the yellowy stuff? With a stick shoved down to the bottom and moved about, white coloring emerged. Hands replaced the stick, and smeared paint up arms to look like long white gloves.

When Dad came home and found this mess he was not overly pleased, but quickly set about cleaning them up with turpentine. That was not nearly as much fun; their arms stung even after washing with soap and water. Another lesson learned.

Fall and winter brought rain and even a little snow, so she spent more and more time indoors playing with blocks, coloring and trying to stay quiet so Edythe was not disturbed. Just what she did Ariel hadn't a clue; but she didn't seem very happy. Ariel hummed and sang little songs to Toby and Teddy Bear, looked at her books, picking out words she knew and later asking Dad about others when she sat on his lap by the fireplace after supper. She liked that he now worked days and not nights. He read the paper, and told her about some articles. They looked at the funnies together and she began to learn to read.

Playing in the snow was great, but it was really wet here, not dry and fluffy like in Minnesota. Toby was not very happy about either rain or snow, and preferred to watch out the window from inside the warm dry porch or better still the living room.

In late fall of 1942, Grandma and Grandpa Johnson celebrated their 50th Wedding Anniversary, and Edythe wanted to be there. She and Ariel boarded a train in Seattle and headed back to Minnesota. Dad stayed in Medina, working and taking care of Toby. The trip was somewhat interesting, but Ariel didn't know much about what she saw out the windows, and Edythe told her to sit still, keep quiet, just look at her books and color, not to jump around. The train itself was fun; there were people to talk with, little paper cups for getting drinks of water, meals in the dining car, and sleeping on a shelf called an upper berth at night.

One morning at breakfast, just as she reached for her milk glass, Edythe again cautioned her to hold onto the glass tightly. She did, and once to her mouth also held it with her lips and teeth. Another instruction to hold it tightly and Ariel bit right through that pretty glass, her mouth full of broken pieces. "Don't swallow; just sit still", and a piece of tissue was held over her lips. Ariel tried to pick the shards out, but her hands were firmly held by Edythe.

Before Ariel could even wriggle a really tall dark-skinned man appeared at the table, and with a wide smile assured her everything was going to be just fine. "Open your mouth and let me have those sharp pieces. It's ok, and that wasn't your fault … not one little bit. I'll get you another glass of milk, and some yummy mashed potatoes. Do you like gravy?" Tears streaming down her face Ariel could only ask with her eyes why he would bring her any much-coveted mashed potatoes, and with gravy; especially when she had done something so very bad. Edythe released her hands at last and wiped most of the tears away with the big white table napkin, tsk-tsking under her breath. "Why on earth did you do that? It's so embarrassing."

That smiling man soon re-appeared carrying the new glass of milk and a really big soup bowl of fluffy potatoes topped with both butter and gravy. "Now, little lady, you drink some milk and eat all these potatoes, just in case one tiny bit of that glass might have sneaked past me and down into your tummy. We don't want it to be there all alone, but completely covered in potatoes, butter and gravy. OK?" In spite of feeling horrible about having been bad, Ariel couldn't help smiling back at him shyly. He was so nice, and hadn't scolded one bit. Later that morning she saw him during her walk through the train; he again asked how she was and if she liked the potatoes. Did she? Those were wonderful. They grinned at each other again.

The 50th Anniversary celebration was quite an event, with aunts, uncles, cousins, family friends and so many people Ariel didn't know, although they all seemed to know her and were so nice and friendly. Cousin Dale and even

Cousins Shirley, Bill and Bob were there; along with Gloria, who was born in Nome, Alaska, and her little sister. This was a major family event, indeed with a huge beautiful cake with candles, cookies and juice.

Grandma fixed a small cup of coffee for her with lots of cream and sugar. She said every Swedish child, and especially her granddaughter needed a good cup of coffee. The train trip back was long, but nothing really bad happened, much to Ariel's relief. She truly tried to be good and not bother Edythe.

1943 arrived and by April 28th Ariel was five years old. In January Dad had bought two acres of land from Mrs. Schoning at the Church. She and her daughters, Doris and Blanche lived in an old farmhouse between Bellevue and Highland. They had about ten acres, with house, garage, barn, pump house and chicken coop complete with several white hens and one very ill-tempered rooster. Mrs. Schoning had been widowed for several years; the girls were in high school, and she had no need for the two acres at the south side of her property. That area had been extra pasture for cows now long gone.

Dad was soon busy drawing up plans for a little house. He was eager to build a house for his family on his own land. And … Mrs. McGhee just might decide to return now that the War had been going on for so long apparently with no additional direct threat to the west coast area.

Also early in 1943, Edythe's mother Hilma suffered a stroke so she traveled back to Deerwood, taking Ariel with her. All the proper nurse uniforms, caps, shoes and pins were also packed so she would be appropriately dressed to care for her mother. Edythe was worried about her mother along with innumerable other things. She didn't talk to Ariel very much, except to scold or tersely instruct her to sit still, be quiet and not ask so many questions.

A new adventure on this trip involved Ariel's walking the length of their train car, struggling to open and squeeze through the heavy doors at the end of each car, crossing over one steel plate to the one for the next car and then getting another heavy door open to explore there. Edythe was frequently napping and wanted quiet, so Ariel often set out on her own to talk with people, look out windows at passing fields, farms, rivers – all new and wonderful discoveries.

Hopping across the open spaces where the cars were coupled together was a little scary because the plates moved side-to-side as the train swayed. The first one took her a while to watch the motion and quickly jump across when they were fairly even with each other. After that it was fairly easy and she moved through several cars stopping occasionally to talk with people and to get another drink of water with a little paper cup, or use one of the tiny toilets. She was having a great time and seeing new things until one door wouldn't open and she was left standing outside on the steel plate. How to turn around presented a new problem to solve. She hadn't thought about that and just stood on the steel plate, holding onto the door, watching trees, telegraph poles and bushes rush past when strong hands suddenly picked her up and she was held close by another tall dark-skinned man wearing a conductor's hat and a seriously worried expression.

"I can't get this door open," Ariel explained, "and I want to see what's in this next car." Then he smiled, which made her feel much better. "Does your Mama know where you are?" he asked.

"I don't know, she is napping and I'm trying to be quiet so she can sleep."

"Well, we will talk with her later about that; but for right now, let's you and I get that door open and check out what's inside; is that ok with you?" It was way more than just 'ok'. He put Ariel up on his shoulder and held her legs firmly against his chest, knocked on the door; it was opened and in they went. There were no seats in this car, just lots of men working standing up and swaying slightly as the train moved.

"Hello, boys, look who's come to visit you", his deep voice boomed, and all heads snapped around to see. They were standing at rows of shelves and cubby-holes, taking handfuls of envelopes from big bags at their feet, and putting pieces into different spaces. They were eager to explain to Ariel just what they were doing, that by sorting the envelopes in those bags while moving down the tracks, mail could be dropped off at small towns along the way to be delivered more quickly.

So that's how letters got from Washington to Minnesota and others back again. Another new thing learned. They seemed to enjoy Ariel's visit every bit as much as she did, but there was work to do as well. Once back up the line of cars to where Edythe had just wakened, Ariel was lifted down to the floor and handed a book to keep her occupied while the conductor talked with her mother.

When they arrived at the station in Minneapolis, Ariel remembered to thank the smiling giant for showing her that Mail car and say a proper 'good-bye' before scampering off the train. Edythe only nodded slightly to him as he wished her a good visit.

Ariel quickly spotted Cousin Dale jumping up and down, waving and grinning. Aunt Bertha and Uncle Cle were right behind him, calling out their welcome. They quickly scooped Ariel up in hugs and kisses, and Edythe seemed happier, greeting her sister and brother-in-law warmly. Bags were soon claimed and they were off to have a good supper, warm baths and a good night's sleep.

In the morning everyone packed into Uncle Cle's car again and headed north, past Mille Lacs Lake to Grandma and Grandpa Johnson's Deerwood home. Ariel had last seen them in late 1942 at their 50th Anniversary, but really didn't quite remember them very well. After hugging her and exclaiming over how she had grown, they were kept quite busy with the anniversary party and she had played with her cousins.

Once at the Deerwood home, Uncle, Aunt and Dale helped get Edythe settled in a downstairs room, then Ariel up in the attic. After visiting with Grandma, Grandpa and Gerda, they had coffee and snacks, and then headed back home. Ariel had hoped Cousin Dale could stay so she would have someone to play with, but that didn't happen. Aunt Gerda presided over the household and said Ariel would be a great help to her with keeping the wood box filled and many more small tasks. Winter had set in, with it very cold weather and that wood box emptied quickly, especially as she tried to keep the house warm for her mother.

Soon Gerda found lots of things to keep Ariel busy. On laundry day she was given clean sheets, pillow cases and towels one or two at a time, to run out to the clothes line where a neighbor lady hung them up to freeze dry. When the wash was all done, tubs emptied and hung up on the back porch, Gerda fixed coffee and treats for everyone. Grandpa joined them at the table, and Gerda pulled Ariel onto her lap for hugs, thanking her for helping. Gerda's lap was so nice and soft, her arms strong and loving. Ariel's coffee always had lots of cream and sugar, and Grandpa usually had lemon drops in his pocket for her. One afternoon Aunt Gerda showed Ariel a shiny brass thimble that just fit on her finger, explaining that it protected the finger used to push a needle through cloth. Each day she helped Ariel learn to thread needles and make tidy stitches on a little piece of cloth held firmly in a hoop, using needle and the little thimble. Gerda had been given that pretty thimble when she was just a little girl, and now wanted Ariel to have it.

That little shiny brass thimble is still a highly-valued sewing box treasure more than seven decades later.

Grandpa had a Bunsen burner on a small table in a corner by the back porch where each morning he put some liquid in a glass tube, added another liquid and then heated the tube over the burner, holding it with a clamp. He did that every day and Ariel liked to watch for the liquid to turn a beautiful deep blue-green. He was careful to see that she did not get too close and burn herself. She didn't know why he performed that exact procedure every day, but he carefully wrote results on a chart. Ariel presumed it had something to do with Grandma's illness, and liked spending time with him and watching.

Each afternoon she would sit for a while beside Grandma's bed and tell her stories about living in Washington State, and playing outdoors with the neighbor dog. Grandma had suffered a severe stroke, was confined to bed, and also had diabetes. No cure, or even much treatment was available then, but she was kept comfortable and enjoyed listening to the childish chatter. Ariel could invent all sorts of adventures, and spin all manner of fanciful tales without reprimand. Grandma just smiled at her in a rather lop-sided manner before drifting off to sleep. Ariel then tip-toed softly out to the kitchen and checked in with Aunt Gerda.

Outdoors there was wood to carry in from the shed, neighbor dog to play with, and lots of deep snow. She used a little shovel to help clear paths on mornings after more had fallen.

One day Dad arrived and Ariel was absolutely delighted to see him. She got to help him with some tasks that Grandpa hadn't been able to do by himself, awaiting arrival of his son-in-law. That was a wonderful time with Dad and Grandpa.

Edythe wore her nurse outfit every day and always had a stethoscope around her neck. Gerda spent a lot of time washing, starching and ironing those uniforms. She also had to hand-wash the precious white stockings and polish her sister's white shoes. Ariel never knew why all that had to be done; neither Grandma nor Grandpa appeared the least concerned about uniforms, nor did Gerda.

After a few weeks Aunt Olga arrived to care for Grandma, wearing regular cotton house dresses and ordinary shoes; stethoscope relegated to a drawer in Grandpa's little table by the back porch.

Uncle Cle came from Minneapolis, and Edythe, Dad and Ariel were driven to their house. She would see Cousin Dale, and that was very exciting.

Tonsils and More

Ariel was quite happy to be away from Deerwood and back at Dale's house where she could play with him and his big happy black and white dog. She loved Aunt Gerda, Grandpa and Grandma, but it was more fun at cousin Dale's. Uncle Cle took several photographs of the Pedersen's, especially of Ariel and Dad, and also a family grouping. No one mentioned anything about tonsils, hospitals or surgery. For some unknown reason Aunt Bert gave her spoons of cod liver oil every day … horrid; but a yummy treat always followed. The War was still going on; sugar and butter, along with meat and other items were all rationed so not many cookies or much candy was available. Somehow Aunt Bert found some sweet for her after each spoon of the wretched slimy cod liver oil.

Very early one morning Edythe woke her up, way before dawn, washed her hands and face, braided her hair very tightly, and Ariel brushed her teeth carefully. She was dressed in a Sunday dress with good stockings and shoes. Her warm coat and hat were by the door, and Dad was also all dressed up in his suit. Aunt Bert still had on her robe and her hair was not combed; but she gave Ariel a big hug and kiss, saying she would see her later. There was no breakfast. What was going on? It was still deep dark outside, and really cold. Dad took her hand to walk down the steps and then gathered her into his arms and carried her as they walked toward the trolley line.

"Where are we going?" she asked, and only then did she learn she was to have her tonsils removed. What did that mean? She didn't have any idea what tonsils might be, what they looked like, or where they were if she even had any. No one had ever mentioned tonsils before, why now? If she actually had any such things, why hadn't she known about them? Why did they need to be removed and why was that taking place in the middle of the night and why a streetcar ride in the dark? Where were they going and without breakfast? What, where and why? Questions raced through her mind. There were no answers. It was cold, dark and the trolley rattled noisily through dark and silent streets. No one spoke; Dad just held her tightly in his arms.

Edythe, Dad and Ariel left the trolley and walked across a dark street to a huge building that Dad said was Swedish Hospital. A surgeon named Dr. Dunlap would remove the tonsils this morning and that should help her not have so many sore throats and colds. Oh … and that was that, no further explanation. Edythe had given Dad a stern look and he stopped talking. His arms tightened around Ariel in a big hug.

Inside the building everything was bright and very white. Nurses in white outfits busily moved about, wheeling rolling chairs, carrying charts, smiling and talking to people; they seemed very cheerful. Ariel had seen nurses at some of the doctors' offices Edythe liked to visit, so she knew what they were. With very little delay Ariel was seated in one of those rolling chairs, hustled into an elevator that quickly went up; it stopped and she was rolled down another hall, through swinging doors and into a large room with beds lined up on both sides. Nearly everything was white … the walls, beds, and even the highly-waxed floors were a light color. This was a really strange place and it smelled funny.

Ariel's clothes were removed and taken away, replaced with a short white cotton wrap sort of thing that didn't quite close anywhere. She was placed on one of the beds with only a sheet over her. Dad stood beside her; Edythe sat on a chair a few feet away and talked with a nurse. The nurse smiled at Ariel and explained she would take a blood pressure reading with a wrap around her arm, and then her temperature. Temperature she knew about and dreaded; but the nurse put a glass stick under her tongue, not up her bottom like Edythe did. That wasn't so bad. The blood pressure wrap was only slightly uncomfortable, and Dad was there, so she didn't say anything.

The nurse wrote something on a paper hanging at the end of the bed, and left. Dad held Ariel's hand and told her he would wait right there until she came back from the operation. Back from where? What was an operation?

No answer. Edythe had looked at him again with that stern expression, and he kept quiet. Where was she going? And why?

Before long another nurse pushed a flat cot-like thing through the door and rolled it up to Ariel's bed. "Well, Good Morning little lady. Are we ready to get rid of those nasty tonsils?" She didn't have a clue how to answer with no idea what was going on.

Dad lifted her from the bed and onto the thing they called a gurney, adjusted the sheet, gave her a kiss and pat on the head. Then it was down through those doors, the hallway, another elevator and long hallway where the floor began sloping downward into a big dark hole.

Ariel was terrified; only tiny dim lights glowed faintly on the ceiling. On and on they went, and she screamed out for Dad, tears running into her hair and ears. More swinging doors and she was in another white room under a huge glaring light. Her arms and legs were tied down firmly; despite her futile struggles. Then a tall man wearing a mask and glasses pushed a stinky white cone over her nose and mouth; there was nothing to breathe but that horrid smell. Clanking metal noises rang in her ears; terror.

The next she knew Ariel was back in that first bed; Dad was holding her hand, softly stroking a hair from her forehead, and smiling. Her throat really hurt so she didn't try to talk. "Are you ready for some ice cream?" he asked, eyes twinkling. Ice cream? Wasn't that hard to get because of the War?

"Today you can have all the ice cream you want, so what would you like, strawberry, vanilla, or … orange sherbet?" Oh yes, orange sherbet – her favorite. She just nodded and tried to smile; her throat was so sore,

Icy orange sherbet slid down easily and soothed both her throat and her mind considerably. Dad stayed with her all afternoon, read stories, and helped her eat mashed potatoes and gravy before tucking her in for the night. He had to go to Maywood the next day, but assured her Aunt Bert and Edythe would take her home in the morning when she would feel much better. She was fast asleep in no time … it had been a very long, confusing and horrifyingly frightening day. But Dad promised ice cream and she had three dishes of the coveted orange sherbet.

The next day Aunt Bert was there early in the morning; Edythe was with her, but stayed by the door talking with a nurse. Aunt Bert helped Ariel wash her face, hands and walk to the potty before putting on her dress, stockings and tying her shoes. Her coat, little hat and mittens were retrieved from the closet and they all walked to the elevator and then outside. Soon they were in Aunt Bert's nice new car and headed for home.

Edythe wanted to stop at a store, so they parked at the curb and she got out. Ariel was not feeling very well and her tummy was churning; she wanted out so she could throw up. Aunt Bert would not let her open the door despite tears and pleas, thinking Ariel just wanted to go with Edythe. No, not at all; no way did she want to go with Edythe. She just needed to get out so she wouldn't throw up in the car; but that door stayed locked. Ariel struggled to stop her tummy from convulsing, to no avail. Up came breakfast, all over her coat and onto the carpet of Aunt Bert's new car.

Finally the door was unlocked and she could escape to the curb, sobbing and slobbering, utterly mortified. Why couldn't she have gotten out in time? After her initial gasp of surprise, Aunt Bert had just laughed, grabbed a rag from the back and mopped Ariel off as best she could. Another rag was found in the trunk and used on the carpet. "Ariel, dear, don't feel bad… you couldn't help it and I should have let you out; you would have taken care of that tummy problem just fine all by your self. Don't cry; everything is going to be just fine. I should have listened to you." She just hugged Ariel who kept sobbing and saying she was sorry.

Edythe returned with her package and immediately scolded Ariel for having been so naughty throwing up. "No, Ariel tried to get out of the car and I didn't let her, so don't you scold her. She knew her tummy was revolting. If you need to scold someone, it is I who didn't let her handle that herself," said Bert very sternly, "and we will be home in just a minute. It's ok…not any real problem at all". Edythe was reduced to clucking and frowning at Ariel. It was a quiet ride those last few blocks.

Back at Aunt Bert's house she certainly did feel better and might even be able to eat. Following a quick bath and clean clothes, she and Dale played with his wooden blocks building all sorts of things and making up stories about their constructions. Edythe went back to Grandpa Johnson's in Deerwood to take care of Grandma again. Dad came from Maywood and told Ariel that she would be now staying with some friends of Edythe's in Milaca and that they would come to get her the next day. He was going to have his legs operated on at that same Swedish Hospital and would not be able to see her for several days, maybe even two or three weeks. That was longer than she knew about, but didn't worry. Dad would find her, wherever she was, so it was going to be ok. Edythe hadn't said anything about Nelsons, Milaca or Dad going anywhere; only telling Ariel to try behaving herself and not cause problems for other people. Then she left.

The Nelsons came to get her and soon she was staying in Marilyn's room and getting to know these folks who welcomed her with smiles and hugs. Marilyn was so pretty, went to school every day wearing pretty clothes, and even had a little bottle of perfume on a dressing table. This was a glimpse of glamour, new in Ariel's world.

Only a few days later another family arrived to take Ariel to their house, so her little suitcase was quickly packed again and away she went, with Teddy Bear to yet another different house to stay with Uncle Art, Aunt Ruth and Cousins Eugene and June.

She didn't remember having seen them before, but they all seemed to know and like her. Everyone was so very nice. Hardly anyone told her "no, that's not for you"; "try to behave"; "why on earth did you do that?", like Edythe. Here she also stayed in June's room…all white and pink with ruffled curtains; even a little dressing table. June took her along on walks into town after school and they visited Uncle Art at his gas station and garage.

Next it was to Anna and Ernest Eckholm's at Uncle Gust and Aunt Frieda's farm. She knew, loved and trusted these folk, felt very good, and liked being back with some of Dad's family, including Clyde, Harvey, Norma and Byron. The big barn housed familiar cows, horses, a big brown dog and oodles of cats.

Johnny and Esther Strombeck came next to pack her up yet again to stay with them. She really liked them, too, even if there were no kids, they had a big barn with cows, horses and many, many cats. She helped Johnny feed the animals and give milk to the cats. Esther let her feed the chickens and help gather eggs. There was always something to do on the farm, and even her cow Bessie was there waiting to have her soft warm nose rubbed. Esther let her help make cookies, too, and those absolutely had to be sampled. Sundays they went to the same little Church and Sunday school where she had gone before moving out West. The little Maywood house still waited on the corner, and the school across the road was open for classes during weekdays.

The months since the train ride from Washington had been very busy and she had been shuffled about from house to house after having those pesky tonsils out – whatever they had been. Edythe was still in Deerwood, and Dad in Minneapolis. Why was she moved from place to place? All the people were so nice to her and made her feel that she meant something to them; there were hugs and kisses, cookies, toys and stories, warm laps and love. Except for Dad not being there, and not understanding the moving about, Ariel's life was quite pleasant during that time.

All the people she stayed with were so nice, they smiled a lot and dinner-table conversation was very interesting; there was some talk about the War, of course, but less about danger and fear than when Edythe was around.

Dad found her at Strombeck's home; she was so happy to see him, able to be in his arms for bedtime stories. Ariel didn't know what had been done to Dad at that hospital, she was just glad to have him back. He helped Johnny with various chores around the farm being more careful than she remembered about lifting anything heavy. Every day he seemed a little stronger, and before very long they packed up their suitcases and returned to Minneapolis.

During the weeks Ariel had been shifted from one family to another and Dad had his operation, Grandma Johnson had passed away. Her funeral had been held, and now it was nearly time to return to Washington.

While in Minneapolis Dad and Edythe went to a tall building, where they all rode elevators to a long hall with numbered doors. Ariel had color books and crayons to keep busy while waiting for her parents to finish talking with a gray-haired stern looking man in his office.

Back in Medina, Dad returned to working at the boat yard, the War was still going on, and he concentrated all his spare time on house plans and lining up available material. Just before Easter they went to the J C Penney store for Edythe's new spring hat.

Dad and Ariel also found little girls' dresses on sale and quickly picked out three; a pink, lavender and blue. The pink and lavender ones were 60 and 70 cents each, but the blue one was more – 80 cents. Edythe said she might have the yellow and green frocks, which were only 60 cents each but definitely not the blue – it was far too expensive. Dad held out for blue while allowing Edythe to put the lavender one back for green. Ariel was totally thrilled with that blue dress and wore it until she simply could not wriggle into it any more. That April also brought Ariel's fifth birthday. They had been in the West for two full years, interrupted by the train trips to Minnesota. Those had certainly been busy years.

Building the House

Plans drawn and materials' lists in hand, Dad began purchasing what he could to start construction. All building supplies were in short supply and many items still rationed the spring of 1943. Much of what he could buy he could also transport with the little coupe. Ariel loved going to the lumber yard on Saturday mornings; the fresh-cut boards all smelled so good. There were hammers, saws, nails and just all sorts of wonderful things at the lumber yard. He had the heavy pyramid blocks and timbers delivered by truck, and construction began. Rigging up a water level with hose and glass tubing, along with a device to determine absolute square measurements, Dad laid out the dimensions of the house. He showed Ariel the lines on the tubing that would indicate when a block was at the same level as the block diagonally across, and those at right angles. Ariel's job was to raise her hand when the water came up to the line on her end of the level, and hold the glass tube tight against the marker pole. This was her introduction to the terms 'level' and 'plumb' which were to be a game with Dad for years.

Once the foundation was established and the long floor joists set in place, building continued on weekends, evenings after work, and any days off Dad might have. Construction progress also depended on ability to purchase materials, still limited by the War. It was not a large house, just 20' by 24', making best use of materials with as little waste as possible. Ariel loved going first to the lumber yard and the house on Saturday mornings with Dad, each carrying a bag lunch. Decades later as an adult the fragrance of warm sunlight on freshly cut lumber always brought back happy memories of peanut butter sandwiches, cookie and, icy cold creek water shared with Dad, sitting on a lumber stack.

Slowly the little house took shape, windows were installed, the roof shingled, sub-flooring nailed, and rooms partitioned. Dad then dug a well at a spot identified by a dowser.

That was a fascinating process, watching the man hold a forked branch in his hands and walk slowly over the ground; looking for places the stick end might bend downward indicating water. He located more than one, but Dad marked the spot where his stick had gone down the quickest and farthest. That would be the well site. Then there was a pump house to build, pipe to lay, a pump to install and more line up to the house. Meanwhile, there was clear cold water in the creek which did quite well temporarily.

Mrs. McGhee had concluded she would be safe living in her summer home again, and so work on the new house became a priority. That she really missed little Toby was also a reason for her return from Florida.

About this time as well, Dad received an important-looking envelope from the law office in Minneapolis where they had spent what seemed to Ariel, hours and hours during the last trip to Minnesota. Inside was a beautiful document with gold swirls, long important-looking words, and numbers. It also had a picture in one corner of a mustached man with medals all over his chest and a crown on his head. "Oh my, who is that?" she asked. With a smile and twinkling eyes, Dad explained he was the King of Sweden and that the document was check drawn on the Royal Bank of Sweden.

"Come Saturday morning you and I are going down to the bank and have a little fun with this check before it gets cashed." Dad chuckled. Ariel had no idea what he was talking about, but it sounded great and she was ready for fun for sure. Edythe just frowned, cleared her throat and muttered something under her breath.

Arriving at the Washington State Bank on Main Street, Dad held her hand as they approached one of the teller cages. With 'hello' and 'how are you today' pleasantries out of the way, Dad pulled out the fancy paper with the King's picture and handed it across to the pretty lady. She gasped slightly, looked questioningly at Dad, "Oh my, what on earth is this? I think our manager might want to see it," and she quickly crossed to a big dark shiny desk where a large bald man was seated. He glanced briefly at the check, immediately rose, put on his glasses and came to the window where Ariel and Dad waited.

"This certainly is not something we see here every day; and it appears absolutely authentic. It truly is none of my business, but would you mind telling me just a bit as to why the King of Sweden is sending you this money?" (He apparently had not realized only the King's portrait, not his signature, appeared on the check,)

This was precisely the opening Dad was looking for, and now with every ear in the building at full attention, he grinned a little sheepishly and paused for a long moment before answering. "Well, not many people know this, but I don't mind telling you. It seems I am a rather 'black sheep' and quite distant member of the royal family. They send me a small stipend from time to time just to stay away here in America. It saves them embarrassment, I guess", he quietly answered, as the grin spread across his face. (If one delves back far enough, virtually every Swede qualifies as a 'distant member' of the royal family.)

The bank manager's eyes nearly popped out of his rapidly reddening face. "Oh, Mr. Pedersen, it is a real pleasure for us to have your accounts here. We just need your endorsement and this will be put into your account immediately." And with that he handed Dad his own gold fountain pen, smiling, chuckling and virtually bowing. Dad was wearing his usual blue cotton work shirt and 'town' overalls, clean, but still work clothes. Ariel wore a quite ordinary little cotton play dress, but they were both treated quite royally.

Back in the little coupe, Dad laughed out loud and hugged Ariel gleefully. "That was fun, now wasn't it, my little Swedish princess," and Ariel giggled. It certainly was, and she easily understood why Edythe had not been along. She would have been utterly mortified by that well-spun tale, with sputtering protestations and criticisms. In actuality the money was the sum residue of an elderly Swedish Pedersen uncle's estate. He had passed away during the War, and Dad was the only surviving heir.

Communication with European governments and legal offices was greatly hampered by restrictions and requirements in addition to battles and ship-sinkings. The tracing of heirs had proven complex as great numbers of Swedes had re-located in European countries as well as to the Americas, some possibly the uncle's relatives and potential heirs. Dad explained the process and finally Ariel understood what all those long meetings with the Minneapolis lawyer had been about. This inheritance had come at a very good time to help with building the house.

Restrictions on building supplies were still in effect and the War continued. Somehow Dad acquired a little here, a little there, and soon the structure was livable–not finished by any means, but they were able to move in. Mrs. McGhee returned from Florida and reunited with her precious Toby. Since they had no real furniture for the new house some shopping was required, at least for a kitchen table, chairs, a fold-down davenport/chesterfield, a couple of chairs and a lamp. Interior walls were insulated and covered with plasterboard. Seams were taped, spackled, sanded and the first coat of paint applied. That helped make it look much better. A temporary cupboard was built for dishes and cookware.

Now that they had acquired land and built a house, another train trip to Minnesota was in order to bring household furnishings still in storage at the Maywood farm. They all went this time and Ariel loved that Dad was there to tell her all sorts of interesting things about the mountains, old mining towns they passed, bison, elk and deer grazing in meadows, eagle and osprey nests, the names of rivers they crossed and sometimes traveled along. He helped her watch which way those ran, first west toward them and then east and away from the train. He walked through the cars with her and talked with the conductor and waiters in the dining car. Soldiers and sailors in uniform sat wherever they could, sometimes on their duffel bags leaning against the walls. Dad always stopped to chat with them, and several put their arms around Ariel and talked about the children waiting at home for them. It had been years since many had even seen their children and they hugged her ever so tightly, sometimes with tears in their eyes.

Soon they arrived in Minneapolis, and changed trains to one going north to St. Cloud where Johnny Strombeck met them. After settling in at his and Esther's home, he and Dad went over to the little farmhouse and checked on things there. Ariel was happy to be back in Esther's pretty kitchen with fresh cookies and milk, the lovely kitties and room to romp about outdoors. After days on the train, she was ready to run through the fields and pick wild flowers.

Johnny and Dad went to town early one morning, not returning until nearly supper time. Johnny was alone in his pickup truck; where was Dad? He soon followed in a shiny blue-green two-door sedan. Edythe and Esther emerged from the kitchen, both smiling, Edythe a little hesitantly. So, just what did this mean? Both men happily explained that they had been able to find this 1941 model used car, in good mechanical condition and at a reasonable price. It was so much bigger than the little coupe, with a larger engine, roomy trunk and even a trailer hitch already installed.

Dad and Johnny hauled some lumber from Foley and built a wooden trailer on an old frame and axle stored in the Maywood barn. It had wooden sides and front so furniture and boxes could fit inside and be covered with a canvas tarp, protected from rain. Before long furniture and household items emerged from the hay loft and house attic, and stacked as tightly as possible onto the trailer. Late each afternoon Dad rolled it back into the barn, out again in the morning as sorting and packing continued. Edythe's treasured Noritake china was carefully packed into the sturdy wooden box that had once contained a cream separator shipped decades past from Sweden, and the wooden top securely nailed in place. Not everything could be loaded onto this rather small two-wheel trailer; some items remained in the attic.

Time to head west again and quick visits were made to the Lundsten and Eckholm farm, Aunt Mattie's and a few other friends and relatives. Good-bye's and best wishes for safe journey, pastries and cookies for the trip, and once more they headed for Washington. The War continued, gas and tires rationed and in very short supply. No side trip into Canada to Judy and Dave's this time, just the shortest route back to the new home.

Ariel had a fine view from her spot in the back of this car, standing behind Dad one arm resting of the back of the front seat. There were some boxes and bags of things back there as well, but plenty of room for her to stand, and even to sit or curl up on the back seat when she tired of standing. Most of the time she stood, watched out the windows, asked all sorts of questions that Dad was able to almost always answer.

With uncanny accuracy, Ariel seemed to sense impending tire failure, and repeated, "I think we're going to have a flat", which most likely was not much appreciated by Dad or Edythe. Unfortunately many predictions were correct, and nine flat tires needed repair along this journey. Dad was quite experienced at fixing inner tubes and kept his repair kit close at hand. The car was jacked up quickly, tire and tube removed, the hole patched and all reassembled. A flat on the trailer required propping it up on one side before jacking up the other to remove the damaged tire. The last box loaded onto the trailer had been the separator crate holding Edythe's cherished china. Being stout and strong, that crate was often used to prop up one side of the trailer; Edythe bewailed the fate of her dishes each and every time.

While Dad mended inner tubes and patched the old tires, with Ariel handing him tools, Edythe strolled alongside the roadways searching for and gathering stones that looked like agates, adding still more weight to the already overloaded car and trailer.

One flat truly required replacement of both tube and tire. They were miles from any town and traffic was sparse at best. No vehicles passed heading west. He patched the tube and tire the best he could, but that would not last long and they could only go very slowly for a short distance, not nearly enough to reach the nearest town. Looking across the open landscape Dad spotted what looked like a telegraph shack in the distance; perhaps he might be able to wire the next town for help.

"Well, kiddo, do you want to stay here or walk all that way with me to that little building by the railroad tracks?" he asked. As if there really was a question. Of course Ariel wanted to go with him. And so, they climbed through a fence and started across a wide open field.

All sorts of bugs hopped up from the dry grass and weeds, birds swooped in pursuit, and it was hot despite a gentle breeze. There were more fences and fields before they reached the telegraph hut. Not at all certain this was actually a manned site, Dad knocked on the door. "Come on in, it's open" came a deep voice as the door swung back. Broadly smiling the telegraph operator thrust out his hand and welcomed them into his little office home. "I watched you two coming from the highway … that's quite a walk, especially for you, little lady." Then he brought out cups of cool water, asking how he could help.

Dad explained his situation of the truly unfixable tire and asked if it was possible to wire anyone in the next town for any chance of buying a tire and tube. The operator went right to work, tapping out messages to the next station where he thought there might be an auto repair shop. That station master telegraph his contacts, and replied quickly. Ariel could not make any sense of the clicking and clacking, but the message was immediately interpreted. A shop had been located … they actually had a tire that would fit and that they could sell. Wonder of wonders. Ariel didn't know much about prayer, except for grace at mealtime, and "Now I Lay Me Down to Sleep" at bedtime; but over and over in her mind during the long walk had been, "Jesus, please let us find a tire". That it may have actually been prayer never occurred to her; she was just talking to Jesus.

Now a tire had been located and the address of the garage written down, along with names of people there who could help. With heartfelt thanks and handshakes, Ariel and Dad retraced their steps to where Edythe waited at the roadside.

After pumping a little more air into the fragile tube and patched tire, Dad cautiously pulled back onto the highway and ever so slowly they headed toward town. Those miles seemed endless. Travel with the heavy load had never been very fast, but now Ariel thought they scarcely moved at all. Dad's jaw tighten with each slight bump, his knuckles white bumps on the steering wheel. Heat waves shimmered on the concrete. She stood silently, hardly daring to breathe.

At last low buildings came into view and the garage with that precious tire was located. This time that box of china was not used as a jack or block. With trailer unhitched, the garage owner rolled a big hoist to the car, raised it and had that battered tire off in a flash. "Wow…this thing really took a beating; it's totally worn out … for sure. You were lucky to make it all the way here; and that's quite a patch job. You used every trick in the book and then some on this one." That poor mangled tire and tube landed in the scrap rubber pile, no possibility of being recapped, patched and used.

The garage owner kept up a steady chatter while working, asking where they had come from, where they were going, and how he would like to travel. He and Dad exchanged information about roads to the east and west. In a flash a new tube and that precious new tire were mounted and secured. Ariel had never liked the smell of rubber, but this strong new tire smelled really good. With the bill paid, many handshakes and "thank you's", they set off again, ever westward and with far greater confidence.

Up, down across the plains, more mountains, rivers, past farms, forests and through towns, wending their way toward their new little house in Highland.

This trip they didn't have a house trailer and so nights were spent in motor court cabins. Accommodations were quite basic and not always very clean. Edythe clearly showed her distaste for the shabby cabins, but in many small towns they were lucky to find anywhere at all to stay. In a few places hotels had existed before the War, but with limited travel and resultant lack of business, many were closed and shuttered. Many roadside cafés had also shut down due to rationing and lack of business.

Finally they arrived; it was good to be back in the little house and hear the cheery bubbling creek sounds again.

Once the trailer had been unloaded, furniture placed in the rooms, dishes and cookware from the Maywood kitchen in the temporary cupboard shelves, and throw rugs on the floors, the little house began to look and feel much more like home. With Edythe and Dad having a real bed, closet for their clothes and chests of drawers, Ariel inherited the davenport for her bed. Her room was planned to have a twin bed built atop big drawers, with a little closet under the attic stairs. Edythe needed real kitchen cupboards and counter tops first.

Late one night the temporary shelves loosened from the wall, tipped and crashed to the floor. Edythe screamed and wailed, shedding real tears. Virtually all the old blue and white plates, bowls, cups, everything from the old Maywood kitchen lay shattered on the bare floor. Very few pieces escaped in usable condition. These were dishes from his and Harold's childhood that their mother had brought from Redwing but Dad just got a shovel from outdoors and scooped the pieces into a washtub. He hauled the whole mess outside; and then swept the floor, over and over.

He made sure Ariel's slippers were by her bed. She was to put those on before setting even one foot on the floor just in case a shard of glass or pottery had escaped him.

Next morning breakfast consisted of toast browned on top of the cook stove, butter and jam. Dad and Edythe drank their coffee from earless cups and Ariel drank her milk from Dad's thermos bottle top. There weren't many dishes to wash. Soon they were in the car and headed for town. Edythe picked out a set of dishes, some glassware and casseroles. Fortunately some of the household things from Maywood were still in their packing boxes and had survived.

Building real cupboards, and attaching those firmly to the walls was next on the list of 'things to do' for certain. Ariel loved helping Dad build things; picking up ends of boards for the kindling box, handing him tools, gathering up dropped nails and screws, and sweeping up the sawdust.

Summer passed quickly as Dad worked on jobs building houses during the days and on their little house evenings and weekends. The War was still going on, and even Ariel sensed it could stop sometime; but when that might happen remained an open question. Most building materials were still very scarce, with many just not available, so progress was quite slow at times. A pump house was built into a space carved out of hardpan on the hillside, and wiring installed so water could be pumped from the well up into the house. A narrow pathway of the crushed hardpan led through trees and salmonberry bushes to a tidy outhouse. Each project completed made the little house better and more comfortable.

Ariel had turned five in April and now, at last, she could go to school. It was so exciting and there were so many things to do before the first day of Kindergarten. She could have walked to school from Mrs. McGhee's house in Medina, but now they lived miles away in the opposite direction, and she would be riding a big yellow school bus with lots of other kids. When Dad talked with someone at the School District offices he learned she would ride not just one, but two buses in order to get from Highland to Kindergarten at the Medina School. That prompted considerable instruction in dealing with crossing the highway to the bus stop, transferring at the Bellevue Elementary School to the Medina bus, and then making the trip in reverse in the afternoon. Ariel was so excited to be five, going to school, and even riding on all those buses; growing up was even more fun than she ever thought.

She would now be out of the house and away from Edythe for hours each day. Maybe she could find some answers to the questions that filled her mind. Why was nearly everything she did or said wrong? Why were treats, toys and candy for other children, not for her? Why was she not allowed to run, shout, laugh out loud, or squeal joyfully like other children? Why was she supposed to sit quietly on the sidelines and watch others having fun? Edythe had stated quietly, but firmly, that such activities were unsuitable and not appropriate for Ariel's participation. But, why? No answer. Somehow, even at a very early age, she sensed those questions must not be put to Dad. Why? Why was she always guilty of having caused someone hurt or harm, even when she wasn't even there? Edythe could, and frequently did, just look at her in a certain way, with a slightly bent head and downcast eyes; Ariel knew she was at fault, again, for something. Would she ever learn what or why?

Edythe delighted in taking prescription medications, and being a trained nurse was well able to describe appropriate symptoms for whatever ailment would garner the desired prescriptions. She also used Ariel in her quest for attention and medications, which worked fairly well until Ariel was old enough to register objections to the doctors at being poked, prodded and prescribed by yet another new physician. Edythe was quite skilled in obtaining '*doctor's orders*' and having those highly desired prescriptions filled at various drug stores, allowing her to access what she wanted. There was virtually no communication between pharmacies in that era, so by using numerous different physicians and drug stores, no questions were raised. She was also skillful in formulating acceptable answers to any query or concern, and then just use another drug store for her next prescription.

Ariel had to regularly accompany Edythe to the various medical offices, some locally in the town, and others at larger facilities and clinics in the city. Testing was not overly prevalent at the time, especially when a registered nurse patient presented with clearly and accurately described symptoms of an ailment for which medication could quickly be prescribed. Edythe's appointments were generally not over-long and Ariel sat quietly in a waiting room.

On one such occasion Edythe emerged, the desired prescription in hand only to find Ariel being fussed over by waiting patients. The ladies were patting her head, smiling at her and each other, and laughing happily over her appearance. "Why, this little doll looks just like Shirley Temple; isn't she just the cutest little thing ever; why--we have our own little movie queen right here." Ariel had heard of Shirley Temple, but didn't know about movies. She was just Ariel. True enough; she had bouncy blond ringlets, a slight dimple, big blue eyes and happily giggled at all the attention she was receiving.

Edythe was not pleased; not one little bit. She yanked Ariel away from the ladies, scowled at her and sternly told her to behave herself. Without another word they were out the door, down hallways and elevator onto the street, and headed for the bus. Ariel's shoulder ached from being yanked, and her upper arm hurt from Edythe's fingernails digging into her flesh.

What had she done wrong this time? She had just smiled politely and answered when the ladies spoke to her. Edythe always said she should smile and be nice to people. What had she done that was bad?

There was, of course, no answer.

Section III

Real School, at Last

Kindergarten was wonderful. From the very first day Ariel was thrilled. Walking up to the highway, carefully looking both ways before quickly crossing the highway, waiting and climbing the steps into the bus, waiting again under a big tree at the elementary school for the Medina bus, and finally through the wide doors, down the hall to her room. Everything in the school building smelled so good, new paper, crayons, pencils, books. She sat on a little wooden chair at the shiny desk assigned to her where her name was neatly printed on a pretty label. There was paper, a sharpened pencil, and a whole new box of color crayons. The teacher Miss Frost was so nice, with a lovely smile, and very pretty. She greeted and spent time speaking with each student individually. Ariel was ready to learn all sorts of new and marvelous things.

Books lined shelves and soon she was able to read some of the stories herself. The only thing Ariel didn't like so much was the time spent playing with toys. She thought that a waste of time when she could be learning. Many years passed before she understood that play had been learning, too. She didn't really know how to play; not with toys and other children. Her idea of play had been helping Dad, stacking wood, feeding chickens, running up and down the creek, catching water bugs and fireflies.

Her toys were a willow branch fishing pole, sickle, small shovel, pail, rake, hammer and nails, end-cut wood pieces for building blocks. Most of her days were occupied with various tasks others did not think of as play. There were weeds to pull and long grass to cut, periwinkles and fish to be caught in the creek and rock dams carefully constructed hold back the water, creating pools. Those were never deep enough for actual swimming of course, but the building process was great creative fun.

Ariel did have the doll sitting on a shelf with her broken foot, but not played with. After all, Ariel had already broken her and there was some dirt on her dress. Only Teddy Bear sat with her on the floor to read books. Play at school seemed somewhat silly to Ariel.

Here she learned a little about interacting with other children, and playing with toys that someone had provided just for that purpose – to play with, not just look at, carefully.

She also learned about bullying from an older boy who rode the Bellevue to Medina school bus. Dad gave her a pretty little bracelet as a special treat, and she was very careful with it, saving it for Sunday school and other special times. Then she wore it to school one day, tucking it carefully under her sweater sleeve.

The older boy spotted it, said it was pretty and he wanted to look at it more closely. Ariel was so pleased, gently removed it from her wrist and slowly handed it to him. He laughed, grabbed the trinket and twisted it into a horrible mess; taunting Ariel by waving it over her head, keeping it away from her and calling her a cry-baby. Tiring of this, he threw her precious bracelet high over her head where it landed at the bus driver's feet. That boy just laughed harder, repeating, "Cry-baby, cry-baby" until the bus driver ordered him to stop. Her day was ruined along with the bracelet.

She was careful to sit at the front of the bus every day after that, far away from the bully who was the only person on the bus rides, or at school who was in any way a negative that first year of school. She loved classes, reading, drawing, writing her alphabet letters and words. Miss Frost read stories in the afternoons, using different voices for each character.

All too soon the school year ended, and she proudly carried home the precious card promoting her to first grade. Dad grinned, hugged her and said she had done a good job receiving high marks her first year at school. Edythe looked at it briefly, only commenting, "Well, it's a good thing you got promoted. Next year you will have to buckle down and learn to study." Whatever that meant it sounded rather bad to Ariel. Dad just shook his head a little and grinned at her so she felt much better about 'next year'.

Summer went by quickly, cutting grass and pulling weeds, feeding chickens, wading and building rock dams in the creek, catching periwinkles and fishing; tramping through the big woods across the road. A tabby with white paws found herself at the little house one day and quickly became Ariel's very favorite playmate.

The thickly-wooded acres were on a corner of the highway and the road Ariel lived on. It was full of tall cedar and Douglas fir trees, vine maples, salmon berry bushes, ferns and tall moss-covered stumps left from huge trees cut decades before. There were notches cut into them at two and three different heights that made climbing quite easy. Dad explained how many years ago long boards were fitted into those notches. One man stood at each end of the board using long two-handled saws to fell those trees by hand pulling the saw blades back and forth. He and Harold had seen that done high in the Cascades in the 1920's when they went to California the first time. There were so many big trees then that no one was concerned about wasting wood.

Now the huge stumps had begun to decay and new seedling trees, moss and all sorts of wild plants grew on them. Small animals made use of cracks in the bark and cozy places that had opened under the long wide-spread roots.

Ariel loved going deep into those woods, climbing up one of the old mossy stumps and lying flat on her tummy, watching over the edge to the ground. Tiny mice, probably voles, lived under the stumps and had tunnels through the layers of dried ferns and grass. They hurried to and fro through their tunnel-runs carrying weed seeds and small grasses. If they sensed a rabbit, snake or any other potential danger approaching they scurried under the stump to hide. Birds of all sorts lived in the woods as well, and frogs inhabited wet areas along the gentle stream. It was a wonderful place for a little girl to spend hours and hours alone. Dad always liked to hear about what she had seen, and answered her questions about the tiny creatures and birds.

The creek meandering slowly through these woods was much smaller than the one below the house. No one bothered to fish there, thinking it too small for trout. One day, watching water bugs hopping about on the surface, and idly checking out periwinkles a good-size trout sped upstream over the rocky shallows right under Ariel's nose and on it went, tail fin propelling it along to deeper water. It was longer than any trout Denny, Alan or Ariel had caught in the big creek. She never saw another fish in the little creek although there must have been some, if maybe not as big.

No mention was made to Edythe about Ariel spending time alone in those woods. She generally spent much of each day on the telephone with ladies from the church, discussing actual or perceived problems and just what actions should be taken. She also spent hours and hours in planning how she could influence various people in the church organization to see things her way and correct the many errors she identified. Edythe's days were quite full.

Dad kept working on the house and Ariel helped by bringing him tools, picking up nails and scrap boards just like at Point-No-Point when he worked with Mr. Boberg. Small pieces of lumber weren't tossed into a burn pile now, but stacked neatly for kindling and starting fires in the cook stove.

First Dental Office Experience

Just who may have identified the need to have the cord between Ariel's upper front teeth removed to correct spacing was unknown. Her front teeth also protruded just a bit. As with the tonsils/adenoids procedure no explanation was given her, other than it was to be removed. Off on a Saturday morning to an office high in a downtown Seattle building. It smelled like doctors' offices and Swedish Hospital. She didn't like that at all, especially when taken into a small room and hoisted into a tall hard black chair with cold white metal arms.

Fear swelled when a tall man wearing a white coat and mask entered and instructed her to sit very, very still; not to move unless he said to. He picked up a glass tube from a tray. It had black lines around it and a long shiny needle at the end. He told Ariel to open her mouth wide, close her eyes and not move, even a tiny bit. A sharp stabbing pain, followed by another and then another, but the needle stayed stuck…why? What was he doing? Her upper jaw started feeling tingly, heavy and strange. Finally he softly patted her arm, and said she could open her eyes; there would be no more needles. The actual oral surgery was completed quickly; but seemed endless to Ariel. Chair armrests were gripped firmly throughout.

At last her mouth and face were wiped clean, the bib removed, and he smilingly lifted her down to the floor. Her mouth wouldn't close properly, and he gave her tissues to catch the bloody drool. It would not stop and was horribly embarrassing; she was making an awful mess. Edythe would not like that at all. He just kept smiling and saying how well she had behaved. How on earth could drooling, not closing her mouth, and unable to speak clearly be good behavior? She could only question with her eyes. He just smiled, patted her shoulder and led her through the door.

Dad stood up immediately, and with a concerned look on his face stooped to hug her, wiped her face with his clean white hanky and whispered that he was very proud of her. Then he stood, pulled out his wallet and removed some bills. The fee for this procedure was $15. The oral surgeon accepted the money, handed one bill to the lady by the phone, telling her it was full payment. With a big smile he then gave Ariel the $5 bill and said she had been so good and sat so still she had well earned the $5. He said it was hers, not anyone else's. In the early 1940's $5 was a considerable sum. Edythe reached out to take it, but Dad said, "No, that is going into Ariel's pocket. " And so it did.

Later a fine magnifying glass was the selected purchase with that $5. Hundreds of bugs, butterflies, twigs, rocks and assorted worms were examined using it; and it held an honored place on each of her desks in banks, insurance and lawyer's offices and courthouse for decades.

Once out onto the city streets again Ariel's concern centered on the birthday party to which she had been invited, card and gift purchased. Dad just looked a little sad, and didn't say anything. Edythe said, 'we will see', which Ariel knew meant "no." She was correct. Despite Edythe's frowns Dad stopped at a drug store on the way home; and came out with more tissue for the still-active drool problem, and a Dixie® cup, ½ vanilla, and ½ the favored orange sherbet, savoring the lovely orange ice which he helped her to eat.

When the stitches were removed, the dental surgeon suggested to Ariel, privately, that gently leaning on her pencil eraser would gradually push those front teeth to straighter positions. It worked; and those front teeth moved together over time. Braces had been highly recommended, however, that would have meant spending almost $100 and Edythe was not about to acquiesce to that. Ariel's front teeth no longer protruded, and in fact were ever so slightly recessed because she became quite accustomed to that eraser against her teeth.

Each summer was much the same until third grade; running barefoot through the woods, and in the creek, pulling weeds, picking vegetables from the garden, cleaning chicken coops, gathering eggs and playing.

At age eight, however, Ariel began to work earning money for her school clothes…picking berries.

Elementary Grades

First Grade was a huge event in Ariel's life. She was to attend classes in the big brick building across the highway from the church, and school was all day, with lunch and recesses.

Even the building was absolutely wonderful, again smelling of paper, sharpened pencils, crayons, books, oiled floors…information, knowledge, questions and answers. She loved school. Her teachers all smiled and said she was doing good work. Her papers were marked with "A" or "A+" and there were no frowns or tsk-tsks, as Edythe did. Even lunches were great. Mrs. Stevenson and Mrs. Granberg cooked just like they did at home and for church dinners. There was fried or baked chicken, mashed potatoes and gravy; stews and soups; roast beef with new potatoes, onions and carrots, fresh-baked rolls, cookies, cake, fresh apples, sliced peaches and milk. Hardly any kids brought bag lunches from home. If not raining, everyone played outside after lunch on the big grassy field and in the woods back of the school. No one gave instructions or organized recess or lunchtime activities. Everyone just went outdoors and played ball, tag, or just ran through the woods and on the grassy playground.

However, no one played or even walked on the front lawn, not even the Principal. Mr. Stevenson and his wife lived just one street north of the highway. Each morning they both walked across the highway and onto the sidewalk just as students and parents did, never stepping on the front lawn grass.

The whole school, all six grades, Mr. Stevenson and the teachers, cooks and even the janitor did walk out onto that lawn one very special day. Students all stood quietly, apprehensive about stepping on the grass and wondered why? This must be a special occasion. It most certainly was. Two 6th grade boys carefully raised the flag and everyone recited the flag salute, standing straight and tall, hands over hearts, as was done each morning before class.

Mr. Stevenson held his hand up high and said he had a special announcement to make. Was it special? You bet. The War in Europe was over. The German army had surrendered and Adolph Hitler was believed to be dead. When the clapping, cheers and laughter calmed a bit, Mr. Stevenson asked the 5th and 6th Graders to come closer to the flagpole and recite the Gettysburg Address. They did so with broad smiles, proud to have memorized President Lincoln's speech. Mr. Stevenson then explained that the Pacific War was still going on and asked everyone to remember to pray for all the servicemen still overseas and their families.

Teachers were in no great hurry to get everyone back into the classrooms and books. One part of that war was over; and some dads and uncles would be coming home. Others were still fighting in the jungles and on islands in the Pacific Ocean. Ariel had only the vaguest concept of an ocean; only that it was really big with waves that never stopped. The sandy beach had been wonderful fun, and they had not sailed on it in May 1941.

Not too long after, everyone filed out onto the front lawn again. This was not such a happy occasion. The 6th Grade boys raised the flag and then lowered it halfway, before stepping back and saluting. Mr. Stevenson had a sad look on his face and cleared his throat a couple of times before telling us that the President of the United States, Franklin Delano Roosevelt, had died. Vice President Harry S. Truman had been sworn into office and was now the President. This meant far more to the teachers and older students than to younger ones, but even they knew it was something big and not a particularly happy occasion. Both World War II and President Roosevelt had always been part of their lives. His picture was in newspapers and magazines and in the hallway at school. Some kids went to movies at the town theater and saw newsreels about the War and the President's many travels to meet with leaders of other countries.

Occasionally films were shown at school. Most were educational and covered science topics, or geography and Edythe had no objection to those. Rarely, however, a cartoon was scheduled and students were to bring ten cents to see the movie. This was an entirely different matter. Edythe strongly objected to movies, be they viewed in a theater or a classroom. Dad was occasionally able to slip Ariel a dime without Edythe noticing, but many times he didn't know there was to be a movie and she went to school without that precious coin. Notes sent home by teachers frequently landed in the wood stove before anyone could see them. Somehow Mr. Stevenson always seemed to know which children would not be able to see the cartoon and each would discover a shiny coin tucked under a book or paper on their desks.

Eventually, the Pacific Theater of the War was ended with Allied Forces striking the mainland of Japan with the newly developed atomic bomb. Development and manufacture of the weapon was so secret that even the crew of the Boeing bomber that flew and dropped it had no idea they were carrying it until they were in the air, well away from their base and headed toward Japan. President Truman didn't know about it until he took the Oath of Office following President Roosevelt's death.

Huge headlines in papers across the country heralded the "End of War". Finally soldiers, sailors, marines and survivors of prisoner of war camps were streaming home. Life returned to normal, bit by bit; rationing ceased, new cars were available for sale, and home building exploded. Dad was busy building new and beautiful houses in new areas that had formerly been fields or woods.

At school Ariel made a few friends who lived fairly close to her house and was invited to their homes after school to play or do homework. These arrangements worked out well to begin with and the girls also were invited to Ariel's. Soon, however, Edythe took longer and longer to grant Ariel permission to spend after school time with a friend or to bring someone home with her. Suitability of this or that girl as an acquaintance or playmate was highly questioned.

The father was known to smoke cigarettes and was even thought to drink cocktails after work; the mother listened to soap operas on the radio while she ironed clothes. The family went to movies, and even played card games in their home. The parents might also go to a different and most unsuitable church, or … even be Catholic. One after another Ariel's school acquaintances were deemed unsuitable and she spent more and more time alone, except for playing in the creek and woods with the neighbor boys, Denny and Alan.

Edythe never knew that when they were not fishing, chopping down alder trees and building rafts or forts, playing football, baseball or basketball, they were holed up in Denny's bedroom reading comic books; those being deemed even worse than movies to say nothing of the half-hour afternoon adventure programs on the radio. Their mother worked full time and the boys had free access to "The Lone Ranger", "Sky King", "Hop-Along Cassidy" and even "The

Green Hornet".

Virtually every kid listened to adventure programs on the radio. Edythe considered them quite evil and detrimental to character-building. Under guise of helping Ariel with her arithmetic, she and Dad closed her door, stuffed a throw rug under it and with the sound turned down, huddled over the little portable radio for at least one or two programs before being informed by Edythe it was time to quit doing homework. She didn't open the door, physically intrude or directly question, but undoubtedly sensed we were listening to those programs she regarded as highly detrimental to good character-building.

Berries, Beans and School Clothes

Another April 28th had rolled around; Ariel turned eight and it became time to earn money during the summer if there were to be new school clothes. Girls wore dresses to church, school, or shopping in town, no pants. Blue denims (JC Penney @ some 65¢), or striped bib overalls (at slightly higher price) were only worn for work outdoors like feeding chickens, cleaning the coop and roosts, pulling up skunk cabbages, splitting wood, or cutting trees and playing in the woods.

Few children in those years had extensive wardrobes; however, Ariel's little closet was exceedingly bare. Each new school year she became more and more aware that other girls in class and at Sunday school were much better dressed, even though their families were certainly not wealthy. By this time the entire World War II was over, rationing had ended and people were eager to buy things they had done without during the War years. Going into fourth grade most assuredly required new garments and Ariel was growing taller.

It was off to the berry fields to learn how to pick strawberries and make money to buy those new things. Mrs. Benson ran the berry field portion of their farm; Mr. Benson took care of the chickens, cows, horses, and hay fields. Sale of fresh vegetables, milk, eggs and big juicy strawberries was their primary source of income. The Bensons also went to the Highland Church so Ariel knew them and her introduction to the working world was easier than it may well have been.

Mrs. Benson started new pickers on the poorer rows near the edges of the field where they picked berries for cannery use, removing hulls and filling flatter boxes only level so they wouldn't be pushed down by another flat placed on top. Picking cannery was messy and soon small hands were covered in berry juice and dirt from the leaves. The leaves also harbored small black spiders and itchy bites were frequent.

The better and more experienced pickers were assigned nicer and more productive rows, leaving hulls on the fruit and filling smaller boxes sufficiently to nicely mound the fruit, shiny tips up for sale in Bellevue markets. Her goal was to pick as rapidly as possible, and advance to picking for market. It seemed to take forever to fill the six boxes in a carrier, then fill the second and take them to the shed, making up a flat. Payment was by the flat, not by the time required to fill it. Each flat was inspected and required to meet high standards in order to qualify for payment.

Despite having blue eyes and blond hair Ariel quickly turned dark brown each summer. Both she and Dad more closely resembled blue-eyed Sioux than Minnesota Swedes, his hair being virtually black. Use of sun block was yet decades into the future, and lotions were not then a part of her everyday life. Naturally oily skin was a blessing along with quick tanning.

Only a single sunburn was experienced; that when long hair was pulled back into a pony tail one early summer day, exposing her winter-white ears to the hot sunshine. By lunch they rather resembled over-done bacon, but Mrs. Benson liberally applied fresh cow's cream. The tender ears healed quickly and she was also given a large-brimmed hat, which hung in the shed by her picking carrier. Those sunburned ears taught her to always wear a hat to protect her face as well as tender ears.

After strawberry season came blueberries. These were picked directly into containers hanging around pickers' necks, poured into carriers, taken to the shed and weighed. Each carrier had its weight written on the end, which was deducted from scale weight to determine the net amount. Payment was based on pounds and ounces. By then, wearing sun hats in berry fields had become habitual, even in Bellevue, during the long hours of picking. Dad took her to the field each morning and picked her up after his work; and then they did grocery shopping.

After berry season and before school started, Edythe wanted Ariel to spend more time playing with dolls and less baseball, sand-lot football, fishing and cutting down trees. She arranged for Ariel to walk to Betsy's for a day where time would be more appropriately spent with suitable Church girls. Ariel was not at all enthused. The mile-long walk was ok, but not the idea of a whole day with Betsy and her little sister. At least Dad would pick her up after supper.

The day dragged on, seemingly forever. Pigs were being butchered that day, so children were kept indoors. Dolls were totally uninteresting and as the afternoon hours passed, strange, sharp smells emitted from the kitchen. What on earth was being cooked? Ariel sincerely hoped it was not something they might be expected to eat; the smell was awful.

At the early supper that mystery was solved. A plate of wieners and an enormous bowl of stringy, light-green slippery substance were placed on the table. Betsy was delighted, "Oh look, Ariel, we're having sauerkraut! It's my very favorite!" Her very favorite? That anyone ate anything that smelled that bad was unthinkable.

Ariel kept quiet and put a very small amount of it on her plate. How could she possibly manage to eat any? Taking nibbles of the wiener, a bit of the kraut, and a quick bite of the plain white bread, some of the meal was consumed, and managed to stay down. Not an easy task at all. She was careful to thank Betsy's mother and father for the afternoon and for supper.

At last Dad's car stopped down the hill at the bottom of their dirt drive. With a quick last 'thank you' she was off running as fast as she could. Her toe caught on a rock and down hard she went, hands, elbows and knees onto the packed dirt. Dad jumped out of the car and started up to her, but she jumped up and pelted down to him. What a mess. Tears, dirt and blood all over face, arms and legs. At least she hadn't torn her dress. Into the car and they were off down the road to a creek where she cleaned up as well as possible. Dad held her close and assured her all would be well; they would say as little as possible about her tumble.

It would be at least another three years before Dad quite inadvertently discovered she was extremely near-sighted. Notes sent home from school about her limited vision had landed in the cook stove fire before he could see them. Cash money was not to be spent getting eye examinations and/or glasses for a child; that was for the church (not necessarily for God's work, but the church). Edythe, meanwhile, had glasses for everyday and a quite ornately framed pair for Sundays and other dressy occasions.

Edythe found an article in one of her gardening magazines expounding the raising of Easter lily bulbs for sale to wholesale landscape and seed companies. Seed-bulbs were ordered. Dad was assigned to roto-tilling a good-sized plot of ground by the garden, and the bulbs were planted. The lilies do not naturally bloom at Easter, but in summer, with the multiplied bulbs harvested after bloom. This was intended to be a reliable source of income. A fairly large number of lilies in bloom are indeed showy and quite pretty; however, they smell--big time. The plant rows also need to be watered and kept free of weeds. Both Dad and Ariel spent considerable time tending the lilies. Whether the bulb project produced any income was never known. The rows of lilies were plowed under after a couple of years; with any volunteer plants that sprouted gleefully yanked up and tossed by both Ariel and her dad. Neither missed them one bit. Edythe seldom ventured onto that part of the property and apparently remained unaware of the diligence with which it was monitored and kept lily-free.

Edythe moved on to another plan involving a small, but productive and potentially profitable blueberry patch. Another fairly large area, near the street, was roto-tilled, blueberry plants purchased through another gardening magazine advertisement, holes dug, water lines and spigots installed and plants put into the ground. They grew, of course, as does everything in the Puget Sound region. Edythe did spend hours appropriately pruning the bushes for maximum production, spraying for pests, and planning the harvest.

For some years, after picking berries at a commercial blueberry farm for which payment was received, there were more for Ariel to pick at home, for free. Blueberries never became a personal favorite. The bushes remained in place for years, to the enjoyment of birds and chipmunks.

Edythe also closely monitored the time Ariel spent in the bathroom and frequency of her visits there. It was the one place inside the house where she could have some privacy and read undisturbed. Books were a major part of Ariel's life and she read constantly. However, Edythe had definite ideas as to the amount of time anyone should spend in a bathroom, which assuredly did not include reading; despite frequent references to it being the library or reading room. She also monitored the reading material, disapproving of most.

Any deemed over-long time spent there by Ariel provided Edythe the rationale for administering soapy enemas; seemingly her very favorite thing to do. Her zeal truly seemed sadistic to Ariel although through many years she was too young to make that actual terminology connection. Protests fell on deaf ears.

At Edythe's command it was up to the attic with the rubber hot water bottle full of hot soapy water, newspaper spread on the floor and the old chamber pot at hand. Edythe was able to better analyze the results than she could have in a toilet; beside which, the bathroom was simply too small. Residual effects of those numerous treatments caused Ariel problems well into her middle age years and finally required surgical correction.

Rocks

Edythe never lost her fascination with collecting rocks. There was the large collection of Lake Superior agates gathered during her early years and carefully kept for some unidentified project. Numerous plans were made for cutting, polishing and displaying, but none came to fruition. Moss agates were found in the Dakotas and Montana; pretty stones at the seashore and petrified wood in Eastern Washington. Fewer than a dozen of the precious pieces were ever cut or polished. All were retained and stored in various boxes, coffee cans and moved time and again. The accumulation steadily grew.

After having a trellis built to support her climbing Blaze roses, Edythe decreed there should be a stone walkway along that display from drive to the door. Many flat stones had already been set aside from time to time, but the hunt went into high gear. Ariel and Dad were designated rock-pickers wherever flat specimens could be found. The piles grew. A trip to Mt. Rainier resulted in a goodly haul, including a long block of basalt deposited in a hillside by volcanic upheaval.

Ariel watched in terror as Dad climbed from one outcropping to another up a steep bank to dislodge the specific chunk of rock Edythe simply had to have. He loosened smaller rocks under it, gave it a Herculean shove, and down it tumbled in a shower of gravel and dust. He barely managed to jump aside and avoid going down with it. She had her rock. Ariel helped lift it into the trunk; a close fit and the rear of the car lowered noticeably.

The walkway construction was undertaken; an edging form put in place, cement, lime and sand purchased. Ariel thoroughly enjoyed helping with this part of the project, mixing concrete and placing stones, shifting them around for better result, and using a long level.

Following the walkway and stone steps, another project loomed rather ominously. Winter snow, rains and run-off swelled the creek and began undermining the hillside on which the house was built. Logs and large rocks were placed upstream of the bend to divert some of the force until waters receded and a concrete and stone bulkhead could be constructed. That required a coffer dam, more water diversion, setting the foundation below water level, and moving more large rocks. Ariel loved working with Dad and this project also taught her skills she would use decades later in building a water feature, large front porch and patio.

The last rock and mortar project they worked on together was another retaining wall on the steep bank to prevent erosion. A planting area was also incorporated in that undertaking. No matter that expanding root systems lead to deterioration of concrete; flowers were installed. Ariel fondly recalled those experiences later doing her own block/brick/rock and mortar projects.

Fall Seasons and School

School remained Ariel's absolutely most favored environment. Books were available, both at the small school library and from the traveling bookmobile. Having become an avid reader, the treasures available from the bookmobile opened marvelous vistas. Traveling librarians frequently questioned her choices, since those significantly exceeded the normal reading levels of her then-current grade. After a few sessions of keeping her in the vehicle and querying her comprehension of books read, they let her check out whatever she wished. When Dad inquired as to what she might be reading, he was pleased at the choices and consistently encouraging. Most library books were kept out of Edythe's sight to avoid the habitual questioning of alleged motive, negativity and criticism. She did not want Ariel accessing any printed material she deemed inappropriate, which encompassed virtually any non-religious text, and even those had to meet her specific personal criteria based on her own narrow interpretation of the favored denominational tenets.

Teachers consistently encouraged Ariel and report card comments were favorable; grades in elementary school were S, S+ and she continually sought to improve on those. School was a positive and she loved being in class, never dreading report card time, as some did. In those days, parental review of cards was required, and confirmed by signature. Feedback was encouraged but not required. Dad always praised the cards, while Edythe only indicated disappointment over the few simply S (satisfactory) grades during elementary years; all should have been S++. (In that era the S designated the desired performance level by educators.)

Later when grading was alphabetic, "A" was regarded by Edythe as 'average' "B" bad, "C" calamitous and "D" never a consideration; who only knows what that designation may have been. Ariel did not receive "C" grades, and very few of the highly-suspect "B/B+" marks.

On completion of the sixth grade, students in the eastern part of the district transferred to Junior High School in Bellevue. Somehow, despite lack of any psychological screening or preparation, all seemed to make this switch from the small country elementary school, to the much larger urban environment for grades seven on. Unaware they needed special help, counseling, or counselors; everyone simply boarded appropriate buses and went to school.

Ariel's only trauma was over what to wear that first day of Junior High. Would a Jr. Hi girl be in a panic over clothes? Of course; it's the norm—was, and is, whatever the current style criteria. She didn't know it, but she was completely, totally and utterly normal. She didn't think anyone else would have concerns or questions because the other girls were all confident, assured, well-dressed, and would just know. Besides, they shopped the high-end department stores.

In that long-ago era, cotton was worn only after Easter; woolen garments donned only after Labor Day. No cotton and only wool after; it was all quite simple and totally unquestioned. White anything only after Easter and never, but never ever worn after Labor Day, other than a white shirt or blouse with jacket or sweater. School started after Labor Day. That was the established order; no one need ask. For grown-up ladies, hats and gloves matched; shoes and handbags matched, period. That's just the way it was; no question. Questions were simply not raised. Without any hint of doubt, Ariel knew cotton was unquestionably out for that all-important day one of Junior High.

So, on this vitally important first day at Junior High in town, which would establish her place in school-related society for the ensuing six years, and possibly life, selection of wearing apparel was extremely important. Ariel wanted to wear a woolen skirt, short-sleeved pullover sweater and a small fake-pearl necklace, with the obligatory white anklets and saddle shoes. That constituted the approved and appropriate uniform of the time. Temperatures in the area in September hovered in the mid to high 70's together with high humidity. It was the Puget Sound region after all.

Logic indicated cooler cotton summery clothing. Edythe insisted that she wear a white peasant-style blouse and full, maroon and gray patterned multi-yard cotton skirt over a layered nylon net petit-coat. No amount of explanation or pleading was effective; so off she went in the totally inappropriate attire. It was absolutely sensible for prevailing weather and temperatures, but completely wrong and inexcusable from the standpoint of proper teen-age fashion of the day. In the annuls of universal history, that faux pas doesn't even make the list; however, constituted a major trauma for a young teen. Ariel was, of course, mortified. The wardrobe gaffe did not escape peer notice or prevent pointedly negative comments. The earth absolutely refused to swallow her. Any slim hope of social acceptance utterly vanished, never having seen the light of day.

Military veterans of the Korean War were beginning to return from active duty and take up where they had left off at being drafted. Two such handsome teachers were on staff during Ariel's 7th and 8th grades; Mr. Hester and Mr. Kester. Every 7th and 8th grade girl fell in love with these marvelously exciting 'older' men, only occasionally paying much attention to lessons in history and math classes. They both coached sports of course in addition to being classroom instructors, only adding to their charm. Ah…how every young girl dreamed, Ariel included.

She also developed a huge crush on Ray Harai who sat directly in front of her in the basement English classroom. Sun shining through a small horizontal window onto his hair was amazing; black turned a deep, iridescent blue appearing to take on a life of its own. His hair was just slightly wavy and unbelievably gorgeous. Ray liked her, too, and frequently telephoned her in the evenings for alleged help with homework. Years later after high school graduation she learned his mother had been highly concerned about her son 'taking up' with a blond blue-eyed Swedish girl. That was most definitely not proper in her estimation.

Shortly after their 10th high school class reunion, Ray and his friend Dennis Hadley crashed a small aircraft on Mt. Rainier. At some future time their remains may emerge from the glacier.

In late summer just prior to eight grade, Ariel received her first invitation for a date. She was twelve; Herb was sixteen, in high school and had built his own car from odd pieces and parts. She had known him for several years, both he and his sister attended Sunday school, and occasionally been part of the neighborhood group of kids fishing, cutting firewood, and building forts in the woods. His whole family attended the church, at which Ariel was then playing the pump organ for services.

Herb telephoned and inquired if she would like to go skating with him at the local roller rink. When she agreed that would be very nice, he then asked to speak with her Dad, who quickly gave his permission. When day and time had been set and Ariel hung up the phone, Dad grinned broadly, winked at her and said, "Now, how about that … looks like you are going out on your first date."

Oh my, she had never thought of that; dates were for the pretty, older girls, not for her. From earliest memory Edythe had made it explicitly clear that she was not pretty, smart, or of any real value, and Ariel accepted that as truth. And now, Dad indicated young Herb also held a somewhat different opinion. This truly was rather exciting; Herb would drive to her house, come to the door, and take her roller skating.

Edythe could hardly object to Herb; after all, his family all attended her church and an uncle was on the Board of Trustees. She was able, however, to alter this very proper and correct procedure and effectively teach Ariel to lie, despite all preaching to the contrary.

Due to her unfounded fear and distrust of the Schonings who lived next door, she insisted Herb not come to the house. She worried that they would 'see', and so insisted that Herb pick Ariel up at the highway, not come to the door. Edythe's instructions were for Ariel to walk down the long drive and up the street to the corner, carrying an empty carton to look like she was delivering eggs. She was to put the carton under a bush or in the ditch when Herb came. That way no one would "see" her getting into Herb's car. Just what the Schonings or anyone else was supposed to do should they notice any such highly incriminating activity was never clear. Herb and his entire family were well-known to everyone in the area, and well-liked. Edythe worried and fretted constantly about what someone might "see" and what any such person or persons might possibly think.

Decades later when Ariel's own daughters were teenagers she recalled that egg carton subterfuge, and how utterly silly it was, serving only to clarify that Edythe placed far greater emphasis on her concept of "*appearance*" and what some observer might possibly think than on truthfulness.

The evening of roller skating was great fun, and only the first of many to follow.

A side-issue during the Junior Hi years that Ariel found amusing, and also provided Dad a good chuckle, was Edythe being asked to participate in the PTA as Chaplain. The position entailed providing an opening prayer at the monthly meetings. If she had ever attended a PTA meeting was unknown.

This secular public school-associated organization was viewed by Edythe as more than a little suspect, highly apt to be engaged in promoting progressive and dangerously new ideas, negatively impacting young minds, and not up-building in her opinion.

For a woman so heavily involved in her church activities, and gravely concerned as to prevailing lack of morals among youth, it seemed reasonable to Dad that she accept this opportunity to spread her view of religion. Not so. PTA met once a month during the school term. Her church prayer meetings were held weekly, on the same weeknight. It simply would not do to miss a church prayer meeting to lead a prayer elsewhere. An insignificant matter to be sure, but more than a bit amusing.

High School comprised the then-standard grades 9 through 12, encompassing all the normal and usual teenage traumas. It was nowhere as much fun as portrayed on the "Happy Days" television series, but not totally bad, in truth. Grades and Honor Society membership were Ariel's primary focus, having realized fairly early in life she would be making her own way in the world at a fairly young age if ever to be out from under Edythe's constant criticism and fault-finding. Her goal: keep grades up, graduate, get a job, and get out.

So, she worked after school and on weekends from early in her sophomore year through graduation. Babysitting during the week and many weekend nights precluded much involvement in school activities. While dating the Sr. Class president, as a sophomore, some football and even a few basketball games were possible. By hook and/or crook, Ariel managed to work on props and production for one school play – what total fun. Nothing interfered with her playing the church pump organ for at least three services each Sunday, teaching a fifth-grade boys' Sunday school class and conducting activities for a Junior Hi Youth Group.

Migraine headaches had begun with onset of menses at age 11, with increased intensity and predictable regularity in the teen years and continuing for nearly two decades. Stress was assuredly a major factor. She was studying diligently to maintain high grades in school, working part-time, sewing her own clothes, singing and providing organ music for numerous church services, weddings, funerals and leading a Youth Group, in addition to having a social life. Meanwhile, Edythe continued criticizing her for not doing enough for the church and not voluntarily donating more of her personal things for the ever-present missions' boxes. Edythe simply appropriated items from her closet and other areas of her attic sleeping area until Ariel was able to lock better things in the trunk of her car.

A member of the Board of Deacons at the church was tasked with being her guide and supervisor for the Youth Group. Ariel soon perceived his interest was not in helping with the program, but getting her off in a side room for purposes other than the kids' program. She tried to relate to Edythe some of his attempts to isolate her, his inappropriate questions and statements along with consistent attempts at touching her, hoping for some understanding and perhaps support in avoiding him. Not so. Edythe was outraged, in her passive/aggressive manner that Ariel would even hint that this fine Christian man was of anything but the highest character and purest intent.

Decades later Dad told her that particular man, so highly regarded, had been discovered in a very compromising situation involving the church secretary. His wife of some twenty-plus years divorced him, was awarded custody of their six children, spousal and child support as well as the real property. The Bible is totally accurate in one area, "be sure, your sin will find you out." Occasionally it just takes time.

Ariel had always believed in God, prayed the standard written prayers, memorized confession, Apostle's Creed, been confirmed and formally joined the church, played the organ, taught Sunday School, sang in choir, duets and soloed. She intellectually understood salvation, and considered herself Christian. That was simply the norm in her life – just the way things were. She did not expect God to pay any special attention to her. Now she began to question just what God's true role should be in her life.

She had been taught to trust in God. Fine, but just what did that actually mean day to day? Why was she so different? Why were the good things, so-called blessings or whatever, consistently reserved for other more deserving people? Why did she carry such a heavy burden of guilt? Guilt about everything, even things she didn't know about—current or long past events far away, in far-flung lands. How and why was she responsible for tragedies, suffering, poverty and hardships world-wide? No answers. Her prayers continued, "please Lord, make it all work out right" and questions remained. Would everything be clear when she reached that magical adult status?

The church senior youth group planned various activities throughout the year, and a ski weekend was one Ariel looked forward to eagerly. She had a pair of used skis, boots and poles. Dormitory facilities at the summit lodge were reserved and car pooling arranged. Ariel could take three or four others in her 2-door sedan and she had money for gas and lift tickets. The old military surplus sleeping bag was still usable, if not very comfortable or warm. Ski clothes were certainly not stylish by any means, but adequate.

Her night-wear, however, was a different matter; pajamas were mere shreds and not even decent. The girls were all assigned to cots in one wing of the dorm, in a sort of slumber party setting. Others would have nice pajama sets and slippers. Ariel had neither. She was well aware of the stack of 20-dollar bills Edythe kept at hand for church giving; those were sacrosanct. No one but Edythe touched those, not even Dad whose wages provided them.

Ariel's part-time work and baby-sitting were sufficient to pay for the weekend fees, food and gas, but not new pajamas. She posed this dilemma at dinner a few days before the trip, asking if she could have a new pair of pajamas. Dad was in agreement; however, Edythe put an immediate stop to any such foolishness. If Ariel was too proud to wear what she had, then she could use Edythe's newer flannel night-gown. There was absolutely no need to go wasting money on new pajamas just to go skiing. What different did it make what she wore to sleep— indeed. Vanity and pride were to be avoided.

Dad remained silent, looking down and pushing supper around with his fork. That Saturday night in the dormitory when the girls all gathered wearing cute pajamas, Ariel huddled on the floor in that horrid flannel gown, at the back of the room as near the door as possible. It was the last flannel item Ariel ever tolerated anywhere near her.

Dating was a part of the high school experience and quite a learning process. Ariel was surprised and more than slightly dismayed to learn early on in this game that some of the nice church boys, whose parents held official positions, did not have the same degree of respect for girls as did the alleged "heathen" boys. Herb, however, was always a gentleman and very considerate. They were part of a group of kids who enjoyed doing things together, and she missed him when he went off to college. During high school, she also dated boys from a religious college, fully approved and highly encouraged by Edythe; highly suspect by Dad, and with good reason.

Despite high-flown discussions of theological fine points, their primary interests centered on parking in the dark on over-grown logging roads to explore Ariel's anatomy. Loftily debating the numbers of angels capable of dancing on the head of a pin frequently initiated their endeavors, which quickly degenerated. Edythe approved of her dating sons of the church deacons and trustees, especially those attending the approved religious college. Ariel favored going out with the alleged 'heathen' boys who behaved much better and treated her with far greater respect.

In her sophomore year of high school Ariel 'went steady' with the Senior Class President, much to the envy of her peers, as well as Junior and many Senior Class girls. He was older, of course, and by all right and proper teen code should have dated upper class girls not a lowly sophomore. It did work quite well, however, as both were rather socially limited by parental restrictions. Neither was allowed to attend school dances, proms, balls, or even after-game sock-hops. Movies were also off limits. So, what remained? Parking for hours in dark woods on old logging roads, allegedly pursuing answers to the weightiest of intellectual and theological questions through long, intense discussion.

Chuck deemed himself quite a Bible scholar and felt it his bound and duty to explain Divine Will to Ariel. Strong emphasis was on the superiority of the male in a relationship and onus on the female to not only recognize that, but be quite subservient. Her innocence and naiveté served well, despite the young man's eloquent dissertations and frequent declarations of his eternal undying devotion.

Ariel worked after school in addition to babysitting, Sunday School teaching and organist duties, which did not leave much time for just hanging out with any girl friends.

Her very first real office experience was in an employment service, where the manager soon recommended her to the local Chamber of Commerce, at no cost to Ariel but a slightly higher hourly wage. This was an interesting introduction to actual office procedures, promotional efforts, business leaders, city officials and multiple-line phones. Through that she met business people in the area and was hired away by a leading real estate firm at a 25-cent per hour wage increase. Saturdays in that office were very busy preparing sale/purchase agreements for newly-built developments as well as older homes. Her opinion of real estate sales agents in general was somewhat jaded and did not change much over ensuing decades. Commission checks were the primary goal then as now, however regulations have altered some practices over the years.

She did make friends with one fellow high school student who lived nearby. Arletta also came from a rather dysfunctional home situation with a stoic and mostly silent father, a younger sister determined to make everyone's lives miserable, and mother who also thoroughly enjoyed ill health, actual or alleged. Much like Edythe, she also claimed inability to get out of the house, or participate in any activities she felt might intrude on her time. She also made swift recoveries for any activities she liked, especially if attention was directed her way.

The girls spent much of the time they could garner away from their homes swapping accounts of their mothers' rather peculiar behaviors. With graduation, however, their ways parted as each sought and found employment they hoped would free them, at least financially, from parental control.

The primary goal of most girls in that era was marriage and children. Very little attention was given to working toward a career, any career. College was seen as prime territory for securing a husband to support her and future children. Studies in whatever chosen scholastic area were quite secondary, but a degree tended to enhance opportunities to marry well and move in upper socio-economic classes. College graduation with a bachelor's degree was a good thing but not an ultimate goal; a large engagement ring was the prize.

Edythe thoroughly and immediately quashed any possibility of Ariel pursuing college other than the church-run entity in Chicago. She desperately wanted to attend the University of Washington. No way would that be allowed; it was a state-run, secular institution which Edythe absolutely knew destroyed proper and correct religious faith through all manner of immoral teachings and emphasis on researching all manner of subjects. Secular institutions also encouraged students to question and challenge established, and more correctly proper, concepts. No. Ariel was not to be exposed to such a sinful environment; she would remain under Edythe's supervision, just as Richard was. Ariel would remain in the family home, employed in an acceptable environment, and not acquire worldly ways.

Edythe's self-imposed role was not an easy one, for certain. There were so many pitfalls awaiting Ariel.

Having voiced her need for employment to be self-supporting, Ariel's high school course of study was summarily shifted from "pre-college" to "commercial". What went unmentioned was that there would be absolutely no information provided as to any college enrollment consideration or possibilities of scholarship application(s) or counseling of any sort. She didn't even know that scholarships required application, and were not simply granted based on student grade point averages. Her GPA was excellent with 4-year honor society membership. No continuing education information was made available to the lower-class "commercial" students by district or high school administration staff persons.

School counselors and teachers confined their work with the "commercial" students to specific disciplinary matters. Any scholastically-related efforts were directed to the better-class and more favored "pre-college" students. If a student indicated a need for employment following graduation there was no staff involvement beyond required subject assignment. Boys were directed to shop classes, girls to home economics and typing.

SECTION IV

Where to Go from Here?

During the mid-1950's an Army Nike Base was built between Bellevue, Kirkland and Redmond, introducing a fairly sizeable number of military personnel to the area. A young soldier and his wife from Kansas began attending the Highland Church, bringing along a Colorado buddy from the base. Edythe was fascinated with them and all were frequent dinner guests. The buddy, Bill, soon asked Ariel out, encouraged by his friends and even more strongly so by Edythe. The boys Ariel had dated were either in college and no longer much interested in mere high-school kids, or had been drafted.

They saw quite a lot of each other, mostly as a four-some with occasional single dates. Bill planned to return to college upon discharge from the service to complete his education and coaching degree, and was a very pleasant fellow. His Sergeant also encouraged him to "put a ring on that little gal's finger" before he lost out. Engagement to Ariel was considered a most beneficial move for Bill's future success in the Military as well as future employment.

Winter break 1955, Pedersens planned a trip to Colorado; Dad wanted to more closely check out this Bill person, his family, background, and all. Winter travel through the Cascades and on into the Rocky Mountains could be tricky in the mid-1950's, but away they went. Edythe was unhappy, Dad quite cheerful and Ariel more than slightly apprehensive. What if his family was wealthy and found her not up to their expectations. The life-long experience of not ever being pretty, good enough, or meeting Edythe's expectations in any manner whatsoever, had not resulted in any degree of self-confidence. No matter the occasion or setting, she consistently expressed only disappointment in Ariel, so apprehension was a rather normal response.

Was Edythe's negativity toward Ariel an attempt to somehow protect her daughter? If Ariel had a lower opinion of herself, didn't think she was gifted in any way, intelligent, pretty, of value, and didn't dream of a full, rewarding future with a worthwhile loving companion and family, would she be saved from heart-breaking disappointment? Edythe had dreamed of more education, advancing socially, marrying into a wealthy prominent family even as she accepted nursing school and hospital floor duty. Her golden dreams had been utterly shattered.

There was no pillared brick house with servants on a tree-lined boulevard; no sleek roadster in the garage; no elegantly garbed, professional, well-connected husband and no high-class social life. She lived in a small house on a patch of wooded acreage with chicken-coop, vegetable garden, cotton house dresses instead of elegant designer gowns; her spouse a skilled tradesman not a prominent businessman.

Was Edythe's approach to parenting protection or merely pernicious disparagement due to personal disappointments experienced? That she was highly intelligent was fact; memory and recall incredible and evidenced by the ability to recall in minute detail perceived sins committed by herself and other years, even decades, in the past. She was adept at tracking which stories she told to specific persons, relating vastly different versions depending upon the setting. If challenged, which Ariel did on occasion, Edythe simply denied any knowledge whatever of the subject, clearly indicating Ariel had mental problems.

The matter of parenting was handled quite simply. No matter what the question, Ariel was told to just "use your own judgment". Later, Edythe responded in a hushed tone, lone tear trickling down from an averted eye, '"oh, no, there's nothing wrong; I'm just disappointed."

By consistently denigrating Ariel and demeaning her husband in public, Edythe presented as the fine Christian woman struggling to maintain in an acceptable and functional situation. An ever-present concern was that other persons, especially church members, think highly of her; she fretted constantly over appearances of any normal and usual activity, lest someone *see*.

At a quite young age Ariel concluded Edythe was not just different from other mothers, women, and also men, but must have significant mental problems. Edythe was quite unable to dismiss the smallest infraction of her expectations as being just the way it was, or merely human nature.

Edythe did not particularly like the Western Colorado area or Bill's family, sighing much of the time and daubing at frequently trickling tears. Only a painfully amateurish Christmas play presented at the community church evoked any hint of pleasure or favorable comment. The stay in Colorado was short.

Los Angeles and visiting a re-located Highland Covenant Minister and family was more to her liking, with Rose Parade attendance tolerated because she could sit with the church group and sing hymns. Ariel tried to appear as separate from that group as possible, having quickly recognized the hymn-singing to be anything but appreciated by the waiting crowds.

A small ensemble at another L.A. church was shy an alto one afternoon, and Ariel wasted no time taking the opportunity of singing with them. They were taping music for a film being produced by North Park College in Chicago, which was on Edythe's approved list. She had numerous contacts there who could report any perceived misconduct by Ariel, should she consent to attend. Having had some casual social contacts, and even a couple dates, with seminary students from North Park; she chose not to. However, it was absolutely thrilling to sing with a group taping music for a film, even though she never knew what, if anything ever transpired from it.

From Los Angeles it was back north, along the then only major highway. Winter storms had played havoc with roads. Ariel was the driver rather consistently on this trip, with Dad tending the map and taking a turn at the wheel now and again. A few miles north of Red Bluff, they had not met any southbound vehicles for a long time and as they approached a bridge, Dad suggested she stop. Hard, driving rain continued relentlessly.

Edythe remained in the back seat as they got out and walked toward the bridge. Inspection showed a deep gap several inches wide between the roadway and the bridge. The other side looked much the same. Dad dropped a few large stones and a length of discarded power pole into one gap, not filling it by any means, but lessening the depth somewhat. He also jumped hard in several places crossing the bridge.

Finally he said they could probably make it if she drove fast enough. What? That was exactly what he meant, and precisely what Ariel did. She backed the car several hundred feet, then floor-boarded the accelerator, aimed for the center of the bridge. "You're doing great – just keep going – don't stop." One loud and jarring thump – smooth sailing – another jarring thump and they were safely on pavement again. Edythe was harshly jolted from her brief back seat nap, tsk-tsking about the rough road. Slowing, Ariel glanced at Dad. A broad grin spread across his face and he reached to pat her hand, still firmly gripping the wheel. "Great job of driving," was his only soft-spoken comment.

A Redding café was still open so they stopped for coffee and a bite to eat. Ariel's hands finally quit shaking just about the time a highway patrolman walked in, shook rain off his hat and coat and indicated he wanted everyone's attention. He said he hoped we were all northbound, because the bridge south of town had just washed out. They were apparently the last vehicle to get over that bridge northbound.

Remaining miles to Bellevue, while lengthy and soggy, were largely uneventful; it was back to work for Dad and school for Ariel.

June of 1956 arrived at last. Donning robes, caps, and adjusting her gold braid honor cords, Ariel and 205 fellow graduates processed to the gymnasium in proper order to receive diplomas. High School graduation was one goal finally reached, bringing with it the joy of having completed that level of education with a topnotch grade point average. That would help in job hunting. An all-night graduation party kept most kids sober and quite safe, entertained, and deposited back at the school in time to get to the daytime jobs some held. Most however, were picked up by luxury cars, by parents, some chauffeured, or drove their own new sport cars, Buick sedans, Lincolns, Cadillacs or Chryslers on home to sleep. The '48 Ford carried a tired, but happy Ariel home to dress for work at the real estate office. Weekends brought house hunters out, especially in good weather and she correctly anticipated plenty of sale agreements to prepare.

Shortly after graduation, Ariel traveled again to Colorado to see Bill and discuss their future. She had saved up money for train and bus fare. This was her first solo travel experience, very interesting and she turned down a marriage proposal from a young Mormon returning from his 'mission'. He strongly pressed his 'suit', praising life in Utah which of course included marriage to him. The first silent question in Ariel's mind was what number wife she might be in that situation. No thank you, for certain. He sadly exited the train alone after a last plea for her to join him.

She quickly realized she truly did not want to marry Bill and move to Colorado either, despite his many declarations of love and promises for their totally marvelous and joyous future together. His family was unlike any she had ever encountered, which wasn't saying much given the isolation under which she had grown up. She also viewed him in his environment, among his friends, and the lack of 'social graces' loomed large; unnoticed during his time in her area. She did not feel comfortable in his community.

She also had absolutely no concept of what love meant. The whispered endearments were pleasant to hear, but were after all, just words. Living in a single-wide student housing trailer in the mountains and hunting a low-paying job cashiering or waiting tables in a college town just didn't have the appeal it seemed to months earlier. Any rosy glow had dimmed. She had her sights set on something more than working in a diner. She wanted out from under Edythe's constant criticism of course; but absolutely not in a marriage to Bill. Doing so could very well be trading the fry-pan for the fire, a big fire.

After all, she was just out of high school; college dreams had been thwarted, but she was qualified for a better career than waiting tables. Caution flags about any future with Bill had popped up all over the place in spite of her misgivings as to her personal value or worth.

Employment and Proposal

High School graduation diploma in hand, all hope of attending University thoroughly quashed, it was time for serious job-hunting. While steering Ariel away from Latin, chemistry and any advanced math courses toward typing, shorthand and bookkeeping, not a word was uttered as to how one went about applying for and finding a job. The engraved cards purchased in addition to the standard graduation announcements at least provided something with one's name to present when initiating an inquiry at a front desk. Basic contact information, high school graduation year and GPA, together with a listing of pertinent courses, office equipment and experience were obviously needed. There had been no instruction in the 'business/commercial' classes touching on resume' preparation. Flying blind, there was nowhere to start but at the beginning.

Working out numerous formats, Ariel finally settled on one and set about preparation. Each one was individually typed; copy machines for public use were still a future thing. Photocopies were just that, individually made and expensive, most often still a black background with white print.

She read the office employment section of the newspaper each day and clipped ads that looked remotely promising, affixing each to the appropriate cover letter and resume'. She visited employment agency offices, signed contracts she didn't understand, talked with people who didn't seem to know much more than she, and went on interviews. Banks had some openings, but wages were extremely low with very little opportunity for advancement. She hand-carried and personally delivered résumés with cover letters, and completed applications wherever a possibility presented.

A call from the Senior Secretary for the Bellevue Schools offered her a job in the district offices working for the Superintendent. She had not applied there;

however her contact information had been obtained through the bookkeeping teacher and she was known from her work during school. This lady wanted to retire the next year and she would love to train Ariel for her job. Without a doubt this was a really good opportunity; right out of high school. Some ladies had worked there for years and were not even being considered for such advancement.

She had done all the mimeograph work for the office during her Junior and Senior years in school in exchange for a B+ bookkeeping grade and no harm to her GPA. Debits and Credits had never made sense to her, and the teacher suggested the trade to meet two goals. The Superintendent needed considerable mimeograph copy and artwork done that his staff couldn't handle. They were not accomplished in the process of cutting the large numbers of stencils required, and dealing with the newer equipment, including ink 'guns' to produce both black and white, and color print-quality copy. The teacher knew Ariel was very good at this and highly intelligent, even if debits and credits didn't automatically register clearly. It seems even some people involved in the finance business have problems keeping those debits and credits straight in some circumstances involving account reference changes. She was also well acquainted with the superintendent and would have no difficulty working for him.

Ariel's employment dream was an office job in Seattle, since attendance at any college other than North Park had been overruled. Her alternate goal was to find an interesting and challenging job, live in a city apartment and present as a very capable and sophisticated young career woman. Bellevue School District was where she had gone all through school; the office was located near enough to Highland that she would have to remain at home with no realistic chance of having her own apartment. The looming probability of ending up like the Schoning 'girls' living in their mother's house all their lives was just too much. Playing the old pump organ at the church for the two morning and one evening service on Sundays, as well as any other occasion at which the organ was scheduled would be part of that life. Each year the Board of Trustees presented her, and the pianist, each with a $5. gift certificate to a local department store; the extent of any compensation. How unlike that was from what she hoped would logically follow her completion of high school.

She accepted the school district offer only because it appeared the only one on the horizon, and started full time employment. From a practical standpoint, Dad supported her decision, knowing that her dreams were far different. Edythe was quite pleased Ariel's salary would not allow her an apartment of her own and so remain under her close supervision. She did have her own car and only Dad held the second key. Her better clothes and any small jewelry pieces she valued were safely locked in the trunk, brought out for wearing and put back promptly. Ariel knew Edythe went through her attic sleeping area while she was at school and now work. That was confirmed by carefully noting locations and placement of specific items each morning and finding those moved in the evenings. Wardrobe items had periodically disappeared as well. Any inquiry was met with a puzzled and somewhat vague, "oh, I thought it was something you didn't want any more, so I put it in the missionary box for (wherever)". Consequently Ariel did not leave any garments she cared about in her wardrobe or in the boxes used in lieu of a chest of drawers; and did all her own personal laundry by hand. Any item added to general household laundry was apt to vanish.

After working for the School District just over a month, she received a telephone message from the Seattle branch office of a Mid-west insurance company offering her the job for which she had applied in mid-June. This presented a dilemma, as she really liked all the School district people, and if the senior secretary did retire as she had indicated was possible, that would mean an excellent promotion for Ariel. In the *senior* office position, she would be supervising staff persons considerably older than herself. However, all that was still uncertain. Current salary was better than banks, but still fairly low by commercial standards.

The insurance company was not well known in the area, but growing rapidly, with plans in place for moving into a new building shortly. Wages…not great, but better than the school district. The major plus for Ariel was the location-Seattle, not Bellevue. She still would not be able to afford an apartment, but she would be working outside of Bellevue, and a tiny step closer to some degree of more independence.

Dad listened thoughtfully as Ariel listed the pros and cons of accepting this insurance company job instead of remaining at the School District. She knew nothing about insurance and the District office was very familiar territory. He finally asked, "what is it you want to do? Stay with the familiar or go for something that may or may not turn out to be what you want to do for the next few years?" While this was not exactly on a level of the motorcycle journeys he had taken with Harold as a teenager, it was at least something she had found on her own, away from the totally familiar and offering another small step toward her goals. Ariel accepted the insurance company offer, somewhat reluctantly gave notice at the School District, and very shortly found herself joining the morning rush of traffic over that floating bridge, through the tunnel and along city streets to an office building.

This was not a very busy place, temporarily housed in a shared space with a fledgling lawyer and an auto insurance agent who smoked cigars. Those things were totally foul; no one liked them, many complained, but to no avail. One day he left a partial one smoldering in an ash tray, went to visit his mother---not expected to return very soon. Ariel located an empty tin can in the back room, ran water into it and suggested to her boss the stinking cigar just might be extinguished if it chanced a fall into the can. He thought it a marvelous idea. The deed was done, and the office aired out; can, water and soaked cigar remained on the agent's desk. Thereafter he smoked outdoors in the alley. No mention was ever made as to the soaked cigar.

With little to do once new insurance applications had been logged in, photocopied, checks listed and deposited, correspondence transcribed from her shorthand, Ariel helped out with typing for the struggling lawyer. She also typed term papers for the Schoning 'girls', both in college at the time; those very young ladies about whom Edythe was so concerned. The branch manager brought in books from his personal library for her to read, and within just a few weeks announced she had completed the required reading for a university level first year liberal arts course. She hadn't been allowed to attend university, but that didn't stop her from learning. This was indeed a good employment decision. The amount of free time slowly decreased as additional sales staff was hired, more applications processed, telephone traffic and written correspondence increased.

The office was moved into a bright and cheery new building across the street; insurance agent to his own separate offices, lawyer to another building, even more sales people hired and business picked up. She now had plenty of administrative work to keep her busy as well as the training of new salesmen. The branch manager was pleased with her work and never hesitated to tell her that, also processing pay increases at regular intervals Receiving positive feedback was still something she did not automatically expect; although that had been the case in school and her part-time work.

Edythe's negativity and criticism continued at each opportunity, especially over supper when concerns were voiced about all the questionable, undoubtedly inappropriate persons with whom Ariel interacted in the business world on a daily basis.

A More Serious Dating Game

Ariel had several boyfriends during high school, with varying degrees of seriousness. Bill had proposed prior to his discharge from the Army. After visiting his family; and spending a few days in his environment, seeing the college he attended, looking into employment opportunities and the student housing, she had opted to remain quite single. As a high school sophomore she had "gone steady" with the Sr. Class President, who went on to a religious college after graduation.

Another fellow from the church was more than slightly serious about a future with Ariel, but that also fell by the wayside when he enlisted in the Air Force to avoid being drafted, and left for the Academy. He had driven a 1936 Packard convertible which leaked significantly in the frequent Puget Sound rain, but was such fun as they cruised up the avenue in slightly shabby elegance. She could dreamily picture herself the Russian Princess Anastasia, with handsome prince in the carriage beside her; the Packard hood was certainly long enough to be a team of blooded black steeds. Tire mounts in the front fenders were particularly impressive, as was the hood ornament.

Years later Ariel readily admitted the car had been more attractive and fun than the guy. Oh well. She had truly enjoyed the foreign films they watched in a tiny University District theater, even if neither understood the various languages and sub-titles left much to the imagination. After the films a tasty plate of fried rice, soup and delicious tea was shared at a charming University District Chinese café. One dollar for the movie and even less for their shared dinner. He wasn't cheap; just rather broke.

One Sunday evening a clarinet quartet from an Issaquah church provided special music for the service. Ariel didn't pay too much attention to the young men, all fairly recent high school graduates, just enjoyed the music and respite from the pump organ. One of the group was a nephew of a Highland Church Deacon, and friend of the Pedersens. This fellow Roger asked his uncle for Ariel's name and phone number, stating absolutely that she was the girl he was going to marry. They had yet to meet.

Roger wasted no time launching his campaign and they went out most Friday and Saturday nights, to a variety of community activities, a few movies; and both sang in church sponsored musical groups. They talked and talked, about everything and anything; he had very strong opinions Ariel didn't always agree with, but went along with rather than appear to argue. He was very decisive, insisted that he pick her up and take her to stores for shopping, and or any errands she had. He started coming to her office immediately after work on nights he had trade school classes or military reserve meetings. Ariel preferred to go home right after work, get through the tunnel, onto the floating bridge and head for Bellevue; but he wanted her to stay and sit in his car to talk until he was ready to leave. In fall and winter months it was totally dark before she started for home, generally raining, and she knew Dad would be concerned. However, she acquiesced to Roger's wishes, for the after work hours, as well as any weekend activities. None of Ariel's suggestions for dates or any weekend activities seemed of interest to Roger and were brushed aside as being quite without merit. She didn't particularly like that, but her wishes had never been considered valid at any time throughout her life, so it did not seem all that unusual or even significant.

She was aware of Roger's increasing demands on her time and control of her life; he telephoned every evening, many times quite late after his school or Naval Reserve meetings, when they had already spent time together after work. She dismissed nagging concerns by focusing on his decisiveness. All her life she had watched Dad just agree, answer with, 'yes, Pet', to whatever Edythe said, and was determined to avoid imposing her wishes on another person, especially Roger. He didn't seem capable of accepting any opinion but his own, very similar to Edythe, though expressed differently. She was determined to be an agreeable person, and acquiesce, not ever to expect a husband to take a back-seat to her.

At Christmas Roger placed an engagement ring on her finger and plans commenced for their wedding. One Sunday morning during the sermon Ariel held the ring close to her face where a ray of sunshine fell across the top facet and examined the diamond. There it was, clear and straight, a line crossing the center of the stone which should have been absolutely clear and smooth. A shiver passed over her; was that flaw an omen of a flaw in her relationship with Roger? Just don't think about it; everything will be fine; he says he loves you. By marrying him you get away from Edythe; and that's enough. The preacher's "Amen" signaled time for her to play the closing hymn and postlude.

Edythe's response to Ariel's engagement had not been overly positive or enthusiastic, merely commenting that, "Well, he isn't all that great, but most likely too good for the likes of you".

Dad was just a little reserved, but quickly hugged her and whispered his very best wishes in her ear after being assured this was truly her choice. He recognized Roger's excessive control while Ariel did not yet acknowledge it; he was concerned for his little girl. There was absolutely nothing he could do to intervene.

The Wedding... And...

As soon as their engagement became known, Edythe sprang into action. This was her hour to shine, to put on a splendid ceremony and reception. Neither Ariel nor Roger wanted a big fancy affair, just a few friends and relatives at the little church – with someone else playing the organ. The old pump organ had been replaced with an unreliable electric instrument, and Ariel's Hammond would undoubtedly be trucked to the church for the occasion. That was done any time the music truly required a decent and reliable instrument. Boards of Trustees, no member able find middle "C", should never be allowed to purchase keyboard instruments for any entity. However, given the nature of boards and committees, that frequently occurs.

Under Edythe's hand the guest list grew and grew; this was her opportunity to pay back perceived social debts, incur more from others, and do it all her way. She was determined this wedding would be a significant event in the community; her plans and her way. In 1934 there had been only a simple ceremony at the little Maywood church, a few relatives in attendance and no décor; coffee and cookies the reception. Edythe had always felt cheated, despite the '30's Depression. At that time many couples were married by a local Justice of the Peace in his office, with absolutely no fanfare whatever.

Ariel wanted warm colors, burgundy, dusky rose and mauve, in soft fabrics her friends could wear for numerous occasions. She preferably ivory velveteen for her simple a-line dress, which of course, she would sew. She also wanted a late fall/early winter date

Edythe had quite different plans, with brown, dark green, pale green and rust tones to serve suitably for her highly-vaunted once-red hair, and a mid-September date. Her chosen dress was milk chocolate lace over rust satin. That custom of the day decreed she not select a dress color similar to the wedding party itself apparently didn't occur to Edythe, or was simply of no consequence; most likely the latter. Colors and shades thereof were to suit her, regardless of any other consideration. Ariel purchased all the fabrics and patterns as selected by Edythe.

Ariel and her attendants sewed their dresses in the fall-colored taffetas. Her dress pattern also was selected by Edythe, and sewn in white taffeta with lace overlay. It featured a high peter-pan collar, seed pearls on ¾ sleeves and collar, with a multi-layered net petticoat. Flowers were also ordered in Edythe's preferred fall tones with brown, yellow, orange, dark green with dull gold tone ribbons.

Invitations went out far and near to one and all, as designated by Edythe. On September 18th the little church was packed. Music played, songs sung, candles lit, and the white runner in place. Ariel stood with Dad awaiting the opening chords of the "Wedding March." She was terrified, gripping her bouquet and Dad's arm in abject fear. She didn't dare meet his eye; he could not be allowed to see the panic she could not completely hide.

"Flee while you can—run—run," surged through her mind. With every ounce of will she silently, desperately beat it down. Flee where? to what? Edythe didn't really approve of Roger and Dad held sincere doubts about him; but, this was Edythe's day to shine, center of attention as mother-of-the-bride. She had determined Roger's family to be of somewhat acceptable socio-economic status, and would simply have to do. For her this wedding was a prime social event where she occupied center stage; bride or groom of minimal interest or concern.

Ariel's mind whirled in panic. This whole thing was wrong, horribly wrong; but she had promised and there was nothing to do now but go through with it. Why didn't the floor open up and swallow her? If Dad knew how she felt, he would grab her and race out of that church in a heartbeat – that she knew for certain. But then what. He would have to put up with and answer to Edythe, his court-ordered controlling guardian for life.

Ariel simply could not reveal the dread rising in her very core. It was altogether too late to run. The doctrinally-appropriate, proper church wedding and reception planned and being executed to provide Edythe her moment of social prominence and importance must proceed.

All the planning and work had been done, arrangements made, funds expended, photographer poised in the aisle, the Minister and Roger waiting at the altar. Ariel lifted her head high, squared her shoulders, put a smile on her face, and with the first notes, stepped onto the runner, gripping Dad's arm for support. He patted her hand and she chanced a brief glance up at him. He was absolutely beaming with pride, smiling down at her. She felt just a little better. She absolutely could not let him down.

She could do this; she would do this. Everyone was counting on her to be the proper bride, and this was Edythe's prime opportunity to exhibit her perceived social status. If she backed out, Edythe would never, ever quit blaming her for every possible potential criticism, snub or disappointment, real or imagined at any future time. This was a Friday, and no matter what she could get through one week and then think about what might come next. She was determined to be the best possible wife – for one week – not permitting any thought of more than one week.

Ceremony and endless reception were a blur; her entire body ached from tension and face stiff from maintaining the obligatory smile. The bouquet was thrown, caught by a bridesmaid, her gown removed and replaced with the gray and black sheath dress she had also sewed. Then they were in Roger's car and off down the highway toward … she hadn't a clue. Nothing had been said about where they would spend the first night of their married lives, or what the following morning might bring.

Roger had never said a word about any honeymoon. They had rented and partially furnished a studio apartment in Seattle, but apparently they weren't going there as Roger to the left and headed south rather than north. He still made no comment as to their destination. She had no clue.

There was silence for many miles until he finally said in a very matter-of-fact way, "Well, I guess we should find some place to stay." Obviously no prior plans were in place. A motel room was located. That first night was essentially endured. Roger certainly lacked any tenderness or concern for Ariel's feelings about his physical demands. Any delusions Ariel may have had about her wedding night were swiftly eradicated.

The remainder of the 'honeymoon' followed that pattern of Roger just stating what they would do and where, without any apparent planning. She never really wanted to remember much, if anything about those few days. She hadn't really comprehended Roger's lack of manners or reasonable social awareness;

they had rarely gone out to eat, and then just occasional burgers at corner cafes or drive-ins. All holiday, special occasions or even just Sunday dinners were meals at his parents' home. A behavioral pattern quickly emerged; he paid very little attention to any opinion she might have; didn't ask if there was anything she might want to do, or see along the way. He drove, he decided, and that was it.

Before returning to their little studio apartment they stopped at his parents' home to pick up more of his things. After serving the inevitable coffee and baked goods, his mother came back into the kitchen with a small jar. She casually tossed it onto Ariel's lap and said, "That, and that (pointing to Roger) are your responsibility now". What on earth did she mean? The jar was crammed full of rolled cash. That was to be the first of several occasions on which her mother-in-law said some rather strange things involving Roger and money. Had that also been a portent?

Years later when a trip was upcoming, she showed Ariel the stash of bills stuffed into coffee cans and hidden under the house. In the event of her death or an accident they might be involved in, Ariel was to retrieve those cans and safeguard the money. She swore Ariel to secrecy, especially from Roger; under no circumstance was he to know it existed. If they died, Ariel was to keep that money for herself and her children, but never tell Roger. Banks were not to be trusted and obviously, neither was Roger.

This was also a somewhat different family. She knew her own was not exactly normal with Edythe holding total control over Dad. She and Roger were both 'only's', which had concerned Ariel from the very beginning. With no siblings, neither had really experienced being part of a family, even though Roger had cousins nearby and had not been isolated from his peers.

The wedding and 'honeymoon' finally over, they settled into the studio apartment. Roger returned to work and both his apprenticeship and reserve training schedule; Ariel set about finding another job. At Roger's insistence, she had quit the insurance office the week before their wedding. He didn't consider it to be a suitable environment for her, and essentially demanded she quit. He was to be the sole breadwinner; anything at which she might work, or any money earned, was insignificant and incidental.

When Ariel had cleared the kitchen and finished doing dishes following their first supper in the apartment, she joined Roger on the couch/hide-a-bed to watch television. The set was a little portable black/white one she had purchased from a co-worker at the office.

Roger became restless after about 7 o'clock that first evening and each evening thereafter, claiming he had to go out for a while. No further explanation was given, and Ariel was not permitted to accompany him. He usually returned after forty-five minutes or an hour, smelling of cigarette smoke. Ariel had always disliked smoking intensely and Roger assured her he had quit months earlier, well before their marriage.

Why did he consistently smell of smoke both after work and after his absence each evening? She only asked that question once. He scowled at her, claiming to have met some acquaintance who smoked, and the vehement anger of his response prevented her from pursuing the matter any further. Roger had only one close friend, and he lived in Issaquah. The only Seattle acquaintances she knew of were co-workers or Reservists, none of whom lived in their new neighborhood. She was not going to nag, harp, question or demand explanations as Edythe had.

The girl from whom Ariel had bought that little portable set some years before worked in an office next door to the insurance business and they had frequently lunched together then. Linda envied Ariel's having a steady boyfriend, and Ariel rather envied Linda's independent status on many occasions. They both wanted to rent an apartment in the city near their offices. After a bit of searching, they had located one that would have been perfect –two-bedrooms, one bath, with little parlor and kitchen on the second story of an older brick building near their work. Her parents were all for it; Edythe put her foot down with emphasis, "Nice girls don't live by themselves in city apartments." The response echoed what Edythe had said about attending University; 'nice' girls don't go there. Being 'nice', as only she defined that was paramount in Edythe's world. Ariel consistently tried to please Edythe, despite life-long failure,

So, Ariel had backed out of the apartment plan and accepted marriage to Roger as the only acceptable avenue of escape.

She was absolutely determined to make this marriage work well. She would do everything right, keep house properly and economically, sew her own clothes (Dad gave her a new zigzag sewing machine as a wedding gift), cook nourishing tasty meals, bake bread and cookies from old recipes, wash and iron clothes correctly, maintain steady employment, and surely everything would work out well for Roger and herself. That determination became Ariel's mantra.

Life in the tiny apartment settled into a pattern. She fixed his breakfast and packed his lunch before vacuuming, dusting and then hunting for a new job. This marriage was destined to be quite different from anything she might have imagined, dreamed or hoped for. She had no friend in whom to confide or go to for any clue as to what a husband might be expected to do or what her response could or should be to make marital copulation more tolerable, if not pleasurable.

Women's' magazine articles were no help. Those tended to focus primarily on means to make a husband (in those days) more interested in his wife's body than in any pleasure she might derive from sex. The premise being that if a wife kept a tidy house, used various products to remain the attractive girl he had married, and be ready in the marriage bed, the husband would then seek to please her. That might well have been true in many instances. Not in this case.

Roger's interest was strictly focused on his access to her at his pleasure, whenever he wished, for his satisfaction. Ariel silently endured. Over the years she devised a number of mind tricks to help her cope with his rough demands and clumsiness. One escape was shopping for groceries—up one aisle at a time, planning menus and mentally placing items in her imaginary shopping cart.

She quickly found a new job in the Psychology School, at the University she had longed to attend as a student, typing mimeograph stencils of instructions for use by graduate students in programming drums for the enormous computers of that era. (Edythe did not approve of course, of the University, the Psychology Department, or computers; however, that no longer mattered quite so much.) Programming instructions consisted of line after line of formulae in Latin and math symbols with very few discernable English words, typed from hand-written pencil copy was highly detailed, demanding, but not always very legible. The waxy stencils were typed in the mornings and proof-read in afternoon hours. Her counterpart was married to a graduate student involved in developing the tests and grading systems that used the information. It was very tedious work, but paid better than insurance office administration, and Ariel saved every extra penny toward a house. Roger did not object to her working at the University for some reason. She had no success in convincing Roger they should open a bank account; he was totally opposed. She knew his parents kept cash in coffee cans stashed in their basement, totally distrusting banks. Ariel had closed her checking and savings accounts at Roger's insistence. She finally convinced him they should at least rent a safe deposit box at the local bank and not keep valuable items in the apartment. They had received cash gifts and she didn't want to chance that slipping away for any purpose, or be stolen in a break-in, but saved to buy a house.

All the 'thank you' notes for wedding gifts were written and mailed within one month. Many of the items remained in boxes at Pedersen's; there was precious little space in the apartment. Christmas cards were purchased, signed by Ariel with both names and dispatched to that same list of people.

One Friday night in early January Roger announced, "I've found a house to buy; we'll go see it in the morning." They hadn't considered any areas for possible purchase, looked at any houses, discussed where they might want to settle, or even looked at any newspaper ads. He talked as though this was a done deal.

Where was it? In Seattle? Issaquah? Or some other town? What sort of place was it? What did it look like? How had he found out about it, and why did this sound so 'done'? No answers were forthcoming, just that they would go look at it.

Finally she learned that a man who worked on the same job site with Roger wanted to sell because he was moving to Canada with his family for some sort of missionary cause. He claimed it was a really good deal for a young couple, and that sufficed for Roger.

Oh. Whose idea of a good deal? No response beyond 'you can see it in the morning'.

First House

Saturday morning they set out to a part of the city Ariel had never before considered venturing into for any reason, whatever. The area had gained an extremely bad reputation during the War and was a place Ariel ever expected to even pass through, much less reside in. Now they were to view a house there? A house they apparently were expected to purchase as their home? The address was located and Roger parked in front of a 1920's or earlier structure with dilapidated and peeling white picket fence, single car detached garage, camellia bush, large cherry tree and huge rhododendron bush. An exterior fireplace chimney on the north side; another, more centrally sited stack topped the roofline from which a thin wisp of smoke drifted. Ragged, dirty-faced children romped about in the long scraggily grass; and weeds clogged the front flower bed overpowering that camellia bush from which last season's dead blossoms had not been clipped. Two bricks were missing from the front step-side; Ariel was not favorably impressed with the initial 'curb' view. That the place lacked appeal would be a gross understatement. The street was paved with asphalt, and driveway concrete … a plus.

At Roger's knock the door was opened by a large doughy-looking woman with stringy, uncombed long graying hair resting on the shoulders of her soiled navy blue dress held together in front by large safety pins. Thick loose stockings sagged at her shoe-tops. Behind her stood a dumpy non-descript man in a dirty shirt and grungy work pants, apparently Roger's co-worker friend.

"Oh good, you're here, come on in," was voiced by these two almost in tandem, and the door swung wide. Evidently an appointment time had been set; not mentioned by Roger. Inside the house conditions were even worse than outside, far worse.

Come in where? was Ariel's first thought. The apparent front room was stuffed with boxes from floor to ceiling, leaving only a narrow pathway to what looked to be a dining room. Roger led the way and they managed the passage to where a table and chairs were centered in front of filthy windows offering a blurred view of the garage and tangled yard strewn with bicycles, wagons and assorted abandoned plastic toys. The woman cleared miscellaneous clothing items and papers from four chairs, simply tossing it all onto a corner pile of similar accumulation.

What could be seen of walls in the room was festooned with dried food scraps; mashed potatoes perhaps? but appeared to be plastered underneath. The dirty windows were leaded, and she had glimpsed what could possibly be leaded glass doors on either side of a tiled portion of wall in the living room. Possibly bookcases and a fireplace? There was an exterior chimney on that wall flanked by tall skinny evergreens of some sort, so it seemed quite possible.

These people were eager to sell and immediately offered a cursory tour of the residence. Viewing the two bedrooms, tiled bath, hall and kitchen was limited at best by the stacks of miscellaneous materials, toys, clothing, books and large Tupperware boxes throughout. Additional loose plastic containers were intermingled with shoes and clothing items. Apparently, the woman was a distributor and also hosted parties in private homes, using the residence as a warehouse. The kitchen was absolutely filthy, and only Roger went to the basement with his friend to look at the oil-fired furnace and electrical service box. Ariel remained in a relatively open spot, trying to avoid touching anything despite the woman's efforts to point out assets of the kitchen. She had judged room sizes by the ceilings only as floor surfaces were completely covered by stacks of boxes, toys, clothing, and who only knew what.

It was actually a well-built structure, circa 1907, and once emptied would provide sufficient square footage. It had to be strong – if only to support the weight of all the stuff stacked floor and nearly to ceiling throughout. What could be seen of living, dining room and hall flooring exposed through worn carpet appeared to be oak, scuffed, dirty and dull; bedrooms, probably pine or fir. Too little was visible to really know. The 150' by 100' lot size was a plus, as were municipal water, sewer and garbage service, a concrete drive to the single asphalt-floor garage, concrete walks, and the yard was fenced. Fencing was in marginal condition, but that was something Ariel knew she could fix. Hammers, saws, boards and nails were familiar territory and a wood fence could always be repaired and painted.

However, she strongly hoped this was not already a done deal and that there would be some discussion with Roger; perhaps they could actually look at other houses in better neighborhoods, and in better condition? Was price not even a consideration? She still had no clue as to an amount having been mentioned, much less considered reasonable, or not.

When Roger emerged from the basement, he announced that they would buy the house. He had not even asked Ariel what she thought of it, and had not attempted any negotiation on price; just said they would buy it at whatever price the sellers had apparently stated to Roger.

Ariel kept quiet, except to quietly state that both her Dad and his needed to view the place with respect to structural condition, the foundation, plumbing, roof, and wiring. His co-worker friend immediately agreed that was absolutely appropriate and most definitely should be done.

Roger glared at her, but grudgingly muttered agreement. Her Dad, after all, was a skilled carpenter and builder with formal engineering training and decades of experience. Roger was a fitter/plumber apprentice. His parents had built two new houses; his Dad had worked in the pipe trade for years, and well qualified to evaluate the plumbing and heating systems.

With no discussion or any further question, Roger said they would buy this house for $12,500, grudgingly agreeing that conditioned only to his and his father-in-law's okay regarding the basic structural condition. Just like that— no attempt at any negotiation whatever; no question or consideration of Ariel's opinion. Roger had decided. She kept silent.

Again, she felt utterly and hopelessly trapped. Just make the best of it; don't make waves; don't disagree. Try to view this decision and the mess in some positive light; thankful to have a job and able to pay for at least some of the trash disposal, cleaning supplies and paint. There would be a lot of work and gallons of cleaning agents and paint required before the place could remotely be considered fit for human habitation. The oil-fired furnace was a big concern in her mind; wood-burning cook stoves she understood, the glass electric panels Dad put in the Bellevue house, and the baseboard heating in the apartment; but nothing of an old oil-burning furnace in a basement with a tank buried in the yard.

Dad was pleased to drive in and look at the structure, concentrating on the foundation, roof, heating, plumbing and particularly the exposed beams in the basement. He pronounced those excellent—massive, mill-cut, closely centered and stout. Once cleared of main floor junk a large man could jump on those oak or pine floors and nothing shook or even creaked. The composite roof also met his approval. The house had been very well-built many years earlier by a master carpenter from Minnesota who lived there with his family. It was well-insulated and the enclosed entry also protected the rooms from cold winter winds and summer heat. The design, construction and general condition were good. Only the contents and underlying condition of the interior presented a major problem, but that was solvable with lots of work. She tried hard to overlook the exterior mess; the interior was bad enough for the present.

Years later it became undeniably clear that only the south half of the house had plumbing connection to the municipal sewer system. The owner, also a plumber/fitter, had made minimal required connections at installation of municipal lines. The north side, kitchen and laundry plumbing, fed to an ancient dry well.

Ariel discovered that one morning by simply draining the kitchen sink; dishwater flowed only as far as the basement floor. No one knew where the drain lines exited the basement. Once the direction was determined it was Ariel's task to break out a section of the basement floor for access to the drain pipe. Roger was too busy. The back yard was dug up, a delicious plumb tree cut down and piping properly installed, some ten years later than should have been done. The house would never have passed the most rudimentary inspection, with the plumbing deficiency being only one such problem.

Next came obtaining the financing. Roger and Ariel had $2,000 for a down payment and qualified for a $10,000 purchase price, but the seller had stated $12,500, with no attempt at counter-offer by Roger. Again, Ariel was not consulted nor allowed any input. Her income was not considered in any financial statement, which was normal banking procedure at that time. Their down payment was sufficient; however, the mortgage could not include the two unimproved lots on the south of the property, only the four with house and garage. They certainly did not want to reduce the lot size and needed an additional $750. to purchase those two lots outright and cover bank charges.

Ariel was expected to come up with that $750 post haste if not immediately. She knew Edythe could easily spare the cash; there was probably that much and more stashed in her top dresser drawer at virtually any given time. That money was for giving to her church.

Having to ask Edythe for money was the most unbelievably onerous thing Ariel ever had to do. She knew Dad would gladly just give her that amount and never expect or want repayment. She also knew Edythe would not permit him to do that. So, the $750 was reluctantly requested and received; the separate lots were purchased outright.

Ariel repaid that amount to Edythe plus quite generous interest, a total of $1,000 from her separate earnings within four months, and well before her first child was born. Nothing was owed Edythe; and nothing ever again, personal, monetary or material was ever requested of Edythe.

Before taking possession of the house, Roger and Ariel drove north to Vancouver, B.C. for a weekend in mid-February of 1959. He was agreeable to visiting a museum and even to riding bicycles through the huge and beautiful park on the north side of the city. Roger was not much for any public display of affection, but held her hand occasionally there as they strolled along sidewalks and in public gardens. It was a lovely trip and the memories savored. Was all that an attempt to make amends for his crudeness about the house? She never pursued the rationale for his pleasant behavior on that occasion.

On a day-to-day basis there was precious little affection shown. He had always been quite constrained in public, but physically demanding in bed. Ariel knew on weekday mornings what that night would entail. If he kissed her briefly and patted her shoulder it meant he expected and would demand sex that night, regardless, not a matter open to question for any reason.

Clearing and Cleaning

Once the transaction closed and they were in possession of that house, the task of emptying remaining trash, scraping, scrubbing and painting began. The former occupants had removed enormous quantities of their personal property and the boxes of plastic products. However, floors were still covered in trash and filth. It was an overwhelming mess; Roger was leaving for his annual two-week Seabee training the Monday after they moved in on Saturday. Ariel had to be at work on Monday at the University.

Roger's mother packed up her grubbies, cleaning and painting gear, and basically moved in for those next two weeks. This corresponded nicely with Roger's leaving. How very convenient for him; two weeks of operating heavy equipment while his wife and mother struggled with restoring the house to somewhat livable condition—the structure he selected and insisted be purchased. He thoroughly enjoyed the annual two-week Seabees Reserve summer training in California. There were new marvelously huge pieces of earth-moving equipment to run, great piles of dirt to move. He not only loved it, he was very skilled and soon placed in training positions. He easily passed various tests and moved up a rank. For him it was the very best of paid vacations.

As years passed Ariel came to savor those two-week periods as well, but for vastly different reasons.

She worked at the University Psychology School Testing office each day, and at reclaiming the house evenings and weekends. Dad and Roger's both joined them on Saturdays, with Edythe making a grand production of preparing lunch. She did not approve of this entire matter at all; condition of the house, that Wilma was helping to clean and paint, but especially the location. She made no secret of her opinion. As usual, Ariel was roundly criticized for having got herself into this mess. She should have known better, but then, what could one expect from someone so inept and with such limited intelligence. If only this girl had ever listened and done anything Edythe's -- the correct, proper and right -- way. Edythe certainly had done her best to point out what Ariel should do from earliest childhood; all to no avail.

Before departing for Reserve Training in San Diego, Roger had moved the old refrigerator out from the wall, disclosing a mound of grease, chicken bones, dog food, can and jar lids, broken glass, plastic chunks, along with numerous unidentifiable items, cooling coil marks deeply imbedded. Ariel flatly refused to clean that, simply handed him a square blade shovel and pulled up a garbage can. He had to have this house; he could deal with the kitchen. Old faded and broken Congoleum flooring was chipped and shoveled off the wood flooring. Several applications of hot, sudsy water and bleach, stiff broom, scrapers and brush finally revealed a pine board floor in fairly sound condition.

A full day of scrubbing was required before Ariel could even think of using the bathroom with any degree of comfort. Shavings of Fels-Naptha soap, bleach and piping hot water were applied over and over; surfaces scrubbed vigorously with stiff bristle brushes. The kitchen stove was immediately deemed unusable, and summarily carted to the dump by Roger's dad. He also came on Saturdays and hauled load after pick-up load of trash to the dump. An electric fry pan, toaster and single-burner hot plate provided the only means of food preparation.

A new stove was purchased shortly after Roger's return, but…only at his Dad's insistence. Though never confirmed, Ariel strongly suspected her father-in-law was also the prime source of funding for that stove—a beautifully clean, new, wonderful stove with double ovens.

When Ariel finally ventured down into the dank basement she was met by still more junk; boxes, old metal objects of indeterminate origin, fruit jars, paper bags and boxes full of papers, broken toys, dirty clothing, shoes and rags, just about anything and everything one could imagine. More truck-loads went to the dump. It all had to be carried up the steps, out the back door, down another flight of steps and then around the house to the drive and tossed into a pick-up bed.

She also discovered that electric service to the house was woefully out-of-date and totally inadequate. The many boxes mounted on the east wall held long, copper-ended, oddly-colored fuses. Large black-handled switches graced others--pulled down or pushed up as power for a specific item was cut or activated. Service had never been updated from the original 80-amp installation in 1907. The electric stove could not be used if the hot water tank was on, or any other heat-producing appliance in operation. Ariel soon became very adept at juggling cooking, baking, water heating and ironing, throwing switches on and off appropriately to avoid plunging the entire place into darkness.

Both her Dad and Roger's clearly explained to him that deficiency should have been corrected prior to the sale/purchase, and could not fathom how it had sneaked past any inspector. Finally Roger reluctantly admitted he had assured the inspector he was qualified to replace the incoming service and would do so immediately.

Service was not up-graded to 200-amp until 1972 when Ariel had to arrange and pay for that when sale of the house could close, the real estate agent be paid, and proceeds made available to finish the Barbaria house. Roger had never even looked at those boxes other than to order Ariel to purchase more fuses. He never seemed to find the time to up-grade the service or even buy the necessary fuses, despite making frequent purchases at hardware stores, spending hours at the fire station, and working on his truck(s).

He had also promised the old chipped, scarred shallow kitchen sink and badly worn tile countertop would be replaced – immediately. After all, he worked in the trade and had access to all necessary materials and required skills to accomplish the upgrade in minimal time at little cost. That original sink and tile remained, vigorously scrubbed, bleached, but still scratched and worn when the house sold in 1972. Thirteen years had not been sufficient time for him to address that deficiency.

The kitchen was narrow, with few cupboards and even less counter space; however, three features were truly valuable. There was a separate little pantry that accommodated canned goods and baking supplies as well as large kettles and baking pans. The end of the tile counter featured a built-in cooler with wire shelving—a screened square opening at the top and another at the bottom; absolutely perfect storage for fresh fruits and vegetables. A small nook off the kitchen accommodated a little table, chairs, the refrigerator, and access to both the basement and back door. The nook was far too small to use for meals, but good for cooling baked goods, mixing bread and cookie dough, and any number of projects. Ariel found a tall cabinet in a second-hand store with shelving, drawers and glass doors for the space next to the pantry. It served well for storing everyday dishes and glassware. It even had a drop down door that latched closed to hide the mixer when not in use. She made use of every inch of space to good advantage; and once painted it was a very cheerful little kitchen.

After the initial and intense interior cleaning/painting and disposal of major outdoor trash, the place looked much better and possibilities began to present themselves. Furniture was limited and Ariel started haunting used furniture stores in search of period pieces that might look good in this early 1900's structure. She purchased a nine-piece dining set from a co-worker at University who was moving to the East Coast. This was a solid oak, beautifully carved set, consisting of round table and two leaves, six chairs, a mirrored buffet and a smaller sidebar. Insert of the extra leaves extended the surface to 58 by 110 inches. The dark wood polished to a lovely matte sheen; and she re-upholstered the chair seats in deep cranberry nylon frieze. Off-white walls and white woodwork throughout the house, cranberry accents, and the dark oak were attractive and well-suited to the house.

One of Roger's uncles gave them several assorted cotton rugs machine woven in period Oriental style together with a pair of small old end tables. The items had belonged to Roger's grandparents. When the old farm house was cleared out following their demise, the twin uncles had argued over those items so vehemently that they did not speak to each other for over fifteen years. Removing the items from the immediate family served to ease the animosity and these middle-aged brothers eventually resumed communication with each other.

The yard was beyond belief even following removal of several large items. Scrap lumber, piles of miscellaneous pipe and fittings, forgotten toys and broken pieces of Tupperware were everywhere in the long grass and weeds. Dead tree limbs, dried up plants and out-of-control wild roses were just the start. When Ariel dug into the first of what appeared to be small mounds of soil she discovered sealed Tupperware containers with all sorts of decayed food product including whole chickens, fish, and roasts. Totally gross doesn't begin to describe what had been randomly buried about the property for reasons unknown. Ariel had never been very enthusiastic about Tupperware; but after this experience refused to ever permit so much as one piece of the product to enter any house in which she lived.

In the early struggle to reclaim this house, Dad spent many Saturdays helping with clearing and disposing, and even Cousin Bill lent a hand. He had come down from Saskatchewan to court her friend Arletta, working on the property during the day while both she and Ariel were at work. Living on the farm and working the land all his life certainly made him highly valued and very capable. He was not then accustomed to just sitting around waiting for time to pass.

One Saturday morning he was standing on a ladder outside between house and garage. Ariel was inside, scrubbing at the kitchen window. Finally able to see through the glass, Ariel gasped, blinked several times, shrieked and pointed at the garage roof. Bill turned, and nearly toppled to the ground. Lying on the roof was a sheep hind-quarter – wool, bones, hoof and all. Would unpleasant discoveries never, ever end? Somehow Roger never seemed to be very involved in the messier aspects of reclaiming this, his choice of real property.

A friend of Roger's family salvaged and re-finished the oak living room, dining and hall flooring as a wedding gift. He was able to clean, sand and restore the beautiful wood with a soft matte finish. It was absolutely stunning and Ariel cared for that gorgeous oak faithfully. Roger did not bother removing his work boots in the evening, or use the back door. He consistently entered through the front door, paid scant heed to wiping his feet, and frequently left a trail of dirt, oil and debris in his wake. His grossly over-weight cousin left pits in the wood from her badly worn high heels, long-minus the rubber heel tips. He complained about Ariel wearing loafers or other flat shoes in the house, claiming she would damage the hardwood.

Something needed to be done about the bare wood kitchen, pantry and nook flooring. A multi-colored roll of linoleum was selected from the 'sale' selection; not the prettiest by any means. Despite the salesman's valiant attempts to present much prettier patterns, Ariel was looking to the future and high probability that food would be dumped, crumbs dropped, and coffee spilled. The pattern she chose would not immediately show every little thing, and once installed it not only looked much nicer than it had on a roll, but actually quite nice. It was easy to keep clean even without daily mopping.

Children...Oh, yes

By early summer of 1959, Ariel had to admit that the queasy every-morning incidents were probably not going to disappear of their own accord any time soon; menses had ceased. In all probability she was pregnant. Another latch snapped shut on the trap.

Roger did locate a physician quite by chance while working in a downtown office building. He didn't know this person, but saw him in a corridor, liked his confident appearance, and made note of his name on the officer door. Ariel made an appointment, hoping against hope her fears might be groundless. Not so; a baby was due in early November.

There was so much to do, and not that much time. She concentrated on the house and yard, paid Edythe back the lot purchase price plus generous interest, found bits and pieces of furniture at bargain prices and refinished those. She sewed her own clothes after a brief attempt shopping in a maternity store, and then set about making baby smocks, little blankets and fitting an old wicker clothes basket as a basinet. Net petticoats from her wedding gown served well as the ruffled 'skirt' with pastel bows bordering the top, white cotton covered a thick foam rubber cushion for the mattress, and lining of the old basket. Placed on a backless wooden chair, the old clothes basket looked quite nice, and at very limited cost.

Ariel had discovered a fabric outlet in the industrial area where sales were by the pound, not the yard. No cutting was done, one simply guessed at yardage, being sure to get enough; consequently there were left-overs. Those were used for other projects; nothing wasted.

She finally gave notice at the University, but worked until mid-October, despite policy of the era that dictated quitting at four months into a pregnancy term. The professor she worked for didn't pay much attention to policy and appreciated her degree of accuracy and strong work ethic; she wanted to keep working and needed the money for improving the house. Continuing her employment served both parties well. Somehow the portion of Roger's earnings making it into the newly acquired checking account did not allow for much paint, landscaping, cleaning supplies, fabrics, or other materials. Car or truck items came first, then mortgage payments, utilities and household expenses.

Roger was working at an out-of-town location and difficult to locate in any instance, so when she realized late afternoon of Halloween that she was in labor, called the company office with a message. She requested he be notified to go home as quickly as possible. Her doctor instructed her to come to the hospital as soon as she could; he was expecting her to be there shortly. Time passed, contractions increased, and still no Roger. Children began knocking at the door for treats, which she handed out with grimaces/smiles. No Roger appeared, and the company offices were closed so she could not learn if he had even received her message.

Just as she had finished writing a note to leave on the table for him, and picked up her old Ford keys to drive to the hospital, Roger appeared at the door; irritated that he had been told to get home immediately. He then would not permit her to drive herself, insisting he certainly would take her. However, he needed a bath and change of clothes first. Roger's baths generally took an hour or more; this one only 45 minutes due to her apparent discomfort.

Her water broke. She headed for the basement laundry tubs and floor drain with wash cloth, towel and clean clothes; was cleaned up and ready to leave again in mere minutes.

Roger then telephoned his parents to let them know it appeared baby might arrive fairly soon, which he could well have done from the hospital later, or any other time that evening. Ariel did not inform Edythe. She would love to have told Dad, but telling one and not the other simply was not possible. She definitely did not want Edythe to show up at the hospital and try to take over. Later would be plenty of time to face that.

Her doctor was highly agitated and concerned when they finally arrived at the admitting office at nearly 8:00 pm; some four hours after Ariel had called him. He took Roger out into the hallway after seeing that Ariel was settled into a room and being tended by nursing staff. She never knew what that conversation entailed. Roger did not seem very happy.

Baby girl arrived at 6:00 am, November 1st; a beautiful, dark-haired, ivory-complexioned tiny 5# plus a 'squitch'. Ariel was delighted and scared out of her wits. What was she to do with this innocent baby entrusted to her care? She hadn't a clue. Never having been cuddled or held in any loving manner by Edythe, she didn't know what a mother should do, was expected to do, actually did, how to act, how to love this marvelous child and communicate that love. Panic rose like bile in her throat.

Baby was placed in her arms and she prayed as never before. "Please God; show the way, how to love her. Tell me what to do, help me, teach me how to hold and kiss and comfort my baby. Please God, show me how to let her grow into a strong, confident woman. Help me to do what is right by her and that she will know I do truly love her, even if I don't have a clue how to show that." Ariel's arms softly folded around the wee bundle and she gently kissed the smooth, ivory forehead. Is this a start, she asked herself. A smiling nurse gently lifted baby from her arms and Ariel drifted into sleep.

Next morning a Pediatrician introduced himself as a colleague of her doctor with his office located near her home. She immediately liked him. He had examined baby and determined her to be absolutely perfect if just a bit on the small side. Not to worry, she will start putting on ounces and then pounds quickly. This baby was exceedingly special in that she could turn herself over from stomach to back. That ability was highly unusual for a newborn, and especially for such a tiny infant. Physicians and nurses throughout the hospital had been able to see her accomplish the feat. No wonder she was always fast asleep when brought to Ariel for feeding. Then with a broad smile, he told Ariel, "this little girl will need to eat at least a half-bushel of soil and bugs before she grows up." What? Ariel was horrified. "Not to worry" he assured her. "By playing outside in the dirt, complete with angle worms and other crawlies, she will develop the immunities she needs to stay healthy all her life." Ariel gazed at the tiny form, ivory skin and delicate features, trying to envision her chewing on a worm. No way. Little did she know. That doctor was totally correct.

Dad was so pleased and proud he nearly burst with happiness; this little granddaughter was his gem. He was so very pleased she had been named Jillian; a favorite aunt had also been a Jillian.

Edythe clucked and fussed, questioning the knowledge and wisdom of each and every move by any medical personnel. Ariel was incompetent of course; that was only to be expected. However, she had thought medical staff to be of higher quality. That had certainly been the case in 1927 when she received her degree. She alone was the expert and it was clear that everything here was being done wrong; little Jillian's small size alone was sufficient proof of that.

Roger's parents were totally pleased; proudly proclaiming this child to be the most perfect ever.

The only draw-back was Roger's obvious and voiced disappointment over her being a girl and not the expected son.

All the Grandparents had suggestions and rationale for various family-related names; Roger basically lacked interest in the procedure. Ariel stuck with her choice made years earlier just in case she ever had a daughter. She wanted baby to be named Jillian Sophia. Jillian for a high school classmate who had been such a pleasant and happy girl, with gorgeous long blond wavy hair and beautiful blue eyes. Sophia for the grade school cook Ariel so admired, and who had given her the Scandinavian cloisonné four-leaf clover pendant she consistently wore. Her hand shook only a little as she carefully wrote Jillian Sophia on the birth certificate form. Roger's family was also pleased with the choice of Sophia, because it was the (now) Great-Grandmother's name.

Again Roger's Mom packed up and temporarily moved in to help. She encouraged Ariel to rest while she tended little Jillian, changing and bathing her, and rocking her back to sleep after night feedings, particularly. She also took Roger to task about the yard; that was where he needed to focus, not just running here and there looking for old cars and hanging out at the volunteer fire station. He did not like that at all; it was totally unnecessary and unwelcome interference from her so far as he was concerned.

He did have trade school classes one night each week, and Naval Reserve meetings as well. It was not long, however, before he formally joined the volunteer fire department, and a scanner was installed in the bedroom. At whatever hour of day or night, the dispatcher would announce the location and nature of a call and designate drivers to respond to drive trucks or report to the scene. Roger stopped at the station each evening after work, returning late at night, expecting his dinner to be ready regardless of the time. On trade school class, or reserve meeting nights he also began bringing single co-workers, or fellow reservists, home for dinner; unexpectedly and without any notice. Ariel quickly learned to cook meals that could be expanded at moment's notice.

With great reluctance Ariel gave up thoughts of any career following Jillian's arrival, and concentrated on being a good and proper wife and mother. Roger had always made it quite clear she was to be a stay-at-home mother. There certainly was plenty to occupy her time. She continued sewing all her wearing apparel and Jillian's, even making Roger's casual sport shirts and boxer shorts. Fabric remnants too small for any other use became patch-work quilt tops, using mill-end by-the-pound blanket fabrics for lining and backing.

An Opportunity, or?

Jillian was just six months old when Ariel received a totally unexpected long distance phone call one morning from the insurance company she had worked for prior to marriage. A Vice President she recognized both by name and voice was asking her to please consider an offer they were making, initially, and quite willing to amend if she found it insufficient. This certainly was a surprise, actually a total shock. She hadn't even thought about that firm or the branch office for months.

He presented a brief outline of their request; first only that she agree to meet with him over lunch or dinner, in her town at her convenience to consider taking the manager position at the local branch where she had worked prior to her marriage. He went on to explain the position came with a very good salary, regular increments, a company car, expense account, full backing by the corporation, bonding, health care and life insurance – just to start with. There could well be additional benefits.

She was speechless; mind spinning and she felt slightly faint. What on earth could this be -- a bad joke, perhaps? No, not at all; he was quite serious. They wanted to keep the Seattle office open; the manager for whom she had worked was being promoted to a higher corporate position, and had unequivocally recommended her to take his place. Wow!! Ariel? the unworthy unintelligent, unattractive, inadequate? He had to be joking.

After all, first Edythe and then Roger consistently made it quite clear she was anything but competent, intelligent or of any value whatever. Roger clearly did not even wish to be seen in public with her, frequently insisting she stay at home while he participated in quite normal and usual activities.

This offer simply could not be true; but, apparently was. The Vice President kept telling her it was indeed a quite legitimate request and that corporate management felt she was very well qualified.

Ariel was silent so long, he asked if she was still on the line, and if she had any questions. Would she have at least a tentative answer to meet with him so he could make travel arrangements?

"Yes," she answered softly, "I heard, and am still on the line."

If she accepted this position, her salary alone would exceed Roger's wages at the present and the reasonably foreseeable future. His would increase as he finished his apprenticeship, but then she also would have salary increases.

Such a situation would not work; not with Roger. He mattered; she did not. That had been quite clear even before the marriage. He had been adamant about his work being important, and providing for them; any employment he might allow her to have was clearly secondary, minimally supplemental to the household. He was the important one and had the only income of any value.

If she even agreed to meet this man over lunch to learn more about the offer Roger would be furious. He would not be able to accept her having been recruited for a highly responsible position, and earning more than he if she accepted the offer.

Even meeting with this corporate officer would be stepping way over the mark and bring down Roger's wrath. She could not take that risk. The thought that such a position could well enable her to leave Roger tickled in a corner of her mind and strongly tempted. No, she had promised to faithfully live her life as Roger's wife and honor his wishes, not her own.

"Thank you so much for your call. The offer is totally unexpected, and the employment proposal you have outlined more than generous. I feel so totally honored even being considered for such a position with the company. However, I have a new infant to care for," she answered with slightly trembling voice.

"Oh, we would definitely help with childcare. That's part of our program, helping former employees return, especially when we have an opportunity to bring someone back who is so highly thought of by a senior manager." Ariel's mind still whirled and swirled. What a fantastic opportunity; she could have a family and a career, an actual career, one she had ever only dared dream about.

Her in-laws would be surprised, probably shocked; Edythe mortified—what would 'her' church friends say. Dad would most likely grin, eyes sparkling, and wish her only the very best, and offering any help she might need.

Finally, hesitantly she answered, "Again, thank you for calling and for making this fantastically generous and wonderful offer. I would be utterly delighted if I were free to accept; however, I just cannot. My husband would never permit it. I am so sorry to have to say no."

"Are you absolutely sure? Won't you at least meet with me so you can have it laid out in better detail and at least consider it?" She again answered, "No", trying to explain that even such a meeting would not only be highly suspect as having some ulterior motive, and be totally unacceptable to her husband. He would immediately accuse her of carrying on an extra-marital affair, and guilty of neglecting of her wifely and motherly duties.

His final attempt was that she at least take down his telephone contact information, think about this, and please call him collect if any even slim possibility existed that she might have a change of heart, however remote. She agreed to that and noted the number.

Ariel's heart was heavy as she softly put down the receiver and checked on Jillian. Such a sweet baby, growing so rapidly, and Ariel did want to be the one guiding her through childhood. Could she have done both? Whether she could balance family and career didn't matter; that simply was not going to happen. Any meaningful employment would have to wait until Jillian was older and more independent. Much work on house and yard remained to be done; yes, she could hire much of that if she had a good-paying job, but the personal price she would pay was far too high.

Just a few weeks after the wedding he had accused her of being unfaithful because she had shared a humorous and utterly innocent verbal exchange with a gas station attendant. She had laughed when relating it at supper; Roger had not considered it amusing at all. Clearly she was not to engage in unnecessary conversations with any men unless Roger was present to monitor her behavior. Yet another snap on the cage lock. Roger had been very attentive prior to marriage, stopping at the office when she got off work on his school or Reserve meetings, and calling her at home the other nights, to check. She had not recognized that as being totally undue control that could easily become even worse. As it had, very quickly.

Ariel realized and finally admitted to herself she had indeed traded the Edythe frying pan for the fire which did not evidence any signs of extinguishment.

When Roger's apprenticeship was completed, a ceremony and banquet were scheduled for members of his group, union dignitaries, and instructors. Ariel inquired if wives, and perhaps girlfriends, were included. Roger was vague about that and claimed he would need to ask. The final competitions started early on a Saturday morning in a nearby city. He indicated he might find out if she would be welcome at the banquet and call her if that were the case.

Ariel arranged for Helene to baby-sit Jillian, washed and set her hair, laid out a nice dress and pumps, filled the gas tank of her old Ford, and waited for a call. None came. Apparently she was not welcome. Roger returned well after midnight.

The following month's union newsletter featured the competition and celebration with pictures of the graduates, all with wives or girlfriends. Only Roger … attended by himself. He was also featured as placing third in the welding competition that included participants from the entire West Coast. Many months later she learned he had also been granted availability of a full ride scholarship at Purdue University based on his training scores, the welding competition and job reviews. He turned it down flat. Accepting that opportunity would have required him to leave the Puget Sound area, if ever so briefly.

In the spring Roger joined a softball team and apparently practiced with them frequently after work. Ariel thought it appropriate that she and Jillian could attend a Saturday afternoon game, bring a picnic lunch, meet other wives, and let Jillian interact with other children. No way was that to occur. Roger didn't want her there at all, claiming those people weren't her kind of people and she wasn't to associate with them. That sounded just like Edythe, virtually a quote from Ariel's childhood, when schoolmates were all deemed unsuitable, and "not our kind of people". If these people were suitable for Roger to participate in sports with, why were they and their families unsuitable for Ariel? As with Edythe, there was no response from Roger. Ariel simply obeyed and stayed home. It was becoming more and more difficult to swallow the disappointments.

And Moving Along

Summer of 1960 Ariel suspected, and then knew, she was again pregnant. This time it was different; she was ill all day every day, and not just a queasy stomach. She felt horrible all over, but carefully kept that to herself as much as possible. Roger was by then part of the volunteer fire department crew participating in area-wide community parades. He delighted in driving the restored 1917 American LaFrance truck. He had not participated in any of the actual work involved in that project, but always ready to drive.

Ariel was assumed to take Jillian and the necessary assortment of items required by a small child, locate the parade site, parking, and be on the sidewalk to view him driving by, no matter what. She would have much preferred remaining at home, doing laundry or yard work, cleaning house – anything but dragging Jillian and all her things to a sidewalk miles away to watch a parade about which she could not possibly have cared less. Rather than being deemed difficult or non-supportive of his interests, she and Jillian went to parades throughout the summer.

Roger's home town held an annual Labor Day celebration with a carnival, salmon bar-b-que, and of course, parade. The vintage fire truck was entered, with Roger the driver. The parade was viewed; and they stayed with his family.

Pain beginning in the morning, continued and occurred more regularly and strongly throughout the day, feeling much the same as labor had, but different – not right. A phone call to her doctor confirmed her fears that she was indeed pregnant, things were not going well, and she needed to be seen in hospital. Roger had made it clear he didn't want to go anywhere until after the Issaquah festivities ended. He was the driver and in charge of the vintage fire truck.

His mother finally instructed him, quite sternly, that he needed to take

Ariel to the hospital and do so immediately, not at some time more to his liking. Reluctantly he drove to the hospital, let Ariel out, and she walked into the Admitting area to seek help. By the time Roger followed from the parking lot, she had been admitted, placed in a wheelchair and was on her way for further evaluation and treatment. Her doctor had been summoned and quickly determined this pregnancy of some four months was well into spontaneously terminating. It was a frightening, exhausting and excruciating night before she drifted into sad, but painless slumber as the eastern sky brightened

Upon learning Ariel was to remain hospitalized, not going back with him that evening, Roger had quickly returned to Issaquah. Next morning he was there for the pancake feed and remainder to the salmon/Labor Day celebration. The vintage truck was then loaded onto its trailer and towed back to the station house. Jillian remained with her Grandparents until Ariel was discharged the following day.

As soon as she was released, they drove to the Grandparents' home to get Jillian. His parents were very concerned Ariel was still not in any condition to take full responsibility for baby and house, but Roger assured them she was just fine and didn't need any help. He barely thanked them for keeping Jillian. Back home they all went.

Follow-up appointments with her doctor determined a corrective procedure was required if there were to be any more children. Without it, Ariel would simply not be able to carry a pregnancy to term. He had developed a new procedure which he strongly recommended for Ariel. She was to be the second patient to receive this new surgical procedure, scheduled for mid-January.

She arranged for Jillian's care with Roger's parents, packed a small bag, caught the City bus and checked in for her surgery. This required a two-day post-operative stay, and she was able to talk with Jillian by phone both in mid mornings and again in afternoons. Roger stopped after work the second day to pick her up following discharge procedures.

She was only back at home a few days when sutures failed and severe hemorrhaging forced a swift ambulance transport to hospital. She was re-admitted, back into surgery, and retained for some additional days. Jillian had once more stayed with Roger's parents while Ariel was hospitalized. This time sutures held, all went well, and her work soon continued on refurbishing house and yard, walking to shop; carrying baskets of wet clothes up from the basement and out to lines for drying.

Little Jillian grew, gaining inches and weight, rolling rapidly across the floor to gain her objective. Rolling from place to place served well until finding her legs at nine months, standing, then off and running proficiently at ten months. She just eliminated crawling as a hindrance in her mobility plan.

When she escaped briefly at a local bank branch and headed for the busy street, onlookers ignored Ariel's pleas of "somebody grab her, please, she's headed out the door". The response was that she was too little to walk; Jillian wasn't *walking*, she was *running*, and fast. One white-haired gentleman finally halted her progress and gently scolded her for running and to stay with her mommy.

From there Ariel carried Jillian to a variety store and purchased a dog harness and leash. That enabled the little runner to move about more freely, be safe, and not have an arm pulled from the socket. She was truly tiny; and holding her by the hand just did not work. Ariel received occasional criticism from older people for "treating that precious child like a dog, for shame". Better she was on that leash than darting out into traffic. Ariel simply could not walk to stores for shopping carrying both Jillian and grocery bags when the old Ford did not run. Any maintenance or repair to her car ranked very low on Roger's priority list.

A truck-load of bark mulch was purchased, initially dumped onto the driveway and toted to flower beds by the washtub-load. Landscape and general yard work continued using an old wash tub in lieu of a wheelbarrow. It had only one handle, so Ariel used pieces of clothes line to fashion another, enabling her to lift and carry it. Landscape and general yard work continued. A wheelbarrow would have made mulch distribution, weed disposal, as well as all other gardening tasks much easier.

She struggled to subdue yard grass with an old reel push mower; filing the blades and oiling it helped a little. Fencing was repaired and re-painted, earwigs, spiders and all. She and Jillian created borders of flowers along all the fences with roses, dahlias, some shrubs started from cuttings, and various bulbs. The place began to look quite nice with very little monetary expenditure. Ariel had no source of income; house and yard costs were eked from grocery money. Roger had agreed to the purchase of bark.

One Friday Roger was home a little earlier than usual with a wheelbarrow in the pick-up. It was an old well-used, heavy construction model…dented, dirty, generously spattered with mortar, and clearly considered a throw-away by the contractor. To Ariel it was wonderful. She could haul much more with this than in old washtubs; and Jillian could ride on top with plants, garden soil and mulch.

Ariel dug out old overgrown rose bushes that had gone completely wild and did not produce blossoms. Some of the roots were huge, spread out all over the grass areas that could possibly become decent lawn, and those had to be chopped off. Roots of one bush were simply too deep, and she had to pull the whole thing out with a chain and her old Ford. Jillian thought that was great fun, sitting on the front seat and bouncing as Ariel tightened the chain and the car bumped over the rough ground. But the huge and ugly bush was uprooted.

Another project was cutting down an enormous and diseased holly tree. Ariel had left Jillian with Helene for an afternoon, and taken the bus downtown to public library to research the problem, hoping for a possible cure. The leaf blight could be corrected; however, the effective chemicals were considered too hazardous to be used by homeowners, or on residential landscapes. To confine the leaf disease and prevent it spreading, that holly had to go. Limb by limb Ariel cut away at it and burned piles of branches. Roger hauled some away to the dump with his truck. Little Jillian found that whole process highly amusing as well.

A puppy had been acquired for Jillian's second birthday the previous November, and was a perfect playmate. An Elkhound Collie mix, he was the runt of the litter, but the most active and first to climb out of the nursery box. He quickly took over guarding Jillian any time she was out in the yard, running everywhere with her and preventing any attempt she might make to go out onto the street.

He required little training of any sort, adapted quickly to a leash and learned not to dig in the flowers. That took a little doing, as Peppy had pulled up and chewed stakes and line marking flower bed borders. Roger had beaten him severely with one of the stakes, carrying him by his fur to each hole, beating him again and again. Roger ceased only when he tired; Ariel's tearful pleas to stop were totally ignored and she was strongly criticized for interfering at all; training the dog was his job, not hers.

Ariel had placed Jillian in a bedroom with a loud radio playing so she could not witness her beloved Peppy's harsh discipline. Ariel and Jillian were his primary concern. He guarded them carefully, even from Roger, placing himself in front of Roger and growling on occasions he deemed necessary. That flower garden lesson was painful for both dog and Ariel. After the garden stake incident Peppy watched Roger even more closely and frequently stood in front of him if Roger approached Jillian wearing even a slight frown.

Another Daughter

Early the summer of 1962 Ariel was again pregnant and realized yet another enormous lock had snapped shut on her life. This pregnancy was quite routine as had been virtually assured by her gynecologist following the early 1961 corrective procedure and re-suturing. She had only the expected weeks of morning sickness and the predictable increased edema due to her saline sensitivity to deal with. Jillian was two, very active, and always wanting to help her mom.

The summer was unusually hot which Ariel definitely did not appreciate; however, there was little that could be done. Evenings were nice, sitting out on the front porch enjoying the breezes off Puget Sound. Occasionally Roger brought part of a milk shake to share when he came from spending his evening at the fire station. The basement remained fairly cool during the day, so Ariel frequently spent afternoons there, sewing, washing and ironing with Jillian playing with toys or outdoors with Peppy.

Edythe was quite elated upon learning the new baby was scheduled to arrive in August, making it quite clear she preferred the child be born on her birthday, August 18th. Baby, however, did not comply, and was born on the 16th, much to Ariel's relief.

Roger had taken her to the hospital, returned to the house, collected Jillian from Helene's and taken her out to his parents' home to stay. After briefly checking on Ariel by phone with the hospital he had gone home and to sleep. Baby was born just before midnight, strong and healthy with soft peach-fuzz hair and lovely blue eyes. Delivery had been text-book. The corrective procedure several months earlier had been totally successful as the surgeon had hoped, and only a bit cautiously predicted. Nurses and doctor were quite uneasy about Roger's absence and insistent that a nurse dial the number for Ariel to then personally inform him of his daughter's arrival. She preferred to just wait until morning, when a staff person could call him, or just let him make an inquiry.

Lacking sufficient strength to dispute with them beyond repeating that she really preferred they just tell him, she took the receiver, and when he finally answered, apprised Roger the baby had been born. She was a beautiful little girl, strong, healthy, longer and plumper than Jillian had been at birth. That his response was less than enthusiastic was no surprise to Ariel. A girl, not a boy.

After work the next day, having had his usual hour-long bath, change of clothes and stop at the fire station, he did view his new daughter. He spoke briefly with Ariel. Minutes after his arrival visiting hours were over, so he didn't need to stay very long. He had no suggestions as to name, having avoided any mention or consideration of a name. His parents wanted her named for an aunt, but also to include Ariel's middle name. She was not at all enthused about that; however, never having liked any of her names. In later years she recognized that having heard those names spoken by Edythe only in negative and highly critical context, her dislike was probably quite normal. Roger also had only used her given name critically; referring to her as 'the wife', or if more directly, using words suggesting she was fat as well as stupid. The given names, as such and outside of that familiar negative context, were actually pretty.

In any event, in future years her daughter might not really like her names, but relatives would be satisfied and happy. And so, this new little one was named Annie Joanetta. She adapted quickly to the pattern of eating, sleeping, and gaining weight. Unlike Jillian however, Annie did not like being held and cuddled, but kicked, fussed and flailed her arms; preferring to be placed in the carrier where she could observe without being touched. Only at feedings did she acquiesce to being held and sometimes, even rocked briefly.

Jillian was totally delighted with her baby sister, eager to participate in her care and anxious to have a playmate. Feeding Annie immediately became story time for Jillian. She loved books and eagerly ran to get her favorites when Ariel settled on the couch to nurse Annie. Holding and feeding Annie, reading a story for Jillian and using one foot to stroke the dog, Ariel was an efficient multi-tasking mom long before any such labeling existed.

Initially Ariel had been concerned about introducing Annie to Peppy, not knowing what the dog's response might be. With Annie on the bassinette, secured by the strap, with rolled blankets on each side, Peppy was brought into the room. This new infant did not turn over as Jillian had done, which was a good thing. Ariel held Peppy's collar as he approached the bassinette, his head high, sniffing inquisitively. He immediately stood on his hind legs, front paws held tightly against his chest, and reached out to softly touch Annie with his nose. Tail wagging enthusiastically; he proceeded to sniff her from head to toes and back again, giving her bare arms and legs gentle licks, all while standing on his hind legs. Finally he backed away just enough to lower his front paws, and looked up at Ariel. He rubbed against her legs, and almost seemed to smile, "this is really <u>my</u> baby, you realize; you can feed, bathe and change her, but she's <u>mine</u>." And in truth, she was. He guarded and watched over her from that day on, but never neglected Jillian.

Ariel had no worries about the little girls playing outdoors alone; Peppy was on duty. He would allow women to walk up to the front door and ring the bell, but not stray off the sidewalk or porch. Men were not permitted to even touch the gate, much less try to open it. Ariel never had to help Peppy with that. He took care of matters beautifully; male salespersons just backed off and went on down the street. The address was undoubtedly tagged, "don't bother/unfriendly dog" or some such.

When Annie determinedly rode her tricycle toward the street, Peppy stood in front of her to halt her progress, barked and even growled. If that didn't work, he took hold of her shirt with his teeth and pulled her back. Meanwhile of course, Ariel had been alerted by his barks, Annie's cries of protest, run up the basement stairs, and was able to give Peppy some assistance in controlling this headstrong child.

Finally the house and yard had been brought to reasonably good condition and Ariel was able to accomplish regular maintenance and painting tasks far more easily. She was becoming less and less enthused about the stay-at-home mom role; longed for adult conversation and ability to earn her own money. Working had been the norm in her life from childhood, picking berries, baby-sitting and then office employment. Being dependent on Roger for household funds and personal expenses was contrary to her nature in every possible way. She began reading employment ads and found several openings for which she felt qualified. Memory of that managerial position offer had been pushed back, surfacing occasionally only to be repressed again.

Both Jillian and Annie were growing up and gaining independence. Ariel's only adult contacts were through a choral group at church where she sang tenor and Roger bass. He determined the persons she was allowed to converse with, and closely monitored her conversations. She did have coffee frequently with Helene the girls' baby-sitter who lived across the street. Roger found fault with their 'coffees', focusing his disapproval on Helene's smoking. That he also smoked was of no consequence; he thought no one knew.

One warm and sunny afternoon Ariel was weeding and transplanting some flowers when her two little girls walked quietly to her side, holding hands and slyly looking at each other rather than Ariel. "Mommy, we think you should go find a job so we can go to Mo's (Helene's) house," they said, almost in unison. What was this? They really meant it. Had they sensed her frustration over trying her very best to be a stay-at-home mom? She had no idea how, but they must have somehow.

Ariel did not waste much time in talking with Helene about child care and actively initiating a very real job search. Interview appointments provided the girls opportunities to spend time across the street at Helene's, something they thoroughly enjoyed, playing indoors and out, helping in their own way with various yard and household tasks. She was delighted having them there, as her retirement from heavy-duty commercial cleaning had been forced by advancing arthritis. Being quite normal kids, both girls found it was much more fun to pull weeds there than at home. Ariel was careful to have meals prepared and served pursuant to Roger's schedule, regardless of the time he might opt to walk through the door.

Edythe voiced her strong disapproval, reminding one and all that she had been a stay-at-home mother all through Ariel's childhood and school years. She had indeed been physically present; however, any mothering of her daughter had never been listed on her day-planer. A vacuum cleaner pulled out onto the kitchen floor in the morning before breakfast was most often still in the same position when Ariel returned from school, her after-school job and stop at the grocery store. Dishes piled in the sink remained unwashed. Edythe had spent daytime hours on the telephone with her church friends, gossiping and endlessly reviewing her many concerns about which church members just might be engaged in what she considered inappropriate activities and behavior. Frequently a large box occupied room center to be packed for some distant missionary post. Edythe was a very busy woman.

Ariel and Dad did shopping after work, prepared most evening meals, fed the chickens and cats, and then gathered, cleaned, candled and packed eggs.

A New Phase

Ariel's first new job was as a title clerk for a new high-roller car dealership quite close to home, and unexpectedly provided a real eye-opening educational experience. She knew nothing whatever about the automobile business, but quickly learned to register sales and file subsequent ownership tracking and title transfers in compliance with state regulations. She also prepared loan documents for bank loans – another entirely new matter. The dealership management was delighted with her; provided minimal training. She just plunged in and was quickly proficient. More and more responsibility quickly found its way to her desk. Added compensation was no part of the increased responsibility, of course.

Titles for trade-ins were not always signed off correctly and legally released by the purchaser of a new car, simply forgotten in the heady process of getting a new car. Trade-in vehicles themselves were sold in multiple lots to somewhat shady used car lots and long gone before Ariel received any of the transaction documents. She had to clear that old car title within a very short time…period; no grace periods and no excuses.

Former owners were also long gone with their new cars and totally disinterested in the old ones; some could not even be contacted. She learned to forge signatures and clear titles for $50 re-sale transactions well enough for the notary to sign and affix her stamp. Illegal? Absolutely; and Ariel was deeply troubled; however, the General Manager, comptroller, and head bookkeeper made it exceedingly clear it was simply a necessary evil of the business. If she should ever be questioned, her response was to be that the signed-off title document had come to her desk executed and notarized. That was the way she had received the sale documents. The title release signatures were good - very, very good.

Before long the General Manager took to telephoning the office on warm sunny afternoons to have Ariel sign his name on specific corporate documents, claiming he just didn't have time to stop there en route to a prior appointment (tee-time). No question ever arose regarding any of those documents either. Ariel complied and became quite expert.

All elements worked smoothly until the Notary gave notice of termination and the comptroller apprised Ariel she would be the next Public Notary for the business. This was not a request that she apply for a Notary license and seal. No. It was a clear statement of absolute fact; no question. Ariel was in a totally untenable position. Notarize her own forgeries? No, absolutely not; prospect of jail time was not attractive. He then demanded she comply; her job depended on her becoming the firm's Public Notary in addition to doing the forgeries to clear those unreleased titles. She had no alternative, from his viewpoint.

Ariel stated calmly that she understood his position and his ability to fire her, but she was not going to comply with his demand. If her job depended on her further compounding already illegal activity then clearly she did not need a job at this dealership.

Actually, she did desperately need her job and pay check; Roger was not working due to his Union having called a strike. What they would do? Going from two incomes to none with no advance warning was an enormous question, but she was not breaking any more state or federal regulations.

The comptroller was not prepared for her response, secure in his prior knowledge of the strike situation and her need of income. He required a highly capable title clerk and was absolutely certain he held the upper hand; that she would obey his demand. He really should have had some inkling of her response however, from another quite recent attempt to place Ariel in an awkward and controlling situation.

He had slipped up behind her at a file cabinet and nibbled on the back of her neck. Her reaction was not at all what he anticipated; no screaming or vocal outburst. She had simply stepped back, silently, a spike heel planted squarely on his instep with, "Oh my…I had no idea you were there…are you all right?" He could only swear, grumble and silently limp back to his desk. Ariel gave her two-week notice of termination in response to his demand she become a Public Notary.

Years later, and under totally different circumstances she did serve in that

Public Notary capacity in law firms, corporate legal departments, and a county courthouse, in two states spanning a period of more than thirty years. Signers had to show identification, appear and sign in her presence as the law requires. No shenanigans.

Neither Jillian nor Annie was particularly happy having both parents at home, at least some of the time. Roger spent the bulk of daytime hours hunting down antique and classic cars, or hanging out at the Volunteer Fire Department. Ariel concentrated on house and yard work, together with diligently searching a new job.

She was quickly hired and worked briefly at a large department store in the candy department, also making and selling popcorn. Popcorn was a problem in that time before gloves were worn for food prep and Ariel's hands swelled quickly from contact with the salt. Merely touching any predominantly saline product caused an immediate reaction. A different temporary position was found for her and the Personnel Manager hoped to keep her employed long enough to find a more suitable and responsible place. She did not want to lose Ariel and made no secret of that.

The Plumbers and Fitters Union settled the strike after a few weeks and Roger returned to his regular schedule of working days and spending evening hours at the fire station. As usual he demanded his dinner be prepared and awaiting him at whatever time he elected to have that served. That a family dinner might be served and shared at a reasonably regular hour was not a matter for his consideration or concern. Ariel's or children's schedules were of no consequence; only his was of any importance and as such, subject to change without notice.

Ariel was soon interviewed for an Installment Loan Department job at a local bank branch, and hired immediately. The retail store Personnel Manager had been very near tears when Ariel quit her job there, but wished her well and acknowledged a bank was a far more appropriate environment for her than big box retail sales.

Ariel started out working collection accounts and scheduling payments to bring delinquent accounts current. This was yet another new experience; a bit frustrating, but soon became comfortable and she actually found it somewhat amusing.

Loan customers she contacted were generally consistent late-payers with lengthy histories of collection efforts. Ariel reiterated the need to pay on time, gently at first, and then more sternly. That all became a bit of a game, each party making, or not making, a move.

She was also able to provide the loan department manager with specific information on loans the car dealership had put together using third-party, "mouse-house", financing for the down payments; one more illegal process practiced by that dealership. Bank staff had not been able to confirm what they suspected and management was delighted with actual customer names. Ariel had accurate information with which they then confronted the dealership. She also knew first-hand of vehicle sales/purchase records having been pulled from storage and burned in barrels behind the body shop. She and the bookkeeper had pulled those from attic storage boxes on specific orders of the comptroller. Those documents all required retention for State-legislated time periods and the company had been doing business for far less time. The pulled and burned sale/purchase documents had not aged out to be eligible for destruction.

It was not long before Ariel was promoted from Installment Collections to the Commercial Department where she worked with real estate transactions, commercial loans, mortgages and reserve accounts. Another task of this area was opening of new checking and savings accounts, and arranging wire transfers of funds. It was in this context she opened a new checking account late on a Friday afternoon for a man she had skip-traced across the country on an installment appliance loan, only to lose track of him in New Jersey. Now here he was right in front of her, holding a fist-full of cash to open a brand new checking account. What a coincidence, indeed. Slowly but steadily that old delinquent loan balance was collected; a loss-recovery coup for Ariel.

Decades later his name appeared in a newspaper article; he had tumbled from the Golden Gate Bridge while working as a painter.

Soon after Ariel was assigned to the Commercial Banking, or 'platform' area, Roger had taken to appearing each and every Friday night before the bank closed at 6 pm. He took up position just inside the door about 15 feet from Ariel's desk, back against the wall, arms folded, silently watching her and scowling. He pointed to his watch if she glanced up. She still had work to do, not things that could simply be dropped at 6 pm and picked up on Monday. Her boss, a V.P. in the real estate department, habitually discovered correspondence requiring dictation and transcription late on Friday just before closing time. Those communications were to be typed, signed by him, and posted before Ariel could leave. That her boss and her spouse engaged in competition for her absolute compliance with their opposing demands caused stress was undeniably obvious. Both appeared to thoroughly enjoy the control they each wielded.

Ariel had a good friend in the Operations Manager at the branch who clearly understood the difficult position Ariel was placed in by these two. There was nothing he could do about it, but understood and encouraged her to just do the best she could to deal with it. Roger's control over every aspect of her life grew steadily stronger and he was well aware of that.

No means of escape presented to allow her to survive and care for her daughters. Divorce was not an option in her then current milieu.

Decades later and in a different part of the state, Ariel and her friend laughed over the absurd situation endured years earlier in that bank branch. It had all been so important at the time.

She realized Roger was never going to let up on his Friday afternoon appearances at her work place, and the demands that she simply leave because he thought she should. Friday nights they were expected to be at his parents for dinner, or a little later, if they had gone to a buffet restaurant.

Parental visits occurred every Friday and/or Saturday night, without exception; often both nights. She was to have the children washed up and ready to eat dinner at an all-you-can eat buffet – no later than 6:30 pm if not going to visit his parents. That she was still not off work was of no consequence. She was sternly reminded of her obligation in loud harsh language. Any thought of Roger's collecting them, washing hands and faces, and possibly meeting Ariel at the restaurant between the bank and home fell outside any possibility of consideration.

Ariel's having to work until at least branch closing at 6 pm did not fit his schedule which she was fully expected to follow. Construction work could simply come to a reasonable halt at or before 4:30 pm; clerical tasks in finance not so, despite what Roger thought.

Ariel was still determined to be a good wife and mother, but her very sanity required adult conversation and mental stimulation; she thrived on learning. She retained her original determination to obey that personal promise —one week at a time, privately reserving the option to pick up the next week, or not. (That 'or not' option was not picked up for just over twenty years.) Besides, with

Roger's penchant for buying old vehicles, she needed her earnings to pay bills. He purchased numerous 1940's and '50's cars, dragged or had them hauled into the yard with fantastic schemes for restoration. Each one was hailed as the very finest yet; but soon settled into the soil, supporting weeds on all sides, to either be sold at loss and/or joined by yet another marvelous treasure.

Deepening Fear

Shortly after Jillian arrived Ariel concluded without shadow of doubt her initial hesitation about Roger and her wedding-day terror had been totally accurate. Annie's birth had only reinforced that knowledge. She came to the ever-deepening realization that what she had erroneously accepted as concern and caring simply masked his need for total control over every aspect of her life. Every moment of each day was subject to challenge; every penny accountable. All the years of desperately trying and failing to please Edythe were not only continuing, but increasing in intensity in her marriage, attempting to please Roger. Control, criticism and fault-finding increased steadily; it was familiar, she was used to that, and accepted it as what she justly deserved because she was simply unworthy. Acceptance did not make it any more pleasant. An inkling began to emerge that these behaviors were abusive. But, she had agreed and promised before God and witnesses; she was stuck.

Still, in the back of her mind, despite valiant efforts to suppress and ignore, were niggling thoughts that she just might be entitled to a few good things. That life might be somewhat enjoyable for her in some unknown manner; that good things were not always just for other more truly deserving people.

No matter what went wrong in Roger's environment, at work, fire station, baseball, Reserves, with his parents or other relatives, at church or even with his vehicles, Ariel was blamed. It, no matter what 'it' was, automatically became her fault, never his or that of simple circumstance. She was not supportive of him and his interests; she was selfish, uncaring, demanding and/or uncooperative—whatever negative trait he deemed suitable at the time.

Even when he angrily stripped out second gear in a new vehicle she was accused of having been the cause. He took great pains to remove gear bits and pieces, place them in front of her and loudly expound on the expense and trouble she had deliberately caused. The ever-increasing blame leveled at Ariel served to further erode her already fragile sense of any self-worth or value as a person.

She also acknowledged that in Roger's increasing level of control over her, clearly he was far stronger physically, taller, heavier and more muscular. Ariel had no tangible defense. He had engaged in what he termed 'just good fun' by tickling her hard and unmercifully before their marriage. That had begun when he insisted on stopping at Ariel's office before his school or reserve meetings, effectively delaying her from going home after work. She was to sit with him in his car, ostensibly to talk, which quickly evolved into his gripping her tightly against him, harshly tickling her. Her protests were ignored, as were pleas to stop. Only when she was reduced to tears did the torment begin to abate; and it was made clear she was the one who 'didn't want to have any fun'. It seemed as though he needed to exhibit his control on a regular basis as reminder. She should have known that was a serious character flaw and his action truly was physical and emotional abuse.

There was no one she could go to, certainly not Edythe, no girl friend. She assuredly could not tell Dad. She just desperately hoped and prayed he would stop doing it. On the rare occasion she queried him as to why he persisted in the tickling when he knew it hurt her, he just laughed and insisted he tickled her because he loved her. That went on for years until his father witnessed an incident and ordered him to stop and never to do it again. That worked. She was eternally grateful to her father-in-law.

Ariel had no concept of what constituted love or a loving relationship. An uneasy tension was the household norm throughout her childhood; no easy conversation at meals; no evidence of any affection between her parents. Dad consistently responding with "yes, Pet" to whatever Edythe said.

No affection had been shown her by Edythe, only discipline and negativity. Dad evidenced his love and care for her by his very soft-spoken, quiet praise for her scholastic achievements, an occasional quick hug of her shoulders, and providing quiet encouragement for her musical endeavors. He carefully avoided openly voicing approval of Ariel lest Edythe overhear.

Many times she felt so utterly confused, befuddled, emotionally disconnected by what was said, done, and what she observed. Just what was love? Could she truly love anyone? She could do nothing right, was unable to please Edythe no matter how hard she tried. A daughter was supposed to love her mother, and she could not muster even a few generous thoughts, let alone feelings of any love, whatever it was, toward Edythe.

She knew Dad cared deeply for her, and did his very best to encourage her without running afoul of his wife. That Edythe could have him re-committed to psychiatric confinement influenced his every word and action; and each late winter he suffered from depression. For years Ariel strove in her own solitary depressing morass of confusion and sadness; who was she, why were there so many questions and no means of finding answers? There was no one in whom to confide; no one could be trusted with any of her questions who would not immediately tell Edythe, or now, Roger.

She had often thought it best she remain single, not risk marriage; most definitely not risk having children. She didn't have a clue how to love a man, a child, anyone, or even herself. She was nothing. Depression was something she battled with every day; it was unfair to inflict that on anyone else.

Only a few weeks following Jillian's birth, Roger's tactics began to change and become more frightening. Ariel experienced severe vaginal bleeding which continued longer than usual and normal following delivery; steadily increasing in both volume and length each subsequent month. Only during the short pregnancy did she have respite. She left their bed frequently many nights to check on Jillian, and attend her own needs as well. Roger began throwing an arm heavily across her throat, or grasping her neck with his hand, ostensibly as a loving and strictly precautionary measure. He also claimed to like her long dark hair, and ordered her to keep it long. The length provided him the ability to tightly wrap it around her neck frequently, hold and pull to restrict her breathing. That too, was allegedly in fun.

She had fainted on occasion due to blood loss; he claimed only grasping her throat to prevent a fall in answer to her questioning that action. Ariel learned to extract herself and get out of bed by going completely limp, barely daring to draw shallow breaths, until Roger moved a bit and resumed steady snoring. She was then able to slowly worm her way to the edge of the mattress, carefully slide to the floor and crawl out of the room.

Roger did not like it one little bit when Ariel cut the long dark tresses far too short to be grasped effectively. His claim of liking to run his fingers through the thick waves fell unheeded.

In the mid 1960's the 1930's movie, "Gone With the Wind" was re-released for the first time to massive publicity and great public interest. Ads for the showings were everywhere, in papers, on television and even radio. Ariel had read the book at least twice, also had a teen-age crush on Clark Gable. She longed to see the movie. This film was also one Edythe declared despicable, sinful, unfit for any audience, and totally immoral. That alone was sufficient reason Ariel wanted to see it. She mentioned this wish to Roger on numerous occasions, noting the local theaters in which it was being screened, the times and that the run was limited. There was no response; not even the usual mutter.

On the last day of the local run, Ariel summoned the courage to ask Roger specifically why it was she could not see this film. Simply going to see it alone was out of the question. Other than church, the only places they went were to old car swap meets, car shows, and the infrequent movie with a race-car theme. For a brief period before Jillian arrived they had gone to silent movies nearby, but that ceased and the theater was closed. Why was it he seemed unable to even consider doing something together that she might enjoy? Ariel was not permitted to go anywhere alone; not even to church without the children, so a downtown theater, at night, was totally out of the question.

She had already checked with Helene and arranged for her to watch the Jillian and Annie in the event seeing the film might be possible; dinner was prepared and ready.

Roger flew into a rage, yelling that she was selfish, demanding, and what did she think was so important about some stupid old movie anyway. When Ariel attempted explaining that she had read and enjoyed the book, he bellowed how stupid she was, the book, movie, and everything else he could think of. Ariel shrank back and said it really didn't matter…she didn't need to see it at all; tears streaming down her cheeks. At that Roger grabbed her antique nursery rocking chair and flung it against the wall, breaking off a rocker and portion of one leg. Ariel fled to the kitchen and began putting dinner on the table. The broken chair remained in the middle of the living room floor, in pieces.

The beautiful wooden rocker had been given Ariel by an elderly neighbor when she was still in grade school, and it dated to the mid-1850's. She had kept this precious piece for years, managing to protect it from Edythe's donating it; now damaged by Roger.

It held wonderful memories of Mrs. Nordby who had also given her a sterling silver cake server as a wedding gift. An especially fond memory was of tiny, frail Mrs. Nordby cradling baby Jillian in her arms at only four weeks.

Ariel gathered the broken pieces into a box and placed those with the chair safely in the basement storage room.

After supper Roger actually carried his dishes to the kitchen sink—a most unusual occurrence, instructed the girls to finish clearing the table before going over to Helene's, and then told Ariel she better fix her hair and change her clothes if she wanted to see her movie. There was no apology about his behavior or breaking of the chair. They drove downtown, parked the car and walked to the theater, found seats and saw the film…in silence. The limited conversation on the return home was painfully casual, everyday, and carefully avoided any mention of the earlier tirade or broken furniture. Nothing more was ever said about that evening.

For Ariel the book together with film version of that well-known work was forever tarnished. The evening had begun and ended badly, and that was all Ariel's fault, as usual, adding another layer of guilt.

Temporary Respite

An opening in the Athletic Department of the local school district was posted. Ariel applied, interviewed and was hired. That served well to eliminate Roger's Friday afternoon glaring presence, scowls, and pointed references to his wrist watch at the bank branch. Whatever she could do to alleviate opportunities for Roger to criticize was worth any and all personal cost to Ariel. She was sorry to leave friends at the bank branch, but eager to lessen the negative in any way possible. Her friend there was a still-closeted gay and very sorry to lose her as an employee, but mostly a friend with whom he could talk more freely. They maintained their friendship for decades. Neither he nor anyone else at the branch would miss Roger's negative presence on Fridays.

The school district position presented yet another totally new environment; and very different type of work, with less stress from Roger, at least initially. His interests were old cars, the fire department, and attempts to involve himself in local law enforcement.

He was quite displeased with Ariel when the Chief began calling on her to provide coffee, cookies, cake or whatever goodies might be in the freezer on the numerous occasions there were late-night large, commercial or industrial fires. Quite naturally the fire fighters appreciated getting coffee and snacks; also unfortunately they expressed their appreciation of his wife's efforts to Roger. When one county sheriff deputy prevented Ariel from entering a fire scene with refreshments, the Chief gave her his 'fancy dress' badge to carry which eliminated all future question and problem. Roger was particularly unhappy at that. He, after all, was the important person, not she.

Roger spent the majority of his non-employment hours at the fire station and apparently didn't even notice that his weekend duty assignments came about more and more frequently. When asked by the Chief if Roger might be available for a weekend shift, Ariel consistently answered, "of course, he can do that; that's perfectly fine, and no problem whatever". The Chief was pleased, and life was so much easier for her, the girls and even Peppy with Roger away from home many weekends. Jillian and Annie only inquired occasionally as to where their daddy was on a Saturday or Sunday. "He's on duty at the station" was a perfectly agreeable answer as well as the truth.

Ariel thoroughly enjoyed her job in the Athletic Department, handling correspondence, preparing manuals and handbooks, designing game programs and setting up an accounting system understandable by coaches and in full compliance with state audit requirements. So much for the admonishment of her high school bookkeeping teacher to 'never even try to keep any accounts or books'. She also prepared change bags for ticket sales and concessions.

The District was comprised of five high schools, nine junior highs and one community college, all the District Athletic Director's responsibility. Football games and track meets all took place at the District field, with several events each weekend, Friday nights and double or triple-headers on Saturdays. Programs for each of the games were prepared and sent photo-ready to the print shop; and multiple change bags prepared for ticket sales and concessions.

Change bags were reconciled on Mondays; receipts kept separate for gate and concessions for each of the several events, and entered on the spreadsheet. Field staff, ticket sellers/takers, and concession workers were also paid from total receipts. Monday mornings during each sport season found Ariel at a long table covered in change bags, with calculator and bank deposit forms. By lunch she had those bags reconciled, cash counted at least twice for confirmation and bagged with deposit slips in hand and on her way to the bank. In the afternoon she cut checks for field staff, ticket, programs and concessions workers.

By Tuesdays Coaches were able to stop at the office any time during their day, check the record for their school's events and quickly determine any profit or loss. Her predecessor had needed all of Monday and well into Tuesday to complete the cash reconciliation and deposit process, occasionally issuing checks by Wednesday or Thursday. Bag preparation process for the weekend games began all over again on Thursdays. The Athletic Department paid all game and meet expenses, with profits used for equipment at the schools. No levy or other state funds were used for the football or track events.

Ariel's administrative responsibilities also included correspondence with area-wide community college athletic directors, and a gymnastics summer camp.

She would have been quite content to continue working at the school district until retirement. However, by summer she could no longer deny that another baby was expected. She had dared relax, briefly, and even pretend to herself that everything was acceptable if not ideal.

Regulations for public school employees had not changed over the years, and she was expected to quit working there if any administrative officials knew she was pregnant and already well past the specified four-month 'quit' mark. Neither the A.D., nor his assistant wanted to lose her; the office was rather isolated from the main building, and so she was able to continue doing what she truly enjoyed. Both men laughingly said a baby posed no problem at all. The crib could be placed in one corner of the office, she could take an extra-long lunch break for delivery, and the Assistant (father of five boys) could handle diaper-changing. She would only need to feed the little one. The Athletic Department could continue to roll along quite efficiently, indeed.

If only that were possible. Ariel would have gone for it in a heart-beat. The mental picture itself was incredibly amusing. Edythe's reaction, to say nothing of Roger's explosion would have been ticket sales-worthy. Too bad it was impossible. Oh, well.

She finally quit work in mid-December anticipating an early January delivery date. Ladies from the main administration building threw a lovely shower upon finally learning of Ariel's pregnancy. She then invited them all to her home for lunch the following week; which came off very well with Annie's assistance.

She ran home as fast as she could after kindergarten class, tripped in the gravel, and badly scraped her knees. She burst through the front door in sobs and tears, frantic that she was causing mommy a problem just before the luncheon.

Ariel gathered her up in a hug before examining the battered knees and for once Annie didn't squirm to get down. "Let's have a look and see what we can do to make you feel a little better now, and then fix that all up right when the ladies have gone back to work. They won't be here long." With a shaky and timid little smile Annie quickly agreed, raised her skirt and pulled down her long sock. The damage didn't appear too grave, so the knees were gently patted with a cool wet cloth, gauze pads placed over each and clean socks pulled up over them. Another quick hug and kiss were tolerated; and Annie opened the door and welcomed the first arrivals. She proudly helped serve lunch and desert, smiling and talking with guests. No one could possibly have guessed she had "owies" on both knees.

Those battered little knees were more properly tended after lunch, stockings removed and gauze pads carefully taken off. Gentle cleaning and application of ointment eased the stinging together with new gauze and another pair of clean stockings for protection. She put up with just one more brief hug, kiss and a candy before wriggling away to play.

Ariel dreaded the approaching delivery, absolutely certain this baby would be physically handicapped, mentally deficient, or most likely both, if even born alive. What had led to such a dreadful conviction? She felt so horribly guilty about not really wanting this child. She finally had a good job she enjoyed, her own medical insurance coverage to which she could add Jillian and Annie at very little cost. A small amount of cash had been squirreled away, hidden from Roger.

Before acknowledging this pregnancy she had again begun to seriously consider the possibility of leaving Roger, taking the girls and somehow making a go of it on her own. Such a step would not be easy. Edythe would be utterly horrified and certain of only Ariel being at fault. Dad would be as supportive as possible; but with Edythe his guardian for life having full care, custody and control over him, he was severely limited. She had no clue as to what Roger's parents' reaction might be. After all, he was their only son. That her father-in-law was very fond of her and supportive she knew. He had reprimanded Roger on more than one occasion, as had Roger's Great-Grandfather. Roger's own mother had made numerous comments clearly evidencing her disapproval of his actions as husband and father. But what their reaction and responses might be to Ariel daring to leave him was quite another thing.

She had managed to function in this marriage one week at a time as she had promised herself to do years earlier, but it was becoming increasingly difficult. She was just plain weary of it all. Pregnancy itself was a drain both physically and mentally. Roger was more and more demanding, accusatory, continually requiring that she account for every moment away from the house and not at work. The Athletic Director and Assistant were both under suspicion of carrying on affairs with Ariel, and even a grocery stop was suspect as some checkers were male. She had even been caught speaking with some on occasion.

Ariel was absolutely convinced that her not really wanting another child would render this baby stillborn, or at the very least severely deficient physically and/or mentally. In her mind there was no doubt whatever. Even if this baby survived delivery and lived, he or she would not be healthy. Ariel knew she would be unable to provide for such a child; Roger would be no help whatever, and she would be totally alone to deal with everything. Her first responsibility was to Jillian and Annie; she would need employment to keep a roof over their heads and food on the table.

She was absolutely convinced that Roger would divorce her when this baby was born in less than perfect physical and/or mental condition, charging her yet again with being unfit as a human being, and definitely not as a mother. She would be on her own, but on his terms, to raise the girls and deal with a severely handicapped child as well; no doubt whatsoever. Her fate was sealed.

No-fault dissolutions of marriage were still a few years into the future, and the most-used accusation in a divorce action was still adultery; a contributing party need not be named or proven to be an accessory. As her due date neared that guilty certainty grew, accompanied by ever-deepening depression.

Her friend from the bank, and his partner invited her to see "Sound of Music" for which they had an extra ticket, and would like very much to give her an evening of music and enjoyment. Ariel was eager to see the film and enjoy good and intelligent adult conversation. Roger put his foot down, firmly. "Absolutely not; you will not go out of this house to see that movie, or any other, and especially not with two single men. No".

She basically sleep-walked through the big family Thanksgiving dinner at Roger's parents and the subsequent visit at Pedersens', just longing for it all to be over, holiday, the baby delivered, and either buried or institutionalized. She had already decided on a child care entity for donation of all clothing, furnishings and baby-related items. It would all be gone. No reminders would remain. Ariel's only plan for any future was surviving to care and provide for Jillian and Annie.

Roger would most certainly rid himself of any responsibility for them as well as her. In his thinking she had to be guilty of prior adultery and he bore no onus whatever to provide for her daughters. She was unaware of any help or legal recourse that could possibly be available. At the time very few agencies existed to provide assistance of any sort to a still-married mother whose spouse was gainfully employed. A man was expected to support and care for wife and children. If a man was court-ordered to provide child support, he was expected to pay that, voluntarily. The mother had to be receiving welfare payment before any enforcement of court orders took effect.

Christmas preparations were even more taxing and wearisome than usual; cards were written and sent, baking was done, gifts purchased and wrapped, all as early as possible while still working fulltime through mid-December. She was utterly exhausted, depressed, and filled with dread. Ariel continued her life-long behavior; stand up tall and smile, always smile.

No change of the established family program was permitted; Christmas Eve required attending Roger's family gathering, with buffet and gift exchange. Christmas Day was also spent at his parents' home followed by a short visit at Pedersen's before she and the girls could be at home.

When finally in their own home, Roger routinely went to 'check things out' at the fire station, which suited Ariel just fine. Jillian and Annie were happy to be home in their own beds, Peppy asleep on the floor beside them.

Two days later they were back at their Grandparents' home, and Ariel was in hospital giving birth to their brother. He arrived on the 27th, a few days earlier than predicted; a beautifully healthy baby boy, strong and perfectly formed. Ariel's dreaded certainties were completely overturned. Roger puffed with pride at now having a son, and not just another daughter. Ariel was utterly relieved, simply grateful her fears had been groundless.

She was also extremely thankful this was to be the last pregnancy, quite happily slipping into blissful anesthetic fog for her tubal ligation. All the documents had been executed and witnessed weeks prior and procedure scheduled immediately following delivery.

Roger had very nearly derailed the entire process in their meeting with the surgeon by casually stating, "Well, if we want any more kids, we can always adopt." The surgeon turned to Ariel for response.

"I truly do not care how many children he wants or may wish to produce. I'm not having any more." The surgeon studied her face for any indication of uncertainty. None was even slightly evident. He then turned back to Roger, "I think your wife's mind is quite made up and not going to change". How utterly true. Ariel was not going to leave the hospital following delivery without that procedure. No way under any circumstances; no matter what Roger might now think he might possibly prefer at some unknown future time. This decision was not about him. She was beginning to feel a tiny glimmer of self-confidence and was not about to allow him to snuff it out.

She had her procedure and before year's end was back at home with baby Ryan. School resumed shortly after the holidays so both Jillian and Annie also came home; both very helpful in caring for their little brother. Peppy was delighted to have another small human under his watchful eye. Ariel's abdominal incisions did not heal as expected, opening wide and spilling infectious liquid. Her surgeon recommended using warm water to clear the major incision region, which eventually succeeded, but resulted in an ugly wide scar. Bleeding also continued even longer than previously and she failed to gain much strength. Jillian at ten and Annie, five both contributed a great deal in helping with household tasks, as well as caring for baby. They helped Ariel carry heavier items, roll the wringer washing machine into position by the rinse tubs, and carry baskets of wet clothes and diapers to the lines for hanging. Clothes lines had been strung the length of the basement, and did allow for drying. With regular family laundry and now diapers, they were full most of the time.

An electric clothes dryer was purchased a few weeks later and much appreciated by all three doing the daily laundry; especially during those dark rainy winter months. The lack of sufficient amperage for a dryer necessitated additional juggling of fuse boxes and switches.

More Medical

Ariel had had historically experienced heavy and lengthy monthly bleeding from age eleven, which increasingly weakened her; only feeling somewhat healthier when pregnant. Her regular, every twenty-eight-days migraine headaches also abated during those months. Declining health did not in any way decrease her housekeeping and gardening work, or prevent her lifting heavy boxes and other objects or pushing the old cars Roger dragged home, ostensibly to restore. Somehow, no restoration occurred. Some were patched together sufficiently to function and Ariel was expected to drive them, oil smoke billowing behind and raw gasoline leaking all over engine compartments. Early 1950's Chevrolets had caught his interest and he seemed unable to pass one by without acquiring it.

A fire truck followed her down a major avenue one afternoon, and after signaling her to pull off the road firemen came running to the car. They were alarmed by the smoke pouring out of the old Chevy, and armed with hand-held extinguishers, popped open the hood. More smoke emitted, but no open flame, much to their surprise. The Assistant Chief just shook his head in disbelief. A gas line was leaking all over the manifold. The fully-manned truck followed her and the children safely home.

That particular vehicle received a bit of long overdue maintenance early the following morning, thanks entirely to those volunteers. They demanded Roger fix the mechanical problems sufficiently for his wife and children's safety.

He was livid about their interference and blamed Ariel for their becoming involved. How she could possibly have prevented their observing smoke pouring from the car was beside the point; it was her fault that he had suffered all that embarrassment at the hands of his peers. How dare she.

One Saturday morning Ariel discovered a hot water pipe leaking at the basement laundry tubs and attempted to close the old valve. It broke and hot water poured onto the floor. Unable to stop the water, she turned off the electricity serving the water heater; at least it would soon be only cold water flowing freely down the floor drain. Her next step was placing a call to the fire station to request help from any available man able to fix plumbing…no matter who that might be. She was not the least concerned about who might show up; whoever, his ability to solve this emergent problem was all that mattered.

Within minutes the first response vehicle pulled up; a volunteer fire fighter appeared at the door, and with a broad grin headed downstairs. He was quickly followed by no less than three more trucks and the chief's car; the basement was filled with volunteer firemen. The Assistant Chief arrived in yet another response vehicle, pulled out a chair and remained at the dining room table. Ariel poured coffee for him and brought out a plate of cookies. A fresh pot of coffee was started.

Bringing up the rear was Roger who also headed for the basement after glowering at Ariel and demanding to know what she was up to; there was no need for her to cause him all this trouble. By this time Ariel had put out another plate of fresh cookies and set out cups for the men. The Assistant Chief told him to shut up and get down to the basement; he had a problem to fix - now.

Roger emerged after a few minutes and indicated he would need to replace a valve at some time and reached for a coffee cup. "Oh, no," ordered the Assistant Chief, "no coffee and definitely no cookies. You get yourself to the hardware store right now and replace that valve, immediately. The crew can have coffee and take the rigs back to the station, but I'm staying right here in this chair until you have that valve fixed and working properly."

That valve, indeed…promised to be replaced years before…was replaced in record time, and only then did he pick up his white hat, thank Ariel for her hospitality and return to duty at the station. Roger was not pleased; Ariel was delighted, but careful to keep that hidden.

Not long after, this same gentleman took umbrage at Roger's snide remarks denigrating Ariel while several of the volunteers were polishing one of the trucks at the station. He picked Roger up by his shirtfront, hoisted him onto the hood of the truck and shook him. "You better start treating that lovely little wife of yours better, and soon, or you will answer to all of us, starting with me." The Assistant

Chief stood 6-feet 5 inches, or more, and weighed nearly three hundred pounds, not one ounce of which was fat. Roger started taking the family out every Friday night for suppers at the local buffet restaurant previously held as a special treat, on the rare occasions they did not go to his parents' house.

While still working in the installment credit area of the bank a few years earlier, Ariel had purchased a beautiful bright red '61 Corvette Roadster with black leather interior. She truly delighted in 'her' little car, and her purchase had also cleared a severely delinquent account from the books. She and the girls fit into this little car quite well, and it even held Helene and groceries for both households on Saturday mornings.

Roger took it one day, ostensibly to have the oil changed. That was unusually nice of him, but Ariel had no specific reason to doubt his intent.

The oil did not get changed, nor was anything lubricated. When he returned it was in a 1963 Corvette; her car nowhere to be seen. Without her knowledge or consent, Roger had traded her car for the Stingray.

That vehicle had been modified for road racing at a local track, and required constant tuning and adjustments along with clutch assembly repair. Depressing the clutch pedal required in excess of fifty pounds pressure; the cotter pins failed regularly. Ariel was expected to replace those, drive it on a daily basis and be pleased dealing with carburetor adjustments, gas additives, and additional service requirements. She was not. When Roger drove it on weekends, the girls had nowhere to sit but on a narrow ledge and banged their heads on the Plexiglas rear window due to his 'jack-rabbit' starts.

There was no way to secure them sitting on the small shelf in the back. Ariel bought plastic football helmets for the girls, which were not very strong, but helped to lessen the bumps somewhat.

After Ryan arrived there was even less room and security; nowhere for baby other than on Ariel's lap, where he also was unsecured in any way.

Roger finally realized in late 1968 a more suitable vehicle was needed if he did not want Ariel using his latest new pick-up to transport herself and the now three children. Again without even mentioning this to her, he arranged to trade the '63 Stingray, together with payment of an additional $500 for a '64 Malibu 2-door sedan. It was a done deal as far as he and the salesman were concerned. That fellow already had a buyer who was eagerly waiting to take possession of the '63 Corvette. However, the dealership manager insisted on having Ariel's signed agreement to this transaction, even though her name was not on the title. She had to execute that agreement document at the dealership. Roger was most displeased; someone was making demands on him and he didn't like that one bit.

Upon leaving the dealership in the newly-acquired Malibu however, Ariel had in her possession a check for $500 and copy of the title transfer request for the Malibu that included her name, not just Roger's. He would not be able to pull off another similar deal. Was he in any way pleased that she had netted a $1,000 saving in this transaction? No, and that remained a sore point for years.

Washington was, and remains, a community property state, despite Roger's unwillingness to acknowledge that. Several years later he still had problems accepting that concept, much less the legality.

The drive home in the newly acquired vehicle was not very pleasant. Ariel had not obeyed his orders, and on her own had negotiated far different terms with the dealership management. She openly challenged his decision and poor judgment; and had prevailed. Roger was outraged.

Ariel frequently pondered possible reasons for Roger's total turn-around in demeanor and behavior. This grumpy, cross and obviously unhappy person was not the one she had married. He had been controlling in many ways from the very beginning, but not completely negative.

There had been some rather pleasant times, increasingly fewer and farther between. She finally had to recognize that when Roger wanted something strictly for himself he was indeed, quite nice to her; otherwise, not so much.

He had been given and offered so many educational and occupational opportunities, and positions he was quite capable of filling that he had either not followed up, or outright refused. What was he so afraid of? No logical or illogical reasons presented, then or ever.

Her physical health continued to decline. Excessive bleeding each month was something that might be addressed with surgical remedies at a later time, but she was still of child-bearing age. Each month she felt weaker and less able to regain any strength. Her doctor listened somewhat casually when she related numerous physical problems, but offered no viable means of addressing the matter for a woman her age; she was still in her twenties. He advocated discussing concerns with Roger and enlisting assistance from him. Ariel knew any such attempt would be a waste of time, effort and breath.

Finally, when Ryan was barely five months old, she bled to a degree requiring emergency transport to hospital. Ariel desperately wanted a hysterectomy, but had just turned 30 years of age and produced only three living children. Minimum age of 35 and four living children were requirements, unless there was a serious medical problem clearly diagnosed and treatable by no other means. Those were basically restricted to tumors, benign or cancerous, not just excessive bleeding and low platelet count.

At her current rate of decline she simply would not live long enough to accomplish either medically stipulated requirement, much less both. Too weak from blood loss to even walk unaided into his exam room in early June, her doctor agreed – it was time.

Little Ryan was installed at her neighbor, Helene's house, Jillian and Annie to their Grandmother's, and Ariel to hospital. The procedure went well despite her extremely low blood supply which required transfusions both pre and post-op.

As usual and expected, Edythe did her best to interfere, questioning the wisdom of this surgery, persistently declaring it to be completely unwarranted, constituting nothing more than selfishness on Ariel's part. She challenged the surgeon's qualifications to a completely embarrassing level, totally refuting his prestigious reputation locally and nation-wide. Dad finally intervened with hospital staff and aided in having her access to Ariel curtailed. What a relief. She could simply lie there in peace and virtually feel herself gaining strength. Dealing with Edythe was always stressful and perceptibly drained precious energy.

Little more than a week post-procedure Ariel was discharged home to recuperate. There was a lengthy list of tasks to be avoided, especially lifting or walking up and down steps. Doctor put it simply – "you can lift the coffee cup, but not the pot." He was of Danish descent and well aware of her high volume coffee consumption. Most coffee pots of the day were electric or stove-top percolators, and heavy. She was to rest, be out of bed only to access the bathroom, and kitchen, briefly, for food and liquids – plenty of liquids including her preferred coffee, throughout the day.

Roger's parents brought the girls in for Annie's sixth birthday, providing the cake, ice cream and gifts. Dad and Edythe brought presents along with more ice cream. Ariel sat and watched as Annie was feted, opened her presents and basked in the attention. She held Ryan on her lap for a bit until be began squirming and was retrieved by Roger's mother. Grandfathers took over clean-up of kitchen, washed dishes and tidied the living room while Grandmothers somewhat reluctantly shared Ryan.

The girls went home with their Grandparents and Baby Ryan back across the street with Helene. Each afternoon she brought him to visit Ariel, who sat on floor cushions in the living room so she could hold and cuddle him when he crawled onto her lap. At 25 pounds plus, picking him up was definitely forbidden.

Recuperation went as scheduled until mid-August when Roger's annual family summer picnic was scheduled. As with any other holiday or event, his mother and aunt were in charge; all-family member participation, while not required by court order, was presumed a given. Short of one's own death, everyone was to be in attendance, and that nearly became Ariel's fate.

She was carried from the house and lifted into Roger's newest truck, belted in, and they arrived at the appointed place over 20 miles from home. Once again she was carried from the truck to a lounge in the shade. It was quite pleasant and she tried to just relax and not be concerned about anything. His relatives swarmed all over the place, greeting her and exclaiming over her weight loss. At 5'2", she weighed a scant 90 pounds. The afternoon was nice; enough food available for a small army, and the lovely sunshine warmed her even under the large tree. It was a long day, and she was glad to get back home and back into her own bed.

Two days later she began hemorrhaging; once more sutures had failed and she was transported to hospital for corrective surgery and more transfusions.

While awaiting the ambulance, Ariel lay as motionless as possible wondered if this time she would simply bleed out and drift into the warm, peaceful and welcoming darkness; it would be so easy.

This time after re-suturing, she spent another full week in the recovery area. Nurses making rounds and asking patients to cough requested only that she breathe – and now please, do it again. Several additional days were in a private room. She truly did not care any more. Even lifting a hand required more strength and energy than she possessed or wished to exert for any reason. Eating was a chore, and she truly preferred not to. She only wanted to be left lying there alone, in peace, not having to talk with anyone, do anything, make any decisions or plans. Breathing was quite enough and she would rather not have bothered even with that if given any choice in the matter.

Needless to say, doctors and nurses were highly concerned, attempting anything and everything possible to stimulate her appetite, both for nourishment and for living. She could eventually heal physically if only she would eat; but the ever-deepening depression was another matter.

Ariel's mind was very active through all this, considering how her three children would adjust to her highly-anticipated permanent absence. She simply did not wish to live and certainly did not expect to do so much longer.

Baby Ryan was just a few months old, well adjusted to his Paternal Grandparents and to Helene who took care of him on the frequent occasions Ariel was too weak to lift him. He most likely would grow up just fine with no memory of her at all.

Jillian was now eleven and Annie six, both also well adjusted to the Grandparents and numerous other adults. They would miss her, but she had worked diligently to prepare them over the years to be quite self-sufficient and well-bonded with other adults. She had not explained her goal in fostering their independence, but truly never expected to live long enough to see them grow up. She had weakened month by month over the years, gained a little strength during each pregnancy, only to slip backward again after each miscarriage or delivery.

She had finally achieved the life-saving surgical procedure and would not be subject to regular, heavy bleeds, but even that thought was insufficient to lift her spirits or improve appetite. She was simply too weary to care; and having briefly glimpsed during one of the emergencies a tiny bit of what awaited her at death, truly longed to experience more of that glory. The colors were both vivid and iridescent, indescribably beautiful, music absolutely glorious, the entire atmosphere loving, peaceful, delightfully active, participatory and she…strong and healthy. Had that been merely an illusion, a drug-induced fantasy? No, it was too real and too wonderful. She simply did not want to live and longed for return to that marvelously beautiful peaceful and loving place.

Her surgeon, nursing staff, hospital psychologist and even the dietician were beside themselves, searching for answers. Every possible medication and dietary option had been attempted to no avail. Some drugs had deepened her depression; others left her too jittery to even sleep; none stimulated her appetite. No medical remedy existed for her lack of interest.

Roger expressed very slight concern. As always his occasional visits were brief, limited to ten or fifteen minutes some nights after work, his lengthy bath and time at the fire station. He consistently arrived shortly before the announcement of "visiting hours are now over." Showing up at all was an inconvenience. He had been rather forced on one occasion to spend a little more time with Ariel, as he needed instructions on check-writing, his preference being that she handle all the checks for mortgage, utility bills, insurance payments and anything else. Not having ever paid any bills or written a check himself, he had no clue. She was too weak to even hold a pen steadily, much less write anything, so he had to 'bite the bullet' and learn; how to mail the payments as well. The process of teaching Roger a simple routine task left her totally exhausted, tears of weakness dampening hair and pillow.

Running out of ideas, her doctor gave her an ultimatum, "Either you eat and consume sufficient nutrients, or we will resort to tube feeding through your nose." A tube through her nose and down her throat? No. That simply was not going to happen, and she forced herself to take a few more bites from each tray presented.

As she forced herself to eat a bit more at each meal strength gradually increased, and the depression began to lift ever so slightly. Finally she was again discharged home to continue recuperation. Roger did carry her up the steps into the house and place her gingerly on the bed. At 90 pounds that was not terribly difficult for him, physically.

Both Jillian and Annie needed to be at home for the early September start of school. They were very capable young ladies, well able to take care of themselves and help Ariel by doing household chores, cooking dinner under her supervision and packing Roger's lunch. Jillian had turned eleven the previous November, and Annie was six.

Laundry however, was more than Ariel wanted them to attempt, especially using the large wringer washing machine and tubs. Those wringer rollers were well-known to capture fingers of adults as garments were placed between for squeezing out wash water and subsequent rinses. She didn't want her young daughters in danger or damaging their hands. Wet laundry items are weighty and frequently tangle in the process.

Ariel was still banned from those basement steps; also from standing at the machine and lifting items into the wringer, then tubs for rinsing, and more wringing before hanging them on lines.

Roger finally took some items to a laundry, mainly his work clothes.

By winter Ariel was much stronger, the girls in school and Ryan gaining mobility. He still liked spending time with Helene (Mo) and her husband (Po). Time spent at their home worked to benefit Po as well. He was recuperating from a heart attack and needed rest. Watching Ryan play with toys, "driving, flying and camping" in large cardboard cartons provided amusing interest, and they both napped on the couch after lunch each day.

Ariel desperately wanted to be at least somewhat independent of Roger financially, and found a part-time job collecting Emergency Room billings for a local hospital. She was not yet strong enough, and Ryan still too young to consider fulltime work. Housework, the yard, sewing, and either preparing the weekly full-course family Sunday dinners or packing everyone off to Roger's parents for those was quite enough. Part-time she could handle, and would also provide not only a bit of income which she could stash, but additional learning experiences as well. If she was to re-enter the workforce, the more current experience she had, the better.

Winter of 1968 became an upper mid-west classic in the Puget Sound area with late January snow piling up nearly three feet on the front yard and still falling at only 8°. The girls were delighted and finally able to hear the snow 'sing' as Ariel had described from her childhood. They loved stepping onto newly-fallen flakes slowly, deliberately and listening while fresh snow fell all around them. Roger even went with them one day to sled on a nearby hillside which everyone enjoyed. He generally disliked snow, but this year it was quite different, fluffy and dry rather than the usual wet, soggy consistency usually experienced in the Puget Sound region.

After one particularly heavy overnight snowfall, transportation in the entire area was brought to a virtual standstill. Children regularly walked to school so closures were not necessary. Roger put weight in the back of his truck and had no problems. Ariel had been getting to her part-time Hospital job using public transportation; however, that was halted and the Stingray was not suitable to drive in such deep snow. (It was traded later the following year) She was scheduled for a regular shift so simply bundled up in warm boots, slacks and sweater, winter coat, hat and gloves, wrapped a woolen scarf around her head and face as she had as a child and set out on foot. Only her eyes were uncovered; frost soon built up from breathing.

Prepared to apologize for being a few minutes late, she was greeted with open-mouthed amazement, "what are you doing here? We had to keep staff overnight because they couldn't get home." Her quite casual response was that she was scheduled to work and just walked after hearing there was no bus service. Her supervisor punched in the total hours of Ariel's scheduled shift; only allowed her a very short time working accounts, warming with hot chocolate, and with a still-puzzled look, sent her home. She still wore a puzzled and concerned look, admonishing Ariel to 'please, please, be very careful'.

That anyone would set out on foot through deep snow for scheduled work was apparently an unknown concept to hospital administrators. For Ariel it was a personal challenge presented and met. She was now stronger than she had been since childhood and reveled in each small feat she could accomplish. Walking just over a mile each way in deep snow was not that difficult; she loved the solitude and time to think.

Time, Friend or Foe

Roger had deemed a camping trailer to be a necessity and needed Ariel's signature on the loan for this, so she was notified, and somewhat reluctantly agreed. He spent precious little time with the children, or at home; perhaps weekend camping trips might improve on that. She dreaded the whole idea of a trailer, having spent months living in the house trailer as a small child. However, a good wife is supposed to support her husband and his interests, therefore no compelling objection was raised. She was still absolutely determined to be as unlike Edythe as humanly possible. Never having been successful in pleasing Edythe, she tried valiantly to please her husband, despite his obvious lack of interest.

Cooking meals, cleaning and caring for children, to say nothing of sleeping in that confined space would be accomplished, somehow. After all, she had agreed to marry Roger even while mentally restricting that to one week at a time. Surely she could stand this for a weekend, right?

A low-profile, 15-foot camping trailer was added to the assortment of vehicles and equipment with rosy promises of wonderful family trips throughout the nation. It had been used in very late summer of the previous year when Ariel was still recuperating from surgical procedures; Ryan stayed with his "Gramma Mo". That trip around the Olympic Peninsula had been ok; not great, but ok. Now Ryan was about 16 months old, and also quite independent. Much of Roger's time was still spent hanging out at the fire station or searching for the next highly-desirable old car.

So Roger decreed they would travel through parts of British Columbia; where surely there would be fine vintage vehicles in the area awaiting his discovery. He had already purchased numbers of old cars, ostensibly to restore and sell for large sums. They were parked in the yard untouched, except for the '50's Chevys Ariel was expected to drive despite very real mechanical deficiencies and downright dangerous mechanical status.

He had also decided to start a bulldozing business working weekends. Without any discussion whatever, he proceeded to locate a piece of equipment and trailer that he simply had to have. His grandfather was convinced the bulldozer was a wonderful business opportunity and worthy of a fairly sizeable loan. Ariel learned of this when the equipment rolled into the drive and was parked under the beechnut tree. He did complete a few small jobs with the earth-moving equipment before his interest in that also faded and the equipment was sold. Grandfather received minimal repayment of the loan if any at all. She never knew, and it was never mentioned in her hearing by any of Roger's family members.

So the trailer was packed and off they went to Canada. The mountains were absolutely splendid as were pristine lakes and tumbling rivers. Ariel was able to capture a few things in her sketchbook for later use. Neither Jillian, Annie, certainly not Ryan, were particularly excited about scenery. They did enjoy camp grounds where the girls could ride their bikes, swim, feed chipmunks and be pretty much on their own to explore. Ryan loved digging in the dirt. There were deer to watch and all manner of birds. No bears wandered close, but they did occasionally spot moose and kept a good distance.

A personal fly-in-the-ointment for Ariel was that Roger wanted sex nearly every afternoon, despite lack of privacy in the small trailer, children playing just outside and frequently wanting attention. Surroundings were anything but romantic; Ariel truly was not interested, and little effort was forthcoming from Roger to inspire any such. That his standard approach of demand and grab failed to evoke her immediate and enthusiastic response consistently surprised and puzzled him. Ariel continued to mentally prepare the grocery lists and shop as her coping method. Encounters were blessedly brief.

Otherwise, the trip was very interesting, educational and the scenery breath-taking, even with everyone rather crammed into the pick-up cab. Other than his Navy Reserve training in California, Roger had not been out of Washington State. He particularly liked a museum at Fort Macleod in Alberta, and little Ryan was enthralled with clambering onto huge old tractors, seeders and some rather odd-looking, unidentified farm equipment. Steam tractors abounded in the early days of taming prairie lands, offering few creature-comforts for the hardy farmers. Huge steel wheels and hard steel tractor seats, with no shelter from the hot sun, sweeping winds or sudden downpour did not make for easy living.

Initial plans were to visit Glacier National Park on return to the States. At the border, Roger's bulldozer business signage still on the pick-up was noticed by the U.S. Customs agent. He apprised them of major fires raging in the Glacier Park area, and strongly suggested avoiding it, as heavy equipment operators were sorely needed. Ariel could see that Roger fairly itched to get in on fighting this major forest fire, operating large equipment and in the thick of the action.

With a pick-up and camping trailer, they would be great candidates for joining fire crews for equipment operation and meal preparation service for those crews. The agent assured Ariel the children would be safely transported to grandparents thus allowing both parents to work on fire control, and they would be compensated. It was only Roger's need to get back to his job that decided the matter. Glacier Park was circumvented.

He reluctantly conceded that shipping kids to his parents, returning late to a major construction project, and Ariel becoming a round-the-clock camp cook with only a 3-burner propane stove in order to provide him the excitement of forest fire fighting was not the best option. Family welfare and responsibility took priority this time.

They camped in a beautiful park in Big Fork, Montana where the girls had a grand time riding bikes and little Ryan played happily in a shallow wading pool, pouring pail after pail of water over his head. That they were all ingesting alkali water never occurred to Ariel or Roger; however it came quickly to mind as they resumed the homeward journey. Everyone was sick. Jillian and Annie fared better, having enjoyed more soda drinks than water as special vacation treats. Roger and Ariel both had chills; stomach upsets and generally felt lousy. They kept drinking coffee hoping that would help, not yet realizing the water used to make the coffee was one source of their problems. Little Ryan quickly fell asleep, lulled by the truck's motion.

Finally arriving at a KOA Campground in Spokane, everyone was miserably, undeniably sick. While Roger, Jillian, Annie and Ryan slept, Ariel forced herself into the truck and down the road in search of a store knowing that once this misery passed everyone would be super-hungry. She shivered uncontrollably and struggled to focus well enough to drive; the roadway appeared to shimmer and swirl. She knew by looking farther ahead that it was truly quite straight.

With a fine roast, vegetables, rolls and Ryan's favorite potato pieces, they would eventually have a good meal – presuming all survived. Roast in the oven and everyone checked on, Ariel collapsed on a blanket under a tree. Toward evening all seemed somewhat restored and ate the dinner she had fixed.

Swallowing the last bites to empty his plate, Roger abruptly announced his departure to attend a stock car race on the opposite side of town. He returned in the wee hours of the following morning.

Next day everyone felt much better after a good night's sleep, even if still slightly weak. On they went, following Highway 2 which after crossing more somewhat desolate country and into foothills of the Cascades, led through the small town of Barbaria. A large tree-shaded park formed the town center with a bandstand and art show in progress. Jillian and Annie found children to play with for a time, walked up and down along Main Street looking in at store windows and located an ice cream shop.

Ariel strolled through the paintings, pottery and crafts on display, keeping a firm hold of little Ryan. At one end of the park he found another little boy with whom to play. Roger had driven off to look about on his own searching for old cars after dropping Ariel and the children at the park. He returned in late afternoon with a very satisfied look on his face, suggesting that they all go to a restaurant for dinner. Ariel hadn't expected that, supposing she would buy something at the local grocery and prepare supper in the trailer. She wondered more than slightly what may have put him in such a generous mood.

The reason for Roger's obvious pleasure was revealed between bites as they ate. He had stumbled upon some old cars. She should have known. He was quite enthused about a 1939 LaSalle ambulance, some old Dodge vehicles, as well as the property owner who apparently collected just about any object found on Planet Earth. As a result, Roger had spent the entire afternoon talking with him.

Much more conversational than Ariel had known in years, Roger lauded this person for repairing old television sets, lawnmowers, teletype machines and even coffee pots, then giving them to elderly impoverished residents in town. This certainly was something not previously seen. Roger was very money-oriented; mainly how much could he possibly spend. Any funds they had in a savings account were Ariel's doing, not his. He did not balance the checkbook, pay any bills, purchased fuel for his truck only by presenting a credit card, which absolved him of any responsibility whatever. Roger simply did not concern himself with any possibility of current or future monetary matters.

They finished a very fine meal, strolled about the town streets in the soft evening air enjoying ice cream cones before settling in for the night in the camping trailer. This was indeed a delightful little tourist town.

Barbaria had been a logging, lumber mill town and major switching point for the railroads, preparing to cross the Cascades. In the early 1900's, a cooperative effort between a lumber company and the railroad actually created the town. A large mill was built along the river; the railroad brought settlers from Tennessee to work both the mill and rail switch yard. Lumber from the mill was used to build a row of small structures on skids to house workers and families. As each family accumulated sufficient funds to purchase property, the little houses were hitched to a team and simply skidded to lots about the town.

With eventual closure of the mill and modernization of rail transport employment opportunities dwindled and the town declined. Ariel had been there once during high school after skiing with friends at Stevens Pass and they had gone down into the town for burgers. It had been very quiet and run down with many store fronts boarded over. Only one dingy café and tavern had been open at the edge of town. The few patrons had eyed the young strangers suspiciously; soft buzz of conversation stilled as these outsiders, and teens at that, walked in, sat down and placed food orders.

In the 1960's the townspeople opted to become a tourist destination with a German and Alpine theme. Taking their cue from Solvang in California, work began. That proved to be a good move, restoration and new construction continued for several years, with ever-increasing business as tourist trade grew. Hiking, biking and golf in summer; skiing and even ski-jumping in winter pulled the town out of economic depression.

While strolling through the art show Ariel had learned it was an open show, with artists paying a percentage fee on items sold. She was welcome to participate, especially on weekends. Some local artists put their works out a few days during the week, with most there Saturdays and Sundays.

Next day found them back at home, Roger off to work, the girls and Ryan at Mo's for the short periods when Ariel painted. School started shortly after and everyone settled into their regular routines.

Ariel entered a painting in a commercially-run art show at a large shopping mall and was immediately asked to take a booth to paint and sell her work on site for the two-week run. What an opportunity! She demurred, and turned it down, not having the required $100 fee. The show sponsor instantly assured her she didn't need to pay that; alleging someone had cancelled at the late minute and he just wanted to fill the now-empty spot. Would she do it? Of course.

Agreeing was one thing; actually getting cooking, laundry and house cleaning accomplished at home in addition to garnering enough framed pieces and materials for a two-week show was something entirely different. She had just two short days in which to do it.

She made it work. An opportunity like this might never again be available to her. Grocery shopping was done, main course dishes cooked and frozen, laundry caught up, and then paints and canvasses gathered. She was glad to have an old standing easel purchased from one of the Barbaria exhibitors. It appeared somewhat professional. With everything packed into the '48 Buick convertible she placed that evening's dinner in the oven, set the timer, chopped salad into a covered bowl in the refrigerator, saw the girls off to school, Ryan to Mo's, and headed for the mall to set up.

A busy time, indeed, but Ariel was eager to see what lay ahead. Roger had not been overly pleased about her spending two full weeks in a shopping mall working an art show; but did not outright forbid her. He just grumbled a bit about causing him problems, and that his meals had better by on time. And… who only knew, she might actually make some money; that was a real positive in his mind.

Was this painting idea going to work, or not. Would anything sell? The Barbaria Park and selling to tourists was one thing; this was a commercial show in an urban setting. Galleries abounded in the area; none of which contained any canvases by Ariel; she was totally unknown.

Roger had been a little concerned in 1968 when Ariel was discharged from hospital following surgical procedures, re-suturing and transfusions, weighing barely 90 pounds and not caring about anything at all. He was also well aware of her life-long interest in oil painting, the sketchbooks filled with pencil drawings. He purchased a small set of oils and brushes that included canvas boards, hoping it might help her gain some strength and weight. That did work quite well and before long she was painting nearly every day and accumulating a small inventory.

This initial invitational show was a success beyond her wildest dreams.

Profits were immediately plowed back into purchase of more supplies, especially commercial frames. More invitational shows followed; she continued traveling to Barbaria on weekends, and sales improved there as well. She devoted time each day to painting and with sales providing for purchase of materials, inventory continued to build. Ariel stashed as much of the proceeds as possible toward her dream.

Just before Christmas that year Roger presented Ariel with a faux mink stole, apologizing with some embarrassment that it was not real fur. She was utterly surprised by this totally unexpected gift and at a complete loss as to a proper response other than to thank him and repeatedly assure him it was quite lovely. It truly was pretty.

Where could she possibly wear it other than to the required family Christmas Eve gathering and next day's dinner at his parents' home? No answer came to mind; they did not have a social calendar, and Roger consistently took great pains to exclude her from his activities. Any dinners away from their home were mostly at his parents', some at hers, or at one of the buffet places opening throughout the region; not any place one wore a fur stole, faux or real. On rather rare occasions they had seafood salads at a quite casual eatery in a nearby city.

There was no circle of mutual friends or close acquaintances with whom they might have socialized. Even a movie was an extremely rare event; definitely no concerts, plays, or banquets other than annual Fire Department functions. The stole was quite unsuitable for church on Sunday mornings. It most definitely was an unexpected gesture. What motive could be underlying was another unanswered question. Was Roger actually attempting something nice in compensation for his general behavior?

While Ariel had never experienced anything like a functional family; neither had Roger. Was this just a gift, or… ? The stole was worn on a rare occasion, but largely consigned to its box. Jenna wore it with one of Ariel's sheath dresses, high heels and lots of jewelry for a church Halloween party. She was quite beautiful, with upswept hair-do and make-up; an elegant young lady at nine.

At Roger's behest, Jillian and Annie were enrolled in weekly Hawaiian steel guitar lessons. Roger contended he had always wanted to play that instrument, so therefore the girls were to do so. Lessons were held in a private home a few miles away. A cabinet maker nearby made frames from scrap lumber and framing molding which he advertised for sale at the guitar studio.

Ariel soon became a regular customer, shopping for frames while the girls were at their lessons. Her inventory of paintings continued to build, ebb as sales were made and then build up again. A few pieces were also displayed in local business establishments, resulting in very limited sales, but at least some exposure.

She also continued traveling to Barbaria on weekends to work and sell her paintings, taking Jillian and Annie with her on alternating weekends, and occasionally going alone. Paintings, sleeping bag and necessary paints and equipment, along with easel were packed into that '48 Buick convertible she had bought at a Portland old car swap meet by selling paintings there. She and daughters slept outdoors at the campground, following dinners in town. It was fun spending time with each, and they met some girls whose mother also painted and sold work in the park. Little Ryan loved staying with his Mo and Po, who by now had become unofficial grandparents.

Suddenly Roger claimed she should have a proper studio in which to work and sell her paintings in their neighborhood. The mall shows and weekend park exhibits had convinced him there was money in that daubing, and he also saw a means to benefit himself. He located a small building on a main road just south of the business district and arranged for Ariel to rent it, even building a sturdy sign identifying it to be an art studio. The building had adequate parking in a graveled lot, two rooms, front facing windows, and after considerable cleaning, was workable. The large windows with northeastern exposure were a real plus.

The primary attraction for Roger was a long open shed at the rear of the property in which he could store his numerous old vehicles, including a 1928 Cadillac phaeton, modified for use as a fire truck many years prior.

Ariel did manage to sell enough paintings to pay the rent and utilities. All costs for her studio and Roger's car storage were her sole responsibility. With the remaining funds she replenished art supplies and bought commercial frames from a wholesaler. Ryan spent his time there playing with toys, talking up a storm with any and all potential customers who found him quite entertaining.

That Barbaria collector of cars, together with just about anything and everything else, telephoned Roger on occasion. He eventually got around to saying he wanted to sell the property and move to an island in Puget Sound. He had no use for real estate sales people, and wanted Roger to buy his place and that included whatever vehicles remained on the property together with sheds full of assorted "treasures". Roger was ready, willing, but unable to do that without financing. Ariel was dispatched to the bank to procure a loan. She absolutely had to succeed.

Several years earlier Roger located a 1920's car he absolutely '*had*' to have and demanded Ariel fork over the relatively small purchase amount. Had he been working at the time that would have presented no major problem; however, he was unemployed, ineligible for unemployment, with no target date for having any income; Ariel also was not employed. Finances were frighteningly limited. Cash reserve consisted of the miniscule amount she had managed to stash into a savings account.

That she would not somehow automatically provide money for what he wanted to purchase was absolutely unthinkable. He refused to accept that what limited funds they had could not be used to buy another old car; children and adults needed groceries on a regular basis and ongoing household expenses like the mortgage had to be paid. He had never forgiven her and used that failure against her repeatedly, building on the ever-present guilt over her inadequacies and incompetence as a human being, and certainly as a wife.

Property values had increased significantly since they had purchased that neglected property and it was now an attractive piece of real estate. She had no problem arranging for a home improvement loan, ostensibly to finish the basement, sufficient to purchase the Barbaria property. She did insist on actually seeing this structure before Roger had access to any money, so a short jaunt over the mountains was made. He could have drawn funds from the bank, but didn't know how to go about doing it; banks were still somewhat suspect to him. Any such dealings he left to Ariel. This time he was dependent on her agreeing to the purchase.

Upon arrival, Bob met them in the yard with a huge smile and welcome. He invited them inside, explaining that he had "cleaned it up so they could see it better."

Cleaned it up? Narrow trails over bare wood flooring led between boxes stacked to unbelievable heights, mainly stuffed with books. A beautiful cat snoozed in one upholstered chair; obviously his bed – well covered in shed fur. Paths had been opened to two other chairs on which Roger and Ariel were invited to sit. Roger plopped down in one; Ariel perched gingerly at the edge of the other; Bob remained standing, taking care not to disturb the cat.

Where had she seen this situation before … but, at least this place didn't smell; no dried food was visible on the tiny bits of open wall space nor was there any discernable evidence of recent food preparation. Actually, walls themselves were marginally visible, quite well hidden by stacks of books and stacks of boxes of books along with items of all sorts…some identifiable, others not.

Bob seemed to know just where everything was in this hodge-podge, even which books were in which boxes, and declared having read each and every one. A large aerial map covered one wall not hidden by boxes, with vari-colored push pins here and there. Those marked sites, or presumed sites, of plane crashes— private, commercial and military craft--throughout the North Cascades region. He also mentioned that the core of this little structure was one of the many built in the early 1900's to house the Tennessee hills/hollows people brought north to work for the mill and railroad. Who knows, perhaps once emptied, cleaned and painted, it could work quite well as a studio. Alternate residential arrangements would be required; children could not live in this place, and she certainly wasn't about to.

With little discussion Roger agreed they would buy Bob's house, and documents were signed. Ariel did not attempt any disagreement and she held the payment funds.

She knew disagreement regarding this purchase would be of no avail, and just possibly Roger might be more interested in spending time with his family once away from the fire department and sheriff deputy buddies. Bob did not want to move right away, but hoped to be settled nearer his mother on the Puget Sound island before onset of deep winter in the Cascades. That was fine; they wouldn't have to worry about snow removal for a while. The roof of the house did not appear overly strong, but then it had withstood decades of winter snowfalls so perhaps looks might be deceiving. Ariel sincerely hoped that was the case.

The early '70's were heavy snow winters in the region and before long Saturday mornings frequently found Ariel and Roger en route to clear roofs and start clearing basic debris from the house. Bob had removed what he wanted and hauled that to his new residence; however, enormous quantities of 'stuff' remained. The kitchen was filled with boxes of surplus food products from local social services that had piled up, one on top of the other, over several years. Ariel became quite expert at testing flour and other grain product bags for weevils. Those deemed relatively free of bugs were packed into the truck and donated to a mission. The 'bug-infested' were hauled to the dump with more to the dump than to the mission. Ariel considered it a major triumph the day enough of the kitchen was cleared that she could sweep a small patch of the worn linoleum. That, however, was just the kitchen, with living room, attic, staircase, bathroom and attached shed yet to be addressed, not to mention large free-standing sheds stuffed full and completely surrounded by mounds of more stuff.

With enough of the structure emptied to allow storage of Ariel's paintings and equipment to work the park art show that was loaded up and transported, just before the season opening. She had sleeping bag, some food and clothing suitable for the show opening; a second-hand-store vinyl-covered recliner chair to sleep in. An old two-wheeled hand drawn cart was located in a shed and thoroughly cleaned for use in transporting her artwork each day. She then made the trek from Seattle on Fridays by bus to work the weekend, returning on Mondays. That enabled her to make some progress clearing more stuff out of the house on evenings after dark when the show closed.

Finally Roger moved the camping trailer onto the property; Ariel brought the old convertible with more painting materials, clothing, and her life became somewhat easier. The trailer was a far cleaner place to sleep and fix meals. She bathed in a wash tub by the Monarch range on which she heated water in the house.

She continued to work the show each Wednesday through Sunday, and at clearing the house evenings, returning to Seattle for a couple days each week. With school out, Jillian and Annie joined her, followed shortly after by Ryan who absolutely loved everything about this new place. He could dig just about anywhere he liked, there were scrap boards, pieces of pipe, car parts and all sorts of wonderful little-boy-toys. Jillian and Annie quickly renewed their friendships with daughters of the local artist. These girls had lived there most of their lives, knew all the ropes, and were ever so happy to introduce these newcomers to the town, river, bike trails and all sorts of things to do. Precious little adult supervision was required and they had a wonderful summer.

On weekends Roger hauled load after load of junk that Ariel and the girls had stacked in the yard, along with items too big and heavy for them off to the dump. He also started digging through the large free-standing, solidly-packed shed, selecting numerous treasures to keep and carting more loads away to the dump. Ariel sincerely hoped no local officials would calculate the number of years being steadily drained from that dump's life-expectancy.

Slowly emerging from the accumulation, it started to look as though this structure could be a suitable studio and … possibly even made sufficiently livable that Ariel and the children could survive a winter in it. She could draw up plans; begin the permitting process for construction of a real house in the spring. Shower and laundry were needed, refrigeration, and something done about relatively decent cupboards. The girls could have the attic for their room, Ariel and little Ryan cots on the main room. She would need to tend fire in the range through the nights for heat. Additional wood was purchased and stashed in the attached woodshed. Certainly not fancy, but doable. Measurements were taken for cupboards and a bid request made. The more work they all did, the more plausible it seemed, all predicated on Roger working and living in the Seattle house, and Ariel painting inventory for the next season..

On one trip back to Seattle for additional supplies and household goods, Ariel and the girls found some carpet remnants that would do quite nicely in their attic space and also as area rugs for the main floor, along with fabric for curtains and bedspreads. While they shopped and loaded the truck with supplies, Ryan played happily with Gramma Mo and Grandpa Po. Jillian and Annie's beds, bookcases and writing desks would all fit just fine and both were beginning to look forward to settling into the upper floor of that old house. Their rooms were in the basement in Seattle; here they each would have a window looking out at mountains, to both east and west.

The arrangement reminded Ariel a bit of the old farmhouse in Maywood where Dad and his brother had shared a similar attic room with views of both sun rise and sun set.

The girls preferred visiting with Helene when it was time to pick up the carpet rolls. Roger's friend Doug helped Ariel load them onto the truck, and on their way back from the store she suggested they have some pie and coffee. A quite reasonable idea, indeed, and they stopped at Roger's favorite coffee shop. Ariel had never been there, but he mentioned it often. The waitress greeted Doug with a bright smile and a teasing question, "well, Doug you rascal, is this your beautiful girlfriend we finally get to meet?" She turned to get the coffee pot, awaiting his response.

"No…this is Ariel, Roger's wife" he answered with a slightly reddened face and sly smile.

"Roger's what?" she sputtered, nearly dropping the coffee, and immediately apologized profusely to Ariel for her outburst. "I'm so sorry, but, we all thought he was single…he never mentioned a wife…brought his son in once in a while… we all thought he was a single dad. I'm so very sorry," she stammered, before hurrying off to bring their pie.

Ariel just smiled and assured her there was absolutely no problem, and that she understood the confusion. Initially she had been surprised. It was minor shock of sorts learning that Roger presented in public as the single parent of Ryan. However, once past that jolt, truly what did she expect? He had not permitted her to bring the girls to his baseball games; insisted they be on sidewalks to view his passing by in parades, hadn't allowed her to attend his apprenticeship graduation ceremony, and carefully avoided being seen with her in public settings. He had also stopped even attending church with her and the children. Just what did she expect?

There had been some hesitation about uprooting from the familiar area where she had begun to garner additional sales of her artwork, and become somewhat known, benefiting from customer referrals. In a new setting she would be starting over from scratch. That had seemed just a bit daunting; however, now she eagerly looked forward to a new start in a new location, more time with her children, painting and selling her work at shows, and…at some distance from Roger. The plan, as she understood, was for him to remain in the Seattle house and work in that area at least until a suitable structure had been built in Barbaria. Her income from painting sales was very seasonal, good during the summer show and dropping to nothing during winter months. At least one steady income was required; money she had saved from summer months would never support them through the winter.

Fire

On Bastille Day, actually very late that night, the old house on which they had all worked so hard caught fire. Ariel awoke in the trailer to the sound of her varnish and hair spray cans exploding, the area aglow from open flame. Grabbing pants, shirt and stuffing bare feet into clogs, she raced out of the trailer to the neighboring house to the west.

That house had actually been built several feet over the true property line and was altogether too close to the now-blazing structure. Getting no answer to pounding on the door and shouts to get out, and to call the fire department, she ran east down the alley to another neighbor who did rouse and call in the alarm. Some help would probably arrive eventually. Realizing the convertible was fully packed with oil paints, canvasses, frames, turpentine and paintings; she found keys and ran to move it…somewhere, anywhere away. As she ran back to that too-close neighboring house she felt the sand and gravel gathering in those clogs, grinding into her feet. Light from the fire helped her find the faucet and garden hose to wet down the neighbors' walls and roof against possible wind-blown sparks. Either they were not home, or sleeping very soundly. No amount of pounding or shouting had brought response, or water beating full force on windows, walls and roof. Fortunately there was only the slightest breeze, greatly reducing danger. But, where was the response? Except for her own labored breathing, water splashing against that adjacent house and increasing roar of flames, the night was silent. Smoke billowed and rose into the starlit sky.

At last a faint siren was detected, its volume gradually increasing. Upon arrival the unit was parked in the alley, directly at the rear of the burning structure with an old wood shed on the other side. The crew quickly hooked up hoses and proceeded to drive flames out of the woodshed and kitchen into the remainder of the little house. But by then Ariel's greatest fear was for safety of responders and the truck parked within feet of open flames. This was a strictly volunteer group, with minimal training, but valiantly doing their best.

More hoses were strung, pumps and nozzles adjusted; gallons of liquid poured into the inferno. Flames receded gradually, and were finally extinguished, leaving smelly smoldering remnants silhouetted against the pre-dawn sky. What a sodden, stinking mess. Ariel's battered feet screamed; pouring sand and gravel out of her clogs helped, but didn't eliminate the pain by any means. Now that things were calming somewhat, she began to shiver and wished she had a warmer garment. Surely she could find a sweater or something in the trailer, but just stood watching curls of smoke rise listlessly from hissing charred remnants of rafters and siding.

The volunteer Chief approached to ask Ariel if she had known what was under the structure serving as its foundation. No, not really, she answered; no one had actually thought about what might be holding the place up, other than a normal presumption of some sort of stone or concrete base. It had been on the lot for decades and surely must have some relatively stable foundation. Roger, the girls, and she had all been totally occupied just emptying the structure of years'-long accumulated stuff – teletype machines, two-way and short wave radios, vacuum tubes, typewriters and parts, radios, television sets, coffee pots and who-only-knew what else. She had hauled boxes of books by the car-load to donation sites. With top down and the back seat removed, a lot of boxes could be hauled in that old Buick. Truck-loads of salvageable surplus food had gone to charity shelters. No one had given any thought to a foundation under the house.

"You probably never would have spent any time in, or even near it had you known," he said; "it was supported by stacks and stacks of old car batteries and one aging tree stump. Good thing none of those batteries exploded, and the stump didn't totally rot away." The possibilities were absolutely mind-blowing. Ariel offered yet another prayer of thanks. Only the old house had burned some personal property, art supplies, along with dreams of winter housing and eventually a studio all gone up in smoke.

No one had been injured and no other structures harmed. A true blessing, but just not very easy to see at that moment. What would Roger say when he learned of this? Once again, she had failed.

Two more immediate things still worried her; where had she put the convertible, and had the neighbors' big white cat Ralph escaped the woodshed? That was his very favorite place to hide out and sleep; he had scared Ariel witless on several occasions by suddenly popping up from a dark corner with a loud yowl. She had learned to look for him in there before getting wood for the cook stove, and praise him lavishly for keeping the mouse population in check.

The sheriff deputy helped locate the car and arranged for her to pass the few remaining night-time hours with the neighbor who had called in the alarm. This neighbor was also Ralph's pet human, and sure enough as she sat drinking coffee with this lady Ariel felt a soft cool nose on her leg and then silky fur. Ralph looked up at her, meowed long and low as if asking what had happened to his nap-shed.

Her daughters were safe at their friends' home, little Ryan at his Gramma Mo's, and Roger also at the Seattle residence. No physical injuries or other property damage had been incurred, the weather was still warm; they had the car, metal garden shed and trailer. The car battery foundation had remained intact and only the house was gone, leaving an enormous mess. Messes were cleanable, and houses could be rebuilt.

It could have been so much worse and Ariel was exceedingly thankful it had not been. But, she had been there; sound asleep in the trailer; unaware until it was too late to stop any flames. Yes, that failure was hers.

Clear, Excavate, Rebuild

The same deputy who had helped Ariel locate her car, calmed her nerves a bit and saw her safely under care of her neighbor, also telephoned Roger later that morning to apprise him of the situation. Being assured his family was quite safe and only the old structure had suffered, Roger expressed his thanks and went on to work as usual. He drove over on the following Saturday to inspect the site and begin working with Ariel on plans for the future. She had been provided a small room courtesy of the local hotel/restaurant for two nights, giving her both bed and the bath facilities, now non-existent at the property. She needed to vacate that room, however, for the weekend when an accordion player used it.

Ariel set her paintings out in the park for the show as usual early Saturday morning, putting Jillian and Annie in charge of 'sales' and returned to start clearing debris. Roger found the girls in the park, gave them money for lunches and then went to the lot where Ariel was already dragging and piling burned boards, salvageable firewood and whatever else she could get out of the mess.

For once he showed some affection hugging her and saying how glad he was she had not been injured, that the girls were fine and no fire fighters had been hurt. Tears streamed down her face more in relief that she was not being blamed than from loss of the structure or the work she was attempting. He had become ever more critical over the years, finding fault with anything and everything. Even when he had angrily stripped second gear of a new car in a blind rage, he managed to blame Ariel for it. She had expected anger and blame, not kindness.

No precise cause of the fire was ever determined. A chunk of kitchen flooring was chopped out and submitted for analysis. That showed petroleum saturation in wood flooring where a gas-powered washing machine had stood for years. Ariel had used every cleaning product she could find to get rid of that petroleum, with limited success at best. She managed to lighten the color slightly, but the oil, gasoline or probably both, were deeply imbedded.

In the process of clearing rooms and attempting to use parts of the old house, some more modern appliances had been introduced with no real concern about the additional load on old wiring. A used refrigerator, electric fry pan, toaster, hot plate, iron, as well as hair dryers and curling irons had been plugged into vintage sockets. Bob had used a variety of electrical implements over several years, a 30-gallon trash can-full of radio tubes had been scooped off the floor, so the matter of adequate wiring and electrical service just never came up.

Old, but reliable, knob and tube wiring had undoubtedly dried out in more than six decades, been bumped about as boxes were stacked and more recently removed from the attic. Rodents had made valiant, but futile attempts at invading the structure, only to be discovered and promptly dispatched by one of Bob's several cats, or possibly Ralph on one of his daily visits. Tiny deposits of black droppings, together with an occasional dried foot, discovered in a corner gave silent witness to their ever having existed.

The local casualty insurance agent had strongly urged Ariel and also Roger to increase the amount of coverage on the structure to something more realistic. That was excellent advice, as the total coverage amount was only $8,000, woefully inadequate in light of the total loss. Her advice had not been heeded, thinking it prudent to delay that until some improvements were in place, such as those cupboards, some furniture, better appliances, etc. Hesitation in this instance was not the better course. When one inquisitive townsperson confronted the lady with the thought the fire may possibly have been convenient for these outsider artsy types, she promptly set him straight, "if that were the case, they would have listened to me and raised the coverage amount. They can't build much of anything with such a skimpy amount." No more was said.

An appointment with the insurance adjuster reviewed what little was known as to the structure history, fire, and value involved. Ariel clarified his only question – that petroleum-soaked wood flooring. The old gas-powered washing machine motor that had stood, dripping, in that spot for years certainly addressed the matter. He referenced the report noting detection of soap, detergents, and bleach residues in addition to petroleum; that those products were inconsistent with petroleum particles. With that one question, not an actual concern, cleared up for him, the matter was concluded, claim approved and payment issued.

Roger returned to Seattle to work and live in the house there; Ariel set about exploring what could be built and ready for occupancy before winter which was approaching even though daytime temperatures still hovered in the high 90's. She truly did not want to go back to Seattle; her studio had been leased out to another business, and Roger had given up his car storage. The Seattle house had recently been listed for sale. They were committed; no real choice but to move forward, decide on what, and start the rebuilding process.

Very few options were available locally that would provide shelter before winter. Contractors were more than happy to bid the job – for the next summer, not by fall of this year. A Boise Cascade pre-cut design was finally located, a contract inked and clearing the lot of burn debris became the highest priority. Pre-cut lumber would be delivered to the site, followed by a crew to do the assembling. Foundation on which it was to be built needed to be fully in place, and rapidly.

Again, Roger purchased equipment to push the old place down and consolidate the rubble. Could a piece of equipment be rented? Of course, but he wanted his own and again talked of unspecified sideline business opportunities. Whatever; the property had to be cleared, debris removed, new foundation prepared, poured, a structure built, and quickly. The burned mess was pushed into a large pile with the goal to burn as much as possible in numerous smaller amounts and reduce the volume needing to be trucked away.

Ariel continued working the art show with considerable help from Jillian and Annie. She could only paint for short periods each morning after setting up in the park and waiting for the girls to wake, have breakfast and then come to tend to sales. With them on duty, and lunch money provided, she returned to work on the burn pile. Each late afternoon and evening she started small fires around the outside of the main pile, garden hose at the ready and tossed blackened boards onto each smaller fire to be steadily if not rapidly consumed. The big pile slowly shrank, and her circle of fires continued long into each night.

Nearing one such midnight hour, while perched atop the pile of charred boards, Ariel's right foot slipped from her wooden clog, and bare heel landed hard on a jagged piece of burned two by four. Strangely, she felt no severe pain, just pressure. Looking down she knew that chunk of wood had penetrated deep into her foot and needed to be removed. Easier said than done, she was finally able to pull it out and hobble down off the burn pile. Blood poured out all over;

that was a good thing serving to wash the wound. So, now what to do. First thing was drench all the small fires so no sparks could fly and catch something else ablaze, as well as hose some of the blood off her foot. Then hop to the trailer and look at this in the light. She had water there, too, an obvious necessity. She probably should go down to the little hospital and have it treated, but the girls were asleep and she didn't want to alarm them. So she simply cleaned out the hole, applied pressure to keep the blood flowing. Poured in a considerable amount of hydrogen peroxide and waited for the bubbling to abate, as did the bleeding. It looked relatively clean and remaining bits of charcoal were most likely fairly clean, having been burned. She folded up one clean white sock as padding and gently pulled the other over toes and padding before cleaning up a bit, checking on the now-cold fire spots and tumbling into bed. Morning found the wound still clean with only slight discoloration. Cleaning the area again, and with less padding over that hole, she was able to pull on a more normal anklet and even walk quite well. She kept the area scrupulously clean and protected, walking normally within just days.

When dimensions for the structure were confirmed Dad arrived to build forms for the foundation and construct the concrete block walls of the basement on which the house was to be built. He and Ariel set the level for footings using a water level he made together with his old transit. Once the footings had been poured, cured and forms removed, serious work began on raising the concrete walls, ensuring correct window openings and readying it for construction of the main floor and loft. Ariel mixed every drop of mortar, using a hoe and the mortar box Dad had built. She carried hundreds of concrete blocks from where the pallets had been unloaded to the areas on which he was working; also carrying 'hod', keeping his mortar board supplied with fresh mud. The piles of sand, bags of lime and cement were close at hand.

Each time Ariel visited the local lumber yard to place another order or pay the bill, she also acquired replacement tape measures. Between Dad and Ryan there was a consistent need. Dad accidentally bumped them into the blocks on numerous occasions. Ryan tightly held those he managed to get hold of, peered intently into an already set block, and dropped the steel tape, listening happily as it bumped and bounced to the bottom.

Ariel chuckled over possible theories and conclusions of an archeologist a millennium or two in the future as to what strange ritual or religion was practiced by *'ancient tribes'* in the 20th Century in placing tightly wound measuring devices at seemingly specific spots at the base of one building. Theories could abound, and thesis written for advanced degrees.

While Jillian and Annie watched over and sold paintings in the park, little Ryan entertained himself at home with scrap lumber, stray odd lengths of pipe and old tools building only he knew what, and digging in the dirt. Everyone was quite busy.

Dad arrived by bus and stashed his personal belongings in another metal shed hastily assembled and placed on a wood platform, sleeping on a cot. Ariel cooked on the old Monarch range, badly warped by the fire and propped up on blocks, but still functional for heating water and preparing meals. They bathed after dark in a galvanized wash tub. Ariel hauled dirty clothes to the laundry behind Front Street.

Dad loved recalling that time, how enjoyable it had been for him and telling his friends that Ariel was the very best hod-carrier he ever had, on any job. Edythe did not like hearing that. When the site was prepared, Edythe arrived to take him back home, tsk-tsking at length about how unkempt everything was, and expressing serious doubts that anything could possibly be livable before winter. They would all simply have to move into the Pedersen house; never mind they still had a fully-furnished house in Seattle. She would take control; Ariel was clearly unfit, incapable of doing anything properly.

Their house, a truckload of pre-cut lumber, arrived and was carefully unloaded. Ariel glanced over the materials and immediately saw the main roof timber was not only twisted but deeply cracked. It simply was not acceptable. The Boise Cascade lead-man also noticed that and a replacement timber was ordered immediately. There was no question, that cracked and twisted piece was not acceptable. It was quite adequate the following spring when cut to lengths for steps in the yard. The crew soon arrived as well, plans were reviewed, plans and measurements checked, and sightings verified.

She was concerned when she saw the crew leader pointing to the corners, then to the plans and talking earnestly with the men. Was something wrong? He asked Ariel if she and her father had actually set the level and dimensions using just the old transit and a water level. Yes. And had they done all the block work? Yes, they had; was it ok? With a broad grin he assured her everything was definitely ok and more; very well done which simplified their work considerably.

The foundation and basement walls were square and level within a 1/32nd of an inch, as checked using much more modern technical equipment than had been available to Ariel's Dad. They didn't have to use valuable time correcting anything and could get right to work on the actual building.

With a crew on site, work progressed rapidly looking more like a house every day. Each morning Ariel set up her paintings and easel in the park, daubed a little at a mounted canvas to appear she was only away temporarily, left brushes and paints open and ready; then returned to her main interest…getting the house built. Jillian and Annie were fairly willing to tend the paintings and work at selling Mom's paintings. They were working to earn commissions toward new bicycles.

On her way back, Ariel shopped for the main dinner course, then fired up the Monarch and by mid-afternoon fragrances of roast beef, baked chicken or a pork dish wafted into the building promising a tasty meal. She served ample and nourishing dinners each evening when Jillian and Annie came from the park and the crew finished work for the day. That little 'extra' of feeding carpenters resulted in several areas of the framing construction being done in addition to the specific contracted tasks, and at no additional cost. Ariel then took her turn at the park after supper to catch some of the tourist dinner crowd, did a little on that same canvas, packed up and came home for the evening. The days were long, physically exhausting and stressful, but rewarding. The house was going up quickly, painting sales were producing some income, and there was real progress being made toward a cozy winterized house. She only hoped it would all somehow meet with Roger's approval.

Basic construction complete and the crew gone, Dad returned to work on the interior. He was determined to make this house in which his beloved daughter and grand-children were to live the best, soundest and most secure possible. Ariel had put in cross-bracing and fire stops that were not included in original plans. Having worked on building projects with Dad, those were definitely going into her walls. Wiring and plumbing were contracted out to local businesses, and with interior walls in place everything started coming together nicely. Dad completed stairways and as much of the interior as possible before Edythe once again fetched him back to her domain. He had regaled his friends, husbands of her church friends, with accounts of working with Ariel to provide her and the children with shelter. Edythe definitely did not like his being the center of any attention, and especially that he touted Ariel's abilities and skill.

Before insulation and sheet rock could be installed the wiring had to be inspected and passed on by a County inspector. That particular official was somewhere out in the surrounding mountains seeking to murder Bambi; no clue as to when he might return. Days were sunny and warm; nights colder and colder with approach of winter. The sole source of interior heat was a small, basically ornamental pot-bellied stove in the living room; water heating and cooking done on the Monarch range outdoors.

Plumbing had been officially approved so at least there was running water; cold, but no hot. Hook-up to the permanent power source required return of the inspector/hunter.

Ariel took Ryan with her to the local utility office to attempt a solution. Electricity to the house was supplied only by a heavy-duty extension cord from the temporary construction pole near the street. Temperatures were continuing to drop, and she desperately needed to activate the electric furnace and hot water tank. "No dice", she was told by the utility office manager; "not without County sign-off." With the only inspector in the County off chasing Bambi for who only knew how long, no reasonable remedy was available. Explanation that she and three children were existing in an unheated structure they could not insulate, with no hot water or indoor cooking did not change the response. These power company staff persons were allegedly powerless to do anything to mitigate the situation.

Wiring had been done by a highly reputable local contractor whose work was well known and documented throughout the county. It was a nightmare with utility staff steadfastly insisting they were helpless. She was completely at the mercy of the absent inspector and local regulations. To come this far in rebuilding only to have everything come to a screeching halt because one man was out hunting. Ridiculous.

Ariel was holding Ryan in her arms, and pinched the soft tender inside of his chubby thigh. His face screwed up and little tears trickled; she pinched harder and he began to wail. She remained standing in the office, pinching Ryan harder to which he howled even louder.

Ariel knew only too well how that hurt; Edythe had sunk fingernails into the soft skin of her upper underarms repeatedly. It had been one of her favorite means of letting Ariel know she was a disappointment and had erred, again.

While Ariel had known better than to cry regardless of the pain, Ryan was under no such constraints. Ariel was counting on that. The utility manager remained adamant; Ariel pinched Ryan even harder, and the noise level rose.

One lineman finally spoke up; said he would go take a look at the place and see if something might be done, at least temporarily. He was out the door in a flash, escaping the office manager, screaming child and weeping mother.

In less than one hour, permanent power was turned on, the temporary pole and meter removed, and the office manager notified. Ariel had stopped pinching Ryan's chubby little leg long before that. She hugged him even closer, kissed his tears and apologized over and over for pinching him, while praising him for howling so loudly.

He truly didn't understand all that, but happily enjoyed his lunch of burger, fries and milk shake before they went home to check on the house. The electric water tank had been activated and already up to temperature; warm air circulated through ductwork. Everything was functional; they would all have indoor hot baths tonight. No more sneaking out to the wash tub after dark.

Roger had hauled rolls of insulation from Seattle on weekends. Sheetrock was purchased locally, delivered to the site, and it was then Ariel and Jillian's job to get that into the house. Not an easy task, but they managed, balancing the material on porch railings and sliding it all in through windows.

Her staple gun normally employed stretching canvasses was put to work securing insulation; sheetrock covered the studs as each four-foot section was insulated. Even Jillian was surprised when she discovered Mom was adept at measuring and cutting holes for light switches, outlets, and nailing sheet rock securely. With interior walls covered and the furnace operational the place was quite cozy and looking more livable each day. Dad came back for a short stay and with some help from Roger framed interior basement walls, hung doors, and all three children had separate rooms.

Before taping, mudding and painting, or carpet installation, Ariel needed to climb the extension ladder and stain the few tongue and groove roofing boards that had remained undone when stain ran out, and the roofing boards had to be put up without delay. Teetering atop the fully-extended ladder, stretching and staining those using a brush taped to a long 1"x1" pole, not missing spots, was unsteady and unpleasant, but accomplished. Jillian and Annie took turns at the unenviable job of steadying the ladder, spotting any missed spots … inquiring every few minutes, "are you finished yet?"

Carpet, wall paneling, drapes, furniture from the Seattle house and a few canvasses hung turned the house into a much more normal-looking home.

Jillian and Annie were enrolled in school, Ryan had a room full of toys, Peppy was also in residence and Ariel needed to paint and frame scores of canvasses to replenish her inventory before the spring opening of the park art show.

Jillian had been given a tuxedo kitten by a school friend In Seattle, and a friendly yellow tabby had been rescued from a local souvenir shop before he could playfully scamper through the tables and send fragile figurines flying.

Peppy learned a hard lesson about fully-armed cats, and soon kept his distance. The black and white kitty had run from him, which was what he expected of any reasonable feline. But he then backed the tabby into a corner from which kitty not only failed to flee, but stood his ground, upright on hind feet and delivered swift right/left/right dead-on hits. Bewildered dog suffered a very bloody nose for his efforts. It was to be a busy winter to be sure.

Christmas was celebrated early and briefly at home the first year in their new house, but early morning of the 24th, they all piled into a venerable vehicle and headed over the mountain passes to Roger's parents' home for the requisite family gathering. Roads were not particularly good, compact snow and ice, with numerous vehicles sliding into ditches; however, the 1940 Cadillac held a steady course despite having only two functional gears-- reverse and second. Never once in crossing two mountain passes did the engine over-heat.

The gears were eventually fixed weeks later. Meanwhile, parking on a downward slope, coasting forward a bit once the engine started allowed use of second gear quite successfully.

During their first winter in the new house, Ariel had waited tables at a local restaurant to keep up with regular expenses and also pay some bills for the Seattle house. Roger was living in Seattle and driving over the mountains on alternate weekends, frequently hauling more materials. He deposited portions of his weekly paychecks, to their joint checking account, but she rarely knew what amounts until the month-end statements were received. Ariel arranged transfer of bank accounts to the Wenatchee branch of the same institution where she could more easily access current information; that simplified matters.

She had consistently maintained custody of the checkbook; Roger just didn't get it – that you need to keep track and enter all amounts, checks written and deposits made. The single experience of having to make a mortgage and utilities payments when Ariel had been too weak to even write her name, much less legible checks, had been entirely too much for him to cope with again.

He had no bank credit card, either. That had been issued in her name in 1963, as a SeaFirst employee, and only one initial spousal card ever given to him. He had promptly charged over $500 on the account for a power lawn mower without, as usual, even mentioning it to Ariel. She learned about the purchase when she checked her account. There was no explanation, and no contribution toward the bill; her name was on the account, she paid. He was never given another after that one expired.

In mid-February, she also worked a small arts and crafts show in Wenatchee attempting to bring in a little more cash. The girls were in school and seldom called in to help at the restaurants during this pre-tourist season. Their earnings were for their clothes and expenses, not to help pay household costs.

Returning home on Sunday with minimal results to show for her efforts, she was shocked to find Roger's truck parked in front of the house. His matter-of-fact statement that he had quit his job and was now permanently residing in Barbaria was not what Ariel needed at that moment.

The Seattle house was fairly empty but with sufficient furnishings for Roger during the week, still on the market and accruing normal utility and maintenance costs, to say nothing of mortgage payments; and now Roger was unemployed. They had no real income; he was not eligible for any type of unemployment compensation, and there were two residences to support. Her restaurant wages were miniscule, tips scanty from the locals, and hours hit-and-miss in February. The park art show did not start until May, and now Roger was here with no job. Just how was she to manage?

To his credit he did immediately set about looking for work, with no contacts in the area and no knowledge of the local job market. It was anything but favorable, and still winter when very little construction of any sort was active. Within a month, however, he did secure a job with a local company and the financial pressure on Ariel eased somewhat.

With advent of spring, snow melt and warmer weather, things looked considerably better. Ariel had just finished their income tax return in early April when the clouds rolled in again and snow descended steadily until everything, including roofs, was deeply covered. Winds howled down the canyon, trees swayed and still the snow fell. As the storm raged even louder, Ariel feared for the roof; walls creaked; the whole place shook from mighty gusts. She raced up the stairs, stuffed the precious tax information into a large manila envelope and tucked that between her mattress and the box spring. If the roof blew off, that return, with healthy refund due, should be safe. Snow began to break loose and slide off the metal roof; a beautiful sound in winter. Now in April, that first loud swoosh/thump was startling, unheard for weeks; but those following were quite reassuring.

Spring thaw, snow melt and heavy rains resulted in quantities of water and mud greater than any Ariel had ever before dealt with, in Minnesota, Bellevue or Seattle. The creek at the Bellevue property had routinely flooded each spring, but water never caused a problem around the house or garage. She had rather enjoyed playing in the rushing water, and building rafts with Denny and Alan. In later years she had helped Dad build a retaining wall to divert water with more large rocks and concrete blocks, set firmly in concrete below the stream-bed and rising some four feet above normal water level. That succeeded in diverting the creek during flooding for many years. Even after it had succumbed to extreme high water and tumbled, it mitigated high waters to prevent erosion.

This was a different matter; as the property sloped from street to alley, where the water stood atop ever-deepening mud. Fortunately the upper area drained well enough to use for parking vehicles. The alley and back of the house, normally accessed, were impassable. Ariel and Ryan spent hours each day with shovels and a hoe, draining puddles and channeling water ever down-slope to the alley and then onto the adjacent vacant property. Ryan delighted slogging about in his boots 'making little rivers', and watching rivulets flow into larger channels in the mud. He learned more about gravity and basic physics in that process than he ever realized. The neighboring alley property was considerably lower and unoccupied for many years which lessened Ariel's concerns about possible damage there.

Late one afternoon Roger drove part-way down the alley before realizing he could easily become thoroughly stuck and backed out to park his truck in front. Gingerly picking his way through the maze of running liquid, he expressed surprise that Ariel and Ryan were still dealing with mud. She just looked at him without replying. She and the children had been coping with it for days; it was still raining; both snow and soil were still thawing. Streams and rivers throughout the entire area were running at flood stage and more; of course there was mud. No grass had taken root in the front yard, and the bare ground could only soak up so much water before gravity prevailed.

Quite unexpectedly Roger made his way to Ariel and placed his arm across her shoulders—not in the 'I want sex now' manner, but just supportive. This was a new experience; Ariel was caught totally unaware, completely puzzled. His comment was not negative or blaming her for the mud, but that she had done a good job trying to deal with an enormous task. He also hugged her just a little, and even though quite strange, it felt so good. She was at a total loss for any answer. Very softly, after a few confusing silent moments, she murmured, "I'll get us some coffee," and handed over her hoe.

Years later she pondered potential for changes in their relationship. Had Roger perhaps given an occasional casual hug, and she been able to respond with something other than making coffee, what might have been different. Another unanswered and unanswerable question.

In April the Seattle house sold; but only after a 25' strip was sold to the north side neighbor, and the 75' south lot to another party, leaving only the house and garage on the remaining 75 feet. Ariel ended up being responsible for closing the sale, as Roger had volunteered for an out of town work project. Ariel and Ryan set out early on a beautiful late April morning. Jillian and Annie were in school and this should easily be a one-day, over and back by evening trip. She did have use of the truck for this trip, as remaining furniture pieces needed to be removed from the house.

The electrical service that had been inadequate years earlier, but never replaced now required replacement before the sale could close. Ariel arranged for that, resolved other less-vital matters of concern, paid the related costs and finally set out for Barbaria. Ryan was exhausted after a long day of travel, waiting around in various offices and watching workmen address the deficiencies as required. The purchaser could now heat water and cook at the same time; a luxury Ariel had never enjoyed. The sunshine of morning had turned to rain in mid day. Approaching Snoqualmie Pass that rain became a steady snowfall.

The ¾ ton truck carried a full load of the remaining furniture items from the house, and with new heavy-duty tires all around Ariel experienced no difficulties whatever traversing bad road conditions. For whatever reason Roger had taken one of his precious old cars to the job and she was able to make this trip in a reliable vehicle. Furniture pieces would never have fit into an old Cadillac or Buick.

Near the summit however, chains were required by the State Patrol. Those were quickly installed by an 'approved' service, the charge paid and they were back on the highway in short order. Barely ten miles down the road, peaceful quiet snowfall was interrupted by the unmistakable clank of broken chain which required a stop. Visibility was non-existent in the heavy downfall, and lane markers had long disappeared. Even being fairly certain she was off the highway, Ariel didn't dare risk walking behind the truck to access a tool box. Another vehicle could easily hit her before having any opportunity to even see her or the truck despite tail lights and flashers.

She pulled heavy hairpins from her head, secured the ends of chain and they set out again. Hairpins broke with alarming regularity; chains were re-connected with still more pins and soon Ariel's long dark hair hung loosely over her shoulders; there were no more pins.

There was no let up in the snowfall, and she worried that the chains would totally break and wrap around the axle, so they limped along slowly and finally approached a service station at the south side of Blewett Pass. Bay doors were closing and most lights out. Upon hearing Ariel's clanking approach, the owner had reversed the door and motioned her to drive in. He immediately saw that the chains had been twisted when put on, and knew exactly who had done so. Up on the rack went the truck and the chains were swiftly removed. Ariel had protested that she could not pay for this service; having spent all but $5 on unexpected expenses incurred closing the Seattle house transaction and then the chain-installation fee.

"Don't you worry about that one little bit. We know who put those on wrong, and we will settle it with him. He's been a problem up there for years." She did have a gasoline credit card, but that was also refused. The truck was lowered and backed out of the bay. Ryan had been asleep most of the time, but awoke trying to figure out what was going on. Ariel still had tears on her cheeks, but the chains were off, and the garage men seemed only concerned that she and Ryan get over Blewett Pass safely and home. They had no problems at all despite ice, snow and wind. Jillian and Annie were fine, had fixed something to eat, done their homework and were sleeping.

Over a year later when Roger was selling that truck he made sure every interested party was aware that Ariel had done *severe damage* to his truck driving with chains incorrectly installed, clearly due to her ineptness and lack of basic intelligence. The purchaser only shrugged and commented he had trouble seeing that terrible damage. It didn't matter one bit; it was a truck after all, and winter conditions can be difficult in the mountains. He had a grasp on reality even if Roger didn't seem to.

Life settled into a relative routine, Roger working for the same HCAV Company, Ariel painting and throwing pottery with her artist friend, and children all in school. Summers saw the girls working in food service and also helping Ariel with the art show on occasion, Ryan busy with youth baseball, swimming and floating the river. Roger became involved in riding with local sheriff deputies more frequently so was seldom at home.

The local area was sparsely patrolled by law enforcement personnel in the best of times, but even fewer were available during late night hours in winter months. As road conditions worsened and much of the traffic was comprised of long-haul trucking, freight trucks and tankers, those vehicles occasionally slid off the twisting icy roads, some ending up in the adjacent river. Answering late night/early morning phone calls, Ariel frequently found the County Sheriff on the line personally requesting help with traffic control. She donned winter gear, woke Jillian briefly to explain her absence, made certain Peppy was inside and headed out to aid in directing traffic and keeping any sight-seers out of the way, freeing officers from that duty.

If Roger happened to be at home, he responded eagerly and would quickly be at the immediate incident scene, elbowing his way in as close as possible.

More often than not, there was only one State Trooper on duty between Stevens Pass and Quincy during late night hours, with a single Sheriff Deputy for the entire county. Just about any vehicle collision or truck slide-off prompted calls for volunteer help, and she became quite skilled.

Ariel spent many cold hours on ice-covered highways waving flares to slow and stop traffic; allowing vehicles to proceed through incident scenes with appropriate cautions. With emergencies dealt with and traffic restored to normal, Roger joined deputies at the café for coffee, or breakfast, at County expense. Ariel returned home to get kids up, fed and off to school.

She was regularly invited to join the 'boys' on those occasions, but didn't dare even have coffee due to Roger's jealousy. It simply wasn't worth more tirades and accusations.

Roger was not often at home and available to respond, so Ariel did, directing traffic and assisting to calm victims.

There were numerous search and rescue incidents during summer and fall, also requiring volunteer response. Frequently these calls also included requests for cookies and/or cake snacks for the deputies who had been on scene for some time, with official food service still being assembled in Wenatchee.

Mountain search and rescue calls also involved driving whatever old vehicle she could get started over remote logging roads to a base of operations. There she assisted with radio communications, food preparation and serving which freed a deputy for actual searching. She also interacted with family or friends of the missing person(s), frequently at the request of officers, as many were more comfortable sharing details, feelings and hunches with her than officers; especially when a child was missing. Seemingly insignificant details were often of interest to officials and helpful in the search process.

Expanding the House

The replacement house plan, marketed and intended more for use as a summer cabin, even with a full basement, quickly proving too small for a family as kids grew, were involved in sports and school activities, and having friends over frequently. The basic plan allowed for rather easy expansion of the living room without any need to change the roofline, just extend it

So an extension was built on the north end of the chalet-style house with large fireplace and chimney incorporated, both for esthetics, supplemental heat and roof support. Ariel had designed the fireplace to be done in basalt, open on the front width and back to about half-way on each side; open corners were supported by two 4" diameter steel pipe pieces some 28" in height. She and the kids hauled rock from Blewett Pass, sorting by size and used to face the fireplace and chimney.

It was a beautiful, unique and very impressive addition to this home and also provided the frequently needed auxiliary heat. Electrical service to the area was frequently interrupted in winter by trees falling over lines, ice build-up, out-of-control vehicles taking out power poles along with numerous unexplained outages. They certainly had experienced that on numerous occasions the first winter, when only a little wood stove and press-to-logs initially comprised the sole heat source. Relying solely on an electric forced-air furnace was iffy at best in winter. The fireplace was quite important following removal of the wood-burning cook stove.

At first the stonemason had difficulty understanding exactly what Ariel had in mind, but as work progressed was highly impressed with her sense of architecture, design and balance. A swing-arm was incorporated so that an iron kettle or cooking pot could be used as well, especially during winter power failures. Word spread about this totally unique fireplace, and several contractors brought clients to see it. Roger took little interest, fussed about all the rocks and the mess, but did dig out a piece of black marble from his stash of stuff to be used in the raised hearth. He had salvaged it when the old Seattle Public Library was demolished, and the slab became a beautiful accent piece in this setting.

The chalet-style house was warm and cozy in winter, especially with heating augmented by the fireplace. Once that column of rock was heated it retained warmth for days.

Cars, More Cars, and Junk Yards

Any hopes Ariel may have entertained as to Roger spending more time with his family and less with old cars with the move from Seattle faded rather quickly. Not only had he acquired a late 1930's ambulance along with purchase of the Barbaria property, but at least three deteriorating 1970's Chrysler products. Shortly after Ariel had begun working the local art show the first spring following purchase of the property, a junk dealer had pulled his tow-truck into the alley one afternoon. Without so much as a by-your-leave he hooked onto one of the derelict vehicles and dragged it away. Ariel returned just as he had returned and was in process of hooking onto another.

Had Roger actually arranged to have the hulks removed? "Oh, no" came the reply; "I've never spoken with anyone but Bob about the cars. He just left them, and I figured no one else wanted them since he didn't. If you are the new people here, I'm just doing you a favor."

Ariel was totally dumbfounded. What sort of town was this? Personal property rights seemed to mean nothing whatever to this fellow. She would dearly love to see those rusting heaps removed, but Roger thought them to be of great value for whatever reason, and would be absolutely furious to find them gone. He would have to sort this out himself. Meanwhile, Ariel firmly instructed the local junk dealer to unhook the vehicle, not return to the property for any purpose whatever unless requested to do so by Roger and had written permission. With considerable grumbling he complied, put most of the dirty parts and debris back, and sped off, tires spinning in the loose dirt.

He had four large vintage vehicles still in Seattle with no place to put them in Barbaria, and ultimately had to admit he had neither use nor space for the rusted Chrysler models. It was not an easy decision for him; he wanted those old cars, despite logic of any sort. That he had absolutely no need or use for them was of no consequence.

Weeks later Roger contacted the man and had him remove the remaining junk vehicles, but only after sternly berating Ariel for not having guarded them more closely.

Years earlier in Seattle, Roger had subscribed to an antique/collectible cars magazine for several years, and through that learned about a cars/parts swap meet in Portland. He actually accessed dates and registration information, immediately signed up and began gathering items to take for sale. He insisted Ariel attend this with him. It was her responsibility as a wife, no question permitted. It was also her responsibility to arrange for child care.

Ariel packed some paints and necessary equipment along with an easel to take along. Just sitting in a booth surrounded by old car stuff was nothing she wished to do, especially not for three full days.

Roger had carted a truckload of old car parts to that event, unloaded the boxes and larger parts randomly onto the floor, neglected to price individual items, or by any per-box indication. Ariel had no idea what he wanted for any of it, nor did she particularly care. Consequently, his sales were minimal; however, he purchased more boxes of parts for cars he didn't own.

She had some framed inventory pieces along with art supplies so she set up her easel, with a few finished and framed pieces displayed toward the back of the booth space. This attracted considerable attention. She worked on new canvases, concentrating on farm-related country scenes and weathered barns in which vintage square-bodied cars and even old wagons were visible in dim corners or under tree branches. Those sold rapidly; several not yet dry.

Just sitting in a 10'x10' space, surrounded by old car stuff was not anything she wished to do for three long days.

Roger's primary focus at the meet quickly centered on a 1948 Buick Super convertible; he absolutely had to have it – no questions, no consideration other than getting it. Could he pay for it? No. However, Ariel had sold several pieces of her artwork, new canvases and those from inventory. It became her responsibility to cover the convertible purchase in addition to motel costs, meals and gas.

The convertible had to be hauled to Seattle by rented trailer at additional cost. Roger was not at all pleased with the outcome of his car swap meet experience. Since the convertible was in running condition, it became Ariel's responsibility to drive and maintain.

Another special acquisition made shortly following the swap meet was a late teens square body sedan, purportedly a Canadian-built Buick, not in running condition. It arrived on a car-hauling trailer and was also placed in the driveway. Ariel searched numerous volumes at the public library attempting to trace engine and body serial numbers to no avail. This very special vehicle turned out to be a hybrid—part Canadian General Motors and part Chrysler product, possibly Dodge. It finally departed, again by trailer returning a fraction of its purchase price, never having turned a wheel under its own power. It had been dubbed the "Canardly Buidge" as it 'canardly' budged an inch.

Meanwhile, however, he heard of a 1941 Cadillac that might be available and his attention shifted once again. It was purchased and added to the growing accumulation. Next to be acquired were two 1948 Buick sedans, which joined the ever-increasing fleet of 'restoration' projects in the Seattle back yard.

Shortly after the Barbaria house was occupied, the wonderfully special old cars transited the mountain passes, some under their own power, and others by trailer, coming to rest in another yard. Both Buicks and one Cadillac were also fairly functional, but required frequent driving to prevent further deterioration due to neglect. Batteries, belts, tires were of concern along with seals that dry with age.

While Roger still lived in the Seattle house and continued working there, Ariel and the children were in Barbaria There she struggled to get at least one of these late '40's vehicles started on frigid winter mornings. Similar to horses needing regular exercise, old cars need to be at least started each day, even if not driven any great distance. Being idly parked for any length of time rendered them extremely difficult to deal with. The six-volt batteries simply did not have sufficient force to turn over the massive and stone-cold engines of old Cadillacs and Buicks, especially in winter. Roger consistently drove his current ¾-ton pick-up truck. One of the Cadillacs had an in-line heater which Ariel made certain was plugged in each night. Light bulbs were placed in engine compartments; hoods were covered in old blankets and sleeping bags.

She also kept close watch on the outdoor thermometer readings, rising several times during the nights to check that and also look for little pointed kitty ears amid the car coverings. No visible kitty ears meant the in-line heater was not working and the cats had retreated to their well-insulated box on the porch. A plugged line meant no circulating warm water. Bundled up in hastily-donned winter gear, Ariel slogged through the deep snow to first check electrical connections and light bulbs; then address the engine heater. Car coverings were removed, the hood raised and propped with a piece of reinforcing rod. Old springs were unreliable (she would be instantly decapitated should one of those massive pieces fall, which they had been known to do) while she reached into the engine compartment. Next, she proceeded to squeeze the water hoses – massaging aging Caddy hoses. Water once more circulating, car hood lowered, coverings replaced, and kitties restored to their beds, all was well for another couple hours. Ariel could return to her warm bed, or resume shoveling if snow was still falling. Falling snow frequently required all night shoveling to keep the off-street parking area cleared. Nights were short and highly fragmented.

One of the old Cadillacs she was expected to drive had a nasty little habit of sticking in second gear. Temporarily correcting this problem also involved raising the huge hood, propping it up, placing Ryan at the steering wheel with instructions to pop the gear shift into neutral when Ariel shouted to him. She was busy attempting to manipulate parts on the steering column.

One necessary 25-mile drive to Wenatchee was delayed when Ariel discovered the battery in that car was about to fall out of the engine compartment onto the road. It was precariously held in place only by the battery cables and a few rusted shreds of the cage. She located some left-over household wiring to create a substitute basket, securing the battery sufficiently to allow driving the vehicle. Ryan was a great help in holding wire, propping the battery and locating safe places where Ariel could hook and bend the household wiring.

Their jury-rigged battery cage held, and was still in place years later when that car finally sold. The purchaser expressed considerable amazement when he raised the hood and observed that battery 'cage'. When he learned that Ariel and Ryan had effectively coped with that problem, he just shook his head in bewilderment. That any husband/father would leave a situation like that unrepaired was totally beyond his comprehension.

Days were spent with normal household duties, shoveling snow, and working to build up her inventory of framed art work for the spring and summer art shows. The local Art in the Park show opened in early May each year and continued through early October. Winter was the time to replenish her inventory; frames and canvas were purchased from Puget Sound wholesale supply companies.

Production painting consumed daylight hours when there wasn't snow to shovel. The stockpile of work available for spring grew steadily. A minimum of 200 pieces was needed to open each season and replenish those as paintings sold. Late Septembers, Ariel and her painting 'buddy' sold off all they could get rid of to start over with fresh inventory for the next season.

She also joined her friend in the pottery, learning to wedge clay and then throw, first on a kick-wheel and then power-driven. Pieces were trimmed, bisqued, glazed and finally fired. They compounded glazes from a wide assortment of chemicals, breathing in all manner of potentially harmful particles; but without apparent harm. Firing the 600-cubic-foot oil-fired kiln required for high-fired pottery usually took a full day and night to complete. A good quiet snowy night was preferable, making the process of regulating the flow of stove oil easier. Small fuel lines inserted into the fire box and blown into the flames by an old vacuum cleaner hose, were pulled at intervals, dripped into fruit jars and flow adjusted with butterfly valves; a hot/cold, dirty task and frequently somewhat tense. They crouched in the snow, wearing asbestos gloves, warm winter jackets and hair secured by cotton wrappers, pulling oil lines from the firebox ports full of roaring flames to adjust oil flow and reinsert the lines. Ariel loved it.

Roger complained that she was wasting time throwing and firing useless pots, only creating an inconvenience for him. The fact that stoneware and porcelain pieces were assets to be sold in the summer art show was of little consequence. Preparation of any sort for a future time just didn't interest him

When not actively working shows, she also worked part time at a local grocery store, and later full time for a dentist, squirreling away money in hopes of escape. How? When? More precisely to the point…could she ever?

Cars, Trucks, Bikes, Garage, etc.

Roger's passion for acquiring old cars increased steadily year after year. Each new discovery was to be the ultimate restoration and win him great adulation at future unidentified car shows. Somehow, not a single vehicle ever received actual hands-on restoration work. Each such find was initially touted as being a rare, very special model and year, possessing unique qualities that would be in high demand years hence when he would have restored it to showroom condition. A new acquisition soon became just one more in the ever-growing hodge-podge of untended vehicles. Most were 1940's Cadillacs and Buicks; however, from time to time old trucks briefly joined the fleet. A WWII U.S. Army truck did run, but lacked minor details of steering wheel and driver's seat. Vise grips and a wooden box served in lieu of those accessories.

One small bulldozer and trailer had been purchased earlier in Seattle allegedly as a source of additional income. That was sold after a few months, but Ariel never knew if any money was repaid to his grandfather.

When the old house burned in Barbaria, Roger purchased another piece of equipment, rather than renting one for a brief time. His uncle borrowed that unit and trailer to use for a church camp project a few miles up one of the canyons. He proceeded to run it out of oil, and so the engine froze up and it no longer functioned. Roger had it loaded onto the trailer and pulled in into the back yard where it reposed for several weeks.

When he decided it should be unloaded, he sat on the seat of the tractor holding the levers, while Ariel pulled it off the trailer with a come-along. She was able to move it, inches at a time, by gripping the handle and hurling herself over the bank edge to gain maximum force from her (then) 120 pounds. Roger issued instructions from his perch. That piece of equipment was also disposed of later, again at considerable loss.

With the house finished to the degree it was livable and fairly comfortable, Roger pushed for building a large shop and garage. Using yet another newly-purchased used back hoe/front-end loader, he excavated a foundation area, built forms and had a 6" reinforced concrete slab poured for a 30-foot by 40-foot structure. The Gothic-style Quonset hut metal-sheathed structure included a large loft quickly filled with boxes of dirty car parts and various pieces of old vehicles. A vintage fire truck, ambulance and the '48 Buick convertible found storage places inside. Two '40's Cadillacs remained outside and were eventually sold, as well as a '48 Buick 4-door sedan. There were splendid plans outlined for restorations allegedly beginning with Ariel's '48 Buick convertible, which he began by tearing apart door panels and removing the radiator.

The wood stove discovered in the corner of the Seattle basement years before had been brought over the mountains and was installed in a corner of the new shop/garage providing heat for the proposed winter car restoration work.

Motorcycles became a new focus of attention, beginning with a Honda 360. He insisted Ariel accompany him on a 'short ride' through orchards and farms in the neighboring county. The bike was not running smoothly, and Roger's plan to correct that was to get it out on the road and 'open it up'. In a small town some forty miles from home, it simply quit running. Having insisted Ariel go along, she was not at home for him to call to bring his truck and get the bike. He had no friends on whom he could call. His shouts and demands were no help; the bike would not run; he had no answers. She was ordered to do something to solve this problem.

Ariel reluctantly telephoned a friend with a truck who appeared in less than an hour, loaded the bike and transported them all back home. For once Roger did not have much to say, and refrained from verbally blaming Ariel for this problem in the man's presence. Once repaired that bike was also sold at considerable loss, and he purchased a 750 model.

At this purchase he insisted Ariel have a bike despite her having zero interest whatever in riding a motorcycle. A used Honda 175 was selected when Ariel insisted it be something she could pick up if and when it toppled over. The bike did serve quite well for errands about town; she used her back pack and the bike for grocery shopping and also getting to her friend's pottery. It was far too small and under-powered for highway use, especially on a cross-state route with heavy truck traffic. Roger demanded she ride her small bike with him on the State Route, which she did…once.

Roger bought, traded and sold a considerable number of new ¾-ton pick-up trucks which he drove. Ariel, with help from Jillian, Annie and Ryan, were expected to use whichever 'wonderful, collectible' car they could get started. Wenatchee was the closest shopping center, and required a fifty-mile round trip. Winter trips were especially uncertain, with the aged 6-volt electrical systems woefully inadequate for starting the huge old engines in sub-freezing temperatures. Vacuum powered windshield wipers frequently failed in heavy snow, and even in rain. Ariel rigged a hand-powered method to operate them using parachute line connected to the wiper blades, running through the wing windows, so a passenger, frequently Ryan, could keep pulling right/left on the line. The wiper blades then moved right and left, not outside to center as they should have; but, it worked.

The spacious garage space did provide Roger the ability to pull engines from the various Cadillacs and do some repair to drive shafts and even perform some few needed engine repairs. He acquired an engine hoist, chains and whatnot; however still required Ariel's assistance. When the hood was removed from a car, with Ariel lifting one side and he the other; all the chains in place, he then required that she stand with one foot on each front fender, and work the lever to pull some 1500 pounds of engine and transmission up off the mounts and frame. Meanwhile Roger was under the car, on a creeper, guiding the load. If she bumped or inadvertently touched a wrong part of the hoist lever while pulling on it, the entire thing would fall on him.

Wild thoughts raged through her mind. What if she slipped? Did she have the lever in the correct position to lift/not drop? If she asked for confirmation of a mumbled instruction, Roger swore and then yelled for her to 'just do it – now!' Slowly massive parts emerged from their mountings, the car body and balance shifted with the weight change; and Ariel's mind reeled. What if….? The weight was more than enough to crush Roger. No emergency services existed, and help of any sort was a long time off.

If he were killed while working under one of his cars, would anyone believe that an accident? She would be a financially secure widow for certain, and far better able to care for her children, in every way; but…she had to live with herself. If she had, or even thought she might have had any part in his death, she would have to deal with that every day and every night of her life. God would know. He might forgive, but she could not.

She had to hold on and make no mistakes; get that heavy engine and transmission up, out, and over to the steel work platform. Roger had to be safely out from under it all before she could think of relaxing.

Why Ariel stuck with the tasks, obeying the rudely shouted orders, ignoring the cold, her aching back and arms, not allowing her feet or a hand to slip was another question never answered.

Much later Ariel listed all those vehicles at her attorney's request. Nearly thirty such 4-wheeled passenger vehicles had been acquired within that twenty-year period, plus trucks, old and new, and motorcycles. When number 29, another Cadillac, rolled onto the property, Ariel had loaded her things into number 28, the 1968 Cadillac Sedan, and rolled out. That did not occur until later, however.

Dad's Passing

Several months after helping Ariel construct the house in Barbaria, Dad suffered a minor heart attack and spent a week in hospital. Ariel and the children visited him there and were highly encouraged by his attitude, good prognosis, and determination to resume normal activities. One thing he did concede to was cutting down on his consumption of amply-buttered sweet rolls, and multiple spoons of sugar together with thick cream in his coffee. He never in all his life encountered a pound of butter or pint of thick cream he didn't dearly love. You only need enough bread to hold up the butter.

When Ariel expressed her concerns over the work he had done on her house, he quickly put those to rest. He consistently maintained those weeks of working with Ariel in leveling the excavated site, setting foundation forms and pouring concrete, then laying block using mortar she mixed; finally building stairways and erecting partitions had been the highlight of his retirement years. No, he assured her, the work was totally beneficial to him in every way. He would not have missed out on that for any other experience. Besides, Ariel was the best hod-carrier he had ever encountered, mixing and delivering mud at exactly the right consistency; and just when it was needed. She had mixed every bit of that by hand in the mortar box he built. Her role also included carrying hundreds of concrete blocks from the stacks and placing them within easy reach for him.

Edythe quite naturally saw everything in a totally different light. That her husband and daughter were enjoying manual labor in building a house while granddaughters were tending and selling paintings in a park without proper supervision was simply not right. Who only knew what strange persons they might encounter in a little tourist town. One could not be too careful.

He made an excellent recovery from this cardiac incident, resumed walking a few miles each day, and looked forward to picking up neglected woodworking projects in his shop. Not so. Edythe forbade his even spending time in the shop sorting materials and straightening it. He was not to use any power equipment, nor allowed to drive his car. She would do all the driving which effectively prevented him even speaking to anyone without her presence for appropriate interpretation and correction. His dry sense of humor was a constant source of embarrassment for her, requiring her to correct and explain what he had really meant, regardless of what he had said.

Before long she had essentially confined him to the house, even putting a stop to his daily solitary walks. Those had been savored and greatly enjoyed; time out of the house to simply be alone, thinking and praying while enjoying the fresh air and exercise. He began writing in order to have some time without Edythe's supervision, but carefully concealed the pages. Since she could not find what he put to paper writing was considered an appropriate occupation and not dangerous. He also conducted regular written communication with individuals in the Covenant Church Chicago headquarters offices. He highly valued this connection and devoted many hours to reading and the writing. His physical health deteriorated slowly, but steadily.

The winter Ryan was in second grade his Grandfather caught a deep chest cold which lingered and developed into pneumonia. By mid-January he had not recovered and began to seriously fail. Ariel spoke briefly with him by phone, with Edythe close at hand to correct whatever he said and quickly take over the conversation.

Ryan was also ill with whatever 'bug' was rotating through the school, and neither Jillian nor Annie in particularly good health with winter sniffles. They kept going to school, sneezes, sniffles and all, but Ryan was home in bed for several days. Weather was typical for winter in the mountains with daily snowfall, compact snow and icy roads, shoveling and snow-blowing. Ariel's only transportation at the time was a marginally-functional '62 compact Pontiac wagon she used for transporting paintings. It did run, but not very well, had no radio and occasionally functioning heater. Roger promised to do something about it, when he had the time.

Late on a cold, snowy evening Ariel received a call from Edythe that Richard was not doing well and she expected him to die within hours. If Ariel wanted to see her father before he passed she needed to do so immediately.

How she desperately longed to hold his hand, tell him how much she loved him, and try to somehow thank him for being her shield, protector and confidant. She wanted him to know she understood how limited he had been by Edythe's control.

However, traveling over two mountain passes that winter night, in steadily worsening weather and road conditions with three children, simply did not make any sense.

Roger was away from home on a job and unavailable in this pre-cell phone era. The girls were better, but still coughing and sniffling; Ryan was still running a fever. Her only transportation was the uncertain station wagon. Snow fell heavily on already slick roads. Travel warnings had been broadcast throughout the day, especially for the passes. Her route involved both a North-South road and then an East-West slightly lower mountain pass. A third choice was closer, but at least 1,000 feet higher with heavier snowfall requiring travel equipment she did not have.

To attempt getting to Dad meant putting her children at risk, especially Ryan. She had no guarantee or reasonable expectation her car would even make the trip without breaking down completely. That could easily leave them stranded in a cold vehicle in winter conditions for an uncertain timeframe. She refused to even consider any possibility of sliding off the road or getting stuck in deep unplowed snow. The first mountain pass was primarily a two-lane road, very limited patrol activity at night, with only one state and one county officer scheduled to cover the entire northwest portion of the county. The interstate was better, but also fewer patrols during nighttime hours. That higher third route was not even a consideration. She always carried sleeping bags and blankets, along with some food and water in the car, but those would not sustain warmth very long in the sub-freezing, windy night.

Did she dare take a chance? Her heart ached to see Dad. The children were all asleep; house silent save the howl of steady wind and sudden gusts pushing at the walls. She paced the floor praying desperately that he would somehow know her thoughts and understand how much she loved him. Those words of love had never been uttered, daughter to father or father to daughter. She knew he loved her, and prayed that he would in some way sense her deep love of him.

Attempting to be physically present with her Dad as he lay dying was by any and all measures simply not feasible. Alone, she would have been on the road immediately, regardless of weather and conditions. To put his beloved grandchildren at risk was foolhardy at the very least. She knew he would not want them to be in any possible danger at any time, and especially not on his behalf. She could not go.

Hours passed as Ariel paced and prayed. She placed a call to Edythe, asking her to please tell Richard of Ariel's love, that she was praying for his comfort and peace; she was unable to come there immediately. Edythe's response was largely unintelligible, and ended with, "well, I guess you don't really care all that much if you aren't coming." Ariel did not attempt to correct her interpretation, knowing any such to be of no avail. Hearing a click, Ariel softly replaced the receiver and wiped her eyes again. She resumed her prayers and finally felt a sense of peace surround her like a cloak.

Ringing of the phone jolted her to awareness and the realization she had fallen asleep on the couch. This was Edythe calling in the still dark early morning to say Richard had passed not long after Ariel's call. He insisted Ariel had been there, holding his hand and smiling, then closed his eyes for the final time. Edythe had immediately corrected him, of course, but apparently he could no longer hear her, or chose not to, because she claimed the soft faint smile remained on his face after heartbeats ceased.

Ariel expressed the normal, usual and acceptable concern for Edythe's well-being, sympathies for her and what she now faced; assuring her they would be en route as soon as travel was relatively feasible. She also hoped to have use of the pick-up rather than chancing the station wagon. Edythe promised to let her know what arrangements were to be made, sweeping aside any consideration of children's health or vehicle reliability. It was a short conversation.

Ariel fixed coffee in the soft pre-dawn light and contemplated future years without her loving Dad; her earthly shelter no longer available. That assurance of being able to call on him should whatever situation become untenable was gone, leaving a huge deep hole in her life. She had not ever dared to ask him for anything, but just knowing that he was there, and she could, had sustained her often. Praying again for guidance and direction, thanking God for the years Dad was with her, that cloak of calm and peace again descended and quieted her overwhelming trepidation. She felt with a certainty he was indeed still watching over her.

The sky brightened slightly and a glimmer of sunlight broke through the heavy clouds. It was time to get the girls up for school and see to having the station wagon serviced, fuel tank filled and car loaded to attempt getting on the road a little later in the day. She wanted Ryan to sleep as long as possible.

They started out in mid-afternoon in the station wagon. Ariel had been able to leave a message at the company office for Roger who was still away. The truck would not be available for at least another day. A note was left on the kitchen counter for him explaining their absence and Ariel presumed he would follow, as they were to stay at his parents' home. Snow had ceased falling and roads were in fairly good condition. The combination of cold temperatures and lack of wind made travel on compact snow and ice quite good.

The Pontiac began to sputter and overheat before reaching the first summit; Ariel was careful to be on a down slope before pulling to the roadside and stopping. Raising the hood revealed a startlingly hot engine, the entire manifold was bright red, almost see-through transparent in places. She had never before seen any engine that hot; cooling would take quite a time before adding any water could even be considered. She broke out cookies and juice for snacks.

Once water had been added to the somewhat cooled radiator they were on the road again, Ariel proceeded very cautiously, paying even closer attention to the temperature gauge. She had Jillian ride shotgun in front with her, helping monitor the temperature as well as watching for animals; Annie and Ryan in the back seat. Annie held her brother closely, ready to follow instructions to grab him and bail out on the left side immediately should Ariel need to brake suddenly and steer into a snow bank. Such a maneuver could result in that snow bank blocking the right side door. Roads were not unduly treacherous in cold temperatures with good compact snow and ice. The engine continued to run extremely hot and Ariel genuinely feared leaking gasoline and fire or explosion at any moment. Ryan complained of tummy problems, not helped by his being in the back seat.

They had made it westbound onto the interstate, just over that summit when Ryan threw up, bringing another forced stop. All the water bottles had been emptied to refill the radiator; however there were snow banks from which hands-full of packed snow were carved out to clean up the worst; Ryan and some of the car interior. At least he felt somewhat better. A motorist soon pulled up and offered help; he had actual water, paper towels and even a few crackers to settle Ryan's tummy a little. All the snacks had been consumed.

Hearing about the engine over-heating problem, he just shook his head in disbelief that a husband and father would expect anyone to drive that vehicle in its present condition. He left only after assuring Ariel she was truly a remarkable woman, highly complimenting the children on their behavior and calm. He was still muttering to himself about her having to drive that 'thing' to her dad's funeral while her husband drove a nearly new truck. Ryan had quite proudly shared information about the new truck; after all, it was new and shiny and he was just a little kid, not yet realizing his chattering did nothing to enhance his father's status in the good Samaritan's estimation.

It was quite late by the time they arrived at Roger's parents' home. His dad met them in the driveway, a look of both relief and anxiety on his face. They knew Ariel planned to leave as soon as the girls were out of school, and now it was many hours later and well into the night. Everyone was hustled inside where Grandmother immediately took charge, with baths and food for the kids. After coffee, Ariel and her father-in-law unloaded the car, cleaned the seat and carpets more thoroughly, and he elicited details of their trip, which should have required no more than three hours, even on icy roads.

As she answered the queries, his expression became more and more stern. Why hadn't Roger at least attempted to check the vehicle? Why hadn't she been driving the new truck, not this old station wagon? And when had he last changed the oil, lubricated anything, or even checked the tires?

Ariel had taken it to the service station that morning for an oil change, lubrication, new air filter and tire check; but nothing was done to adjust timing. Roger insisted he alone was capable of correctly performing that task; and that old wagon wasn't of much value anyway.

As she answered the queries, his expression even darker. Why hadn't Roger at least attempted to adjust the timing on the vehicle? Well, he never quite found the time to do that

The answers remained much the same. There never seemed to be enough time, and he needed his truck.

Ariel knew he would be displeased enough over her having had routine service done. She wasn't about to enlist the services of a trained auto mechanic on her own, and Roger never felt that necessary for any vehicle she drove, but carefully avoided mentioning that to her father-in-law. He was upset enough without further details.

Back inside, he pulled his wife aside and talked quietly with her for some time. She had finished getting the children fed, bathed and put to bed, then sent Ariel to a recliner with an afghan and big cup of hot coffee…the cure-all for any Scandinavian in any situation.

The next morning Ariel was given keys for their car to drive to see Edythe and inquire as to funeral arrangements. The station wagon was still in the garage and she was absolutely forbidden to even consider driving it until it was declared road-worthy by her father-in-law.

When Roger arrived that evening he was met by his father, not permitted to set foot in the house, grabbed by an ear and steered into the garage. "You are not leaving this garage until that car is fixed—no coffee, no dinner, nothing. Do you understand? Your mother and I cannot and will not allow you to endanger your wife and our grandchildren by your neglect."

That old station wagon was fixed rather quickly. Somehow there was adequate time. Roger was hungry.

Her husband's funeral provided Edythe time to shine and bask in all the attention afforded a new widow. She fairly purred as accolades regarding her kindness to her spouse as well as the entire community were related. The little church was full, and a goodly number of attendees followed to the cemetery. There the minister continued praising Edythe, saying very little about the deceased.

In giving the basic obituary facts, he noted: Edythe, the grieving widow, the numerous half-brothers, their spouses, children and grandchildren were all named along with cousins; Richard was pre-deceased by his parents and brother. After a somewhat lengthy pause, the minister happened to glance down and see Ariel, Roger, Jillian, Annie and Ryan seated in the second row. "Oh, and Richard is also survived by a daughter, son-in-law and three children." Ariel quite silently, found that highly amusing, knowing Edythe had provided all the family-related information and reviewed it with the minister prior to the services.

A reception at the Pedersen home followed grave-side ceremonies. Ariel was seated on the organ bench when the minister joined her and again launched into glowing praise of Edythe. She was an absolute saint in his eyes. He quite casually mentioned Mr. Pedersen, to the effect he had apparently been an active church member for several years. He did say he had not been very well acquainted with her dad.

Ariel looked him full in the face and calmly responded, "You never knew him and haven't the slightest clue as to who he was, or anything of his character, to say nothing of all he did to establish your church, build and nurture that congregation throughout his life. He also gave up his own income for months to build the education addition superintending volunteer help."

"On two occasions, he traveled at his own expense to Alaska to build mission station structures in Alaska. That particular sacrifice cost him dearly in reduced pension benefits due to the failure of your denomination to fulfill their commitment to him." The man just sat, somewhat stunned, mouth slightly open.

With that Ariel rose and left the room. She much preferred to help wash dishes than listen to anything more that preacher might have to say.

The return trip to Barbaria was delightfully uneventful. Ariel was ordered to follow Roger; she and the children in the now more-smoothly-running station wagon…Roger driving his new truck alone, able to smoke.

Further Deterioration

The art show re-opened as usual the first weekend in May and Ariel was busy setting up and painting in the park every day. In early childhood years, Ryan played nearby. Tourists strolling about town and through the park were quite taken with him, chatting and some even getting down with him to converse about what he was constructing and the toy trucks he favored. A conversant, well-behaved and pleasant child certainly was not a deterrent to sales of Ariel's paintings.

As he grew up he preferred being with friends, checking in with her at the park throughout the day and updating her on his activities. Riding bikes, playing ball, and just hanging with his pals kept him busy after his list of chores at home was completed.

With school vacation, Jillian now wanted real work, not tending paintings. She was quickly hired by one of the numerous restaurants even though she was still too young. Business people in town were not overly concerned about some "minor legalities" such as age, gladly providing jobs for kids capable and willing. Tourist season required many extra hands and the population was limited. Job openings during the tourist season outpaced qualified applicants, and many kids filled the gaps.

Annie spent much of her time with friends, riding bikes for miles and miles. She also had household tasks each day and spent some time with Ryan when he tired of hanging around in the park. Before long she, too, found a 'real' job waiting tables in a local restaurant.

Both girls were excellent workers, glad to be earning their own money for clothes and things they knew Roger would never buy for them. They also realized the money Ariel earned from paintings paid for many household expenses as well as their shoes and school supplies.

Annie was not a particularly happy teen, worrying about her size, weight and that clothes, especially shoes, were hard to find. Jillian favored Ariel's build, both were slender, standard dress and jeans sizes, and could wear pretty shoes. Not so Annie. As she developed it was clear she would retain a much sturdier build, more like Roger's family. Decades later old family photos confirmed that with a Great-Grandmother's picture showing a lady who, with change of clothing style and hairdo, could have been Annie's twin. Buying shoes for her was a challenge at best as her sturdy feet grew. Fortunately during the '70's kids were allowed to wear jeans for school; that helped. She never really accepted that she simply was not the same size and build as her sister or mother, and felt quite cheated.

During the mid-70's gas shortages Roger arranged to stay with Ariel's Seafirst bank friend and his companion in Wenatchee during the week. Ariel purchased as much gas as could be stored in the available cans, using a car bearing odd-numbered license plates on for odd days and the even-numbered plate cars on the even days. That provided gas for him to transport to Wenatchee and share with Richard and James as token payment for his weekly board and room. They both much preferred that Roger go home on Friday nights; however, he routinely stayed, inviting himself out to dinner with them.

One beautiful summer Saturday morning Roger announced he was going to go by motorcycle (the second and larger bike recently purchased) to check out various junk yards for cars and parts, and be gone most of the day. Both Jillian and Annie were working. Ryan stood by with a hopeful look on his face, but Roger said nothing about his going along. Ariel spoke up for him, clearly stating it was an excellent idea and that Ryan would love to go with him. "No, that's not possible," was the terse reply. Despite Ariel's query as to rationale, he offered no explanation – just "no". Ryan was crestfallen, but didn't say a word. Just what was Roger up to and where, indeed, was he going? No answer ever to that question.

Ariel took Ryan with her to Wenatchee for a bit of shopping, lunch at a fast food place he liked, and then to Rocky Reach Dam with loaves of stale bread for the birds. An afternoon touring a power generating facility and feeding ducks with mom is not the same as zooming over highways and side roads on a motorcycle and tromping through junk yards, but Ryan was a good sport about it. As an adult in his 40's he clearly remembered that disappointment and steps Ariel took toward mitigation.

Both girls spent more and more time with friends, working on weekends, and also going to and hosting overnights. In the small town transportation was usually on bikes, or walking in small groups. Gradually a few of Jillian's friends acquired cars, allowing a wider range for their activities.

Late one Friday night/Saturday morning, Ariel received an alarming call from one of the deputies that Jillian was at the little hospital following a vehicle accident. "No, Jillian's in her room, asleep" Ariel protested. She had checked on each of the children less than an hour previously.

He then asked that she do so again, and he would stay on the line. She discovered pillows arranged under blankets, not her daughter. The deputy assured her Jillian's injuries were minor, but that sutures were required and he would fill in more details when she arrived at the hospital, which she did within minutes. Jillian received stitches over one eye, and was horribly embarrassed and ever so sorry about the entire matter. Those egress windows in each bedroom intended solely as quick escape from any potential fire also allowed for sneaking out for late-night adventures. Jillian was not cited for under-age alcohol consumption because the officer was certain Ariel would address that matter. Not so for some others involved in the drinking and driving fun that resulted in a vehicle off the road and in a creek together with multiple injuries, mostly minor.

A very contrite Jillian was allowed to go home, drink more plain water and be tearfully tucked back into the bed she sorely regretted having left.

Ariel did not call Roger in Wenatchee until a reasonable breakfast hour. During the gas shortages, he had been staying there during the weeknights, but not returning home until later on Saturdays.

That morning, she spoke with Richard, asking him to simply inform Roger that he was needed at home; the emergency had been addressed, however he needed to come home as soon as possible. The message was delivered.

Roger continued a leisurely breakfast, with seconds on food and coffee before casually departing. Some two hours later Richard called to inquire how everyone was, presuming Roger to be there. He was not. Richard's concern was immediately apparent and also grew; neither had any idea where Roger might be.

After being assured that Jillian was not seriously injured, and was sleeping off her ill-considered adventure, Richard tried to soft-pedal the degree of his consternation as to Roger's delay. He found it alarming as he had left their house hours before, more than enough to drive 25 miles. He did recall Roger mentioning car parts, tried to reassure Ariel, and urged her to please call him if there was anything at all he or James could do. They both cared deeply for Ariel and the children.

Years earlier, in Seattle, Richard provided Ariel transportation to their work at the bank; frequently picking up the little girls in his arms and carrying them across to their sitter Helene's house. Both men felt every bit as protective of Ariel's children as they did their nieces and nephews.

When he finally arrived after noon, Ariel was totally distraught, with all manner of possible disasters having churned in her mind. Roger immediately criticized her for even suggesting that he should have come home hours earlier when he had been notified. Just what was her problem, anyway? And why was Richard worried? Why had he called? It was none of his concern.

He had car parts to buy and a wonderful vintage vehicle to check out. He did eventually go downstairs, wake Jillian and talk with her at some length in her room.

Roger's criticism of everything and anything increased steadily. Jillian graduated high school and Annie was now a junior; Ryan still in grade school. Both girls had winter part-time and full-time summer jobs in retail and food service. Jillian managed a gift shop for several weeks while the owners traveled in Europe. Annie waitressed very successfully at local establishments, garnering good tips in addition to her wages. Ariel worked two winters packing fruit at the local warehouse, then in retail grocery, finally as front office and x-ray tech for a local dentist. She also kept painting and building inventory for future shows.

The girls now bought most of their own clothing and learned to make good choices. Sometimes the early lessons were difficult, but in time those were very helpful. Ryan played every possible sport, except football; he had never liked the concept of hitting and being hit, hard. That was perfectly fine with Ariel. She still sewed most of her clothes, purchasing jeans occasionally on sale.

More and more old cars rolled into the yard; occasionally Roger sold one only to make room for one or two new acquisitions. None was ever restored despite all his grand plans. Included was his stated desire to purchase a flatbed truck on which to haul those wonderfully restored treasures; to where was not identified. He also planned to mount a camper unit on that truck and expected Ariel to be thrilled at the prospect of a transient life in a truck. She was to paint, frame and sell her work while he showed off his cars and searched for still more to add to the collection. A visit to an antique car museum had evidently prompted the idea he would have sufficient funds to acquire something similar. To whom were paintings to be sold in ever-changing environments? From where was the money to come for travel? To acquire still more old vehicles?

He never comprehended her lack of interest, much less flat refusal to even consider such a plan. The concept that becoming established in the creative arts arena, with ability to sell pieces on any regular basis required being established in a locale, not transient, had never entered his mind. She had just begun to have her work known, recognized and acquired in Seattle when he had initiated the move to Barbaria. Now his scheme was to pick up and basically become transient? Work by unknown painters does not sell very successfully.

He had fully expected her to be thrilled with a transient lifestyle. He could do that any time he wished; but Ariel was not going. His wishes had always come first; not this time. Besides, there would be no income. She would need a good-paying full-time job in order to meet rudimentary expenses, and their children should be able to expect some degree of financial stability. They were still in school and there was no provision whatever made for college. He had resisted all thought, much less implementation, of saving any money, to say nothing of investing for their future. What was Roger thinking? Or was he thinking at all of anyone but himself and what he wanted…right now, never mind later.

Rape by Cop

Roger's participation in the local Sheriff posse centered primarily on riding with deputies evenings and weekends, further limiting his time with family, or doing much toward his promised restoration of the old cars. His absence also meant any household responsibilities were further neglected. He was included in all the social events held by deputies, with Ariel's attendance not only clearly expected, but she was also specifically and personally invited. That did not meet with Roger's approval. However, showing up stag would have been totally unacceptable to deputies and other posse members.

One deputy was regularly designated to remain sober at the social events and make certain everyone got home safely. He frequently called upon Ariel to help provide transportation. The huge old Cadillac she drove was excellent for transporting the entire Little League ball team and all their gear, or a bunch of drunken lawmen.

After one such party Ariel drove miles and miles over the snow-packed, icy back roads, delivering deputies, some of their wives having left the gathering earlier. She finally arrived home with only Roger draped across the back seat, snoring loudly, too drunk to even sit up. The warm car quickly turned cold in the sub-zero temperatures, and would soon dip even further. Attempts to rouse Roger were not successful. Briefly, Ariel entertained the idea of simply letting him lie there, half-slumped on the floor; nature would soon decide his fate. She certainly could not be blamed for his drinking to the point of being comatose. He would not be aware or suffer in any way…just keep on snoring in the freezing car. She didn't need to do anything, just stop trying to wake him enough to move.

No, that couldn't happen. She still had to live with herself and sleep with herself at night. Single status would assuredly be better for her, and probably for her children; the constant criticism would be gone along with pain of being otherwise largely ignored. Her life would be so much easier; and he had excellent insurance. She just needed to walk inside, check the kids and cats, bring the dog indoors, turn off lights and go to bed. How simple. Ariel hated the thoughts that had not crept, but raced through her mind tempting her to freedom from the trap she had so purposefully entered years before. .

No, she couldn't walk away; she had to keep trying, had to get him into the house where he would be warm and either sleep off the alcohol, or vomit at least some of it…not freeze to death. He was too heavy for her to carry, or drag down the slightly sloped path, much less hoist up steps.

Ariel changed from her party clothes, donned jeans, warm sweater, winter boots, jacket and gloves before trudging back to the street and opening the rear car door. It took many hard slaps, pulling arms and tugging his feet out the door before she achieved any response whatever indicating Roger was even still alive. Respirations were very slow and shallow.

He finally muttered a few oaths, berated her for bothering him but was obviously alive. Why didn't she just leave him alone; she always bugged him and got in his way; never letting him just rest and sleep. The familiar grumbling and negativity assured Ariel he would probably live…with a significant hang-over. She would miss that…needing to be at work in a few hours.

She finally wrestled him out of the car, propped him up as best she could on the slick pathway and rather shoved him in the direction of the steps and front door. A few halting staggers were accomplished before he veered to the left and crashed face first into a massive pine tree. That impact restored sufficient awareness to allow Ariel to guide him back down to the path where he crawled up the steps, across the porch and through the open door. He actually managed the way to his room and flopped fully dressed, on his bed

What had happened to Roger? She certainly hadn't married this grumpy, consistently negative, totally uncommunicative person, now dead drunk. Granted he had never appeared a brilliant intellectual or particularly sensitive to her, but had been able to calmly discuss events and consider at least an opinion other than his own on occasion. That he considered his point of view to be superior in most instances had always been a given, but he hadn't immediately shut others down. Where had that other person gone? No answer.

She should have figured out during the dating period that he was quite inept socially, but that was something that could be addressed, social awareness and manner improved with time. Certainly possible as both presumably matured and grew, both personally and in their relationship. One aspect had escaped her; both people needed to mature and want to become more knowledgeable, discerning and perceptive. It was clear no answers would be forthcoming this night.

Ariel washed up and crawled into her sleeping bag on the living room floor. In just a couple hours, she was scheduled to work at the grocery store.

It seemed like barely minutes before Ariel was jolted awake by loud pounding on the front door. She jumped up, grabbed a throw around her and turned on the porch light. A uniformed, armed deputy identified himself and ordered her to open the door; he was looking for someone. Clutching the fluffy throw, Ariel complied and he stepped in…turning off the porch light as he did so. What was this all about; she knew him of course, but what was he doing in her house?

Wearing a serious and stern expression, he claimed to be looking for his wife. Did Ariel know where she was? Was she here? What? Looking for his wife, here? Why? Ariel had no idea at all where his wife might be, but certainly not at her house. She scarcely knew the woman. Why would that woman be in her house?

This guy was on duty, so had not attended the party. His wife had, along with a couple other wives of duty officers. From Ariel's casual observation, she and her friends seemed to enjoy the party; drinking and dancing in a perfectly normal manner. Why would he think Ariel knew anything about her plans; they certainly were not friends, having met only once before.

Nothing he said made any sense whatever; but, he was uniformed, armed, well over six feet tall, far stronger than she and obviously in control.

He took a step closer and his expression changed. He took hold of her arm, pushed her around the stone fireplace toward her sleeping bag bed on the floor. His side-way thin half-smile left little doubt as to intent.

Jillian, Annie and Ryan were all sound asleep in their basement rooms and Peppy had joined Ryan in the farthest location from the front door. Roger was completely passed out fully dressed on his bed, having barely made it into the house; not a source of any help in normal circumstances, and definitely not in his present state. Besides, Roger considered this deputy his pal, his good buddy.

Ariel gritted her teeth and silently submitted to being pushed down to the floor, her gown pulled over her face, and legs forced apart. "Just don't think about anything; don't fight; stay quiet; don't make a sound; it won't last long and he will leave. He can't be here very many minutes, he's on duty and has to check in regularly." One thing she knew for certain; she would never, ever forget his leering grin as he lunged on top of her, gun belt digging into her flesh and thrust his fully-engorged penis into her. This lout lacked even a shred of decency.

Thankfully it was brief. He rose, adjusted his trousers and gun belt, and flippantly thanked her, waved as he closed the door and said "see you later sweetie, good night".

"Oh no, you won't," she hissed and curled up on the floor with a bit of sleeping bag over her shoulder. "You won't ever see me anywhere outside a crowd in a very public place," her silent pledge.

She knew that her only protection was silence and not ever encountering him anywhere, alone. She certainly could not file a complaint against him, he was an officer of the law and his word would be accepted without question; hers highly suspect. Roger would not believe her; he frequently accused her of carrying on affairs with any number of men. He talked about her allegedly numerous affairs during his ride-along nights with deputies. Some of them were acquainted with Ariel and knew Rogers was lying through his teeth.

However, in that day society in general still presumed a woman to be at fault in any such situation, having enticed some hapless man by her feminine wiles, manner or attire. No, Ariel must remain silent, never even hinting at having been raped by a local cop in her own home.

The jerk was a sheriff's deputy, permanent resident in the area, not apt to be going away anytime soon. She would undoubtedly encounter him again as long as she remained in Barbaria. A most unpleasant certainty.

More than twenty-five years later she first spoke of it and to her utter amazement, was not only believed, but tenderly comforted as cleansing tears flowed. Times had changed and also her environment.

Still Things Worsen

The already sparse communication between Roger and Ariel dwindled further, becoming virtually non-existent; limited primarily to his accusations, criticism and strong disapproval of her. Ariel maintained as much silence and distance as possible.

At one point, however, Roger suggested they take a trip together, and he mentioned New Orleans. She briefly wondered if perhaps he wanted to make some attempt at an actual relationship at this late date. One neighbor had observed Ariel doing most of the physical work at the home, and that Roger didn't spend much time with her or his children. She had also been seen chatting with Roger a few times; and he was definitely not smiling in response to whatever she was telling him.

Ariel had once commented on wanting to see that part of the country, thinking in terms of warm fragrant breezes and carriage rides under magnolia blossoms, listening to improvisational jazz in bistros, sipping wine at sidewalk cafes, and touring period mansions. In those daydream scenarios Roger was quite absent.

For him to now suggest they travel any distance in each other's company was absurd; they were scarcely on speaking terms.

Ariel replied in as calm and non-accusatory a tone possible that she truly did not wish to do that. First of all there were no discretionary funds available to pay for such a trip; she had enough trouble managing normal and usual household expenses with what of Roger's earnings made it to the checking account and her meager earnings. She paid many bills from part time grocery store pay. His monthly gas credit card bills alone were astounding.

The primary reason, as she also tried to explain it is not where one goes, or what one does, but with whom, that makes travel or everyday life enjoyable, or not. She clearly did not wish to go anywhere with Roger. The every Friday at the same local restaurant, and obligatory holiday dinners with his parents were more than enough to endure knowing everything she said or did was subject to critical review and blame.

So the short answer was, no, she did not want to go to New Orleans with him, or anywhere else for that matter.

Some months later he wanted to purchase a larger Hammond organ as an alleged gift for her. A nice gesture, perhaps, but again, where would money for such a purchase come from? Additionally, there were two Hammond Spinet organs in the house already. Where could a third, larger instrument be placed? Also, when might she have the time to use it, between working at the store, painting for the outdoor art shows, changing the works in various Puget Sound galleries, keeping up the house and yard, attempting to parent children? This idea was neither practical nor logical.

Was he beginning to think she might be less than delighted with him? Weird way of showing that, but after all, it was Roger.

Ariel pondered at times just what went on in his head that produced these apparently sudden wishes to go somewhere, buy another unwanted and unnecessary item that she was supposed to like. If he knew of an extra dime in household coffers, he immediately spent a quarter and charged the difference. What was he thinking?

At the retail grocery she volunteered to make pizzas early mornings, return home after Roger had left with the lunch she packed and left on the counter for him. Then the kids were off to school, and she did laundry, painted a while until school was out. Ryan had time with friends, the girls worked for a couple hours, and they had homework. She then set the table, put dinner in the oven on the timer, and returned to the store before Roger's return from work. It was only a few blocks from the house, so she frequently walked, enjoying the solitude and exercise. She worked until closing, counted out the tills and put cash and checks receipts in the safe, and locked the place for the night. Long days, but more peaceful than could be achieved any other way she could think of. Just hard work was no problem; being constantly criticized, and on guard, was.

Ariel also met weekly freight trucks in the wee morning hours, caught boxes from the unloading chute and stacked the incoming merchandise. Some of the male drivers found it amusing to send heavy boxes, especially canned goods, down to her with an extra shove. Most only tried that once when they saw she was quite capable of catching and stacking those, never stopping to rest.

A Side-step?

Ariel stashed as much of her earnings from the market and paintings sales as possible. She truly feared for her financial future. The slowly-accumulated bills were secreted in an old trunk in the loft where she painted. Roger never questioned her handling of the finances, so long as she did not expect any increase in deposited amounts from his wages regardless of incremental pay increases or significant overtime. Bills were timely paid and he enjoyed the resultant good credit rating; he had money in pocket to spend whenever and wherever he liked, primarily purchases of more vehicles, and rounds of drinks at his favorite haunts. How all that occurred was none of his concern.

While still working part-time at the retail grocery and only beginning to dare contemplate a possible change in her life, she met a wholesale/retail businessman who imported specialty products from various parts of the globe. He had come into the store hoping to speak with the owner; and in whose absence was directed to Ariel.

In addition to the wholesale import business he also owned a small retail outlet in the Puget Sound area featuring specialty import foods. As he was branching out in that market he wanted to put some of the import food items in Barbaria. The location presented an opportunity to test tourist traffic interest. He felt it would be a good business move there and also benefit his Puget Sound retail outlet from tourists having found product they liked while vacationing and perhaps want access in the Puget Sound area. Having visited this store and seeing how scrupulously clean it was maintained and the volume of tourist traffic, deemed it quite suitable for his product lines.

With the owner away tending the wholesale and dairy end of the grocery enterprise, he made his pitch to Ariel. He found her utterly enchanting, quick to follow his presentation, ask appropriate and sometimes probing questions regarding his businesses and the accounting processes involved relative to this small store. He considered this outlet, well situated in a tourist area to be one in which to introduce his line of imported product to the region. She gathered his business card; print materials, clarified accounting information, took copious notes, and politely informed him the packet would be presented to the owner upon his return.

Would she consider having dinner with him? "Thank you for the invitation, but no," she replied, quickly explaining that she was married and had a family.

His response was that presented no problem, it was only dinner with perhaps more detail regarding his business proposal. She just smiled and shook her head – "thank you, no". He would be returning to the town in a few weeks. Perhaps they could at least meet for lunch; he made no secret of being totally smitten with her appearance and obvious intelligence. Ariel was stunned, barely able to hide her consternation. What was he saying? She concentrated on bringing this meeting to a close, thanked him for the presentation, and quickly but politely showed him out.

What to think of that? Nothing. He had to be slightly demented. After nearly forty years of denigration, she knew what she was. None of those glowing attributes related to her in any way. She went back to trimming, wrapping and pricing beef in the meat room.

His words had sounded nice of course, but he was a salesman first and foremost, not likely ever to be seen again, and that was just fine with Ariel. Even if he did return for whatever reason, no good of any sort could possibly result from even speaking with him on any subject but product marketing.

She was so very wrong. Only a couple weeks later he returned, ostensibly to talk with the store owner about stocking the import product line. After a brief conversation, they shook hands concluding business and he appeared to be leaving the store. Ariel was busy stocking and facing shelves, only glancing up occasionally. He was a rather handsome fellow, and looked to be somewhat younger than she … but, whatever; no concern of hers.

Next thing she knew he was at her side, smiling and saying how good it was to see her again, followed by more compliments. She truly did not know what to do about this.

No, he was not going to give up and kept contacting her every few days with no pretense of conducting business with the store owner. He had learned she painted in oils and had some work on display in galleries in the Puget Sound region. Would she consider placing some in his retail business? Well, yes, she supposed that could be done; more outlets in that region could result in additional sales. Arrangements were set for her to see his retail business and consider placing work there on her next trip to re-supply area galleries.

Over the next several months, she made the usual trips to replenish galleries and picking up occasional checks here and there for items sold. She had placed a few pieces with the sales rep for his retail outlet, and some of those also sold... surprisingly well. After a few such visits, she also enjoyed dinners with him at very nice restaurants, wonderful conversations, some pampering she thoroughly enjoyed and a bit of light romance. They even danced in hotel lounges...a totally new experience for Ariel.

Yes, he was younger than she, by some five years. He wanted to take her to Hawaii for one weekend; oh no, she simply could not do that. Ariel just knew if she dared, the plane would go down. Her name would appear on the manifest. Her sin of daring to enjoy herself and have fun would most assuredly find her out. Beside which, she was by now, actually involved in an extra-marital affair. Any aircraft she might dare board would most assuredly crash; that was an absolute.

This man said repeatedly how much he loved her; she was beautiful, even gorgeous; he was proud to be seen with her on his arm. Wow ... was this different? Totally. She didn't quite believe all of his compliments and praise; but did begin to feel slightly more confident about herself. Maybe Edythe and Roger were not totally accurate in their evaluations of her as dis-functional. After his declaration of intent and actually wedding her, Roger never wanted her company in public, nor to be seen with her, preferring to present as a bachelor; this man wanted to be seen with her, in private and in public, openly in front of everyone. Entering gourmet restaurants with Ariel, he fairly beamed, an arm around her and requesting the best seating. She was treated to the finest accommodations, including spa visits. He sought her input when shopping for a new luxury vehicle, being certain her preferences were included. Was Ariel confused, along with being delighted? To be sure; but was any of this real?

He also wanted her to divorce Roger, and marry him; he could provide for her every wish and loved her, just as she was. He absolutely could not understand why she would ever feel inadequate in any way. How could such a thing have happened? Ariel explained as best she could – that was all she had heard since earliest childhood; naturally she knew that to be accurate. Not so, was his consistent answer, not at all.

While in town he had made a point of finding out just who this Roger person was, and having overheard him talking to a local merchant judged him to be a total clod, unworthy of Ariel in every way.

No, Ariel had married Roger "for better or for worse" and had to stick it out; at least for the *one week at a time* program under which she had managed for years. Friday to Friday, she could do that. And she had accomplished that, one week at a time for nearly twenty years. The 'worse' she understood, where was the 'better'? No answer.

This persistent fellow had to be refused a number of times before he finally accepted that Ariel was not going to leave Roger, at least not for him, or in the reasonably foreseeable future. Eventually he accepted her statements as irrefutable fact. She ended their relationship, realizing all too well it would serve no benefit to either of them in a longer term.

While fully realizing she had broken her marriage vows, Ariel also had to admit the affair had not only been helpful, but even necessary to provide her a degree of self-confidence otherwise totally unattainable. Surprisingly, she felt minimal guilt despite her actions which were absolutely contrary to all her beliefs.

Later she spoke with a local minister and questioned why this affair did not cause her more mental and spiritual anguish, when it most definitely should have. He also knew Roger and was well aware of his involvement with local law enforcement, lack of any apparent interest in family as well as his frequently openly-voiced disparaging remarks about Arial along with his sexually-explicit comments made to waitresses while dining with his family. The minister listened most thoughtfully to her brief review of childhood, the marriage to escape Edythe and assessment of her then-current mental state before quietly answering very calmly.

"We are each a child of God, whom He loves and cherishes. He gave us free will, instructions, and commandments for guidance. I strongly believe there is God's perfect will for our lives, and His permissive will which is at times divergent; but in no way diminishes His love. You were disparaged, criticized, demeaned and put down for decades, left without any degree of self worth by people who allegedly should have loved you. You stepped outside the marriage vows, absolutely; however, did your husband not have equal responsibility for his vow to love, honor and cherish you? Did he keep that vow? I know him well enough casually, to think he did not; an opinion reached from observing him and his actions these past few years. He only tore you down as a person with constant criticism and blame; not only in private, but frequently in the public community. Witnessing consistently negative behavior by one parent against the other presents a negative perception of marriage and family for children, both boys and girls. They learn from parents how to treat others, and unfortunately the poor examples seem to be adopted quite readily.

Another man was able to give you some appreciation of personal value, self confidence and courage to live life more fully and joyously. A non-theologically appropriate means granted, and his personal motives may not have been completely praiseworthy, but appear to have been quite effective. You achieved significant mental and emotional healing without harming your children or calling attention to yourself. Seeing their mother becoming a stronger more optimistic and positive individual can only benefit them. As an acquaintance or as a pastor, I cannot stand in a position to judge you poorly or negatively.

I cannot accept that God places any of his children on this earth merely to survive and endure until freed by death. We all are created in His image, loved by Him, to serve Him and do His will – in whatever circumstance and manner that may be. And yes, many times the pathway is dim; we only see one day at a time."

Ariel was stunned; she had expected a massive dose of condemnation, and received instead additional affirmation that she was at least a somewhat viable and functional human being.

That brief affair had been scary, thrilling, utterly terrifying and marvelously wonderful; she had learned so much, primarily about herself. She had ended it on her terms.

Jillian Marries

Ariel had carefully saved earnings from the retail grocery job, and being paid in cash under the table had made that much easier. Later she stashed wages from her dental office job. She had a little over $3,000 saved to help her get away and survive financially for a while. It was a pretty good plan that should have worked. However, that was derailed.

Jillian had been taking classes at the community college and working in accounting at a Wenatchee department store. She had also been dating a son of the School District Superintendent. Ariel had tried desperately to steer Jillian away from an early marriage, stressing the need for higher education, and how she regretted her own lack of a degree. Jillian had nodded politely, and verbally agreed; however, she was soon engaged and planning a mid-August outdoor wedding. She had absolutely no clue as to her mother's stash of get-away money hidden in the loft trunk.

Ariel strongly encouraged the idea that they simply live together first before marrying, or parting ways if that didn't work well; better to give the whole thing a try. Mentally in anguish, Ariel quietly outlined the advantages of giving the living together concept a chance. If they were blissfully happy, totally compatible and eager to spend the next decades together, raise children, and eventually hold hands rocking on a front porch in the sunset…great. By all means, marry. If not…better to find out before both lives were further complicated – personally, legally and financially.

Jillian was utterly horrified at that suggestion, refusing to even consider it. Wedding planning progressed despite all carefully cautious attempts at logic. Ariel astutely avoided criticism of Jillian's choice despite his personality being amazingly similar to Roger's and in many ways, Edythe's. They were very controlling personality types, just different in the manner of implementation. Daughter followed the path of selecting a spouse most like that of her dominant parent, as had Ariel.

The selected site was a beautiful, lovely setting on the Fish Hatchery grounds along the river, a backdrop of tall trees, with potted asters and myrtle at an archway. Jillian paid for half of her dress cost, Ariel picked up the balance.

She also paid the bulk of costs for having the basement of the house finished, along with invitations, venue, reception refreshments and flowers, all of which virtually wiped out her get-away stash. Roger contributed $600 toward finishing of the basement, and then created quite a spectacle at the reception, turning pockets inside out, claiming his daughter's wedding had 'cleaned him out'.

The groom's car had suddenly developed some sort of mechanical problem just before the wedding, so Ariel gave Jillian her credit card along with keys to her Cadillac to use for their honeymoon. Both were returned in good condition.

When threats of being declared insane and placed in a mental institution, along with not-so-veiled death threats increased, Ariel knew a decision about her own situation could not be delayed much further. Holes had been found on the top side of her old station wagon tail pipe. She used that car for hauling paintings rather than the Cadillac when gas prices were high and supplies of fuel short. It got far better mileage when it ran. That tie rods showed signs of having been filed, was also noted when she had the vehicle serviced, not waiting for Roger to do it. A garage employee brought it to her attention, commenting on how strange that was – not something they saw, regardless of poor general vehicle condition. Roger routinely serviced his truck and could easily do the same for Ariel's old station wagon, but never quite found the time. Was it possible he wanted those to be discovered by a third party, perhaps so Ariel would realize some of the capabilities available to him? That remained another open question.

She had purchased the '68 Cadillac to use for working more distant art shows. It held all her work and supplies with adequate room for sleeping if she hadn't sold enough pieces to afford a motel room.

She hated the thought of a divorce. That simply was not part of her background and absolutely unacceptable. She had promised to spend the rest of her life with Roger. Besides, how could she survive financially? When sales of paintings went well that was one thing; in off seasons, there simply was no money. There were no outdoor shows during cold months, mall shows few and far between, with gallery sales woefully uncertain in the best of times.

Shortly after their marriage, he had begun making very specific negative comments – directly, and to other people. He consistently remarked on her being unattractive, over-weight (some 110#), unintelligent and totally incapable of accomplishing anything. He referred to her as a 'pumpkin' or 'the wife', if at all; never was any remotely endearing term used.

By the time Jillian arrived he clearly did not wish to be seen in public with Ariel or Jillian, except at his parents' home and family gatherings. The criticisms and demeaning references echoed what Edythe had said throughout all her childhood and teen years. Roger frequently asserted that only by reliance on his abilities, earnings, skill and expertise did she have a roof over her head, clothes on her back and food to eat. She had never argued or disputed his assessment or Edythe's … it was precisely what had been insinuated, implied and specifically stated consistently from her earliest memories. She was inadequate in every possible way; that was familiar and within her comfort level. She did wonder on several occasions why she was so utterly unworthy in her home environments, while considered intelligent, efficient and quite competent in school and workplace situations. Another unanswered question, or maybe just one in a series of same.

Most of her carefully hoarded get-away cash had been spent on Jillian's wedding and finishing the basement before Roger's relatives began arriving for the occasion. His $600 contribution had helped, but not come close to covering basement finishing by any stretch; and she had wedding expenses. Jillian covered half the cost of her dress, which she should not have had to do in a normal family. Ariel had simply peeled off currency to pay for dresses and fabrics, flowers, reception expenses and builders. She now struggled to build back some cash reserve against the probability she needed to flee in a hurry.

Finally one afternoon when there was no one else in the house, and after berating her over some new alleged failure, Roger angrily shouted that he had all her so-called friends ready to testify against her in a sanity hearing, she would be put into an institution for the remainder of her life. She would never see her children again; she would have no money whatever. No one would help her. She would remain incarcerated in an asylum, period, end of discussion. Reality hit, hard.

Even he knew it was not feasible now to have her committed involuntarily as Edythe had done to her husband Richard in 1935. However, he was well aware the distress this threat caused Ariel. Her Dad's nominal sharing of his year in the Stillwater Insane Asylum was clear in her memory, as Roger knew it would be. He had played his best hand in this game of total control, having no clue that in actuality Ariel was not quite the timid, stupid, incompetent and inept mouse he wished.

His tirade went on, "You can't do anything on your own. Without me you will starve. No one will help you. You are damn lucky to put your feet under my table."

She sat frozen on the arm of a love seat; looked straight into his face, "this is 1978, not 1935, and you simply cannot have me involuntarily committed; it won't work. There is no possible way you can prove me a danger to myself, my children or anyone else. Your scheme will not work."

A look of horror on his face, Roger raced downstairs, threw himself on the concrete floor, screaming, banging his head and fists on the floor. Ariel sat, immobile on the wooden love seat arm until she was certain he had stayed downstairs. Ever so carefully eased down from the love seat and crawled to the bathroom, violently ill.

He wanted to do to her what Edythe had done to Dad. She simply had to escape. He had been quite careful about not inflicting noticeable physical abuse, but the mental and emotional abuse had truly become unbearable. She immediately started searching for an affordable apartment in Wenatchee.

Ariel also began a serious job search. Her dental office work paid $3.75 per hour and that only after a recent 25-cent per hour increase. A pleasant environment and extremely nice person to work for, but it obviously was not sufficient to support herself and Ryan. Wages in Wenatchee were not high by any means, but better than Barbaria, and she needed to relocate. There must be at least some distance from Roger before she could feel at all safe. Even twenty-five miles would help, though she would have preferred twenty-five thousand.

An apartment was rented; payment of the two-months' rent and deposit seriously depleted her funds. Each day she loaded her old Cadillac with personal property, first her art supplies and easel, framed canvases, then pottery, and most of her clothing. Many items came from the loft, and their absence went completely unnoticed by Roger. She purchased a set of commercial dinnerware, service for eight, at a home furnishings sale, which was swapped out for her hand-thrown pieces. Roger had always dismissed porcelain and stoneware that Ariel had made and fired as inferior to any commercial product, and of no actual value. He made no comment as to the new table settings.

A limited number of pots and baking pans were also removed, together with her grandmother's cast iron fry pans and vintage Dutch ovens. Not a single question came from Roger, which was what she expected; after all, he just did not open cupboard doors or kitchen drawers. She was not about to leave her Grandmother's cast iron pieces for him to destroy.

She also purchased new wardrobe items for Roger, slacks, shirts and even underwear and socks. He might want to go 'a-courtin' and would need decent clothes. No questions were posed regarding his dresser drawers filling up or the content of his side of the closet increasing while hers shrank.

The physical aspect of their relationship had never been particularly thrilling or adventurous, diminished to being nearly non-existent for months. One evening when Ariel was hanging his freshly-ironed shirts in the closet, Roger grabbed her and demanded sex. Her immediate, but calm, quiet and firm response was a simple, "No". His rage erupted, but apparently something about Ariel's firm answer and expression prevented him from any further action against her. He tore out the back door and down the stairs to his garage. Ariel could hear tools and car parts hitting walls and vehicles; finished ironing and hanging clothes with trembling hands.

Departure

Early morning on a regular work day, Ariel handed Roger his lunch and thermos with the calm statement, "I'm leaving you today, and will not be living here any more." His expression did not change and nothing else was said. He just took the lunch items from her, walked down the steps, started his truck and roared down the alley.

She cleaned the kitchen, vacuumed carpets, scrubbed both bathrooms, saw Annie and Ryan off to school, and then went to work at the dental office. She had called the one person she hoped was still a friend and asked for help. They had painted in the park, thrown and fired pottery and hiked the Cascades together; Ariel prayed she could be counted on.

Could she? Absolutely, and she would bring another of their hiking pals, a strong young fellow with another truck. They both would not only be willing, but utterly delighted to assist in her long-overdue escape. Time was set for noon; no dental appointments were scheduled that afternoon so she would not cause her dentist a major problem.

Ariel had index cards each listing items to be removed from the loft, main floor, and basement. No time would be wasted in decision-making or searching. Time most assuredly was of the essence.

The dye was cast. There was no turning back.

SECTION V
Choice

How Did She Dare

How did Ariel dare try to escape the second oppressive situation in her life? She had fully accepted during her forty years through the alleged fine, upstanding Christian parental relationship of her childhood and subsequent marriage to Roger, that she was totally unfit. She simply did not measure up in even the remotest manner. For decades she had been told repeatedly by Edythe and then Roger that she was unintelligent, ignorant, stupid, of no value in either house, and not the least attractive in any manner whatever.

Other than school teachers and employers, only Dad offered her any encouragement, severely limited by Edythe's control. Any positive comments from teachers only elicited stern instruction that she must improve. Favorable comments her Dad made were made very quietly to Ariel alone, not within Edythe's hearing.

Many times Ariel heard Edythe sigh and lament to one of her church friends that she, "simply must do something about Richard." Just what she must do was never stated, and for years Ariel had no clue. When Dad finally told her about being committed to the insane asylum and then released into Edythe's care, custody and control for life, she understood what Edythe meant. She could have him committed if she wished.

Years later Ariel realized that to be untrue, especially in light of significant changes in both state and federal laws pursuant to mental illnesses and patient commitments. Regardless, it had a chilling effect.

That highly negative evaluation had simply been part of her very being. She was inadequate in every respect. Dad was gone.

School and work situations had been decidedly opposite.

Employers appreciated her abilities, skills, intelligence and willingness to exceed their expectations. The grocery store owner for whom she worked insisted she be a signatory on the business checking account. He left all the business and accounting matters to her when away on business trips.

Edythe, and then Roger, derided and brushed aside any positive references to Ariel. Roger actually questioned his children's parentage, but backed off when Ariel challenged him to simply obtain a blood test. Each child's blood type was of record as was hers; his on old Navy Reserve information. DNA testing had not yet been developed.

From where then, did she acquire the courage and just plain daring to even attempt an escape? From what she knew; but into what? What could she do to support herself and children? Jillian was married and employed, but Annie in high school and Ryan still dependent. There were no available employment opportunities in the town that paid living wages; apple-packing, waitress and clerk jobs, part-time office positions, all very low-paying. Her job with the long-established dentist was one of the best to be had at $3.75 per hour.

Extrication

Her flight from Barbaria that early afternoon in late October was utterly terrifying. She just knew, not thought, Roger would kill, or have her killed, before she could reach the hoped-for safety of the little apartment. He had joined the posse shortly after moving to Barbaria which enabled him to ride with local law enforcement. He considered the deputies his close friends. Staging a one-car traffic incident, investigated and declared accidental due to driver error, would be simple to arrange. Roger could easily accomplish that, including an iron-clad alibi with credible witnesses to his being miles away at the time. In Ariel's present state of mind, the possibilities, though more than slightly off-kilter, were ominous, utterly real and endless.

The 25-mile stretch of highway along the river provided numerous easily available accident sites. Having Ryan in the car with her could possibly thwart him, but that was iffy at best.

There had been so many dire and quite specific threats. The directly stated threats to kill her and get her out of his way so she could no longer hold him back from some marvelous but unstated achievement, attempts to choke her with her own hair which would not leave such obvious physical marks, clear evidence of tampering with her vehicles and finally threatening her with asylum confinement. That had been the final impetus forcing her to flee.

She had taken less than $100 from the joint checking account and left the checkbook on the kitchen counter. The savings account of $56 was closed; she used that to purchase black pumps and a blazer on sale. Job search was the next major hurdle. She and Ryan had purchased flatware and a few groceries, which were now carefully put away.

Nearly three years later, on the witness stand, Roger angrily pointed at her with the accusation she had "cleaned out *his* savings account." Judge looked at her, questioningly with a raised brow, and asked for her reply. "Yes, Your Honor, I withdrew the entire $56 with which I purchased shoes and a blazer for my job search." He just smiled, and indicated Roger should continue with his testimony.

Locking the apartment door that first night, Ariel reveled in a new sense of freedom, of self, and safety. Even with severe lack of funds, no job and Ryan to provide for, she felt more upbeat and hopeful than she ever had in all her life.

She had taken the small old black and white portable television and soon Ryan was perched on cushions watching a cartoon while she fixed their supper. His bed and many of his toys were set up in the smaller bedroom; she would sleep on those cushions in the larger room once Ryan was settled. She had also taken the love seat and left the long couch in Barbaria; both items in dark vinyl and plain wood that dissembled for easy moving. A teak dinette table purchased at sale, and four vinyl chairs Richard and James had given her, coke bottles and plank shelving pretty much completed the furnishings. Art supplies were stacked in her room.

She hoped Ryan would at least consider transfer to a Wenatchee school; standards were significantly higher and he would have far more opportunities, scholastically and in sports. Quite predictably he did not want to change schools in November and leave his friends. For the next month she took him to school each morning and worked at the dental office.

Leaving her job with the dentist was difficult for both. He liked her work and appreciated her having made considerable changes to update and improve administrative procedures. She really enjoyed working for him. He and his wife were instrumental in her beginning to see that married life did not need to be perpetually grim. They were delightful and happy people she truly liked.

She was able to find a replacement person for her job, mitigating the doctor's need to initiate a search process. She had worked with Judy at the grocery store, knew her to be bright, capable and highly desirous of better employment. In addition, she wore the same sizes Ariel did; uniforms all fit, which saved him money there, as well. He still hated to see Ariel leave, but had some knowledge of Roger's general demeanor, and understood her reasoning.

Judy picked up the office routine and procedures quickly during the short period of training, and continued working in the dental office for several years. She quit only after meeting a recently-arrived Swiss farmer who had found her when a toothache brought him to the office. They were soon happily wed, living on his farm and enjoying travels to Europe. Judy's first marriage had also been to a Finn, and dissolved years earlier.

Winter was on its way with rain, wind and finally snow. One morning as she and Ryan set out for the 25-mile trip to school and work, several inches of new snow blanketed the roads, quite sufficient to make driving hazardous. First snow is always an open door for accidents as drivers re-learn how to drive in it. Tires on her big old Cadillac were bald, smooth, with only traces of tread visible, not a good combination.

Ariel cautioned Ryan to sit still, and please be quiet as possible. She eased out onto the highway. Quiet was a difficult task; he was 10 years old and this was the first snowfall of the season. He understood though, and tried valiantly to keep silent knowing his mom needed to concentrate fully on controlling their vehicle, while avoiding others that occasionally slid toward them. He kept watch on vehicles following in the side mirror.

Able to remain silent only so long, he softly said, "Mom, you know that truck behind us?" "Yes, son." "It's not there any more; it's in the ditch."

Ariel just nodded, and silently to herself, *Oh thank you son, for sharing.* Gripping the wheel even tighter, daring to glance briefly in the rear view mirror, she did notice several cars following; none appeared eager to pass. Twenty-five miles had never been so long before. One by one several of those following cars and trucks were noted by Ryan, very softly, to have disappeared off the road. She kept going at the steadiest pace possible, barely turning the wheel smoothly, ever so smoothly and cautiously, never touching the brake pedal unless in neutral gear, then barely, softly tapping the pedal.

Ariel had always preferred a standard transmission and being able to rely more on gears and compression for slowing, not brakes. This was an automatic of course, but it had not taken her long to determine that applying braking to front wheels while rear wheels were in 'drive' and pushing a vehicle was a most effective means of skidding, not slowing or stopping. Gearing down the huge engine in this old Cadillac merely upped torque on those rear wheels: not helpful at all. They finally arrived safely, Ryan at school and Ariel at work. This was her final week at the dental office and would be her last paycheck.

Snow fell sporadically throughout the day, with considerable accumulation for the return to Wenatchee. Ryan walked from school to the office and gave an update on snow depth as well as traffic problems in town. Ariel drove to the house to await Roger's return from his work. She needed her winter tires and those needed to be put on the car. Roger was surprised to see her there, waiting for him. She greeted him in a pleasant, if slightly cool manner, and informed him the winter tires were a necessity and must be installed. Strangely he did not argue or criticize; just pulled the tires out of the garage jacked up the car; put the winter tires on, bald ones in the trunk.

Ryan begged to stay the night, to play in the fresh snow with his pals and come back with Ariel on Friday. First snow of winter is so special in many ways, and she was not going to deny him that pleasure. Roger assured her he would prepare something for supper or take Ryan out for burgers. Not the most nutritious perhaps, but food.

With the quite well-used, but slightly better tires on the car, Ariel headed home to her safe apartment with a far greater sense of confidence than ever felt previously; not limited just to tires. She had faced Roger who had not grumbled, growled, or blamed her for anything, just installed the tires and quietly cautioned her to drive safely. This in a tone he might have used with anyone in winter. Wow. She had not even been accused of causing the snowfall.

Ryan absolutely refused to consider changing schools, so each weekend Ariel drove to Barbaria late Sunday afternoon so he could be ready for classes there on Monday. Heart heavy and face streaked with tears, she headed back to her sparse, but safe, apartment. Serious job hunting continued early each Monday morning.

Her resume was edited and several copies typed in preparation for answering available job advertisements. Each was individually typed on the old IBM Selectric she had purchased from a good friend. Cover letters were written to personally deliver with resumes to firms that included street addresses in their ads. Phone calls were placed to others to set up appointments. There were not many openings advertised, but she zealously followed each one that seemed even slightly plausible. Her total cash assets amounted to $600, carefully wrapped in foil, tucked under a small package of frozen food, and had to last. She had used the $56 of joint savings to buy decent shoes suitable for a professional office. It was money she had managed to save from selling a painting, but was legally considered community property. She knew Roger would lay claim to it at some point.

Her efforts to find employment did not meet with early success, nor did anything come of her search at the local State Employment Services office. Finally, she resorted to signing with a private employment agency; at a cost, but she needed a job, and quickly.

She used the car as little as possible, with its 12 mpg in town and over 25-gallon tank, gas consumption was a very real concern. Walking not only saved the precious, dwindling cash, but was excellent therapy and exercise. As she walked, Ariel repeated the silent mantra: *You are a worthy person, you do have value. You are entitled to live.* Gradually she even began to believe that, at least a little bit. Smiles began to more often replace worry lines, even as her financial resources shrank.

Her entire body ached, particularly her back and hips. It felt as though her thigh bones had been screwed into the wrong sockets. Walking was painful, but she kept at it. Gas was expensive. Her backpack used for hiking in the mountains now served to carry groceries.

Her friend Richard with whom she had worked at the Seattle bank branch had transferred to Wenatchee several years earlier. Roger had stayed with him and James during the gas shortage period; Ariel was doubtful at first if they would remain her friends, or perhaps support Roger's position. She needn't have feared; both were definitely in her corner and totally encouraging. Years later Ariel still wondered if she would have had the courage necessary to pursue the divorce and survive the years she referred to as "single blessedness and abject poverty" without their friendship and help. Both were true friends.

Employment, Law, and Dissolution

The employment agency sent her out almost immediately to interview for a bookkeeping job at a law firm. She was both delighted and rather amused that this was a bookkeeping position, precisely what she had been strongly advised by a high school teacher to never even consider. In fact they had struck a deal by which she received a good solid "B+" grade in bookkeeping in exchange for doing mimeograph stencil typing, art work and production for the District Superintendent's office. Now she was to interview for a bookkeeping job. A chance is a chance regardless of prior concerns, and certainly not one to turn down.

The interview process was short; Ariel started training in her new job the following Monday. She had a job! Salary was not great, but a whole lot better than nothing and this was an entirely new venture, also an introduction to the legal field. Little did she suspect her remaining employment years would be in law offices and courts, with brief detours into domestic and global marketing.

That she had been hired immediately by a law firm was in and of itself highly amusing. For years Roger had insisted she was certifiably crazy, complained to his cop buddies that she was completely nuts, and then threatened to have her committed. Now she was employed by lawyers. Let him put that in his stinky pipe and smoke it. After all, *everyone knows* law firms only hire crazy people – right.

Ariel started by doing client billings where her prior installment credit and collections experience was very helpful. Some of the business accounts were seriously in arrears and the overall delinquency percentage higher than she considered appropriate for a small four-member firm. When clients and their attorneys move in the same business and social circles, live in a relatively small community, and have been long-time acquaintances, there can be tendencies on both sides toward leniency regarding payment and collection. Ariel was not hampered by any such or expectations of laxity by anyone; she always paid bills on time. She had a strong background in collection, both in banking and retail business.

Besides, she didn't know any of these people, didn't move in their social circles, and didn't much care if they didn't like being prodded into payment. She followed the banking format of adding reminders to past due statements that the account was to be brought current, and enclosing written notations specific to each account 120 or more days past due. Before long the percentage of over-age accounts decreased with a corresponding increase in gross receipt totals; a change quite pleasing to the partners.

She was also introduced to real estate transactions, drafting purchase/sale documents and conducting closings. Filing and recording of documents became her responsibility, and soon presenting orders and conducting foreclosure sales.

Large orchard contracts frequently required computing two and three interest rate amendments per year during this period of high and rapidly- fluctuating interest rates. Each of the changes involved calculating new monthly payment schedules for the amended rates. In this pre-computer age, all those were hand calculated and typed, individually. Fortunately copy equipment had become office standard so at least carbon paper and onion skin secondary sheets were no longer involved.

As her responsibilities increased so did her salary slightly, although far less than did the level of responsibility and expertise. She drafted documents establishing new businesses, filed corporations with the State, and maintained annual corporate records books.

Bankruptcy proceedings were added to her responsibilities, with opening cases and tracking of assets and liabilities, attending initial hearings, opening interest-bearing investment accounts and monitoring bankruptcy trust accounts. Some bankruptcy trust accounts involved short-term re-purchase investments placed with Wall Street banks at rates of 17% to 20% during the height of the late 1970's and early 1980's high interest rate period. The firm also handled retirement investment Trust accounts for local individual clients which required monitoring, appropriate amendments, with each account maintained separately. She also computed quarterly State and Federal taxes, submitting her calculations to the private accountant for review. The numbers of bankruptcy trust and individual trust accounts increased to set this particular firm in the position of the one local firm best qualified to handle trusts. All that was Ariel's responsibility, for which the lawyers garnered credit. Partners and Associates alike knew she was still working to divorce Roger, and definitely struggling financially. She could not afford to quit this job, and they knew it. Pay increases were small and infrequent.

Weekends that Ryan stayed in Barbaria found Ariel working diligently at the office all day Saturdays and after church on Sundays. She was not compensated for any of those hours, at an overtime rate or even straight time. The lawyers were quite pleased. She still lacked sufficient confidence to admit she was doing the work of at least two people; the need for extra hours was not due to her inability. There simply was more work than any one person could handle.

One fruit packing company bankruptcy for which she became responsible involved both real and personal properties with the requisite separate trust accounting. Opening deposits for each were in the $5 and $6 million range. These funds were invested at very high interest rates for short time periods with East Coast banks, carefully monitoring each of the many separate designations. Trust account balances increased steadily both from Ariel's re-purchase dealings for each, and new deposit amounts as the bankruptcies proceeded.

One branch vice president at the bank decided to merge the separate trust accounts to access a potentially higher return. He had accessed the accounts information while both Ariel and the specifically responsible bank employee were on vacation. Arrangements for high-interest re-investment of funds had been put in place to cover the time period, blocked to any other persons. He decided to circumvent all normal procedures, ignoring protocol. His action violated both banking and bar association rules, placing both the law firm and bank in jeopardy. He had no approval from any source; none would have been available had he inquired.

Upon discovery, Ariel and the bank branch employee with whom she worked spent hours and days sorting it out as well as possible. That V.P. was ordered by lawyers and senior bank officers to never again even go near Trust accounts of any nature if he wished to remain employed. Previously he had smiled and greeted Ariel as he did all customers; after this fiasco he kept his head down if he noticed her in the lobby, diligently studying a paper on his desk.

The firm's lawyers basked in their prominence; Ariel just kept all the investments, trust accounts and records straight. One particular concern was maintaining the required separation of the firm's general fund accounts from office-related individual client Trusts. The lawyers certainly understood their fiduciary responsibilities, but were not always spot-on with timing of the authorized draw amounts, tending to want those draws a bit earlier than perhaps appropriate.

She received the sporadic small salary increases and life became slightly less stressful financially. She still saved every possible dime and dollar, and savored the day she could finally purchase renter insurance and minimal vehicle liability coverage. No coins received as change from purchases were spent; all landed in the stoneware crock, and saved against emergencies.

Ariel was also tasked with attending continuing legal education seminars, providing appropriate instruction for the stenographers. One held in Spokane focused on probate scheduling and closing of estates. In addition, she was to research word processing capabilities for the office, including service availability and staff training. She was not at all confident that her little Fiat 850 Spyder would make a trip of that length and voiced that very real uncertainty. She had sold the '68 Cadillac for a mere $300 some time earlier, unable to afford gas or servicing. The Fiat was very economical, particularly since it did not run very consistently. Reluctantly, the managing partner gave up keys for the company car; she also took Ryan with her, providing him a little trip and also for his companionship. Her previous trip to Spokane had been to the '74 Exposition and had not included any familiarity with the city in general.

The CLE seminar was extremely informative, particularly as she had absolutely no formal legal training. Word processing equipment was also found that included four-hour response for service. Nothing even close was available in Wenatchee where mag-card systems were then considered the ultimate in technology. The Videc 1800 utilized a standard IBM keyboard and 8" diameter discs on which text was saved to a side 'A' or 'B'. Volume was limited, but a vast improvement over each and every document being typed individually. Simple arithmetic capabilities also were included, which eliminated hand-calculations being transferred and possibly transposed.

The managing partner only agreed to the acquisition when Ariel pointed out that the word processor eliminated hiring another steno and the additional costs of benefits. It didn't get sick, have kids to worry about, receive any personal phone calls, or take vacations. The greed light-bulb activated in his brain.

Training on the (then) innovative apparatus required three full days, included in the purchase price of $15,000.

She was given an 'office manager' title – no pay increase, and tasked with correcting some of the bad habits acquired by stenos over the years, long personal phone calls being chief. Her attempts met limited success with the primary offender who spent much of her work day conducting personal business and dealing with teenagers together with an ex-spouse's perceived problems. Ariel attended numerous additional CLE sessions, using her weekends, and sharing the updated legal requirements. She received no compensation for attending, information gathering or providing that to staff verbally and in print. Direct expenses for travel, food and lodging were reimbursed.

The client billing process included services for several small business accounts. One such business was the branch office of a major financial corporation located just a couple blocks from the law firm. The Senior Branch Manager Tom met frequently with one of the partners and she noticed him in the office from time to time. She was involved with any court action required by his office; motions and orders for judgments and occasional foreclosures. The firm also handled the probate when his wife passed away. He spoke with Ariel frequently by phone pursuant to his collection accounts that required legal work. They worked quite well in *"good cop – bad cop"* roles to bring some of his habitually slow-pay accounts to more consistently current status. When that did not succeed, default documents were prepared which she then presented in court with the supporting documentation for issuance of the judgment.

Ariel continued to struggle on $1,000 per month, gross. Her apartment rent was $250, with all utilities extra. Then there was car maintenance, haunting of sales for appropriate professional wearing apparel, clothing for Ryan and taking him to an all-you-can-eat fish place when possible. Ariel provided fare money so he could come to Wenatchee by bus on Friday afternoons. She tried to find some boys in the neighborhood about his age to shoot baskets and ride bikes, was able to treat him to a movie occasionally and find things to do that he liked.

Her friends Richard and James had a bit of land on the lake behind Rocky Reach dam, and many summer Saturday afternoons were spent there with Ryan swimming, learning to water ski, picking rocks to reinforce the breakwater, playing backgammon, and just enjoying summer. Winter months were more difficult, and many afternoons she bought stale bread for mere pennies; they went to the dam and fed the water fowl. Ducks of all sorts, geese and some birds they couldn't clearly identify wintered there, knowing ample food was available. The dam also featured an exhibit area with a wide assortment of interesting information, historic and interactive equipment relating to discovery and development of modern electric generation and transmission. Sundays they were in church where she sang in the choir, visited local parks, hiked a bit before Ryan returned to Barbaria.

Those years definitely were her period of single blessedness and abject poverty. Somehow neither she nor Ryan actually ever went hungry, but it was very close on occasion. That crock of coins religiously saved was tapped many times for essentials.

A Friday or Saturday treat was dinner at an all-you-can-eat fish place often found a 'second' piece of fish tucked into Ryan's pocket for the twenty-pound 'kitten' they had adopted. He always seemed to know when they went to the fish eatery and was at the door awaiting his treat on their return.

Dissolving a Marriage

First of all, that is not always easy to accomplish; particularly if only one party wants to dissolve the legal relationship, is willing to invest the necessary time and effort, and the other party steadfastly refuses to cooperate in any way. State statute actually makes the process quite simple, predicated however, upon some rudimentary degree of cooperation by both parties.

With employment secured, Ariel had sought advice from the leading family law attorney in town. To her query as to what was the reason Ariel wanted dissolution, this lady was astounded by the answer. Ariel had not gone into any great detail, just that nothing she did was ever right, or ever good enough. No matter what went wrong, or not in accordance with his wishes at home, Roger's work, anything and anywhere, it was her fault. That she failed to put sufficient starch in his blue chambray work shirts to deflect welding sparks served as just one example.

The lawyer fairly shouted, "What the @%#^$&#* do you mean? Doesn't his employer furnish leathers for the welders?"

"Oh, yes" Ariel responded, "but Roger doesn't want to use those. He wants the shirts stiff enough to not require leathers. I never did even that to his satisfaction."

Upon declaring that demand to be totally insane, beyond any degree of logic or comprehension, she immediately began drafting documents. All the while keys of her typewriter clickity-clacked at high speed and ashes drifted off the cigarette dangling from her lips. Ariel could clearly discern the muttered oaths spewing forth. The woman's range of profanity was utterly astounding; but, through it all document after document emerged. Concern about Ariel's eligibility to draw on Roger's SSI earnings at some future date was quickly put to rest. Ariel had extended that privately-held1958 *one week, just until next Friday*, for a full twenty years and six weeks prior to fleeing. She qualified under the then 20-year co-habitation requirement.

Her attorney was also highly concerned about her ability to support herself until a settlement could be reached and any funds that might be available from it. Community property, including real property required fair distribution under a decree of dissolution. It could take time; neither she nor Ariel had a clue as to how much time.

Documents drafted and filed, Roger was served. That really sent him into a blind rage – How dare she do this to him, to him … of all people?!?

He finally read the Summons sufficiently to understand he needed to respond timely, or Ariel's attorney would accomplish the deed through a Default action and he would have no say whatever in the matter. Roger hired a lawyer just before the deadline; Notice of Appearance was entered to stop the clock and an Initial Answer filed later. For a brief time Ariel brightened and her attorney hoped for some cooperation. She wanted a quick resolution to what she deemed a totally untenable situation. Roger's attorney was a reasonable person and one with whom she had worked numerous times with quite acceptable results in her paralegal position.

That attorney was every bit as unsuccessful as Ariel's in obtaining cooperation from Roger. Each responsive document prepared by his counsel remained unsigned until deadlines were reached and beyond. Of necessity extension motions were filed while the attorney struggled to get Roger's review and signature. He finally petitioned the Court to allow him to fire his client and withdraw. Petition to withdraw was granted; the Commissioner granted the motion and noted on the record it was the first such request he had ever heard during his private practice or decades on the bench.

Roger finally was accepted as a client by another office, and initially some degree of progress was made. Members of this new firm held Ariel's counsel in the highest regard and sought to get the matter settled; they absolutely did not want to go to trial against her. The whole process took two years and seven months, plus a full day's trial in Superior Court. Fees mounted unnecessarily high due to Roger's refusal to cooperate with his counsel or obey any court orders. A Judge or Commissioner could order anything he pleased; Roger simply paid no heed.

The presiding trial Judge brooked no nonsense, despite Roger's numerous attempts to discredit Ariel with wild accusations including alleged public drunkenness, poor housekeeping, child neglect, overly-permissive behavior, financial instability and on and on. He testified under oath she had never supported any of his interests, been helpful to him in any way, caring only about herself, never him.

He made sure the Court heard about her reading of "Psychology Today", stressing his point that this alone was sufficient to prove she was mentally ill and needed to be institutionalized. The Judge spent several minutes intently studying something of intense interest on the floor at that bit of testimony.

Roger failed to realize that Court personnel including this Judge were well acquainted with Ariel from her frequent visits to the Courthouse in the normal course of her paralegal employment.

They were also well aware of the sparse coverage available for traffic control in outlying areas from Sheriff Deputies and State Troopers, particularly during winter nights. Those officers knew the value of volunteer help in directing traffic. They knew of her help in handling communications at search and rescue situations, and providing needed nourishment for responders. They knew Ariel had repeatedly been out on icy roads in the dead of night, freezing cold, snow and wind, slowing and halting traffic with flares to enable trained responders to deal with incidents. They knew who was on scene and taking directions to be of assistance, with some of those winter incidents having been casual courthouse chatter. Roger didn't want to light flares and take on traffic control. If present, he wanted to be right in the middle of any traffic accident, especially any involving injuries, and then hang out with officers at cafes later.

Also of record was Ariel's having barely kept the real property out of foreclosure by the bank: Roger having failed to make the $54. per month loan payments timely. Additionally, the County had initiated foreclosure action for non-payment of real property taxes. She sold the 11-piece antique oak dining set to pay the taxes. He also had not paid property insurance premiums. Ariel scraped, scrounged, and sold her 18 ct. gold and diamond ring to pay the delinquencies once she learned of them. Roger made a major issue of *his* having faithfully paid homeowners insurance premiums. In actuality he had made a long-delinquent payment the day before trial, with instructions to the local agent to delay notification to Ariel until after the trial date. He offered no explanation for failure to make mortgage or property tax payments.

The Judge did not consider his testimony plausible, and noted Ariel had receipt for the insurance payment in hand at Court, along with the envelope and her copy of Roger's receipt she had found the day before reposing in the agent's out-going mail tray. That agent had tried to prevent her from picking it up, claiming it would be inappropriate for her to do so. The Judge's one raised eyebrow indicated what he thought about that. She also presented receipts for real property taxes and mortgage payments she had brought current.

Judge Vann was not pleased with Roger's attempt to discredit Ariel and paint himself in a glow of responsibility and credibility. He was quite well acquainted with her from appearances at Court on behalf of the law firm where she worked. Just what was this Respondent trying to pull? Whatever, it wasn't flying with the Judge.

Roger had brought Annie and Ryan to the trial, planning to use them in testimony against their mother. Judge Vann did not address Annie, who had sat in the back glaring at Ariel; but called Ryan into Chambers and spent considerable time talking with and listening to him.

Meanwhile the attorneys were working to divide up personal property from the lists Ariel had provided. Roger did not bother to list anything … it was all his after all. He considered her art supplies and completed works to be of no value, so made no claim to any of that. Ariel had listed the collected vehicles, including the Buick convertible she had paid for by selling paintings at the Portland car swap meet. She most definitely did not want any part of the large garage-full of parts or tools, just her little wood-burning stove that was installed there.

Judge finally re-entered the courtroom, ready to render his decision. Ariel was granted her dissolution and full custody of Ryan, the real property in Barbaria and personal property as listed and divided between the parties, together with change of name to one of her preference. Roger was ordered to pay $75 per month child support and receive an appropriate share of proceeds at such time the real property might be sold. Child support would be nice, but Ariel knew better than to count on ever receiving it.

Roger was devastated. The Judge simply did not understand. Everything was his. The real property was his alone; all the furnishings, all the vehicles, all his tools and old car parts – everything. She had been his property; she had run out on him and deserved absolutely nothing.

Judge Vann calmly, clearly and deliberately corrected him; then turned to Ariel and her attorney with a question. He was aware her daughter Annie had taken Roger's truck back to Barbaria with Ryan so he could play in a baseball game. He fully realized it was an unusual request and understood completely if she said *no*; but would Ariel consider providing transportation for Roger, since he was without other means? No public transportation existed in the region at the time.

"Certainly," she assured him. That would be no problem whatever, as she needed to pick Ryan up and hoped to see him play at least part of the game as well. Judge Vann fairly beamed at her while trying to maintain his dignity and decorous legal demeanor.

Her attorney chuckled, very nearly laughing out loud. Roger's counsel spoke firmly, instructing him to behave himself completely. "If you say or do anything the least bit inappropriate at any time, Judge can, and most likely will, cite you for contempt of court. It will not be a good thing and you could quite easily find yourself in jail. Is that clear?" There was no audible response from Roger.

Descending the broad courthouse steps Ariel's only regret was that Dad was not here with her, but knew somehow he was watching and very happy to see her finally free.

He had passed away in the mid-1970's ostensibly from pneumonia. Ariel always believed he just couldn't take Edythe's control any longer and actually died in self-defense. The official certificate listed "pneumonia and long-term congestive heart failure" which were physical. Ariel always believed his very soul had become too weary to continue and he consciously opted for heaven and home. She had paced the floor and prayed the night he passed, asking only that God grant his wishes and take him home free of pain. He had insisted to Edythe that Ariel had been there that night, but was summarily corrected. True, she had not been there physically, but most definitely present spiritually.

Roger now had to squeeze into her tiny orange '72 Fiat 850 Spyder and endure Ariel's driving for what had to be the longest 25 miles of his life. It was a relatively silent drive, top down, in gorgeous June afternoon sunlight and soft warm breezes. Ariel absolutely loved it.

And then, Implementation

Roger had been given a month to relocate, remove all his personal property including all garage/shop contents with exception of the wood stove, comply with the distribution as entered in the courts records, and provide Ariel all keys to the real property and Buick convertible.

Ariel gave notice at her apartment and began the process of sorting, packing and gathering cleaning supplies. She also arranged through her attorney a time and date for Jillian and Annie to be at the house with her and Ryan to take items each might want from storage trunks. There were numerous trunks and large boxes in the loft containing antiques, school memorabilia, bone china and silver and much more. None had been selected by Roger from the personal property lists, and she wanted to be certain Jillian and Annie particularly received things important to them; Ryan's interest was limited, but he selected a few things. The rest could be used, gifted or sold.

Roger had never stored anything in the loft where Ariel had established her refuge, painted and kept art supplies; he considered it all of no value. The trunks purchased over several years specifically for storage, were tucked under the eaves, lining both sides of the loft. When Ariel took possession of the house, several trunks had disappeared, with contents dumped into the few remaining or scattered on the floor.

Roger was also court ordered to provide Ariel one-half the family 35-mm. slides and photographs. She never received a single one.

Keys for the house and garage/shop were to be turned over on date certain at the end of the one-month period granted Roger to remove his cars, parts and personal possessions. It came as no surprise to Ariel that no keys ever materialized. She had retained one Buick key found stashed in a jewelry box so at least that was available. The car did not run, of course, since Roger had begun dismantling it for some unknown reason.

That she would change door locks in any event was a given; however it might have been a nice gesture had he complied with the order. She and Ryan nailed bracing against upstairs exterior doors, blocked a basement window to open just enough that Ryan could squeeze through, removed the locks and took them to a locksmith for re-keying.

The entire house was a filthy mess and would now be hers to clean and try to restore. The cleaning and restoration of the first house came immediately to mind; another mess she had not created, but needed to clean.

More cleaning supplies were gathered. She and Ryan worked on this every late afternoon and evening. She arranged for very early morning at the office, leaving as soon as possible in the afternoon for daily cleaning efforts. Initial vacuuming helped slightly, but the carpet was truly grim. Why had she chosen something so dull and ugly?

Upstairs bathroom required hours of scrubbing before she would even consider using it. Downstairs she gingerly opened that bathroom door and slammed it shut it immediately. She had never seen such filth, not even in primitive gas station facilities on the prairies in the early 1940's; it was unbelievable. Before attempting re-entry, a 5-gallon bucket was filled with hot, soapy, sudsy ammonia water. She pushed the door open barely enough to splash the entire contents onto walls, ceiling and into the shower stall; slamming the door tight,

Fortunately the floor drain was sufficiently open and functional; in part due to the gallons of hot water and cleaner, and most of the more liquid grunge eventually seeped down. She could then scoop out solid residue with a shovel.

After several repetitions, she dared to actually step into the remaining mess, with broom, mop, scrub rags and still more hot soapy ammonia water. Bolts were so rusted a hack-saw was required to remove the toilet seat before it could be consigned to the trash.

Ariel had offered the still-functional dryer to Annie, asking only that she pick it up when Ryan and she were at the house cleaning. Instead, Annie simply entered by jimmying the block on a basement window and removed it. She had not answered any phone calls or spoken to Ariel after the trial. She had not acknowledged Ariel's calls, or even her offer of the dryer, other than to basically break in and take it.

Ryan worked on clearing debris from the basement bedrooms discovering toys he had thought lost forever. Most basement contents found their way to trash cans in the alley for pick up by garbage trucks. A carpet shampooer was rented for a Saturday. Three sequential scrubbings of the carpet restored it to a degree Ariel had doubted possible. No wonder she had chosen that particular texture and color; it was really quite nice now relatively clean. Was there hope of getting this place back into livable condition? Slightly more each day, but still a real brain-straining stretch. Was she doomed to forever clean houses left filthy by other persons?

Her apartment rental agreement came to a close, and the move was finally accomplished with help from her good friends, Richard and James. They also offered the use of their little Corvair truck along with more muscle power. By mid-August Ariel and Ryan were in the house, with fall and winter closing in. Despite the clearly-worded court order, nothing much had been removed from the garage/shop; an old Corvair sedan, minus wheels, remained under the deck, directly in front of the basement door. Roger made no attempt to move any of the vehicles, or the vast quantities of car 'stuff' everywhere in the garage/shop, in the garage loft and scattered about on the property. There was no room to park the little convertible under cover.

Ariel and Ryan located a discarded power pole in an adjacent alley and dragged it home. They cut it in half and by jacking up one end of that Corvair hulk, placed a piece of pole under the frame, balanced, then rolled the vehicle back, tipped one end, placed the other log. By balancing, pushing, tipping, rolling and moving the pole pieces they managed to get the hulk repositioned nearer and parallel to the alley. With that out of the way Ariel could at least park her little car under the deck somewhat out of the weather.

Only under threat of yet another Show Cause action and court order, did Roger slowly start clearing out some of his accumulation from the garage/shop. Ariel had the wheel-less hulk removed by a man wanting to restore it, so she didn't have to look at that any more, or pay someone for towing. Roger was unhappy about her getting rid of it – big surprise…he would simply have left it there…until???. Getting rid of it was a real plus; money was very tight and she could not afford the necessary costs to hire anyone to clean up the property.

She had a small load of firewood delivered and began splitting that, stacking it under the deck. Winter temperatures would require supplementing the forced-air electric furnace with use of the fireplace in order to reduce utility costs. The normal and usual procedure in this area was to simply leave one's axe, wedge and sledge hammer at the chopping block, as they were used virtually on a daily basis. There never had been need to lock those items away. One evening she discovered the sledge to be missing. The axe had been given to her by Dad before her marriage; and the wedge was also his gift. Neither of those had been moved. Only the sledge was gone; interesting, but hardly a mystery. Most likely it had been purchased with community funds; never listed or addressed, however.

Just before payday, Ariel lacked the $7 price of a new sledge at the local hardware store. She had maintained an excellent credit account there since originally moving to town years before, and presumed she could put this $7 purchase on account for two to three days. Not so. She was flatly denied. Roger had burned this store account so badly the manager absolutely refused. It didn't matter one bit Ariel was now a single person, no longer married to Roger, and it had been she who paid the account in full each month for several years. The answer was a resounding "no". She was utterly humiliated. On payday she purchased a new sledge at a Wenatchee hardware store, never again to enter the local Barbaria establishment.

There also was no great mystery months later when two plaid lap robes vanished from another old Corvair she used to get far enough toward Wenatchee to catch a ride. The vehicle had no heater and was parked at a café lot; only the robes missing one evening. Roger made no excuse about removing them; they were his, period. That Ariel or a passenger might need those (not new by any means) robes to keep warm was of no interest to him. He had reclaimed his property.

Just getting to and from Wenatchee each day for work presented nearly Insurmountable challenges. Her little Fiat was extremely temperamental, there was no public transportation available and she had marginal success in arranging private transportation. Several male residents did work in Wenatchee, and commuted each day; however, she quickly learned the local wives did not want their spouses allowing Ariel to ride with them despite her insistence on making cold green cash payment for rides. She found that ridiculous; she needed to get to work and had less than zero interest in '*their*' men. She probably should have anticipated that reaction however, as several husbands from the town had mysteriously appeared at her apartment door in the Wenatchee years, with offers of comfort in her alleged loneliness. "Sorry, guys, not interested, not one tiny little bit, not ever under any circumstance, no matter how you might think alcohol could achieve compliance with what you want."

Finally she had been able to purchase that somewhat functional Corvair, no heater, but it did run and faithfully started each morning. Minus its heat shields, the engine absolutely roared, choke engaged at all times. Adjusting speed over icy roads was a matter of constantly judging road surface, shifting out of drive to neutral for a time and then back into drive when control was regained and speed sufficiently reduced. Lap robes had provided a little comfort until being retrieved by Roger.

One morning a deputy with whom she was acquainted pulled her over, and asked if she was having problems. Problems? The question was laughable; of course, but precious little she could do about the matter. After looking at the vehicle, he just shook his head; there were too many infractions to count. He cautioned her to please just be careful, while knowing full well that's exactly what she was doing. No other deputy or trooper ever did more than smile and wave when meeting that faded little vehicle on State Route 2 after that. They were fully aware of the help Ariel had been directing traffic at accident scenes and assisting in mountain searches, also providing snacks.

If lacking direct knowledge, also strongly suspected Roger tended to ignore court orders. They knew him quite well, and he had been dropped from Posse involvement.

Thankfully she had no additional encounters with that deputy allegedly looking for his wife in the middle of the night following a 'cop' party. There was no acknowledgement of any nature from him on the highway.

Ariel and Ryan struggled with snow removal, keeping the house heated, getting to school and work through the long winter months. Ryan was frequently late for school, going back to sleep after Ariel got him up and having to leave for work. The school office staff steadfastly refused to communicate in any way with Ariel, despite having her office phone number, home number and address. They telephoned Roger who did nothing; a Wenatchee phone number was long distance so not used.

Ariel was unable to obtain any school-related information, about upcoming events, schedules, or even report cards; she was simply ignored by the school, teachers and staff, as far as her son was concerned, despite awareness of her having been granted full custody. Teachers did not answer any questions she asked, or provide notices of any activities, trips, supplies required; they simply ignored her existence. Roger did not forward any school-related information.

When confronted by his attorney he simply shrugged that off as being of no importance and absolutely no interest to him. He didn't care what Ariel might know, want to know or have any right to.

The courts had ordered him to pay $75 per month in child support, and to do so through the County Clerk. Ariel received one payment of $75 which was immediately used to purchase basketball shoes for Ryan. Only years later when Ariel sold the property and proceeds were distributed per court order, did Ariel receive the ordered child support. It was nice, of course, but not really needed at that point.

Ryan went to the Grandparents' with his sisters for Christmas; Ariel sent the usual Christmas bread with them, and small gifts she could afford. Snow continued to accumulate on a daily basis, so shoveling certainly gave her plenty to do to keep busy. There wasn't much time off for holidays in the law firm, which suited Ariel.

Christmas Eve found her still at the office late in the evening working on a real estate transaction for a client from Chelan. For reasons never adequately made clear, several documents required drafting to be filed on December 26th at the very moment the courthouse opened. Everyone else on staff had family celebrations; not Ariel. Documents completed and executed, this client drove Ariel home to Barbaria shortly before midnight in a blinding snowstorm; he then turned around to drive to Chelan. The extra hours of work were uncompensated in any monetary way. The client was very grateful for her willingness to go the extra mile, and had flowers delivered to her office the day after Christmas. They were lovely, but in truth Ariel would have more welcomed whatever money they cost.

Ryan was given a puppy for his birthday, three days after Christmas by his father and Jillian's husband. No one had mentioned a puppy even being a possibility; he was a cute and absolutely precious little dog. Ariel could hardly afford to feed Ryan and herself, much less a puppy. There was no shelter or fencing to protect him. It was a nice gesture and he was absolutely adorable; but, had anyone considered the upkeep, potential vet bills, anything connected with caring for this little fellow? Of course not. That was Ariel's problem.

She cobbled together a shelter from scrap boards, charged fencing at the lumber store where fortunately Roger had not defaulted, bought food, found food and water dishes in the still-cluttered garage/shop, and put a rug in his little shelter under the deck. It would stay dry and he was out of any wind, so should stay warm.

The snow continued falling and both Ariel and Ryan continued shoveling. Ryan worked to keep the Fiat and/or the elderly Corvair running as much as possible so she could get to work. He also started working on the '48 Buick that was awarded his mom. She had bought the car originally, and it was also awarded her at the trial. Roger had begun removing engine parts, radiator and also tearing apart the doors for some unknown reason.

As he attempted to reattach an inside door panel, Ryan discovered a 4-leaf enameled clover pendant and piece of delicate broken gold chain. He took it into the house and asked Ariel if she knew what it was and why it had been inside the car door. She squealed with delight, hugging her son and lifting him up in her arms, though he was now taller that she and out-weighed her.

This small piece of jewelry had been given to Ariel by Sophie Granberg when she was just seven. She had worn it faithfully for decades; was heartbroken when it had caught on the window edge and vanished. Now it was restored; what a blessing. That little pendant meant so much to her.

In early January during this same dead of winter time, the washer suddenly quit functioning; hot water tank began leaking, fiberglass ductwork drooped alarmingly from the basement ceiling; and her little convertible less and less willing to function. Standing in the basement, Ariel was totally overwhelmed. Her earnings at the law firm were woefully inadequate to replace the washer, tank, or do anything about the ductwork other than attempt patching that together with still more tape. Snow continued to fall, Ryan did all he could to keep the car running; they chopped wood and shoveled snow every day. Ryan was still frequently late for school, still falling back to sleep after she left for work. She was exhausted. School staff persons never once called Ariel, despite having her direct office number; they occasionally telephoned Roger…who did nothing.

Standing in the basement one Saturday afternoon, feeling utterly helpless and hopeless, she quietly uttered a completely inapt prayer of desperation; "Lord, I need help; I've done everything I know of, and there isn't enough rope left to tie a knot and hang on. Please show me what to do."

With just that, she picked up the shovel and went back outdoors. Would her car start on Monday? She and Ryan could walk to the Laundromat, grocery store and Church. Her office and only source of income was a twenty-five mile trip one way.

SECTION VI

The New Year and New Opportunity

Ariel had worked with Tom, senior branch manager of a major finance institution ever since her first week at the law firm. He called frequently regarding seriously delinquent accounts, status of collection efforts by the law firm, default actions and foreclosures. Their daily conversations were consistently business-related dealing with delinquent loan accounts and discussions as to appropriate legal means to resolve them. They never discussed any personal matters, or indicated in any way either even had lives outside their respective offices. She saw him occasionally in the corridor when meeting with his business and personal attorney. Her view was that of a somewhat sad-appearing individual, not much given to smiling or evidencing any expressions of humor. His physical appearance was quite similar to Buddy Hackett, and a tad of Walter Matthau. He presented in a straightforward businesslike manner with an agenda to be addressed; little interest in pursuing any non-business matters.

He had lost his wife of some 16 years to cancer just over a year prior. The firm had handled the closing of her estate which also brought him to the office. Ariel had no personal interaction with him as all their conversations regarding accounts were by phone.

So she was totally surprised when in the course of reviewing delinquent accounts by telephone one afternoon, and with no preamble, he asked if she would consider having lunch with him the next day; he had something to show her and a question to ask. What was this all about?

She had turned down numerous lunch and dinner invitations from several car dealers, lawyers and other local businessmen during the months since escaping Roger. Very few of those men had been single, but she knew Tom was widowed.

The adopted kitten 'baby' Chester, now a 25# muscular and well-furred gray cat, served well in avoiding dates. Ariel had quietly replied to each unwanted, unexpected and most pleasant invitation, thanked them for thinking of her in so complimentary a manner. She was certain the evening, or whatever, would indeed be lovely; however, she was involved in a relationship; and didn't want to jeopardize that in any way, or ever hurt Chet's feelings.

When asked who "Chet" was and what he did, as they didn't know him, she replied that he rather kept to himself, didn't go downtown much at all, but hiked, climbed and really enjoyed hunting. The image of a large, robust outdoorsman, most likely armed to the teeth was instantly established; no further explanation required. Thus, she smilingly managed to spare fragile egos, dodge detail, and avoid queries as to any possible future date.

And in truth, she was indeed quite involved with Chet who, curled into his pillow next to hers, purred softly in her ear every night.

She handled collection matters for Tom's office, and considered him a quite responsible and reasonable person. There was no place in Wenatchee from which she could not walk back to the office if need be and this was just a workday lunch after all.

She agreed. Tom audibly signed with relief and arranged to pick her up a little before noon the following day.

She briefly reviewed the probate file, confirming Tom to be a financially responsible individual. Her next step was to pull a credit report from the Bureau office located immediately below hers in the same building. She occasionally lunched with the clerks and they were happy to help her check out this McPherson fellow. Reports were more easily accessed then, especially those from a law firm employee. Slight bending of procedure perhaps, but these ladies didn't want Ariel to be misled by some possibly shady banker type.

The report was excellent; his affairs all appeared totally in order, with nary a hint of dark secrets lurking undercover. After Roger, Ariel was taking no chances, not even on a short daytime meeting.

They had a lovely lunch, and over coffee each watched the other warily to see if a pack of cigarettes might emerge. None did, and Tom brought out a slim packet of colorful brochures.

Hesitantly he explained that these pamphlets briefly outlined a company-sponsored cruise on which he hoped she would consider accompanying him. He didn't expect her to answer immediately, just look through the brochures and give his request a fair chance. Of course, she would give this matter her attention and serious consideration. With just cursory glances through the material, she agreed it all looked quite lovely and she would review it all carefully. With that it was time to go back to their offices, and she thanked him for the delightful lunch.

Now what should she do? Well, he didn't smoke which was a huge plus. She was not about to waste even one minute on any man who smoked. Her hunch was Tom would not have much time for any woman smoker either, having lost his wife to lung cancer … she a long-time chain smoker.

Ariel's immediate mental response was – he's a pleasant sort of fellow away from addressing delinquent accounts, a nice lunch and totally lovely thought, that of a cruise; but … for her? No way; she didn't deserve anything like that. After all, she had conducted an extra-marital affair and was divorced; there could just as well be an "*A*" branded on her chest – and not for "Ariel".

There was simply no question; good things were for other people, not for her. That had been drilled into her from earliest childhood, first by Edythe and then continued by Roger for the following twenty years, a firmly-imbedded perception blunted only slightly by that wonderful forbidden affair. She savored memories of that delightful, scary interlude. He had always said the most wonderful things, insisted she was beautiful, intelligent, and talented. He treated her like royalty; but, it was an affair after all, not real life. She had managed to keep it all secret, so far as she knew. That she was unworthy and undeserving was a given; and had been all her life. Good things were for other people, not the likes of her.

Besides, if she accepted this offer what sort of example would she be setting for Ryan? At 14 highly protective of his mom; and convinced he could get his parents back together. He just had to work at it despite all evidence to the contrary; he kept hoping.

Ariel showed all the cruise brochures to Ryan that evening after supper and outlined Tom's invitation for her to go on the cruise with him. She rather expected Ryan to object; after all, she and Tom certainly were not only unmarried, but they really didn't even know each other very well. That alone was sufficient reason for her to refuse; it was contrary to everything considered the least bit proper, correct and acceptable to her very core.

Traveling together would certainly require sharing accommodations. She wanted to know his thoughts about mom going off on a trip with a man he had never met and she knew only from her employment.

Ryan's immediate response was totally unexpected, "Mom, get real. If you don't go, you're nuts." What? Her son was all for this, and she wasn't even remotely sure if she should even think about it. Ryan had it all figured out in just minutes; he could stay with a neighbor for those few days, take care of the house and his dog; all would be well. It was "go, Mom – go". Ryan pinned that down further with, "if you don't do this you'll regret it the rest of your life."

Out of the mouths of babes for certain. He could not have known what a prophetic statement that was. And also unknown, how prophetic it was for himself and his own maturing and development. Ariel fought her own doubts, fears, inadequacies and decided to take the chance.

Tom was very pleased at her decision, and grinning as shyly as a teenager, asked her to dinner that Saturday evening. After all, he said, "we should go on at least one date before flying and cruising together, right?".

Snow fell steadily throughout Saturday. A lovely bouquet of flowers arrived early in the afternoon.

When she telephoned Tom to thank him, she also cautioned him as to the bad road conditions rapidly developing. A mere snow storm did not deter him, and they enjoyed an excellent evening. Months later he confessed having feared her call was to cancel their dinner date, and that he had still felt totally insecure about her actually accompanying him on the cruise despite her having agreed to.

He truly did not know Ariel very well yet. Little did he realize; she had promised, therefore she would….and did.

She did not yet know how little he liked driving, especially in winter on snow-covered, icy roads.

Tom insisted on taking her shopping for a new suit, appropriate for travel and for introduction to his corporate environment. This was still in an era when people dressed up for travel, meetings and corporate dinners. A lovely neutral tone suit and colorful blouse were selected and served well for years.

And so, she borrowed luggage from her painting and pottery friend, gathered her few summery outfits and set out in dead of winter on what became a new phase of her life. She had no clue.

First, a Cruise, and then ...

With snow shoveled, bags packed, Ryan and his list of things to look after during her brief absence safely under watchful care of her neighbor, Ariel was on her way ... first to Wenatchee. Tom placed her bags in his car and they headed for the local airport for the brief initial flight to Seattle and then on to California to board the cruise ship. Thick fog with heavy snowfall had enveloped the entire area delaying flights both in and out. It did not lift and with their flight finally cancelled, drove quite safely to Seattle on roads not all different from normal winter conditions.

After checking in at the hotel, they joined the other company employees for the meet and greet gathering before dinner. Ariel was more than slightly nervous; what would Tom's co-workers think of her. She didn't know anyone but Tom, and even him quite casually only through business. This was a major corporate setting and an entirely unfamiliar environment. One lunch, one dinner and a brief shopping trip comprised the sum of their social interaction. What had she been thinking?

Stand up straight, think 'tall', and just keep smiling. This familiar, oft-used coping method seemed to work very well here as in previously encountered unfamiliar circumstances and environments. Don't ever let anyone guess you are terrified.

Tom proudly introduced her to one and all, grinning broadly and relishing the responses of friends and co-workers on his good fortune in having such an attractive lady on his arm. He also made certain they all knew she worked in one of the best law firms in town, saw to all his legal work, and was adept at handling the company's Trust accounts. He praised her to the skies in this corporate setting, a totally new thing in her life. Ariel was at a complete loss for words, and mentally shrank hearing all this praise. So her responses were limited to being so very pleased to meet all of them, and how very nice it was to be there with Tom. Just keep your head up high and smile, smile, smile.

Dinner was excellent, wine flowed freely and the evening's entertainment delightful. This was a whole new experience; and she didn't quite know how to handle it; just smile. Could she possibly adapt to situations like this; only time might tell. Thoughts raced and tumbled about in her mind from mere apprehension to sheer panic. From absolute certainty of being struck dead by lightning to an occasional glimpse that this could possibly become a part of her future. These people appeared quite normal, chatting casually, eating, and drinking, all very pleasantly. No one seemed the least concerned that she was here with Tom or indicated negativity in any way about their relationship. Was this sort of casual acceptance possible?

Roger had not wanted her to attend any social functions with him. When she had been specifically invited by third parties and actually attended, he distanced himself from her as much as possible. On occasion she even drove to the function by herself; having been specifically invited and not wishing to be impolite.

Tom held her hand as they moved about the room, ensuring she met everyone, especially all the senior corporate management persons and their spouses. His pleasure and pride were unmistakable. This openness in a mutual environment was an entirely new experience for Ariel in every way possible.

Obviously, there was one room at the hotel and would be one stateroom on the ship. Nothing to do but smile pleasantly, try to remember at least some of the new names she was hearing, perhaps even a few of their titles; and remain very, very calm. Retreat was not an option. Smile.

Back in the hotel room, Ariel was more than a little apprehensive. There was one king size bed. It would be totally unrealistic to think Tom would shake her hand, wish her pleasant dreams, turn his back and pull covers over his head. But, what might she expect. Her mind whirling aimlessly, she finally calmed, and recalling her marriage to Roger, firmly told herself, "this is for just a short time; he truly is a nice fellow; just take one step at a time."

She instructed herself somewhat sternly, "after all, you were married to Roger for twenty years by taking just one week at a time. You put up with his blunt rudeness and crude behavior for two decades. This trip is even less than a full week, and Tom is a basically kind person. You can do this … relax."

And so she slipped quietly between the sheets, took several slow deep breaths and waited.

Tom stroked her cheeks and neck, kissed her softly, and quietly spoke of ordinary everyday things—dinner, snow and the drive over the mountains; how proud he was to have her with him before even touching her shoulders and arms. He was ever so gentle, stroking her back, gradually easing her tension before even attempting any further advances.

Their first night together didn't set off any fireworks, but certainly was far more pleasant than Ariel had ever dared hope. Tom slept soundly, snored up a royal storm, and woke with a sort of silly grin on his face in the morning. He just couldn't stop hugging her and holding her hand wherever they went. This truly was something new, previously experienced only briefly during her 'side-step' with the broker. She was reminded of that experience now by Tom's gentleness and caring. Who only knew; she might even become accustomed to this kind of treatment. It was altogether nice.

Tom's late wife had been so very ill for so long, passing more than two years earlier and he was not hesitant in sharing how lonely he had been. His three cats were nice, and needing to care for them every day had kept him from hanging out at taverns every night after work. However, even he had found kitty-cat conversation not overly stimulating or particularly rewarding. A real live lady was much more to his liking, in ways not totally limited to conversation.

Ariel was definitely not an experienced air traveler, having flown just once before as a teenager on a brief commercial flight. At no time during the entire 27 minutes of that flight did all four engines function simultaneously. They took turns.

First one and then another would sputter, shut down, remain inoperable briefly, then re-fire. Altitude rose, then dropped, rose again, but not too much and it seemed to Ariel the craft barely missed tree tops and flag poles. That experience had not inspired much confidence or enthusiasm for future flights. She would do her travel by car, thank you just the same; and she would do the driving.

Tom knew she was nervous, and had been quite relieved when they had to drive Seattle, even thought it meant crossing the pass in heavy snow. The small local airline connecting to SeaTac did not enjoy a particularly great reputation for safety, referenced locally as 'crash-cade". However, there would be no driving to California.

He steered her into the bar nearest their departure gate and ordered a double bourbon and water. Ariel protested: "it's the middle of the morning, way too early to drink." "Never mind the clock, you need some relaxant; this variety is quite legal, available and effective, so just get it down … but slowly", he cautioned.

Despite her consternation, Tom was right. Years later, however Ariel still insisted her fingernail gouges must remain visible in that boarding tunnel.

Tom held her hand firmly as soon as they began to taxi toward the runway, not releasing her until they were airborne; she smiled at him and finally let out a soft somewhat relaxed sigh. It was a lovely and totally uneventful flight, with beautiful weather the farther south they went, a smooth landing. Next stop – boarding the ship.

Was this real? Ariel looked up at the beautiful, sleek white ship lying at anchor, crew and passengers moving about, walking up the gangplank waving and calling to friends, music playing over speakers. Everything was so festive. Was she really here, in the line to board? It didn't seem possible. Tom assured her that all was quite fine, and yes, they were going to sail south along the coast and into Mexican waters. Not for very long, as he had initially explained at their first luncheon. This was a corporate perk trip, and they only spring for so much. Ariel was having enough trouble accepting that she was being given this opportunity, with no expectation other than she relax, enjoy and have fun. A totally new concept in her experience. That had certainly been the case so far … once she calmed and quit worrying.

Even during her brief affair there was need for constant awareness less she be seen by someone who knew both her and Roger. To the best of her knowledge that had not happened. Now there was no apprehension; she was a free person.

Bags were located at their cabin door and quickly moved inside. To say space was limited is kind. Tom commented they would have to step outside just to change their minds, but no one anticipated spending much time there in any event. Clothing was quickly stashed in the tiny closet and drawers before they set out to explore a bit and be on deck for sailing. With paper streamers at the ready they stood at the rail to release those over the side. A band played, whistles blew and the ship's deep blasts signaled departure. Streamers flew in all directions, hawsers retracted and the ship gradually moved away from the pier.

This was real; but, Ariel pinched herself just to be sure.

Food was amazing in both quality and quantity; at buffets and in the dining room. As soon as any slightly open area appeared on one's plate, a waiter was at hand offering more delightful choices. That Tom rather closely resembled comedian Buddy Hackett and somewhat Walter Matthau, led to much finger-pointing and whispering in the dining room. Buddy had recently re-married for whatever number of times, a blonde, and Ariel was blonde. Curious looks and whispering increased. Tom's former son-in-law, also a branch manager, so closely resembled Paul Lynde it was spooky, even walked like him, which garnered still more attention. Then, their waiter could have doubled as Dom DeLuise. The Captain quite enjoyed it when their group dined with him on the designated evening. He readily admitted was much easier more fun and less demanding having celebrity look-alikes on board than the actual personages.

Time on board was spent sunning, swimming in the pool, watching dolphins and the occasional whale, lying around on deck and thoroughly enjoying the warmth. All the company employees on board lived in either the cold, snowy northerly interior areas, or the chilly, damp regions of the West Coast. The sunshine was wonderful. Escapees from winter rain, wind, snow and fog logged hours soaking up that gorgeous sunshine and turning brown – or quite red in some instances.

They awoke to find the ship docked at a Mexican city, where a day ashore was scheduled. Somewhat alarming at first sight was a long line of armed soldiers, ammo belts across their chests and rifles at the ready. Crew assured all passengers there was no cause for alarm; this was just standard procedure for any non-Mexican-flagged ship entering port. Once routine governmental regulations were cleared, the gangplank was lowered, and passengers spread out onto the streets where vendors eagerly waited with all manner of goods.

Ariel had been into Mexico just once in 1955, with Dad and Edythe; however, they had left the car in Calexico and walked across the border into Mexicali. She had thought Calexico dirty until they walked through the Mexicali market area.

This seaport was also not sparkling clean by any means, but ever so much better than Mexicali. School boys were all in white shirts and dark slacks or shorts, girls in starched white dresses and colorful sashes; beautiful dark hair braided. How on earth did their mothers accomplish it? Laundry facilities appeared extremely limited, often consisting of a slow-running, rather muddy creek with bushes serving as driers.

Tom and a regional manager, friends for years, had the objective of locating a specific bar in town that was quite a tourist attraction; Ariel and his wife Pat followed behind them, stopping at intervals to scrutinize interesting merchandise displayed on the sidewalks and windows of small shops. The bar located and drinks ordered, it was vodka for the men, red wine--no ice for Pat and Ariel. Neither ever figured out the significance of this particular place, but it was rather pleasant. It simply existed as '*the one place you absolutely must go*'.

The town market was very interesting and of course items were purchased both as gifts and personal souvenirs. Lunch was excellent. Tom bought a lace tablecloth and colorful woolen blanket for his mother; earrings for Ariel over her protest that he not spend money on her. Before they realized it, the day had sped by. It was time to return to the ship and dress for dinner.

Was it possible to 'OD' on Lobster? That was a question she never expected could possibly arise in her life, for sure. Lobster and the drawn butter arrived by the platter. All the meals were excellent, as was the live entertainment. Ariel could scarcely believe she was really there, enjoying all the amenities, and encouraged to do so. A delightful new experience for certain. And to make it all even better, Tom was a truly nice person. He drank more alcohol than she was accustomed to seeing, but was a happy individual, even when tipsy. This also was something new. When Roger had any mixed drinks he turned sullen, even more negative and belligerent.

Two of Tom's friends virtually cornered her against the rail one afternoon on deck and clearly expressed their concerns as to Ariel's motives and intentions regarding their best friend. They briefly reviewed their long history with him, his late wife, her daughter, and some of Tom's dating experiences, particularly with the lady originally set to be on this cruise. They knew absolutely nothing about Ariel other than Tom had met her at the law firm where she worked with his delinquencies and handled court appearances. They most definitely did not want their pal hurt by some selfish, greedy little gold-digger.

She was more than slightly intimidated, actually a bit apprehensive they might toss her overboard. She didn't know them at all; but quickly realized they truly cared about Tom. Their only motive was to protect him. She concluded he must indeed be an all around good person to have such loyal long-term friends, and one an ex-step son-in-law at that.

All too soon, the cruise and this delightful interlude came to its end, and they were again headed to Eastern Washington and more snow.

Arriving home, Ariel discovered Ryan's puppy had been taken from his enclosure. He was missing one afternoon when school let out. Despite searching the animal shelter, placing ads in both the local and Wenatchee papers, searching the town on foot and by car, no trace could be found. This was a problem without a solution. Ryan finally accepted that his little pal was gone; he and Ariel both held onto the mental picture of his having found a good home and was a happy little dog. He had only been theirs for a very few weeks.

Her little '72 Fiat Spyder was neither designed nor built for winter driving conditions in the mountains. The south of France, zipping around curves in warm sunlight along the Mediterranean was far more suitable. Ryan spent many evenings in the garage trying to coax it into starting and running better and with greater reliability. He was learning much more about car repair and maintenance than any of his buddies; but, the hard way; no instructor, no books and no help except for mom. She had some experience with old Buicks and Cadillacs, but didn't know anything about the little Italian car that was of much help.

En route to work one morning, however, the tiny vehicle suddenly started spewing forth steam, lurched, jerked and came to a stop at a long-closed gas station still several miles from Wenatchee. Opening the 'boot' in the attempt to see what could be wrong this time, provided Ariel no clue, whatever. She managed to get it started again and limped back home.

There was no way to get to work; no public transportation and no known townspersons commuting to Wenatchee with whom she might get a ride.

She had no choice but to call on Tom for help; the most difficult telephone call ever. The only time she had asked Roger for anything was to come home when Jillian had been injured, he had simply ignored the request for over five hours. Now she had to ask someone for help; and she didn't really know him all that well. Sure, they had driven, flown, sailed and slept together, but she had no concept of how he might respond to her needing help. What would his reaction be?

There being no real choice, she carefully dialed his number, hung up the phone, briefly contemplated calling one of the lawyers at his home that she would not be in. No, that was not an option; there were too many client matters needing her attention. She needed her job and it required her being on site each day and even weekends on many occasions.

There was no working from home in those days--no computer networks even thought of much less in existence.

Reluctantly she again dialed Tom's number and waited. He was surprised to receive any call that early in the morning, especially one from Ariel. She apologized profusely for having to bother him, finally explaining that her little car had apparently died and she was without any means of getting to work; would he consider driving up to get her?

"Of course, I'll be happy to," he responded the instant she quit apologizing long enough for him to get a word in. "Just give me a few minutes to finish shaving and get dressed; I'll be right there. I'm glad to help and you don't need to apologize at all." What a different response. She still felt horribly guilty about having to ask and causing him inconvenience; it was after all a fifty-mile plus round trip.

In what seemed simultaneously forever and virtually just minutes, Tom pulled up in the alley and stopped next to her still-steaming little convertible. Ryan had not yet left for school and met Tom at the back door. Together they pushed the Fiat into the garage, neither having any hint as to the further car adventures they would share, with that vehicle and numerous others. How she would get home this day and to work for the following was a question begging some sort of answer, also to be addressed later.

Tom came to her office at noon, picked her up for lunch at his house, and explained how her transportation situation would be taken care of. She was to drive the little Dodge Dart. It might not be the most exciting vehicle on the road, but ran beautifully and had good winter tires. He would use the gas-guzzling Chrysler for his short daily commute. She was also to bring laundry to his house in the mornings, dry it during their lunch, rather than using any public laundry service. She had admitted to the 'dead' washer and laundry situation during the morning drive to Wenatchee. Tom had queried her at some length as to other things at her house might not be functioning very well, in addition to the Fiat.

As days and weeks passed they grew closer and found they really liked each other, shared similar values and hopes for better times in their lives. A real plus ... they both liked cats. Ariel had her 'Baby Chester', all 25# and more of him, and Tom's kitties were Sabbath, Jasper and Jasmine. They had complete run of his home and controlled his life. He was quite possibly the best-trained "pet human" on the planet. What kitties wanted, kitties received.

Snow melted, days grew longer and Tom found many ways to help Ariel and Ryan. She continued driving his little red car, now nick-named Donny Dodge. Ryan kept attempting repairs, finally discovering that the Fiat had thrown a rod. That was far beyond his ability to fix even if necessary parts could be found locally. Tom called his friend in Olympia (the ex-son-in-law who had cornered Ariel on the cruise), and enlisted his help in obtaining parts. Those simply were not available in North Central Washington. With needed replacement parts in hand, the Fiat was towed to the same shop in Wenatchee where it had already spent considerable time.

One of the mechanics wanted to purchase it, despite being extremely familiar with the vehicle and its numerous problems. He offered significantly more than Ariel had paid for it some three years earlier. His offer was accepted immediately. It hadn't run when she bought it, and didn't when she sold it. When it had functioned it had been such fun, and she truly would miss putting its top down and zipping along winding roads.

The '48 Buick convertible, however also was not in running condition due to Roger's having begun to tear it down. Covered in dust it occupied a corner of the garage. What was she to do about that? She certainly didn't have the money to hire a qualified mechanic put it into running condition and didn't know what Roger may have done in his initial efforts at alleged restoration. Had he removed parts that could be easily replaced, or difficult to even locate due to the vehicle's age? It would just have to sit there until who only knew.

With major snow melted in the region, Tom took her to the Lake Chelan Yacht Club where he maintained a cabin, and leased a slip for his boat. One week of tent camping following his and Rose's marriage convinced him that club membership and a leased cabin/villa space was far preferable. They had maintained membership and villa accommodations for years.

They walked the clubhouse grounds and he showed her the slip where the boat would be moored for the summer, and reviewed some of the numerous activities held each summer. There were so many things for kids to do there, too, so Ryan would definitely not be bored. Tom's late wife and her son had spent their summers there and enjoyed it tremendously. This woodsy retreat on a lovely lake was only about 45 miles from his East Wenatchee home, an easy commute during the week, and great place to spend weekends.

One late May afternoon, returning to their offices after lunch and having finished Ariel's laundry, Tom suggested she and Ryan move into his home as soon as school let out. It was plenty big enough, with a pool in the center of the structure, close to schools and more than adequate room for Ryan to have friends visit both in town and at the lake. He outlined the many advantages for both --- the commute would be eliminated; Ryan's opportunities for better schooling and greater participation in sports; Tom's household appliances all functioned; he had two vehicles that also ran well. It simply made more sense. He was convinced this was totally logical, and put forth an excellent case, also pointing out he wanted their company. He was absolutely correct in all respects.

Tom needed someone in his life to take care of. He had married Rose nearly twenty years before, and raised her son as his own. Jim was now in his early 20's, with a good job, his own house also in the same area and engaged to be married. Tom was widowed and truly didn't want to be alone any longer; Ariel was divorced and struggling to support herself and Ryan.

Roger had made only one child support payment, in that princely amount of $75. No further payment had been forthcoming. Court orders meant nothing to him. He simply ignored them. The state support enforcement agency only assisted single mothers on welfare at that time; no way was Ariel ever going to apply for that. Begging on a street corner would come first.

That one payment had immediately gone for Ryan's basketball shoes. He needed more than a single pair of sport shoes. Shirts, jeans, underwear, socks and school shoes, jackets and all, were consistently outgrown rapidly; no to mention other school expenses. Tom was more than willing to take on raising another boy, and take care of his mother. All Ariel needed to do was accept his invitation and simply move in, immediately. He would rent a truck and it would all be very simple.

Just up and move to this man's home? He had to be joking, didn't he? She just couldn't do that. It wasn't right, correct, proper, or even acceptable in her estimation.

"No, I don't think so" she answered softly. His offer was totally generous, absolutely logical and certainly genuine; however, she just could not accept the invitation to share his home. To have helped host his annual open house party Wenatchee's spring celebration, cleaning, cooking and serving for days, greeting scores of people she didn't know from Adam's off-ox was one thing. Moving into his home, on a permanent basis, was quite a different matter.

Besides, her major concern was Ryan. He was still young and forming his ideas of morality and appropriate adult behavior. Roger had brought a number of women, some more than slightly strange, into the Barbaria house for occasional nights. According to Ryan most did not return a second time. Ryan had questioned Ariel about his father's practices, and she had been hard pressed to come up with any reasonable answers; just that Roger had to live his own way. She did not want to set an equally bad example; although a permanent move to Tom's home actually was quite different. No, just moving in with him simply would not be the right thing to do.

Tom was silent for only a moment before asking a bit shyly, "Well then, why don't we get married?" His late wife Rose had actually been his fourth wife, so the idea of marrying again presented no major hurdle for him. His first marriage lasted only six months; the second was to a single mother with two children. This broke up within months, and then they had re-married before divorcing again. That second time, she had her kids in the car and Tom held the two little dogs securely in his arms as she drove away.

He had met Rose through her work at a service club; a single mother and son Jim for whom he gladly assumed a parental role. Now Jim was on his own and doing well. They enjoyed over sixteen years together before Rose passed away. Tom was rattling around in a four-bedroom house with a pool in the center; three cats for company. Even weekends at Lake Chelan weren't much fun for him alone. The yacht club membership consisted of couples and families, not widowers.

Tom was admittedly lonely and didn't want to remain alone. He needed someone to care for; Ariel clearly needed a caring and capable person in her life, despite her determination to succeed, both financially and personally on her own. She had a job and was able to pay basic expenses for herself and Ryan, but anything beyond bare bones simply was not possible.

Dad was gone, and other than her friends Richard and James she had no one on whom to rely; having served as third person 'cover' for them on occasion and enjoying summer days on the lake. They remained supportive, but also had lives of their own.

Jillian had married, moved a hundred plus miles away and had plenty to deal with in her own life. Annie shunned Ariel completely, refusing all overtures, even reasonably polite communication.

Edythe maintained her consistent criticism of Ariel, by telephone and in writing; not only believing every negative comment Roger and Annie uttered against her, but was also convinced those to be greatly understated. She knew Ariel was far worse, and berated her in lengthy letters. She continued finding fault with her having divorced Roger, working full time, and worst of all, Ariel drank wine. That had been a major criticism since the 1968 hysterectomy, re-suturing, relapses, lengthy hospitalizations and a doctor's instructions to regularly consume the *'evil liquid"*. No medication had been found to calm nerves and improve her appetite. So her surgeon had specified wine with clear instructions as to dosage and frequency.

At any possible opportunity Edythe sternly and relentlessly queried Ryan about his mother's *alcoholism*, and preached the evils of drink. Ryan lost all respect for his grandmother the more she criticized Ariel; he knew how she struggled to keep the roof over their heads and food on their table. He felt she was quite entitled to a glass of wine – when it could be afforded.

Ariel had never requested anything of Edythe since having no choice but to borrow the $750 to purchase the extra Seattle lot decades earlier, and truly wished to live her life without any input whatever from her. Edythe had been repaid a full $1,000 in less than four months; $250 was not a bad rate of interest.

Ariel and Ryan visited her when they were in the Puget Sound area to rotate and replenish gallery paintings; but as briefly as possible. Ryan didn't want to see Edythe at all, but understood it was the polite thing to do; and if he refused the grandmother would make life even more miserable for his mom. Ariel could only imagine the reaction should Annie inform her that Ariel had taken Ryan and moved into some man's house, married or not. She was finally coming to the conclusion that there truly was no pleasing Edythe, regardless of what she did.

Ariel recalled the desperate prayer uttered months before when she had pleaded with God for help ... to show her the way. Was Tom the answer? He hardly fit the "knight in shining armor" image, and the obligatory mighty white steed was a little red compact; however, he certainly had come to her rescue ... and, he was nice, a kind and caring person. They had fun together. She continued to ponder this somewhat casual proposal of marriage. No way had she expected candles, flowers, or Tom down on bended knee; actually not a proposal at all.

The major element in this life-changing question was that she did not want to set the same, or even remotely similar, example for Ryan that Roger had done and continued to do. He had women of all ages and descriptions in and out of his place on a revolving door basis. Her painting friend in Barbaria was only one person apprising her of his current habits, though she truly did not want to know.

Ariel had to do right by Ryan; she could not fail him. Jillian was married; Annie was living with a local logger in Barbaria. Ryan was fourteen; a difficult age for a boy trying to make sense of adult relationships and his role in the universe.

She was silent for nearly a mile before softly answering, "Well, yes, I guess we could." It was hardly a fairy-tale proposal or acceptance. Tom had asked her to marry him and she had accepted. They smiled at each other a bit shyly, and Ariel quietly giggled.

Plans were formulated immediately. They set a June 11th date; school would be out. Tom's good friends, the same who had cornered Ariel aboard ship and questioned her intentions toward their pal, were invited with their wives, of course, the minister engaged, a ring purchased, the short 'to-do' lists consulted and items checked off as tasks were completed. This was definitely planned to be a simple ceremony with a very limited guest list.

With school out for summer vacation, Ariel and Ryan moved most of their things out of the Barbaria house to Tom's in East Wenatchee. Tom deemed yard sales to be utterly absurd, total waste of time and effort; however, when Ariel explained if they held one at her house, people would actually pay them some small amount and take the unwanted possessions off the property. No dump fees were required; no packing. To the senior branch finance office manager it did at last make sense. He brought a cash box and set up at a card table, smilingly accepting bills and coins, slashing price tags willingly. The assortment of excess possessions rapidly dwindled.

Their plans for a simple, small and quiet ceremony were quickly turned upside down. Everyone catching word of the impending ceremony joyously insisted on attending; the little church was filled.

Suddenly realizing no décor of any sort was in place, she purchased flowers for the bridal party at 4:00 pm for the 7:00 o'clock ceremony. The florist all but fainted dead away when she finally realized the wedding was to be that very day, and in only three hours. Then she understood why only flowers on hand in her cooler had been considered. Ariel and Ryan picked pink and yellow climbing roses from the yard, and covered coffee cans with foil for altar décor.

Ryan drove Tom and Ariel to the church in the Chrysler, not yet in possession of a driving license, of course. A local Deputy met them on one street, smiled broadly, waved to Ryan, and flicking his light bar in passing. It seems even the local lawmen had heard of the nuptials. While unacquainted with Tom, they all knew Roger quite well. Ryan also provided the music by playing a Bach tape on Ariel's little portable stereo player

Tom's step-daughter helped Ariel prepare finger food snacks, cracker trays and set up a small bar in Ariel's house for the reception. All those in attendance were so very pleased these two had found each other, were first and foremost good friends and now officially a couple.

Months later Ariel learned her friend James had opened the church door to step outside during the ceremony and virtually pushed Roger off the steps where he had been crouched at the door, listening. Rather strange behavior for anyone, and even more so for an ex-spouse.

It was soon clear that together Tom and Ariel still had far more furniture and household goods than they needed or could possibly use. In addition to his house, there was the lake cabin, also well stocked. Household items were shuffled between Lake and house, resulting in still more excess. Another yard sale seemed the logical choice; especially since Tom claimed no sentimental or emotional ties to any furniture pieces or household goods. Early American style items with green plaid upholstery and ruffles predominated in the East Wenatchee house; Ariel's few pieces were of simple design and straight lines. Tom liked those mainly due to lack of fussiness.

After clearing cupboards and closets at the cabin, restocking with some extras, and in general taking inventory of their useable and excess household goods, a sale was set. A two-day stint in a larger population area eliminated more of the excess and with donations of left-overs simplified their lives considerably. Furniture and general household goods held no great importance for Tom. He liked his home environment to be simple and easy to care for.

Home décor and landscaping didn't hold his attention for long. Clean, tidy and trimmed were his only requirements. Clean, uncluttered and functional were just fine. Gradually the two households merged in a quite comfortable manner.

The only cloud was Ryan's steadfast refusal to also move, enroll in an East Wenatchee school and live with them full time, visiting Roger on occasion.

He thoroughly enjoyed time at the lake, swimming, boating, water skiing and meeting kids his age from the area. Summer was excellent; only in September did his insistence on staying in Barbaria come to the fore. At the time, neither Ariel nor Tom knew about the grandparents' June visit and their dominating influence. Roger's mother issued declarations, and everyone obeyed. She informed Ryan he must stay in Barbaria with his father, regardless of what any judge may decree or court document contain. It was his duty to take care of Roger. She issued commands and her word ruled, well into her 90's.

In his late teens, Ryan finally told Ariel that the paternal grandparents had been in town the weekend of the wedding to support Roger. They drilled into Ryan that he must stay with and take care of his father regardless of any insignificant judge's decree or orders. They didn't know anything about the man Ariel was marrying, only that with a Scottish name, he obviously was not Scandinavian, which was reason enough to be highly dubious of him and his motives suspect. They were willing to, and did, use their grandson in those efforts despite harm to his personal future and education.

Roger did not know, or ever learn, how to cook anything, relying on cheap fast foot outlets for the majority of meals. Donuts, toaster-thawed items or dry cereal served for morning; milk availability was uncertain. Nor did he pay any attention whatever to Ryan's educational progress, lack of same, or future wellbeing. The grandparents had no education beyond Eighth grade. Roger had deliberately shunned post-secondary education opportunities, and they apparently saw no need for Ryan to pursue any. Therefore, he must remain with Roger in the small town with its limited opportunities.

Ariel had taught Ryan how to prepare a few items so that he would not be helpless in a kitchen, but his menu selections were somewhat limited. Money for groceries also presented a problem. Roger's employment was subject to lapses, and he had no clue about grocery shopping.

Before Ariel's escape one contractor had kept Roger employed year-round despite the usual lack of jobs during winter. He didn't want Ariel and the children to undergo stress from lack of income. Having grown up in the area he was well aware of the scarcity of employment available to Ariel. However, with Ariel no longer in the picture, Roger had lost that job as well.

When he had no money for groceries, fast food on a credit card was the option. Lack of employment and income did not deter his frequenting a local bar and purchasing drinks for other patrons as well as himself. Those practices resulted in Roger gaining significant amounts of debt, extra weight and Ryan's diet severely lacking nutritional balance.

Decades later Roger's mother apologized to Ariel in tears, for having interfered. She came to like Tom a great deal and even told him what a blessing he was in Ariel's life, also acknowledging that Ryan would have benefitted significantly from more of his influence. By then, of course, Ryan was out of school and been deprived of educational, social and health advantages.

Ariel had put her house up for sale, and accepted a lease/purchase agreement from an East Coast couple relocating to the Cascades region. That worked out beneficially for both parties. They maintained the property well and made lease payments promptly. Ariel's life, financially of course, but more importantly, emotionally and personally improved tremendously. Ryan remained a concern, but she and Tom continued to include him whenever and wherever he would agree. He was a bit resistant to their marriage at first and didn't always agree with Tom. He was a teenage boy, and typically still thought he could get Mom and Dad back together if he just worked at it. That wasn't going to happen, but he didn't want to give up the thought entirely. This concept had been strongly encouraged by Roger's parents, primarily Ryan's grandmother leading to their insistence that he remain in Barbaria with Roger.

Later, Ryan came to appreciate and highly respect Tom. Roger's mother had liked him as soon as she met him later on, recognizing his care for both Ariel and Ryan. That recognition and appreciation came much later. She apologized for her interference in all their lives, and this was a lady not much given to apologizing for anything.

Three Decades, plus

Their lives settled nicely into a very satisfactory routine; both working in their respective positions, sharing house and yard maintenance, and enjoying time at the lake. He and Rose had followed that same pattern of both work and both play. This was another entirely new thing in Ariel's life, but she adapted. Tom had immediately set about convincing her that she too was fully entitled to fun and enjoyment. Life was not all work and no play. It was not criticism and blame.

Gradually she relaxed, allowing herself to laugh, smile, sing silly songs at parties and chat freely. New, but nice, and she enjoyed this unexpected phase of life. Tom was so caring, gentle and loving, only wanting her to be happy. She felt safe at last; how could she not trust him. Was this the love she had sought, never really hoping to experience it? Nightmares dwindled to near obscurity. When one did waken her, Tom's snoring reassured her that all was well. She was safe.

Very early in their relationship Tom had shared his history of petit mal seizure incidents. He was regularly monitored by a neurologist and absolutely faithful about his medications. He had experienced a couple incidents prior to their marriage, and sporadically thereafter. These were mild, absence-type incidents and were of minor inconvenience; provided he was not driving. Tom did not really enjoy driving and very shortly Ariel was at the wheel a majority of the time. Piloting the boat, however, remained his responsibility.

The first full summer following their marriage was busy beyond all expectations. First his step-son Jim and fiancé set their wedding for July. Tom and Ariel hosted the rehearsal dinner at their home, with even more guests than had attended the annual Wenatchee Festival in May.

The wedding was in a local church with reception on the lawn of the bride's family friend. Late that night found Tom and Ariel still in their festive garb, returning from a 24-hour grocery store with more beer. Ariel's long dress was folded up on her lap so she could drive; Tom held a case of beer on his lap and there was more in the trunk; gas gauge hovered on "E", and area gas stations had long since closed. Would they make it all the way back to the festivities? Somewhat apprehensively they looked at each other in the dim dashboard lighting and burst out laughing, "neither of us is biologically responsible for any of this – what on earth are we doing." That memory brought chuckles for years.

Next on the calendar was Edythe's 80th birthday. Her sister Olga and brother Fred traveled from Minnesota by train. Ariel met them in Wenatchee late at night, with Ryan driving the large sedan. Tom was at the lake with his buddies and their wives from Oregon and Western Washington who had stayed after the wedding. They would all be down in the late morning. Well after midnight, the train finally arrived, late as usual.

The elderly siblings and luggage were somewhat briskly removed from the car and placed on the loading platform, slightly disheveled, with puzzled looks, searching the small crowd for someone to meet them. Both Conductor and Steward retreated immediately, bounding up steps into the passenger car; and the train pulled away.

Ariel immediately hugged them both and steered them toward the car where Ryan waited with doors open. He had grabbed their bags and quickly stowed those in the trunk.

Once everyone was seated, Ariel's aunt turned and asked her if it was her new husband at the wheel. "No, Aunt Olga, that's my son Ryan, Tom is up at the lake and will be down later." Her next question came quickly, "Then who are you?" Oh dear, not only was Uncle rather vague and addled; but Auntie as well. "I'm Ariel, your sister Edythe's daughter, remember?" Her face remained rather expressionless.

Meanwhile, Uncle, seated in front, turned to Ryan and announced they had to hurry because he needed to grease all the dozers before the morning crew arrived to start clearing trees. He was back several decades in Alaska building the Alcan Highway, or perhaps the DEW-line; certainly not in Wenatchee in 1983.

Ryan shot Ariel a startled look; later admitting he nearly headed for the local hospital and some help with these two elderly relatives. Neither apparently had clue one as to time, date, location or reason for being wherever it was they were.

Once over the river and home, Ariel and Ryan concentrated on getting them settled into beds for the remainder of the night; Tom and his friends would be down from the lake mid-morning. A generous slug of whiskey, very little ice please, and Auntie was quickly and contentedly asleep. Uncle's clothes had gone immediately into the washer and when showered, he was tucked into a pair of Tom's pajamas and asleep in moments. Travel had been hard on both elderly siblings.

Ariel woke after a brief nap and left for work placing Ryan on *'guard duty'* with strict orders to stick with Uncle every minute he might be awake, get him dressed in the cleaned clothes, and absolutely not allow him to wander off. Who might have a clue as to who, where, when, whatever Uncle might be by morning.

Auntie slept until late morning, and was quite content to sip her coffee and daintily nibble on sweet rolls after her shower. Ryan didn't worry much about her, quite content to sit in a comfortable chair watching a daytime program she favored. Ryan accompanied Uncle Fred faithfully as he toured the yard and short distances on the street, commenting on the lack of progress on adjacent property. The trees had not been cut, no roads punched through; time was running short, and where were crews? Apparently he was still in Alaska; that 'raw' land was the East Wenatchee Golf and Country Club.

Tom knew immediately something was amiss when Ryan met him at the door with, "man, am I glad to see you!" Ryan was always courteous, albeit still just slightly reserved with Tom, but this was something else, as he quickly discovered. Tending to Uncle kept them both busy for the rest of the day and well into the evening. Tom abandoned Ryan to solitary guard duty only long enough to transport Auntie to the hair salon. They were both delighted to see Ariel after work.

Next morning everyone was loaded into the car. Auntie and Uncle were slightly more rational after another full night's sleep, and the entourage headed for Bellevue and Edythe's 80th birthday celebration at her church.

The church ladies did a beautiful job of planning and preparing the entire thing. Tom was attentive to Edythe even though she introduced him to her friends by various names, many being those of long-dead relatives. He just smiled, shook hands, and helped old ladies with refreshments, carefully pouring more coffee, providing cream and sugar along with additional cookies. Jillian, Annie and Ryan attempted fading into the background after the initial receiving line was concluded, responding politely to repeated inquiries as to their identities. Many in attendance could not possibly image that 'little Ariel' was all grown up with children of her own. They remembered her as a pretty, but quiet, little girl with blond ringlets; and later as the young lady who taught Sunday School, sang and played the organ.

Before leaving home for the celebration, Ariel contacted her cousin in Minnesota regarding Uncle's level of confusion and they arranged for another cousin to transport him from the reception to the airport and fly him home. His daughter would meet him at the airport in Minneapolis. A name tag with his name, destination and daughter's contact information was attached to his shirt. She had somehow thought the trip visiting with his sisters and nieces would serve to improve his mental state; not so.

With travel arrangements set, Olga and Edythe safely back in her apartment, Tom, Ryan and Ariel fled for home along with Jillian and Annie. Sister Olga spent a few more days with Edythe at her church-run condo before leaving again on the train. Tom had done yeoman duty plus in dealing with Edythe, relatives, her elderly friends and the entire production.

A few weeks later Ariel received a letter from Edythe complaining about how tired she was, and accusing her sister of having stolen a favorite bra, and that she was only thankful the ordeal was over. Not a word about her many church friends who attended, the many cards and wishes, to say nothing of the considerable effort they had expended for her birthday reception or how very nice it was. All the cards, food, flowers, friends and accolades brought only complaints...par for the course.

The remainder of the summer was considerably calmer, with time at the lake, various social events there and in town, visits from friends and of course, their jobs. They settled in to a quite comfortable and normal life together. Ryan still insisted on continuing school in Barbaria, spending weekends with them and becoming a little more acquainted with the somewhat larger town. Ariel sang in the Methodist Church choir, and having joined there was soon appointed to various commissions and committees. Ryan attended Sunday services with her; Tom only occasionally, primarily when she did solo or small group musical numbers.

Tom's sporadic and totally unpredictable seizure incidents continued with no discernible pattern; all relatively mild with medications adjusted from time to time. No major concerns were expressed by neurologists who readily admitted lack of medical knowledge as to causation or possible cure; only medication and monitoring.

Ariel made significant improvements in Tom's diet; he lost weight and felt much better than he had when heavier. Lean meats, less beef, more fruits and vegetables, salads were increased; burgers, fries and shakes diminished. She was watchful of his rest patterns, guarding against his becoming over-tired; stress was also a factor she tried to mitigate where possible.

Corporate stress and ever-present push to put more business on the books regardless of quality was beyond her control. He tended to fret and stew over some things, while firmly declaring they didn't bother him at all.

It had taken some time for her to figure all this out, and so began to keep a log of events and circumstances preceding incidents, on the chance that might be helpful to his neurologist. His work emerged as a likely source of most stress; not surprising in the finance business. Corporate emphasis was consistently placed on ever greater short-term outstanding loan growth, with delinquency ratios deemed less important. Tom firmly held the concept that moneys borrowed were to be moneys repaid in compliance with terms of the executed documents. He never understood the corporate logic of making loans that held little chance of being repaid. His consistently-held concept was that valid, repayable loans together with a low delinquency ratio constituted sound business practice, resulting in predictable profit.

Ariel's real estate paralegal position in addition to billing, collections, accounting and trust duties had grown considerably over the years, and should have been shared with at least one other staff person. The managing partner of the firm refused to hire anyone, nor would he consider reasonable compensation for any female employee. After overhearing him state unequivocally that no @#*^%# woman was ever going to be paid more than $1,000 a month in *his* office, Ariel began job-hunting.

When she quit and the full scope of her duties became clear to the other partners, two people were initially hired to replace her. They soon needed help and a third was added just to handle the real estate transactions, foreclosures, incorporations, accounting and collections, quarterly taxes, individual and bankruptcy trusts. So much for the managing partner squeezing out ever-more production for less compensation; other partners finally learned that could only go so far.

Additionally, that lawyer faced repeated reprimands from the State Bar Association on a number of occasions over the years for improper rulings and derogatory racial comments when he was appointed to the District Court bench. One year he filed and ran for the Superior Court Judge position; being soundly defeated.

This fellow was also chair of the finance commission at the Methodist church and made much of his high standing there. Ariel found it rather interesting and ironically amusing; particularly as law firm community gossip about his office management tactics together with ever-increasing court-related problems and official reprimands filtered back to her.

After working briefly for a quasi-governmental job-training entity, she was hired by a County-wide Port District primarily focused on economic development.

Travel - Pacific Rim

Her lease/option agreement for the Barbaria property had worked very well for months, with payments arriving timely. She deposited the checks, sending the correct percentage amount to Roger each month. Her lessees were delighted with the chalet style house, and decided to exercise their purchase option.

On receipt of the full payment, Ariel again forwarded Roger's percentage to him promptly. He had made only one $75 child support payment, which served to considerably reduce the percentage due him from a statutory 50-50 split.

Years later Ryan told his mom that the moment Roger received that check, he raced to the local bank branch, deposited it, withdrew cash and then rushed to Wenatchee to begin spending … on anything and everything that he could find. Not a solitary dollar was saved.

Ariel received the major percentage of proceeds pursuant to property distribution court orders. She put some money into a growth fund together with cash value of the life insurance policy Dad had taken out for her years earlier. She had no debt; the first time in her life she had no pressing fear of her financial future. Any debt she might acquire would be hers.

Tom was consistently responsible financially. He did not ever purchase anything he could not pay for; quite unlike Roger who would spend a quarter if he only had a dime.

She and Tom began to think of traveling and considered several possible destinations. They were in no great rush, spent time gathering bits and pieces of information, looking through the atlas and pondering. Tom was still managing the finance company branch and Ariel in economic development.

Her economic development job involved property management for a large incubator building, marketing industrial park properties, securing industrial revenue bonding, preparing grant applications, bid requests, project monitoring, organizing decades of resolutions and motions passed by the board of directors, none of which had ever been codified. Commissioners and the manager relied solely on memory with respect to actions taken and projects authorized over the decades of operation. There was some written record; however, no reference listing or indexing existed. A sizeable assortment of topographical, plat, and various county maps of existing roads, those vacated at prior times, and proposed road improvements were simply stuffed into a basket, unlabeled, unidentified and unlisted in any form. Finding a specific item could only be accomplished by someone recalling what the rolled-up paper might look like on the outside, or the color of the rubber band.

Office administration had been under the direction of a woman who apparently wanted total control of any and all information pursuant to the port district; she, and only she, knew what and/or where information was stored. She went to a medical appointment one afternoon and never returned to the office. It was Ariel's task to make sense of all of it so records and information could not only be available upon reasonable request, but also comply with more current public records requirements. It was an enormous job.

She also became acquainted with business owners and entrepreneurs interested in relocating to the area. One such was an inventor and manufacturer of equipment used in paper manufacturing processes. He had worked in that field for several years in Europe and was looking for properties for his business as well as residence. One requirement was sufficient land to accommodate horses, cattle and buffalo. Having lived in Sweden and Switzerland, he also wanted a mountain setting. Despite diligent searches, that was not to be found locally; he and extended family moved to Idaho. He was a very pleasant person, highly skilled, an inventor/builder of paper manufacturing equipment. His family was closely involved in his business enterprises, and Ariel found them to be very nice friendly people, assets in any community. However, when they all packed up and moved, she didn't expect to see them ever again.

Neither Tom nor Ariel had ever visited the Southern Hemisphere or Asia. After weeks of searching and inquiring, Tom located a Pacific Rim tour that included all air and ground transport arrangements, accommodations, most meals. This appealed to both and arrangements were quickly made; passports obtained, together with necessary visas, and packing commenced. Ariel smiled and even giggled as she sent the check off; that she was actually going to fly off to distant places was amazing. She actually had the money to pay for this trip, and they certainly would not starve as a result. To be off on a trip with someone she loved, and who truly loved her was even more amazing; sending little shivers of joy up and down her back.

A niggling part of her brain chided her for spending money on pleasure; she should save every penny for … what? Old age? She hadn't expected to see thirty, and here she was at forty-seven, married to a man who valued her, wanted only her happiness; with sufficient assets to have some fun, not just worry about bills. Wow! What a change. Could this become habit-forming?

Tom had reluctantly agreed she could pay for this trip; but, the next one was definitely his treat. The next? They had yet to depart on the first. Tom had virtually rescued her financially, provided a lovely home and everything she and Ryan could possibly need. He had even paid off Roger's long-delinquent legal fees. He did not want the fledgling lawyer cut out of hard-earned income.

Ariel was less anxious on this flight by very small aircraft to Seattle, but somewhat apprehensive watching the co-pilot look out the window, flip through pages of his maps, glance out at the terrain and flip more map pages. Even Tom expressed minor concern. It was Ariel's turn then to provide a miniscule shred of reassurance; identifying trailheads she recognized and assure him she knew the way out should they crash. His wry grin did not convey any great desire to test her mountaineering skills. A very real benefit of living in Barbaria had been hiking in the Cascades. She had also participated in a few official searches for lost hikers, children, and rock climbers. Before long though, the mountains were crossed and they landed at SeaTac.

Once in California from Seattle, their trip started with a flight to Tahiti; landing on a narrow airstrip barely above crashing ocean waves seemingly inches from the water. This truly was an exciting introduction to the tropics.

Descending to the tarmac, sultry air slapped their faces like steamy wool blankets; but everything was absolutely beautiful. Flowers, colorful birds, fluffy white clouds in a cerulean sky and lush vegetation everywhere. This really was a paradise, even at the airport.

Hotels all appeared to be single storey buildings when viewed from the streets. Building codes on the island restricted building heights to that of palm trees. Multi-storey hotels were constructed from top to bottom; starting at street level and descending to the beach. The entire island seemed to jut abruptly from the sea. There were valleys and more level areas among the peaks that provided for town, residences and farm land.

Exploring on foot became a bit wearying in the unfamiliar heat and humidity, despite being incredibly interesting. To rest at bit, they boarded a village jitney on its regular schedule around the island perimeter. This presented delightful views of farms, beaches, birds and animals, some identifiable, some not. Bread, milk and mail were delivered to isolated farms in boxes mounted on posts at the ends of overgrown lanes. Fences constructed of tree trunks and branches had sprouted, so even the fence posts were lush and green. Pools, beach and hotel accommodations were great and food splendid.

From Tahiti they flew to Sydney for a lay-over and flight to Auckland, which appeared quite similar to pictorial views of towns in Great Britain, with friendly people and beautiful scenery. The stay included a harbor tour on a catamaran where they were not only allowed, but encouraged to take the helm, briefly, for another new experience. The tour continued inland, with stops at a Maori village for a thermal-cooked banquet and cultural performance.

They traveled farther down the North Island to sheep ranches, a glow-worm cave and under ground river float near Rotarua. Ariel swallowed her claustrophobia and stepped into a tiny craft for a fantastic underground float through the glowworm cave. Presence of an overhead cable that could be used for exit served to reassure. It was not needed. Small glowing creatures hanging from the ceiling provided an amazing sight in addition to illumination.

A short flight aboard a vintage DC-3 brought them to Christchurch on the South Island. What a marvelous country.

A lovely afternoon there found them relaxing on a balcony overlooking the city park, enjoying wine and crackers, watching horse-drawn carriages leisurely traverse pathways. This city was beautiful with architecture closely resembling what she thought London might look like. Would she ever go to Europe? The initial "oh, no" thought faded at the possibility that it just could possibly happen. She had begun to perceive the future could possibly hold all manner of unexpectedly delightful experiences.

Ariel struggled a bit to accept that she was really on a trip, thousands of miles from home, seeing all manner of new things and enjoying new experiences with someone who loved her and truly cared for her. Life was so very good.

Back to Sydney, their next stop was a sheep station in the outback and demonstration of sheepherding by most efficient dogs. They had amazing ability to respond instantly to whistled signals and carefully manage the large flocks. Sheep quickly obeyed without exhibiting any fear of the dogs, whatever.

Then it was further south to Canberra, and Melbourne. Each stop was a wonderfully new experience; places they had only read about and located on the globe. Now here they were, walking the streets, meeting people, enjoying new foods, basking in the sunshine, strolling on white sand beaches … actually … two very ordinary folks from Washington state. Ariel had to pinch herself frequently to be sure she wasn't dreaming. And to be here with Tom was truly wonderful; he held her hand, they hugged and kissed – frequently for no reason whatever.

Steadily Ariel eliminated more and more negativity from her mind. Tom was proud of her and her accomplishments in the business world, her painting and in music. He encouraged her and she began to acquire a little more sense of confidence. Where first Edythe, and then Roger, had consistently criticized anything and everything she did, Tom complimented. They both had found fault with her in every possible aspect of life; he encouraged and promoted her interests.

He had particularly appreciated her support and reinforcement of his corporate obligations in the finance field. Unlike Roger, Tom wanted her with him at corporate functions and was proud to enter conferences with her at his side. They truly were a good fit.

Singapore was next, including a luncheon at the vintage hotel, savoring those world-famous Singapore Slings at the very place they had been invented, and in the gardens under which solid silver serving pieces were hidden during WW-II. Japanese and German officers had been wined and dined there in luxury, without a clue the famous fortune in silver carts and trays rested directly beneath their feet.

Elderly women moved efficiently through the streets constantly sweeping with long bamboo and grass brooms. Ariel had acquired gemstones and finished jewelry items along the way, and Singapore was no exception. Coral in Tahiti, Tom bought opals for her in Australia; and here she watched a skilled craftsman create a beautiful amethyst and gold pendant. It was purchased the moment he finished. His broad smile reflected his pleasure; at the sale of course, but also that Ariel had watched him create it and appreciated his skill enough to purchase the piece.

Their next stop was Bangkok, where the annual water cleansing festival was in full swing. Canal water was scooped up using any and all available containers and tossed to allegedly wash all the past year's sins and problems from those being so 'sprinkled'. The activity was quite playful; however canal water was absolutely filthy, incapable of much 'cleansing' to be sure.

Tom's clothes all went to the hotel laundry. Ariel rinsed hers out in the tub and hung them on the shower rod to dry, fully expecting her dress to land in the trash. It came out beautifully clean and ready to wear without a bit of ironing required.

Dinner that evening was a sunset cruise aboard a 300-year old rice boat; gorgeous views and absolutely delicious food, the origins of which no one queried. Some dishes were identifiable; others not. No questions, just enjoyment of the splendid entrees, appetizers and desserts, together with excellent wines.

They visited temples, viewed the Royal Palace and barges across a canal, and of course, purchased trinkets, including small prayer bells, from the ever-present children peddling trinkets.

At one temple, Ariel left her shoes on a step and went inside while Tom sat in the courtyard taking in the scene and enjoying the sunshine. Several well-fed cats lounged about under trees, others idly strolling; but all somehow appeared to be waiting. A robed priest emerged from the temple carrying a large, beautifully decorated pottery bowl, and placed it under one of the trees. Cats all immediately perked to attention, but only sat up, watching, and didn't approach the bowl which obviously contained something of interest. One large and stunningly handsome tuxedo tom slowly stood, stretched, yawned and languidly stepped toward the decorated bowl. Carefully sitting beside it, he reached out a front paw and picked through the contents. Having selected a suitable morsel, he deliberately lifted it to his mouth and ate. This pawing, choosing and quite dainty devouring was repeated until he was satisfied; each tid-bit having been specifically singled out and consumed. Only when he meticulously cleaned his paws and whiskers, slowly rose, and casually strolled to a choice resting place did the other cats approach the dish to eat. None individually selected each bite; they indiscriminately plunged heads into the bowl and ate whatever they could get hold of. Tom found this highly amusing; particularly in light of their four cats at home, none of which would stand back and let another dine first. When Ariel joined him and heard the account the big tuxedo tom was curled up under the tree enjoying his nap, the end of his tail twitching ever so slightly at random intervals.

Waiting on the tarmac for departure to Hong Kong, Ariel first realized her apprehension about flying had utterly disappeared. The only concern this time was if a pilot, any pilot, might be boarding anytime in the foreseeable future. Total confusion among the crew dominated the cabin, with stewards darting forth and back. A last, pilot and co-pilot ambled across the tarmac and boarded. Finally in the air and on the next to last lap of their tour, Tom regaled her with tales of being in Hong Kong, Japan and Korea during his time in the Navy. There were so many things he wanted to show her, places to take her where he had been years before, if indeed, those still existed.

Hong Kong was truly an adventure and they walked miles through streets lined with shops, wafted incense smoke and sent printed prayers aloft at shrines. They gathered all manner of goods in what had to be the largest shopping mall on the planet. They rode the ferry from Kowloon to Hong Kong, then the counter-balance up the mountain and enjoyed high tea on a beautiful terrace overlooking the harbor. Much had changed since Tom's time there in the early 1950's. But many places remained quite as he remembered.

High-rise buildings of all types rose beside hovels, much as they had seen in Bangkok. The harbor was filled with junks of all sizes and descriptions, living quarters, cottage industries, fisheries and processors, floating markets, anything one could think of. The tides were expected to change out harbor waters, including whatever had accumulated, twice daily. Since entire families lived and worked aboard, waste materials abounded; the water not exactly the 'wild blue ocean'. Somehow, the harbor and its' residents continue to survive.

Tom sought out a tailor and was quickly measured for two suits, one dark and the other lighter gray; and also for custom-made boots. Ariel purchased a suit in rather neutral soft blue/gray tweed with just enough color to go well with a burgundy silk shell, ivory or shades of blue. She also found a silk dress, skirt and blouse on the tailor's sample rack at excellent prices.

Hunting out bargains had always been a habit, never to be abandoned throughout her life. She had picked berries and beans as a child to buy school clothes; purchasing garments at full retail pricing was not a consideration. No matter she was half-way around the world on a once-in-a lifetime trip, and all merchants "spoke fluent plastic". Cost-effective was a life-long mantra, and would remain so. Classic styles that would not be out of style and price were always her goal. All their purchases were delivered to the hotel next day accompanied by a gorgeous bouquet of orchids; a totally different experience from department store shopping in Wenatchee, Washington for sure.

Strolling down Nathan Road, he suggested they rest a bit and have a drink, expertly steering Ariel into a topless bar. The bar girls were indeed, topless (not that it mattered all that much). Tom ordered a glass of white wine for Ariel, sake for himself; and the drinks for the girls that were part of the program. He had truly expected Ariel to be at least somewhat taken aback; however … that just did not happen. While Tom sipped his sake, Ariel her white wine, and the girls their tea (in hard liquor glasses) the bar girls and Ariel talked about raising children, housing, fashion, schooling and other normal 'girl-talk". So much for shocking his church choir-singing, organ-playing wife. With a somewhat wry grin, he paid for all the drinks, left a good tip and the stroll down Nathan Road continued.

Jimmy's Kitchen had been highly recommended as 'the' place to eat in Kowloon, and they found that to be totally correct. Atmosphere abounded; there were autographed photos of early stage and screen stars, notables, opera divas, famous explorers, best-selling authors, generals, admirals and you-name-it covering the walls. Signatures occupied all available spaces in between framed sepia, black-and-white and occasional slightly faded color photos. The food was absolutely outstanding; piano/vocal entertainment, excellent. They even had a second order of Brussels sprouts; who on earth does that? Tom hadn't even known what Brussels sprouts were until he met Ariel. Those Jimmy's Kitchen sprouts were off-the-charts delicious.

At no time over the following decades however, were they able to come to any agreement as to the gender of the vocalist/pianist. It remains forever another of life's unanswered questions. Whichever, whatever, whoever, the music was great and the food absolutely splendid.

Ariel still struggled with the reality she was in Asia, enjoying travel with Tom; and he had planned it all with her pleasure his main goal. How had she been so fortunate? So unlike her earlier life.

Tokyo was their last stop before heading home, another outstanding experience with more shrines, palaces, parks, canals, water birds and beautiful flowers to be enjoyed.

Tom had briefly visited the Ginza years before on liberty, and wanted to see how that had changed over the years. He thought Ariel would enjoy seeing that unique area of Tokyo, and he was correct; the little she knew about it was rather mysterious. Having decided to take the rapid rail metro, they received excellent directions for getting there; the return trip not so explicit. They had a great time; the train sped over miles above and underground. Sight-seeing and shopping there was great.

Finally, with loudly protesting feet, they found the correct line for return to the "My City" terminal in the center of Tokyo. With subway map in hand, valiant effort was made to determine the appropriate station for getting off. "My City" terminal did not appear in English or anything similar on the map, and fearing they would go far beyond, they grabbed a random stop, and climbed long steps to the surface in hopes of seeing something familiar. No luck. Everyone wanted to help these confused Americans, and *everyone* allegedly spoke English. Not entirely true.

Many blocks, seemingly miles, later they finally spotted "My City" in the distance. Once there, all that remained was locating the bus stop (2) sign that would take them back to the hotel. The searched for the highly visible Subaru automobile sign in the distance, a landmark for locating it. Bus stop (2) was apparently located on the opposite side of this huge subway/train/office/ shopping mall/residential structure from where they stood on throbbing, aching feet with no landmark Subaru sign in view.

This massive building complex was at least 6 blocks long and who only knows how many wide. Rail tracks of all sorts and in virtually uncountable numbers stretched across the width, entering and exiting at various elevations. The interior consisted of shops in which many families lived, manufactured and sold product; restaurants large and small; medical/dental/legal services; anything and everything one could possibly imagine. No main corridors or straight lines existed to provide direction; and *everyone spoke English*, yah, sure ya-betcha. Smiling, bowing, everyone truly was eager to help, all to no avail.

After several unsuccessful attempts at descending broad steps to a lower level, walking what they desperately hoped was directly across that lower level, and ascending more stairs only to discover they were still on the wrong side, there was no choice but to remain at street level.

With shoulders to the wall, at least figuratively, Tom and Ariel walked, walked and walked, ascended rickety steps to an equally uncertain elevated walkway, shared with bicycles towing wagon-loads of poultry, women with heavy burdens on their heads, school children, small donkeys patiently plodding with loaded wagons, and every form of non-motorized transport, known and unknown over the myriad rail lines. Trains roared in both directions barely under their feet. Carefully descending more rickety stairs, they resumed walking, walking and walking.

Tom mused about "Sixty Minutes" sending a crew to Tokyo years in the future to do a segment on the strange elderly American couple that had been aimlessly wandering "My City" for decades.

This shoulder to the wall plan worked eventually; they located the (2) sign, and gratefully boarded a bus for the hotel.

The last evening in Japan was quite special; a delicious multi-course meal, live entertainment, wines, and flowers everywhere – a delightful ending to a wonderful Pacific Rim journey.

Both Tom and Ariel were ready to get back home, and back to work. Tom had to buy a large suitcase to fit everything in for the flight home, particularly his new suits and boots. Most of Ariel's purchases folded and 'squashed' down well; helpful, but Tom's additional bag was an absolute necessity.

It was a long flight, smooth and uneventful; but, they were both very happy to be back in the U.S. Customs was not a problem and soon they were winging their way to Seattle and then the East Wenatchee Airfield. Home at last, and delighted to be there.

What a great trip; wonderful experiences; rolls and rolls of film, and great memories. Ariel still found herself wondering just a bit if it had all been a splendid dream; but no, it was real and the beautiful memories could not be taken away by anyone. Besides, she had proof in roll upon roll of film to develop. Tom had given her a new Pentax camera for Christmas and she had put it to very good use. She cringed slightly at the bill for developing all those photos, but what wonderful memories of their adventure.

Another Adventure

Less than two years after their month-long Pacific Rim tour, Tom talked frequently of his strong desire to go back to Australia and New Zealand; and this was to be his treat as he previously promised. He again set about making arrangements, which they both now felt comfortable doing on their own. Once more he spent the time necessary to seek out routes, accommodations, car rentals spending long hours on the phone; and quite soon had everything in place. They would be able to spend more time in the chosen places and to see things that were skipped on the Pacific Rim tour.

Ariel could scarcely believe all this was really true. She was going places, seeing and doing things with Tom she never thought possible. He wanted to spend time with her, go places with her, and proudly introduce her to his friends, acquaintances and business associates. It had taken her some time to fully accept that he did love, care for and cherish her. Tom had taken the time and put considerable effort into achieving Ariel's relaxing and acceptance of his love and care. She began to understand what was meant by love. That a real and loving relationship truly is as described in the New Testament: mutually supportive, accepting, unselfish and not pride or ego-driven. Tom enjoyed doing for her, and she for him, a two-way bonding she had never before experienced.

Language would not be a problem these U.K. countries, even if they spoke Americanized English rather than that more proper. Tom had been medically retired due to his petit mal seizure episodes, was rather casting about for activities to occupy his days, and planning another trip was perfect. Ariel was still working at the economic development entity, quite frustrated at the consistent hesitancy of the manager and lack of results in acquiring new business enterprises for the region. She seriously considered quitting, but few, if any realistic opportunities were available in Wenatchee.

Her frustration at the office was partially due to the lack of genuine effort put forth in development and promotion by the very entity for which she worked. The manager's goal was rather consistently focused on attending meetings, whenever and wherever they could be found. His daily goal was completion of the cross-word in the local newspaper. It was not much of a problem to arrange two-week' vacation.

They were able to fly out of East Wenatchee to Seattle without any weather interference, and on to California to board a Qantas fight to Sidney. Here they were restricted to the international (holding pen) area for some time before going on to Auckland. The long flights had left both exhausted, but totally hyped and definitely not ready to sleep. Ariel's only real concern was that interruption of Tom's eating and sleep patterns could bring on a seizure. Nothing to do about it if they were to travel; just hope none would occur, and if so, be mild.

Having been in Auckland before, they felt secure in hopping on public transportation and downtown they went, soon finding a friendly-looking and very active pub. Both had consumed generous quantities of complimentary wine on the Qantas Sydney to Auckland flight, and more drinks were really not necessary, but one each was ordered. Then a gentleman at the next table realized they were "Yanks", pulled up a chair to join them; and the party was ON. Additional chairs were drawn up and more and more people joined to welcome then and ask questions of these traveling Yanks. That first fellow and Tom had both recently been "redunded" from long-term employment they had enjoyed, put on pensions and each felt they had received the short-ends of corporate sticks. As more locals joined the conversations, more drinks appeared, another table was added for still more people. Talk about a warm Kiwi welcome.

Ariel finally was quite ready for sleep, rather suspected Tom might feel the same, and whispered, "I think we better slip out and try to find the right bus back while we can still walk". Tom glanced at his watch, did some quick flight/ time zone calculations, and agreed. It took several minutes to extract themselves from this friendly bunch, and when Tom located a waiter to pay their bill, was told, "Oh no, there's no tab; welcome to Auckland and enjoy your stay." Neither was ever absolutely clear on how they got to the right motel and their room that night/early morning/whatever hour it was by whichever time zone.

By mid-morning they were awake and felt amazingly well, all things considered. With map in hand, a car was rented and Ariel started out onto an unfamiliar city street sitting on the right side of a left-hand stick-shift vehicle, on the 'proper' side of the road, carefully following a car with local license plates. Tom attempted to read the map, and indicate turns to put them on course for Bay of Islands at the northern tip of the North Island.

A broad six-lane motorway led north out of Auckland, well marked and a beautiful road. Ariel gained more confidence as they proceeded, and felt she was indeed getting the hang of this 'proper' driving. Making left turns onto two-lane roads, into the correct lane, required considerable concentration, especially remembering to look carefully for traffic approaching from the opposite unfamiliar direction. Right turns into a far-left lane, without being clobbered presented yet another quandary, but successfully executed without incident.

The farther north they traveled the narrower became the roads. First lanes decreased from six, to four, to two; fog lines and then center lines disappeared. Narrow bridges abounded, marked with triangular "Give Way" signage—black lettering against a gray background. Giving way to on-coming vehicles was virtually automatic. Someone could possibly be traveling in their direction kilometers head, and plan to cross that bridge. Extreme caution was a given.

Stopping in a village to ask directions, they discovered the annual Kiwi Festival to be in full swing. It appeared the entire population was participating in the parade as it proceeded down the main street, seemed at an end, but then the lead band rounded a corner and it all went by again. It was a real treat to join those locals not marching, and enjoy the community-wide, old time celebration along with delicious hand-dipped hard ice cream cones. Ariel bought a small porcelain espresso cup at the art show and wrapped carefully. Enjoyment was the order of the day, including a hearty and delicious lunch. Chinese take-away was not needed out here in the country-side; the food was delicious.

Back on track they found the 'highway' narrowing even more, edges resembling lace where asphalt chunks had disappeared. Upon reaching Bay of Island and checking in, just at dusk, Ariel learned the route they had taken was considered hazardous by the local population. Townsfolk didn't drive it after dark, ever. Oops. True it was narrow, on cliffs high above the sea, minus any hint of guardrails.

Oh well, they had survived despite Tom's pleas that she slow down no matter how many lorries were trying to drive up the tail pipe or over the top of that rental car. His consternation was due, in part, to sitting on the left side of the vehicle, in the left lane, traffic speeding by on the right, seas crashing some 200-feet below on massive rocks, and no guardrails. Ariel was facing oncoming traffic on her right, and closely behind, but spared views over cliffs. Tom also had only a side view of a speedometer registering kilometers rather than miles per hour … none of which the least bit helpful.

Bay of Islands was absolutely beautiful, clear iridescent blue water, gentle waves on this sheltered side, islands of all sizes and shapes scattered about in the sea as though tossed there by a playful giant. On a boat tour of the islands, which included going through a tiny tunnel in the rocks, they also learned several of the small islands disappeared at high tide, only to reappear at low. Beach campers paid close attention to tides and which beaches were not suitable for overnights.

Nearly every house had gutters, downspouts and barrels for storing rainwater. Municipal water supplies were also refilled from rainfalls as dug wells were somewhat salty on these small islets. Tom was not overly enthused about the available restaurant fare in town restaurants, nor was Ariel; they relied more and more on Chinese take-away for meals. Pastries and coffee were excellent, and Tom really enjoyed the bottled fresh milk delivered to their room each morning. Rudimentary kitchenware, coffee and assorted cereals were supplied for breakfasts, with freshly-baked hot pastries available only a door or two away.

From Bay of Islands they traveled south again, stopping at villages, sheep ranches, and just poking about the countryside. Small streams trickling down hillsides were lined with gorgeous white and pink calla lilies that blended with the white sheep grazing in deep green meadows. This was absolutely beautiful country. About half-way down the North Island, their route traveled east along a pristine lake abounding with graceful swans, ducks of all sorts and colorful birds of unknown types, but beautiful. The eastern coast looked much like the eastern U.S. coast of the past, with small cabins, fishing villages, lovely beaches with grassy dunes and easy access for strolling and finding shells.

Back in Auckland they turned in the rental car, enjoyed a delicious seafood dinner on a deck overlooking the sea, strolled along the waterfront, and settled in for an early night before leaving next morning for Sydney.

The flight from Auckland back to Sidney seemed shorter for some reason; perhaps being well rested and not exhausted from hours of airplanes and terminals had something to do with that. They did some touristy sight-seeing and shopping in Sidney before flying north to Brisbane which they had not visited on the first visit to Australia.

They found this a very cosmopolitan city, with excellent dining, interesting pubs and again, very friendly people. Ariel also attended Sunday services at an Anglican Chapel which closely resembled many Protestant services in the U.S. Chapel was the 'low' church, and cathedrals the 'high'. Somehow, she knew God did not make such distinctions even though humans tend to.

This rental car was an experience in itself; an automatic transmission with which Ariel was neither familiar, nor particularly comfortable; and enough rattles, rumbles and hesitations for her to seriously question its road worthiness. A print placard on the dash assured drivers that in case of any failure, they had only to telephone and assistance would be forthcoming in prompt and timely manner. "Okay, let's hope we do not need to test that", was Ariel's unspoken response. Finding a telephone could also be a question in this pre-cell phone era.

She did feel considerably more confident about her driving though, still on the 'proper' side of the roads and from the right side driver position; it had begun to feel almost normal.

Brisbane probably has more bridges and small car-ferry crossings than any other city on the planet. A major river twists and turns through on its way to the sea, and just happened to be at high flood level at the time. One road brought them to a ferry crossing reminiscent of the Vantage ferry on the Columbia River in 1941, albeit without surrounding cliffs. This one held all of four small cars.

They visited animal preserves, petted kangaroos, wallabies, anteaters, koalas and even fed many species. Roos, particularly become quite friendly when they sense availability of food, nibbling tidily from open hands. Koalas are definitely not soft and cuddly, but stiff-coated and reek of eucalyptus. Ariel and Tom were very glad to have purchased the cute, soft and fluffy stuffed Koalas in New Zealand to ship home. Moreno wool had also been shipped, along with a large four-pelt sheepskin.

One morning they boarded a large catamaran for a day on Tangalooma Island, complete with white sand beaches that felt somewhat like cornflower underfoot. Iridescent blue/green water lapped gently on the sands, pleasure boats were simply pulled, or run, safely ashore on the sand; passengers stepped out into the warm gentle waves. It truly was a paradise; very difficult to leave at day's end.

Another jaunt a little south of the city was to Beenleigh and old-fashioned greyhound racing. Owners accompanied each dog to the start, and ran to reclaim them at the race finish. One pup slipped his leash following a race, jumped the fence, streaked across the infield, and triumphantly caught "Rusty". His red-faced owner had to walk over one-half the track to retrieve the bouncing, tail-wagging and obviously happy dog. That pesky speeding 'rabbit' hadn't got away from him after all.

A commuter flight carried them to Cairns and the Great Barrier Reef, their final stop in Australia. A catamaran cruise took them out to the Reef where they viewed sea life in a glass-enclosed submarine, snorkeled and had a marvelous day, including a prodigious buffet. Vast numbers and varieties of fish, coral and sea animal/plants totally defying description; in every size, color and shape imaginable abounded. Tiny bright, iridescent, black-finned fish to huge smooth, lumbering groupers, interspersed with orange, red, yellow, green, blue specimens large, medium and small, none seemingly the least concerned about the humans among them.

When all passengers and crew had eaten their fill and then some at the buffet, every morsel of left-over food was tossed overboard to those waiting fish. All sizes, descriptions and colors swarmed the sea, and some tiny, darting, brightly-colored varieties hardly more than brief flashes as they flitted about to eat, while avoiding the ever-present danger of being eaten, themselves. Somehow it all worked out. Within minutes all traces of the buffet disappeared and the various schools dispersed, ensuring excellent viewing opportunities for the morrow.

Cairns offered numerous attractions for tourists and the local population. Beaches were short distance from town, again absolutely gorgeous, waters clear and warm; soft white sands, with clothing optional. A vintage train of open-air carriages traversed the steep mountainside, crossed more spindly bridges than ever thought possible, and arrived safely in the charming village of Karunda. Tom opted for a beer at the local pub and people-watching while Ariel toured a butterfly sanctuary.

Glassed-in, with all manner of plants and trees, vast numbers of butterflies freely abounded and somehow narrowly missed landing on visitors ... most of the time. Slightly intimidating, but absolutely thrilling, one large splendid creature perched briefly on her shoulder.

This was rain forest territory with jungle growth encroaching on all sides.

Wreckage of an actual downed WW-II fighter plane could be glimpsed just a few yards from the edge of town; not as a tourist attraction, but just left there, rusting away where it had crashed.

Pub walls stopped about four feet off the ground; poles supported the thatch roof, and rolls of bamboo could be lowered if winds happened to accompany rain. Otherwise, shade and gentle breezes provided a totally satisfactory environment. When Ariel joined Tom for a glass of wine he indicated some of the bar occupants he had observed. These people appeared to have spent a good deal of their time at the pub, and several groups of younger folk arrived at intervals in vintage vehicles, purchased box wines and then just disappeared into the dense jungle.

A small theater performance by indigenous local actors was not only well done, but wonderfully informative about the tribes living in the Outback for centuries before any whites arrived. They provided interpretation of ancient drawings on cave and cliff walls that portrayed major events of earlier millennia; face painting, dances and instrumental music imparted a bit of introduction and understanding of native culture.

Bus transport returned them to the valley floor descending an extremely narrow strip of steep, winding pavement. Gouges on the rock clearly evidenced the difficulties in successfully maneuvering any large vehicle over this route; not enhancing any sense of safety, but they made it.

Having already experienced a non-stop flight from Tokyo on their earlier trip, and comparing mileages/time zones, etc., they had opted for a short stay in Hawaii on the return leg of this journey.

Hawaii

Tom had been in Hawaii briefly while in the Navy, but never as a civilian; for Ariel that had been only a far-off, no-possibility dream. Spending a couple of days de-compressing there seemed a highly logical plan. Bags collected and out on the sidewalk, a taxi arrived; "what's he doing?" gasped Ariel as the driver sat down on the left, not the right, side. "Its ok" laughed Tom, "we're back in the States now, and I'm glad you're not driving just yet". Decompressing in Hawaii was a wise choice and very pleasant. Their hotel balcony had an unobstructed view of Diamond Head and the ocean – totally beautiful. Drinks on the balcony at sunset---perfect.

Both wanted to visit Pearl Harbor, and found the tour very moving as well as informative. Ariel vividly recalled December 7, 1941, and that if not for Edythe's rejection of sailing the Pacific, she would have been right here at Pearl on that date.

Following the tour, Ariel again rented a car—automatic transmission, but left-hand drive in the right lane. They explored Oahu a bit, crossing through the mountain tunnel and up the sea-side highway. They were both impressed by the changes in vegetation, multitudes of flowers and lush landscapes. Beaches were rather rocky, with the sand-enhanced hotel beach access being the only one found comfortable. A good night's sleep also served well to re-establish time and place.

Both Ariel and Tom were quite ready to get back home and try to make up with the kitties having been 'abandoned' by their humans yet again. They had not been neglected in any way, but the human opinion did not match that of cats.

Relocation

Home again in East Wenatchee their lives resumed a normal pattern, with Ariel at the development offices where she had been able to use earned vacation for the trip. Tom continued tending the house, cats, and helping transport a friend who was recuperating from a stroke. With spring weather there was considerable yard work both at the house and at the lake cabin.

Weekends at the Lake were great with boating, activities at the Yacht Club, and entertaining friends. Tom had given Ariel a kayak for her birthday and she had great fun with that, especially going out early in the mornings as the sun rose. Ducks abounded on the lake; frequently swimming alongside as she also paddled the lake and explored small inlets. Any dry bread she may have brought along was quickly gobbled.

Tom finally agreed to try it one afternoon when they had towed the kayak uplake to a sheltered moorage for an afternoon of picnicking with friends. This sheltered bay with absolutely no wind or waves was not a usual condition on this particular lake. He gingerly placed one foot into the little craft, hung to both the kayak and Ariel's arm, carefully eased onto the seat and pulled his other foot inside. He reluctantly accepted the paddle and sitting stiffly upright slowly dipped each blade shallowly into the water. He eventually moved out a bit, rounded a brushy outcropping, and disappeared. Ariel returned to the sandy beach and their friends.

Everyone continued swimming and playing in the warm water, chatting, having drinks, snacks and basking in the beautiful sunshine. Time passed. Ariel suddenly realized Tom had been gone around that bend for quite some time and started up a trail to look for him. She soon spotted him coming toward her on foot, carrying the kayak, paddle, wearing a not overly-pleased expression.

So much for kayaking … he had managed to get out in shallow water without falling, pull it to shore and carry it. His kayaking days were over. Ariel did not suggest they purchase another and paddle to the head of the lake for beach camping.

The cabin provided so many good times, with friends, or just the two of them. Ryan joined on many occasions along with his friends. There were parties, cook-outs, club events, all sorts of pleasant times. Jillian and her family came occasionally and the children began referring to "Grandma's Lake" as a neat place to spend days playing in the water and sleeping outdoors on the deck.

Driftwood pieces were garnered from the lake and used for creating the natural landscape efforts on the cabin site. Each mountain summer storm brought drift from the mountains that gradually made its way down the narrow waterway, hazardous for careless boating, but a great asset for interesting additions to the cabin site. Those also helped hold the steep bank areas and provide places that soil could be added and plants take root. Ariel had never thought she would purchase bags of soil, pull out enough large rocks to create holes in order to plant small bushes. The ground was basically rock, and plants struggled to grow. Logs 'captured' from the lake were excellent material for her attempts at creating a green space and fire-barrier around the cabin.

Her kayak was excellent for towing driftwood logs and interesting pieces of old root formations that provided bank stability, framework for vines as well as nesting places for quail. Resident deer made pruning of bushes, including roses and raspberries, totally unnecessary. They even ate cedar and walnut branches. Ariel was convinced they watched from behind pine trees as she unloaded and planted the various flowers and shrubs brought from the home yard. In spite of the deer, she managed to introduce enough plantings to secure the steep bank areas and install a primitive drip irrigation line.

Evening meals were frequently taken on the deck and many included visits back and forth among neighbors. Ariel generally had a large pot of spaghetti, a meat and bean dish or stew on the stove and salad in the refrigerator. Casual potlucks sprang up, unplanned, with good conversation, drinks, some card-playing, families and friends.

These were indeed, excellent times. Ariel had never hoped to enjoy a life like this. Old fears and doubts sank into the past where they truly belonged and could be ignored. Only occasionally did pesky negative questions creep in, unbidden, that this newfound happiness was undeserved, future recompense to be required.

She was determined to suppress all those old, negative thoughts and fears … enjoy and become accustomed to these good times adapting to life with Tom. That he loved her was an absolute and he never hesitated to not just tell her, but demonstrate that. Was it all real?

This non-threatening, low-stress, loving and sharing way of life was most pleasant. She sincerely hoped she and Tom would have many years together, growing old and enjoying each others' company. He had, after all, promised her a dull life married to him. She had truly experienced more stress, problems and foment in her forty-plus years to suffice for a lifetime. Dull could be a very good thing.

In her job at the economic development entity, Ariel had previously worked with a European businessman, inventor and manufacturer who wanted to settle in the North Central Washington area, establish his business and also raise livestock. A requirement had been suitable pasture accommodations for buffalo and a considerable amount of general acreage for a large residence, barns and assorted outbuildings as well as garden, orchard and landscaping. Ariel had consulted listings, real estate sales agents, traveled the area and walked properties on her own hunting for available land. Despite all efforts the local search had been unsuccessful and he had acquired acreage and excellent pasture land in North Idaho with the desired mountain setting.

Shortly after Tom and Ariel's latest travels, he returned to Wenatchee and contacted Ariel with a request that she consider working for his company, assisting with their becoming established in Idaho. This offer was based largely on her familiarity with the revenue bonding processes, legal documentation, corporate structuring, her verbal and written communication skills, and her efforts to locate properties for him. "Ariel, you talk government, and I don't," was his definitive explanation. That ability to 'talk government' would certainly be quite useful in dealing with state, county and local entities in initial processes and even more with federal requirements as the company grew with product shipped globally. He had decades of experience in dealing with European governmental entities, but not with individual state or federal regulations in this country.

Tom was initially surprised at Ariel's being recruited, but fully supported her checking it out before giving any answer, considering her well-qualified and more than capable. A positive and encouraging response from a spouse was fantastic, and something she had never experienced from Roger, to be sure. She gave this offer considerable thought, also recalling employment opportunities received in past years and turned down because Roger would not have allowed her to accept. She was not about to cast Tom in that light. He thought her to be intelligent and capable of taking on whatever she chose to, and was unabashed about saying so, to her or anyone else. He was not overly enthusiastic about Idaho, having lived there years before, but not going to stand in her way if this was something she wanted to do. Her economic development entity job had become just that, a job. One of the better paying available in the area, but no longer very interesting, and certainly not a challenge.

She had organized office procedures, purged decades of files into archives; codified decades of motions and resolutions. A desk book had been created for administrative purposes. Someone else could step in with little if any interruption in service.

She dearly loved Tom; he was a genuinely nice, kind and caring person and they loved each other. He had not only rescued her and Ryan, but worked diligently at caring for them both, showing her in more ways than she could count that he loved her and it was not only okay, but expected, for her to enjoy life and have fun. She was not to blame for the problems of the universe. Tom was an absolute dear, not perfect, of course, just delightfully loving and human; and she was extremely happy. If push came to shove, and a job offered, did she want to uproot and move again? Time would tell.

And so, Ariel visited the Idaho business, fell in love with the area, accepted the employment offer and rented a little condo on the lake; a beautiful spot. Having her own apartment was something she wanted to do at 18; and now that very personal dream was coming true at 50+. The apartments rented during her time of 'single blessedness and abject poverty' had been basic temporary refuges, that never felt like any real home. The struggle just to pay rent, utilities and food had consumed energy and the majority of her earnings. This was a completely different time, place and phase of her life. A new job in a new location with new challenges and opportunities; and the company was in process of planning and building a new manufacturing complex. This could be a very good thing, or… Again, time would tell.

She was not about to let this opportunity go by as she had with the insurance company offer years before and the Wenatchee bank trust department opportunity. Tom didn't attempt to stand in her way at all; encouraged her to go for it if this was of any interest whatever to her. He was retired and more than capable of caring for himself temporarily. His support was a major plus.

She and Tom worked out a schedule by which Ariel drove home to East Wenatchee or to the lake cabin, on Friday afternoons, returning to Idaho late Sundays. When days shortened and temperatures cooled, they alternated weekends, Ariel driving west one weekend, and Tom hopping on the train for Idaho the next.

After a few months, he tired of the train commute schedule and wanted to move to Idaho as well. He put his house on the market. Ariel located a rental house that accepted cats, and he began the process of relocating to Idaho.

She missed Tom. Though the condo was fun; it was time to be together again. Having separate housing, post office addresses in separate cities and even separate states had been unique and even more than slightly amusing, but temporary.

The rental, located at the base of Schweitzer Mountain was of relatively recent construction, but for unknown reasons not at all well-insulated. Winters are cold in Northern Idaho. Lying in bed at night the cold breezes were clearly felt. Also the structure was sited only about 50 yards upslope from a set of very busy transcontinental railroad tracks that carried in excess of two dozen trains per day. The owner-builder had intended to live there with his family, but soon relocated, probably due to the frequency and noise of the all day, every day train passages.

Tom had been highly concerned about those trains and the kitties being flattened by locomotives. His fears were immediately put to rest when Whitney (white, long-haired, 25 lbs+) cautiously ventured onto the lower lawn only to suddenly leap straight up, do a mid-air 180, dash across the lawn, up a set of stairs and flatten himself against the slider door in total panic.

Somewhat later, Tom heard and then saw the approaching engine and long line of box cars. Whitney had felt the earth shake under his paws and didn't like that one bit. He wanted in … immediately and preferably on Tom's lap. Kitties all stayed quite close to the house and safety. That concern was firmly put to rest.

Winter came early, with several inches of snow on the ground by mid-November. Packing wood up a rise from the garage/storage shed to feed the auxiliary basement heating stove, shoveling snow and trying to stay warm required constant attention and grew old rapidly. The house was equipped with baseboard electric units, which together with lack of insulation and higher electricity rates, meant using the basement wood heating stove on daily basis.

Roads were not plowed in the county road areas, nor in town either, as they later discovered. Large, new, bright and shiny trucks equipped with wide, shiny silvery plow-blades rested safely under protective shelter at the edge of town.

Tom and Ariel also learned rather quickly that '*county*' road was synonymous for '*dirt*' road, possibly graveled, but definitely not paved, or plowed. Ariel skied over two miles to work one morning after a heavy snowfall, when she couldn't even get her car to the street, equally impassable. Communications from the German offices required immediate responses; delay of any sort not being an option. A mere three-foot plus overnight snowfall in Idaho was of absolutely no consequence or concern to anyone in Germany. Skinny skis solved the dilemma. By day's end, roads were traversed sufficiently by trucks to be drivable and Tom could pick her up along with her skis.

Ariel then found a house for sale, closer to town, on a paved street, insulated, with forced-air electric heat in addition to a good wood heating stove, and a great floor plan. She arranged for a conventional mortgage in her own right, and upon closing they moved once more. A nice house and large lot in a good neighborhood was a great improvement for both, and even the cats; no roaring, rumbling, whistle-screaming trains to disturb their naps or threaten even one of their nine lives.

Much to the surprise of the new U.S. Company President, Ariel was able to garner the attendance and ribbon-cutting expertise of Idaho State Governor Cecil Andrus for Grand Opening Ceremonies. He was definitely enthused about job creation in the area and especially the wage scale of this new venture. Northern Idaho needed new and expanding businesses, and his ribbon-cutting would provide him and the state with great publicity and excellent photo ops.

Visiting German corporate executives were highly impressed upon learning of the Governor's participation, and quite naturally presumed an upper-management male had accomplished that significant feat. The senior German executive specifically requested meeting this top-level, highly qualified executive who had been able to access such a high-ranking government official.

A bit of macho pride was painfully swallowed upon his learning a lowly female administrative assistant had simply picked up the phone, spoken with the Governor and personally invited him. He graciously accepted immediately; willing and delighted to participate in welcoming the new business, a long-established international corporation, to his state was even more noteworthy.

German corporate enthusiasm was quickly subdued upon learning a mere woman had arranged the entire event, site preparation, appropriate refreshments and beverages, including participation by the state's highest elected official. Northern Idaho not being German and operating in a quite different manner was a concept that remained totally mysterious to them. No German corporate officer ever said a word of acknowledgment or appreciation to Ariel.

She fondly recalled Governor Andrus' graciousness years later when he passed away at 85, having served in a Presidential Cabinet position and four terms as State Governor. His life began in very humble circumstances, making good use of available education, rising to positions of considerable power and influence; never losing track of his roots and genuine concern for people and the environment. His early employment was logging, hands-on in the woods of Northern Idaho.

Despite all the distractions provided by moving twice, settling into a new-to-them house, maintenance and improvement projects, the large yard that emerged from winter snows, Tom remained depressed over his medical retirement status. He had been employed, part and full-time since grade school age, as had Ariel; work was the norm for both, not retirement, especially at a relatively young age. As his depression deepened, seizure activity increased as well.

Just shy of three years on her job, Ariel gave notice at the European-based company complex, and began preparations to leave Idaho. What she might find for employment was a big, wide-open unanswerable question.

At this same time, a number of OSHA and Idaho Safety complaints were made against both manufacturing division companies. One company designed and built the weaving equipment then used by the other in weaving and joining the endless belts for actual production of paper product. OSHA and individual states were beginning to implement quite stringent requirements for safety procedures in manufacturing and production facilities. The filed complaints required both federal and state mitigation together with institution of industry-specific training procedures and retention of manufacturers' safety documents for every product on site.

Management heads of both companies were at a total loss regarding compliance and in complete quandary as to response. They both turned to Ariel. She agreed to remain long enough to mitigate the 18 specific citations, clear those with both state and federal regulatory agencies, compile compliance documents and write safety procedures for both companies, on contract basis.

Her house sold quickly without difficulties; a duplex unit was rented in Spokane Valley and the move back to Washington rapidly accomplished. For a time she commuted 150 miles round trip each day until delivering the clearance documents from federal and state entities together with training materials and compliance procedures volumes to both companies.

Another Move

Ariel was once more without employment or immediate prospects. Her filed application for unemployment was denied. One Idaho entity executive, temporarily assigned to the Idaho facility, testified she had simply quit her position voluntarily without any cause. He denied any knowledge of the serious conflicts existing between German and U.S. business procedures, and that all had been quite wonderful. "Dat voman" had just left for no reason. He was believed; she was not.

Tom seemed slightly less depressed in a larger community environment and turned his attention to unpacking and settling in. The now four cats were quite pleased with their new digs, sunning on the deck, eyeing squirrels that frequented the railings searching for nuts and peanut butter, and visiting the adjacent unit, accessing an open slider door from the deck. Fortunately the building owners really appreciated Tom and Ariel as tenants, and actually liked having the cats around. Interaction with the squirrels provided additional entertainment in addition to on-site rodent control.

Ariel went job-hunting yet again. Employment opportunities were somewhat on the slim side; and she abruptly terminated more than one law office interview when it became quite clear the lawyer advertising paralegal and/or legal assistant positions also had quite non-professional duties in mind. A generous assortment of allegedly Christian magazines in the reception area occasionally turned out to be a clue as to lawyer intentions; none of which involved her singing in a church choir or leading a Bible study group. Where had she seen this camouflage before … indeed.

She found work as a marketing director for a local steel and plastics design and manufacturing firm. Her primary area was in Lottery point-of-sale plastics, together with bulk food distribution systems. The position required travel throughout the U.S. which was another new thing for Ariel. Initially Tom was very supportive, staying home and taking care of the kitties; quite pleased to see her to the airport and meet her there again upon return. She rather enjoyed being out and about, traveling on her own, presenting product lines to corporate executives and even a few boards of directors. Lottery point-of-sale marketing also involved attending trade shows in cities never before visited and more new experiences.

She contacted the state and provincial lottery offices by phone and provided print materials with photos she took and mounted with descriptive information. Color copies at the time were more expensive than photo print copies, and Ariel called on her prior experience in lay-out preparation for sports programs years before at Highline Schools for presentations.

At the plant, she formed a very good and friendly working relationship with the Purchasing Agent, Marie, a single mother raising three children. Ariel also kept a pair of coveralls in her office so she could easily provide some non-skilled help in the shop when needed. No prior 'director' type staff person had ever pitched in when things backed up in production and shipping; the crews appreciated her willing efforts.

House Hunt... and Depression

Tom was not overly pleased living in a rental duplex and started looking about for real property. Ariel's Idaho house had sold quickly, and despite the relatively short time frame had turned a fairly decent profit. The duplex owner was also a real estate agent, and before long he located a rancher with most of the requirements on Tom's list; primarily a level lot, fenced yard and 2-car garage. Not exactly what Ariel had hoped for; however, this was something Tom had found on his own and she felt it was very positive for him. It could very well be an emotional boost for him. She would just have to deal with a '70's rancher, tiny kitchen, limited counter space and dreadful interior décor. Except for the physical dimensions of the structure, refurbishing and updating were quite doable and since the basic structure was sound, plumbing, wiring and heating systems quite functional, it would meet their needs, at least for the immediate time. She hadn't wanted a large or showy house, but just something not quite so utterly ordinary as this 25-year old rancher.

The large yard, corner lot and the secure fencing were definitely on the plus side. Tom was so happy and that was a true positive after his months of depression. He did have a wild fantasy the cats would remain safely in the fenced back yard and not venture out beyond it. The fenced yard certainly provided them more than adequate room for being outdoors chasing butterflies and bugs, together with protection from dogs. However … cats have quite definite ideas as to what constitutes their territory and fences have little or no impact on their actions.

It took a very short time to arrange the purchase, packing commenced, and once again, they moved. Also once again, it was dead of winter, complete with deep snow and howling wind. With help from the Engineering/Design fellows, moving was accomplished on a Sunday. Ariel left early Monday morning for a marketing trip through Eastern Washington, parts of Oregon and then Western Washington. It was an altogether good time to be on the road. Highways were well maintained and her car handled beautifully in winter. Tom had most boxes unpacked and contents put away when she returned. He did an excellent job, with only some kitchen cupboard contents needing to be rearranged months, and even years, later.

Back at the office, however, things were not quite as pleasant. The President/ CEO began calling special meetings in his office at the end of virtually every day, allegedly to discuss future business opportunities. Attendance by Marie and Ariel was required. No rationale was ever provided. Occasionally one or two of the Engineer and Design fellows were included briefly, and summarily dismissed. His basic intent and purposes for the after-hours sessions became increasingly clear as time passed. At each such after-hours meeting, having dismissed any design/engineering men, he immediately brought out glasses and bottles of liquor, pressuring the 'girls' to drink with him. His disappointment was obvious when they politely refused, citing responsibilities at home, and as tactfully as possible reminding him it was after office hours.

Ariel truly liked her work, the salary and commissions were good; and did not want to leave. She was out of town calling on existing customers and updating contacts fairly frequently and able to avoid some of these 'meetings', but not so Marie.

Meanwhile Tom's depression had slowly returned. He was utterly bored once they were settled in the house, a second bath had been installed, walls painted, some trees removed and the entire place spruced up after years of neglect. He still experienced seizure activity that seemed to result from, or was exacerbated by his depression and self-induced stress. He lacked any specific interests beyond the kitties and watching sports on television, and increasingly fretted over minor details.

When he became peevish and increasingly distrustful of her work demands and even time spent grocery shopping, she quietly, but firmly, informed him the behavior was totally unacceptable. She calmly but decisively reminded him she had lived with one grouch for twenty years and was not about to repeat that. He needed to find something to occupy his time; quit picking at every little thing and openly exhibiting jealousy, or he could be single and every bit as grumpy as he wished.

Ariel feared she might have triggered still more stress and depression and thus increase frequency and intensity of seizure activity. Those had not been a problem thus far, and unlikely to be, unless he happened to be driving. Even one minor incident could easily become a disaster. She prayed that would not occur; but his insistence at knowing exactly where she was every moment and what she was doing had simply become too much. He was obviously stewing and fretting, creating stress for himself. Stress being the greatest contributor to seizure activity, something needed to change.

She clearly stated her concerns about his depression, the slightly veiled accusations made as to what she "might be up to", people she worked with and where she was after work, why she went to the office so early in the mornings, and why she frequently wanted to go to a shopping mall. Any phone calls she received at home from co-workers resulted in close and lengthy questioning. This was becoming more and more like a re-play of Roger's endless interrogations about her daily life. She had endured that similar scrutiny and constant demand to account for every minute of each day from Roger and was simply not willing to do it again. Ariel was a different person now than she had been years before; she was far more confident and positive.

She calmly informed him she had absolutely nothing to hide; requirements of her marketing director position were completely professional. Communication among persons with whom she worked was occasionally needed and appropriate outside actual office hours. Early morning office hours were necessary to contact East Coast customers. She was not the least interested in any involvements outside their marriage. He simply had to find something to do with his time other than dream up imaginary jealous fantasies; be that some part-time employment, volunteering … whatever. Find something with which to occupy his mind and hours besides just feeding cats.

She did not express anger, just the absolute necessity of his doing something other than fretting about what she might possibly do or want to do. It was truly a simple matter. Nevertheless, old familiar guilt and responsibility crept in.

Tom just stood there silently, for several very long minutes. Ariel's fear and apprehension grew. Had she exacerbated his stress level by openly expressing her own feelings? What would be his reaction be to what pretty much amounted to an ultimatum? Would what she had finally expressed trigger more seizures?

Nothing for even more long minutes, and dinner preparations continued in silence. Local television news served to cover the lack of usual conversation. No comments from either Tom or Ariel.

Next morning with arrival of the paper, Tom secured both the sports and advertising sections. Over coffee, Ariel scanned the headlines and local legal pages before heading out for the office. What might she find in the evening? Question without answer.

Only days later, Tom shared what he had been up to; scrounging the newspaper employment ads diligently and finally locating one for a part-time 'financial oversight' position at an old long-established company in town. Would Ariel help prepare a cover letter and update his resume? Of course.

Opting to hand-deliver his information, an immediate appointment was set, and after talking briefly with the owner Tom went to work the following Monday.

It was perfect; the corporate accounts were a mess, delinquency rate off the charts, hours were at Tom's choosing, with parking provided. Less said about the pay scale the better; but, there was some compensation. He came and went as he pleased, and most importantly, he had something to do each day other than invent suspicions about Ariel. He now had business-related financial topics and experiences to share.

Required to create a title for this position, they came up with "Special Assets Officer", which upon presentation of his business card, led to numerous queries, and many opportunities for a bit of fun. No one quite knew just what a "Special Assets Officer" was. It didn't matter. The title did precious little, if anything, to indicate specific duties, but opened great opportunities for a bit of humor, a business-oriented identity, and enjoyable conversation.

Before very long, company billing statements were being sent out timely, payments received more promptly and the delinquency rate brought under control. While that never quite reached as low a percentage as Tom would have liked, the company owner was delighted. These accomplishments made him feel better, more confident and his depression lifted somewhat, resulting in fewer seizure incidents.

Another major plus included with his job was the presence of homeless cats in the alley parking area. He soon began placing food and water dishes out for them. Next, of course, was having Ariel build a little shelter so the kitties could dine more comfortably out of any rain and/or snow. A plus for businesses in the area was the free rodent control, effective despite employees leaving all sorts of food scraps around, and an Asian restaurant being somewhat careless about securing garbage can lids. Not a single mouse was ever seen inside the stamp and signage business in all the years Tom worked there. Cats do rather efficiently control rodent populations.

For Ariel the marketing of product and plant had lost the team environment initially experienced and enjoyed. Those feelings were echoed by her friend Marie; working conditions for both became steadily less comfortable. They particularly objected to the unstated, but clearly recognized, requirement to drink with the boss after work. In time they both departed that entity and found other positions.

After leaving her marketing director position Ariel took on a few temporary placements selling video surveillance systems for one company, and developing marketing tools targeting local businesses. For another company, she sold nuts and confections, among other products, to local outlets … even the county jail, at times wondering just what lay ahead in her future. This particular environment was unique in nature and also included working carefully, along with other employees, around an in-house extra-marital situation that had a quite negative effect on general employee morale. Sticky and icky. She kept looking.

She had often been faced with totally new environments, unfamiliar businesses, equipment and processes, learning strictly on-the-job with no training, and no formal education beyond high school. She had taken a few evening classes in real estate law, writing and corporate communications at the community college level. Seminars at university level had focused on continuing legal education and business communications, but she had no degrees. The question remained, now what?

Private Law, Court, Private Firms

Not surprisingly, it was back to the legal field, this time as paralegal in the family law arena of a very busy, high-pressure office environment. Again, Ariel walked in, was shown to her office and basically left to figure it out on her own; new formats, documents, procedures, systems and court procedures.

Once having paid a hefty retainer and accepted as a client at this firm, an individual met with Ariel for information intake, document preparation, financial distribution considerations, meeting the attorney again at courthouse for various hearings or at trial. Frequently Ariel provided counsel with a physical description of the client, along with pertinent reminder as to children if custody was an element, to prevent embarrassment and confusion. Occasionally she needed to be present at court to identify the client for her attorney. She worked at this office for three years with ever-increasing responsibilities, particularly with document filings and court appearances for presentations.

She spent a good deal of time at the courthouse answering dockets call, filing all manner of documents, meeting with opposing counsel in settlement attempts, some of which were quite successful. Throughout all, she learned far more about the law than she had ever expected, or necessarily wanted, to know. The long hours, considerable volume of high-profile clients, and ever-increasing demand for more billable hours led to her low-profile search for another position. She was expected to clock a minimum of 50 billable hours in a 40-hour work week.

Salary was based on standard forty hours per week with all manner of promises made for compensatory time for the considerable amounts of overtime. Somehow it was never deemed convenient to grant that comp time. Vacation time was never deemed appropriate either due to volume of cases and workload. Lunches rarely occurred; a box of crackers in a desk drawer sufficed.

Unexpectedly an opportunity presented when one client was most anxious to get her dissolution of marriage finalized and move to Florida where she had family. She worked as Bailiff for a Superior Court Judge who was terminally ill and keeping that condition totally under wraps.

A deal was quickly worked out with the Judge's highly appreciative approval. Ariel's client, his then-current bailiff, would get her divorce, she and her children could move; Ariel would then take over the Bailiff position. The Judge was totally pleased; he did not have to post a position, or interview anyone. He was acquainted with Ariel, knew her work as a paralegal, and she was familiar with courthouse procedures. She knew the Judges and court staff persons; it was a good move for all concerned.

Only the eminent lawyer for whom Ariel worked was not overjoyed; she had to find a replacement paralegal. She also chose to delay payment of the several weeks' vacation compensation due until the 'gap' week between jobs passed, so Ariel was not financially able to use that time for a short road trip to photo old barns and other sagging structures in a nearby mountain pass. This lawyer was not accustomed to having any unexpected changes made to her plans, and habitually took any available steps to interfere with those of other persons.

Ariel really enjoyed the courtroom position. Jury trials were particularly interesting and enjoyable. She liked interacting with the panel members, explaining the system and how every facet worked in harmony, each in its separate and equally important role. The only fault she encountered in this environment was courthouse politics for which she had no interest. The deputy clerk assigned to the department, however, thrived on gossip and possible power-play plots. Having desperately wanted to be the bailiff, she turned her attention toward undermining Ariel, planning to oust her and thereby get the job. Her plan failed despite herculean effort.

The Judge spent less and less time at Court as his health deteriorated. His last major case involved a medical malpractice bench trial, during which Ariel resurrected her shorthand skills and took copious notes. She had thought those to be merely a means to use rusty skills, but as the case slowly progressed, Judge increasingly sought out her notes and recollections. He semi-retired shortly after rendering his decision, subsequently hearing only a limited number of dissolution cases. After reviewing his notes and decision regarding the terms of the matter, he relied on Ariel to assign orders documentation to each lawyer in compliance with his decision, ascertain the accuracy and when satisfied, bring the completed documents to him for signature. She then filed the originals, conformed all appropriate copies and distributed those to counsel.

The deputy clerk and reporter were not at all happy about the degree of trust placed in Ariel; the clerk wanted to be bailiff, and the reporter was her ally. Ariel was the outsider and destined to remain so. No problem there; she certainly did not look to them for friendship or any social interaction.

Judge fully retired, traveled briefly, and his health steadily deteriorated. Ariel maintained communications with his wife, and cautiously answered questions from his Courthouse associates and friends. At the funeral his widow related that both Judge and she had regarded Ariel more as a comforting angel specifically sent to help him through his final months in office, not just a bailiff.

The judge replacement process had taken several weeks before the Governor appointed a Court of Appeals Commissioner to the Superior Court bench. As an Appellate Commissioner he had spent several years reviewing cases, researching previous case law, the latest revisions/reversals and delving into nooks and crannies of law, in his quiet private office. Years earlier in private practice, he had only appeared before a Superior Court Judge once in his career. Now he had been appointed to the Superior Court bench where he would be hearing cases.

Bailiffs in Superior Court serve at the pleasure of the sitting judge; he opted to retain the staff in place. No new job search this time; and with this new judge also came an advance in salary, which was very welcome. Ariel had taken a pay cut from private practice. He made no secret of his pleasure in working with Ariel and her knowledge not only of the courts' systems, but acquaintance within the courthouse and the legal community. He also appreciated her verbal and written communication skills dealing with other judges and lawyers in coordinating court schedules.

They worked very well together, neither having any great appreciation for courthouse politics, pompous lawyers, frivolous filings or delaying tactics. His wife was delighted to find Ariel's rather dry humor somewhat similar to the Judge's; they could each make slightly sarcastic comments in chambers without his getting in trouble at official 'judge meetings'. His penchant for somewhat caustic comments had been a very real concern for her. Judge and Ariel could safely make comments in chambers without causing even potential harm to any fragile egos.

Motions calendars in the department became known as 'thunder dockets". Matters were heard, testimony given, documentation reviewed, decisions reached, orders entered, cases closed. Judge had noted from files reviews the date at which Ariel had left the private firm and a replacement began drafting documents. He deemed the latter to be of considerably lesser quality.

This Judge was subsequently appointed an Appellate Judge following nearly three years on the Superior Court bench. "Apples" as it is commonly known does not have individual assistants for each Judge. Superior Court Bailiffs (now Judicial Assistants) serve at the pleasure of the Judge, and the incoming one for this department brought her own assistant with her. So for Ariel, it was job search time again.

Tom's concern was obvious and only added stress for him by worrying about her; it was a vicious cycle, which was of major concern to Ariel as well. He had worked in finance for the same corporation through its various name changes for nearly forty years. His part-time job with the stamp and signage firm was apt to last as long as he lived, should that be his wish. The more current business practice whereby skilled people could change jobs every few years without significant damage to their career paths was completely foreign to him and he found it very troubling. Ariel just kept on finding new employment no matter what, and he truly did not understand that seismic change in general business practice.

Law Offices and Hospitals

Tom truly enjoyed his part-time work, feeding the ever-fluctuating band of alley cats, and keeping up with the numerous changes in the downtown area. He continued to keep very regular hours and meal times, paying close attention to good nutrition, mediation doses, and keeping stress at as low a level as humanly possible.

Ariel quickly found another paralegal position with a downtown law firm after leaving the courthouse. She was working with financial entity default matters with which she was quite familiar, now had fairly predictable hours and able to continue using public transportation most of the time.

Tom had on occasion mentioned experiencing minor chest pain, none of which had been either severe or long-lasting. No, he wasn't going to call his doctor. He used public transportation most of the time, driving only to a local transfer station to catch the bus, and then walking about two blocks from drop-off to the stamp company each mid-morning. One morning he telephoned Ariel because the chest pain had been more intense, and wondered what she thought could be the problem.

After asking a couple questions as to when the pain occurred and what he had been doing, she answered, "First of all, I'm not a doctor, and unable to diagnose over the phone in any event. Call Berdine (primary care physician) and get it checked."

Obviously he did, as his next call was from the hospital where he was being prepped for a procedure. An arterial stent was to be placed. Ariel was assured by the attending physician that he would be going into surgery within just a few minutes, and expected to return to his room a little later in the afternoon. She could see him there and expect to take him home by early evening. Well … that certainly was quick.

A call to his primary care doctor confirmed that he had presented at her office, been examined and immediately put in a wheelchair and shipped off to the hospital by way of sky bridges, elevators and corridors; not walking. No one had deemed it necessary to apprise Ariel, apparently considering it all quite routine. Or, perhaps Tom had assured one and all he would call Ariel, thereby saving them time; then simply delayed doing so. That was a definite possibility.

When Ariel arrived at his room he was back from the procedure, which had gone very well, fully cognizant, and only slightly miffed about all the fuss, and the rush. He had been quite ready to dress and go home when an unexpected bleed occurred just as she arrived and that was in process of being controlled. The reasonable course was for him to stay the night for observation to be certain that blood vessel was not going to 'pop' again.

Ariel retrieved his evening medications from home ensuring all would be on schedule. The last thing she wanted him to experience was a seizure incident, however mild it might be. Next afternoon Tom was up and about, very ready to get home. He did take it easy over the weekend, and was back to work on Monday. Little did either of them realize this was just the barest beginning of his medical problems and further adventures.

He also began to experience occasional rather sporadic and relatively minor intestinal bleeds, which his doctor thought could be due to an ulcer. Medications were prescribed for that along with attempts to alleviate arthritis pain.

The arthritis medication was highly advertised as being totally wonderful, absolutely safe and appropriate for use by one and all. Tom took the prescribed dosage for two days, one tablet on the morning of the third day. Ariel was speaking with him by phone, he at home and she at work, when there was a muffled thumping sound and the line went dead. She shut down her office area, bolted out, fortunately having driven that day and sped home.

Only an axe murder scene could otherwise describe the kitchen. Tom was on the floor, barely conscious, blood everywhere. He had crawled up the stairs, unable to stand. Ariel got him up off the floor and into the bathroom, cleaned him as well as possible, into a towel wrap, some loose clothing, into the truck and to the hospital emergency room in absolute record time. He was again admitted and kept overnight, receiving a number of transfusions.

Neither Tom nor Ariel, to say nothing of the physicians involved, had any clue this scenario would repeat and repeat over the next years, more often than not without any new medication having been involved. Labeling for that arthritis medication now carries a warning pursuant to possible causation of intestinal bleeding along with other side effects. Suggestion at the time that intestinal bleeding could possibly be a side-effect, occurring shortly after ingesting the drug, was adamantly denied by several physicians. Denial continued for a number of years after Tom's experience, subsequently amended substantially, as bleeding is now listed as a possible side effect.

He recovered quickly, rested at home a few days, and returned to his normal and usual schedule, as always carefully adhering to his prescription dosages and schedules. He was now able to walk the short distance from the bus to office without any discomfort, thoroughly enjoying the morning exercise.

A later attempt at lowering his cholesterol levels introduced a Red Yeast Rice supplement recommended by his primary care physician. Only seven capsules, taken as directed, were required to bring on another severe bleed situation. This one occurred at night when Ariel was at home and able to get him to Emergency again in record time. Only one transfusion and a couple days' hospitalization were required. Tom missed a few days from work, but was soon back on his regular schedule. Red yeast rice was also added to the growing list of products to be avoided.

In 1999 Ariel found another paralegal position at an office quite near their home in Spokane Valley and no longer commuted downtown. She worked there four years before giving notice the summer of 2003.

This firm handled general litigation as well as estate planning, probate actions and real estate transaction, all of which were familiar territory. She enjoyed a considerable amount of variety in each work day, court appearances, document preparation and interaction with clients, as well as legal research.

One major litigation case involved attending city council meetings, note-taking, filings in federal court and maintenance of a full set of document copies duplicating those filed with the court. Before public records were available on-line, document hard copies had to be purchased through the clerks' office and were unavailable for days subsequent to filings. Ariel pulled the Court files and made copies through the local Bar office, thereby maintaining an easily accessible document source for the numerous lawyers involved.

This position was just challenging enough to remain interesting, involving considerable research at the county-site law library and considerable interaction with the courts, clients and other law offices. Here as well there was definite need to update procedures and improve maintenance of client file information.

However, one of the lawyers exhibited several 'shades of strange,' being entangled in an extra-marital affair within the firm, clearly disruptive to the practice. The allegedly secret and totally private affair was not nearly as hidden as either party believed, and generated endless queries from other law office staff persons, lawyers, court personnel and even judges.

She also encouraged her rude, demanding and generally ill-mannered children to run about in all areas of the office, chasing each other, shouting, and playing on office computers containing client information. Ariel's concerns steadily mounted. There was highly-confidential information easily available to those children, inadvertently, without any malicious intent on their part; but nonetheless, confidential. That lawyer was also somewhat lax about trust account draws, as well as billing clients at her rate for work done by Ariel. The work environment steadily deteriorated.

She did not want to stay in that situation and be caught up in potential litigation tangles or State Bar concerns over practice irregularities, especially those easily involving client data and trust fund accounts.

A week's vacation at the ocean provided her time to decide what her course of action might be. Walking along the ocean beach cleared her thoughts, and firmed her decision to give notice immediately upon return.

Excellent plan; however, that same week, the senior partner (other party in the office liaison) and by far the most capable and competent lawyer in the firm suffered a brain aneurysm from which he was not expected to survive. The lawyer with whom he was involved begged Ariel to stay, at least until there was some idea as to the outcome. Her help was needed with several cases and upcoming trials. Consequently she worked there nearly six additional months before making her escape.

The senior partner recovered well physically; however, he never practiced law again. On occasions he visited the office, looked around briefly and then sought out Ariel for documents she might have requiring his signature. At times, early on there were such, and he was quite pleased at that. Before long, however, the cases on which he had worked were resolved in some manner and nothing needed his attention. Ariel occasionally had him sign off on meaningless pages consisting of draft text which were then destroyed. He liked signing whatever she put in front of him. She was much relieved when she could finally leave that situation.

Tom continued to work part-time downtown, driving mid-morning and mid-afternoon, and feeding his alley cats. Ariel was out of work nearly four months, busy with various improvements to their house and yard, in addition to actively searching and interviewing for another job.

That same lawyer, party to the extra-marital affair who had begged her to stay to aid in dealing with the pending case load, challenged her claim for unemployment. She denied Ariel had given any reason whatever for terminating, just up and quit. In actuality, the problem of her children had been addressed by all staff members with the senior partner numerous occasions. His attempts to control the children were totally unsuccessful. They continued to have free run of the office.

A telephone hearing on the denial of benefits was set with an administrative judge. Ariel prevailed. Final determination included an additional and completely voluntary statement by the hearing officer: "Plaintiff's testimony is highly credible and factual; respondent's testimony significantly fails to disprove. Benefits awarded the Plaintiff." Ariel began receiving unemployment checks while her job search continued in earnest.

She was hired by a large energy management and consulting firm in the contract law and contracts department, at 65+ years of age. Ariel wanted to continue working and build up her Social Security account. This office location meant commuting downtown again, but she was able to rent a parking spot in the covered garage, settled in and thoroughly enjoyed this new environment. Her initial responsibilities were to organize the legal contracts department, locate numerous missing documents, and search for patent and a considerable amount of trademarks documentation. She established files for corporate clients, filed, purged and/or archived stacks of client and vendor documentation, located missing corporate documentation including original patents and trademarks. She set up renewal and fee payment schedules for U.S. and foreign trademarks. Original patent and trademark documentation was filed in binders as it was discovered or duplicated, some printed from federal web sites.

She also found original patent documents stuffed away in cabinets, straightened, pressed and framed those for display. When no original documentation could be located, either in the carelessly stacked materials scattered throughout the building or through the patent attorney, she retrieved information from on-line records. Hard copy binders were compiled for each patent and the myriads of trademarks.

Tom experienced a significant seizure incident one mid-week day while working accounts at the stamp and signage company, 911 was called and Ariel notified later. Upon arrival she found Tom ensconced in the transport vehicle, an EKG in process and vital signs being monitored. She identified herself as Tom's wife, to which the EMT responded, "Oh, you must be Evelyn, he talked about you." Ariel laughed and grinned, "No, Evelyn was wife No. 1; I'm No. 5. You need to come farther forward in the rolodex".

"Oh gosh, I'm so, so sorry," he sputtered, turning several shades of crimson. Tom was quite coherent by that time and grinning broadly. "Not to worry" responded Ariel, "I truly find it quite amusing. Perhaps he's going for Henry VIII's record – we'll just have to see. So far I'm in pretty good health."

Ariel's only real concern was that Tom's mind and memory had flipped so far back – over forty years; that had not happened before that she knew of.

Tom had refused to be transported to any hospital and now that she had arrived he was even more adamant. The crew persons were highly concerned as to what would transpire later. Ariel finally convinced them she was very familiar with the onset, duration and outcomes of Tom's seizures, and quite capable of dealing with this situation. With considerable reluctance they finally removed the monitors, helped him get his shirt back on, and allowed him to leave with her. Rather than another hospital transport, he was happily on his way home in her convertible, top down in the warm sunshine. After additional hydration and a short nap Tom was feeling fine. They returned to the company parking lot to retrieve his truck.

He was back at work the next day, feeding the alley kitties and suffering no ill affects whatever beyond some embarrassment.

Ariel was concerned about this particular incident and discussed it with the neurologist by phone. He had nothing new to offer regarding causation or treatment; especially with respect to the petit mall incidents Tom historically experienced; those being more difficult to control and virtually impossible to predict. No significant changes or recommendations; just try to keep his schedule as regular, and limit stress much as reasonably possible. Medication dosage was increased only slightly.

Tom eventually quit his job after the stamp and sign business was sold and new management dispensed with all basic bookkeeping practices including timely issuance of billing statements, never explaining rationale behind that decision. New ownership/management failed to comprehend the normal and usual business practice of issuing billing statements, maintenance of accounts, or payments at the local office. Their approach anticipated receipt of payments of unstated amounts voluntarily sent by customers. They apparently expected customers to just send checks; based on some amount they might possibly locate on a shipping slip; precious few did. Somehow that new management was unable to explain just why their program didn't work very well and that income along with profit had suffered. Delinquency rates soared; however, those were no longer Tom's concern.

He did continue driving into town each day to feed the kitties and be sure they had fresh water. Ariel remained at her job with the energy management firm, and fully intended to remain there until basically being shoved out the door at some point in the future. (From reviews and salary increases that shoving did not appear to be on the near horizon) She had been over 65 years of age when hired by this entity, quite pleased to see her retirement funds building up, and in no hurry to retire.

It was in this corporate/contract law setting the next chapter of Tom's medical adventures unfolded and Ariel's life took another abrupt turn into still more uncharted territory.

More Hospital Rooms, etc.

A mid-June Canadian jaunt was planned to celebrate their 25th wedding anniversary. Tom made all arrangements for an extended weekend at a British Columbia hot springs. Ariel had no problem whatever getting a few days off work; a neighbor was happy to check the house, feed the kitties and take in mail and papers. What with all the relocating, Ariel's marketing-related travel, employment changes and just life in general, this would be their first trip together in several years. And, since Tom had been married on four previous occasions, several mutual friends were surprised at the swift passage of 25 years.

So much had happened. Ariel liked telling their story her way; that she was wife number five, frequently eliciting raised eyebrow responses. Was he going for Henry VIll's record, or what? Actually, his first marriage lasted barely six months. Tom had wed one lady twice, taking care to have the two little dogs in his arms at the second divorce, when she drove away with her two children. The dogs had been the primary reason he married her the second time. The children he could well do without as they were totally undisciplined and resentful of him altogether. He expected them to behave with some degree of courtesy and consideration for their mother and at least without open hostility toward him. They had found that most definitely not to their liking and were not at all shy about letting him know it.

He was again single and found that far better; the little dogs were good companions. He frequented bars, fast food outlets, together with the Elks and Eagles clubs to which he belonged.

It was at the Elks Club bar he met Rose. The soon wed and were together for over sixteen years before she succumbed to cancer. His marital track record was really not as bad as it first sounded. He had most willingly taken on raising her son and made numerous attempts to adopt Jim as truly his own. Unfortunately her ex would never agree, but had no problem ignoring child support orders and later hitting up both Tom and his son for money. He even refused to allow the adoption in exchange for the money he wanted; a bribe? Absolutely. Tom was perfectly willing to do just that and buy him off, but to no avail. Now Tom was quite determined to make Ariel's life as pleasant as he was able and do his best for her son.

Ryan clashed with Tom as a teen while in generally rebellious years but came to value his judgment. Seeing his mom happy and treated well helped him understand somewhat and better appreciate how her life had improved after leaving and divorcing his father. His respect for Tom grew slowly, but steadily, greatly appreciated by Ariel in the months to come.

Jillian also was now extremely pleased with Ariel's marriage to Tom, despite Edythe's disparagement and also the interference by Roger's parents. Tom's obvious love and caring for Ariel had won the siblings over slowly but surely, and both were pleased at their mother's obvious happiness. Annie had not openly expressed an opinion one way or the other, opting to ignore any invitations to join planned activities.

So with plans made, and reservations confirmed; only packing bags and filling the gas tank remained. They would have a lovely extended weekend in Canada.

Returning from lunch with Jillian on May 22nd, a voice mail message informed Ariel of Tom's having been in a single-car vehicle incident and transported to the hospital Emergency Department

She heard his voice in the background, turning the air purple demanding he not be transported anywhere. Deputies were to just call Ariel; she would take care of him and everything else. They could go on about their business and leave him the #%@&$#*@ alone.

He had suffered a seizure incident returning from feeding his downtown 'alley cats', and stiffened, with truck at full throttle, muscles and nerves in left-turn mode and out of control, plowed into a concrete block wall.

Ariel was somewhat reassured at hearing his vehement protests. Obviously he was alive and fully conscious. Anyone critically injured could not have such anger, control of language and/or volume. Objections overruled, he was transported to Emergency.

She made a swift trip to the E.R., and found him being treated by hospital staff. With his bruised hands treated, x-rays taken along with a number of tests, he was admitted on his doctor's strong recommendation and Ariel's insistence. Effects of the wreck would become more painfully evident once the adrenalin wore off.

When Ariel spoke with the Deputy later by phone, he assured her Tom had been quite a handful, determined to remain at the scene and await her arrival. With a chuckle, he said they finally were able to get Tom onto a gurney and into the ambulance without having to cuff him, but it was close.

Tom had totaled his little truck and very nearly himself. He had seized while driving despite prescription medications faithfully taken, regular monitoring by his neurologist, being well-rested, not under specific or identifiable stress. Fortunately he had been traveling alone on a one-way by-pass in light traffic. No other vehicles or pedestrians were involved, to the amazement of the deputy on scene. Thus began another new phase of both their lives; details fortunately unknown at the time.

Later the insurance adjuster indicated passenger side floor boards had been raised up some 4" to 5", the entire right front of the cab smashed; and he couldn't understand why injuries had not been more severe. When Ariel viewed the truck remains to remove Tom's personal property from it, she too was amazed that he not only survived, but apparently with relatively minor injuries. Seat belts were secured and both air bags had deployed. Those alone were responsible for most of the bruising in addition to saving his life. Without those bags and the belt, results would certainly have been quite different.

The June trip was cancelled. Seizure control medication was changed with new drug and dosage slowly phased in, gradually reducing the former to avoid a sudden change and also to monitor the new drug for any adverse reactions. None was experienced and healing progressed.

He suffered severe negative side effects from one new prescription pain medication at home after discharge which resulted in no less than eight far more severe seizures in one day. Ariel had carefully guided him in trips to the bathroom, ready to catch him at any point. He was extremely sore and quite weak, in addition to the seizures. He had resented her concern, of course, and rebuffed all concern claiming he didn't need any help.

The seizures occurred randomly, as usual, but these were quite different, not being the more simple petit mal absence seizures, but full-blown grand mal events. He stiffened, jerked, his eyes rolled back, and breathing ceased. Calling for assistance was of no avail; Ariel shouted at him, slapped his face – hard, demanding that he respond. Amazingly, he did each time, puzzled and sharply questioning why she was yelling at him, unaware she had also struck him, hard. He insisted he was just fine other than having sore muscles and bruises; she was to just relax and not worry about him.

On a later return from a bathroom trip, they were in the hallway with Tom using his walker and Ariel close behind. He began to seize and pitched forward, not back; Ariel was unable to stop his plunge to the hardwood floor, walker skidding against the wall. She first checked for obvious injury to his right arm as he had landed on that before collapsing onto his chest. He quickly regained consciousness and wanted to be rolled onto his back; a pillow and blanket provided some comfort. Ariel immediately checked his blood pressure. Initial reading was low and the next more alarmingly so.

He wanted to get up off the floor and onto the couch … not an easy task, and B/P was even lower. It had been a nasty fall at best. A call to 911 brought emergency response, ambulance transport and hospitalization. That specific medication was added to the growing list of prescription and OTC supplements to which he reacted badly.

Ariel rushed to the ER, locating him in a secured area being attended by a surgeon and several nurses busy inserting a tube into his chest cavity. Fluids flowed freely into plastic collection bags. Blood supplies had been ordered and immediately upon receipt, replacement began. Once stabilized, he was admitted.

Fluids were drained from his chest cavity, and no less than a dozen transfusions, half of them plasma, replaced lost blood. Recuperation commenced once more. He was again back in hospital late June/early July for treatment of congestive heart failure. Recovery from the three inter-related incidents lasted well into winter.

With each hospital emergency room visit and hospitalization, particularly gastrointestinal bleed incidents, Ariel became increasingly aware that attending physicians and nurses frequently had already formed very definite ideas as to proper diagnoses before any examination was done or test results available. None paid much, if any, attention to what the patient or spouse attempted to relate regarding current symptoms, medical history, or anything relative to their even being at a hospital for the current emergency treatment. This was particularly troublesome each time she rushed Tom there with a bleed incident, which he now experienced with increasing frequency.

Medical personnel completely ignored the fact he was passing bright fresh blood, not dark, granular, old material. For several years doctors insisted his problem was upper tract, i.e., ulcer, acid reflux, Barrats syndrome or some such. None would consider a lower gastrointestinal problem with some even suggesting a psychological rather than physiological causation. Bright red fresh blood is truly not a frequently-occurring psychological phenomenon despite all efforts to dismiss physical evidence to the contrary.

Ariel had been raised from infancy under the strict edict that, 'the doctor is *always* correct in every situation, not to be questioned in any way at any time.' However, as Tom continued to experience the GI bleeds and no factual diagnosis was determined, she spoke up more firmly, insisting they at least listen to and consider what was actually occurring. Her concerns were voiced softly and somewhat hesitantly at first and ever more boldly as time passed with no diagnosis. Questioning of medical authority was another totally new element in her life, but one that would continue to develop considerably over ensuing months and years.

Tom had served in the Navy during the Korean "Conflict", in aerial surveillance over the Pacific as an Ordnance man aboard Neptune prop-driven craft. A Neptune reunion scheduled for San Diego in September seemed a perfect get-away opportunity for both. Again, Tom made and pre-paid all arrangements for their rail/air transportation, accommodations, and side-trips. Extra days were reserved to enjoy the beach and sunshine before returning to the chilly fall/winter seasons in Washington. Ariel had plenty of vacation time available, and the office was now organized so that her absence would not immediately cause any great problem.

His older brother's health had deteriorated rapidly in a relatively short time, and Robert passed away the second week of September. Ariel determined she could drive across the state; they could attend the services, visit briefly with family, return to Spokane and still keep their schedule for flight and rail travel to San Diego on September 18th. Kitties would just have to enjoy the 'pet hotel' an extra few days. A tight time schedule, but she could do it, and Tom could sleep during much of that drive, and hopefully stay sufficiently rested. He would be under some stress, of course, but far less than if he tried to do any of the driving, or not attend his brother's services. He expressed deep concern over Ariel's long driving hours, but agreed that upon their return, she could sleep quite well on planes and trains.

Tom still felt so terribly guilty about his wreck and health problems having spoiled their anniversary plans. He truly wanted this California trip to be relaxing and fun for both, and especially for Ariel. Her office work load was heavy in an extremely busy but pleasant environment. As in prior offices, more and more responsibilities seemed to unerringly make their way to her desk. New state and federal insurance regulations had created additional demands for corporate documentation, records submissions and retention in addition to increasing compliance procedures, all involving the legal department. Ariel, corporate counsel and a part-time steno comprised the entire department. There were over 500 employees at the headquarters offices and several more sales and service people located coast to coast. It was a busy place. Client/customer numbers grew steadily, each new entity requiring documentation and tracking procedures.

Early the morning of September 16th, Tom mentioned just not feeling 'quite right', nothing specific, just a little off and he might call Berdine (primary care physician) later. Ariel vetoed that immediately, insisted he take two aspirin, get his pants and shoes on and himself into the truck ... now. This sounded like a heart problem in her estimation; and better addressed hastily. Emergency was once again the first stop, then admittance to a tower room, multiple tests and ever-more consultations.

The early morning of September 18th, Tom was in surgery undergoing a triple by-pass procedure.

Travel plans were again cancelled, for his brother's funeral and all arrangements for San Diego. Ariel ordered flowers for the funeral services they had expected to attend, red roses for each living sibling with white blossoms representing those deceased.

She also mailed appropriate cards and consulted with Ted's sister to formulate a mildly-worded explanation for their absence, as his family was quite stressed enough. The elder brother had been ill for several months, in and out of hospitalization with slight improvements followed by relapses prior to passing. His wife had age-related health concerns together with early on-set dementia. She would certainly require additional care now, physically and mentally in attempting to adapt to being widowed. Close family members had undergone recent cancer surgeries, extensive treatments, and some continuing treatments with uncertain prognoses. None needed an additional matter of conjecture, and concerns for Tom.

He had been hospitalized numerous times over the years due to seizure incidents in addition to frequent gastro-intestinal bleeds, so the concocted story of his having '*some tests*' and that Ariel was taking care of everything was accepted without question. Tom had been hospitalized so many times over a rather short time period that no one was overly concerned. They were somewhat aware of the dead-of-night trips to emergency rooms, treatment and occasional admittances to hospital, and Ariel's bringing him back home. It was a reasonably well-accepted pattern.

Meanwhile, what was anticipated to be a rather routine procedure unfolded quite differently. Ariel was at the hospital pre-dawn to be with Tom before the procedure, holding his hand and sharing a prayer as he was being transported. The surgeon reassured them both this triple by-pass procedure was necessary, would relieve Tom's discomfort and provide him excellent quality of life. He foresaw no major concerns or complications in this quite routine procedure, indicating he fully expected to chat with them both later in the afternoon in the Cardiac care unit. Assurances from medical staff persons further reinforced this expectation, and several voiced their highest respect for this surgeon as being the very best in the city. Some had family members his skill and procedural abilities had restored to health against all odds.

From the moment of his entry to the surgical suite, routine normalcy ceased. Tom went into total cardiac arrest at the initial administration of anesthesia, with absolutely no prior indication of any imminent problem. Response was instant with surgeon and staff administering closed, then open, heart massage, connecting to all the necessary systems to keep adequate blood-flow to brain and organs. Once stabilized, the procedure itself was classic and completely successful from a medical/surgical standpoint.

The full six minutes that elapsed before all equipment was in place and blood circulation restored was of major concern carrying high uncertainty as to outcome. He remained medically sedated following initial evaluation at conclusion of the procedure. Ariel's meeting with the surgeon was not what either had expected or hoped for. He did not promise any rosy outcome, particularly in light of those six highly traumatic minutes. Tom's condition was precarious, he was very weak, being kept under sedation, and only time would tell as to any degree of recovery.

Late night of the 18th Ariel received a phone call that a second procedure was required to install an arterial assist pump, and would she authorize that. Of course … there was no question. His heart was weak and rhythm irregular as well. Tom spent the next nine days on full life support, non-responsive to any stimuli, not exhibiting even the slightest clue of regaining consciousness. His entire body was enormously swollen; fifteen medication pumps clicked and clacked their contects into his body through tubes and needles taped to virtually every possible location together with oxygen and feeding tubes. Additional lines monitored heart rate, blood pressure, oxygen levels, with yet more tubing to remove bodily fluids; arms and legs secured in restraints. His prognosis was extremely guarded at best.

During the surgical procedures and while watching Tom, the monitor screens and IV pumps in the Cardiac Intensive Care Unit, Ariel kept busy with yarn and crochet hook, busily making afghans for donation.

Flying fingers and the increasing numbers of rows quieted some of her panic-driven thoughts and served to keep remnants of calm and sanity intact. Tom was her rock; logical, steady and resolute, caring and loving, he was proud of her, considered her intelligent, attractive, a valuable and beloved asset in his life. She needed him; and knew he needed her. Why did all this have to happen to him? He truly deserved far better. She wasn't yet able to even think she also might deserve better. There was no answer.

Each morning Ariel was at the hospital before 5:00 if possible, to access updates from his surgeon and CICU staff. From hospital to work until mid-afternoon, then back to the hospital to spend time at his bedside, speaking softly, stroking the top of his one free hand, working on those afghans and watching the overhead screens. Tom was truly wired for sight and sound, with every possible physical function, input and output, addressed and monitored. A breathing tube fed in oxygen, gravity-flow feeding tube dumped gray semi- liquid substance into his stomach; wires and tubes were taped everywhere. Only the faint rise and fall of the sheet provided any indication he still lived.

The many consultations among his primary care physician, cardiac surgeon, neurologist and cardiac specialist were unsuccessful in determining any positive changes; prognosis remained unrelentingly grim. Of major concern in the event he might possibly regain any degree of consciousness was that crucial six-minute period at the onset of the procedure and now failure to regain consciousness once sedation had been gradually curtailed and then halted. Neurologic damage was deemed a given; with only the degree in question. All that was predicated on the unlikely possibility he ever woke.

One Friday evening the medical conclusion was reached to do a full range of evaluations and a brain scan the following Monday. With those results known, it would then be Ariel's decision as to continuation or cessation of life support. It was not realistic to continue that full support course indefinitely with no indication whatever of any potential positive response.

Her telephone conversation with his Neurologist was not remotely encouraging. He had treated Tom for nearly two decades, was familiar with what Tom would want for his future, and did not hold back his prognosis or build up any unrealistic expectations. It was both his personal and professional opinion that if Tom ever regained any degree of consciousness he would, at very best, be in a permanently vegetative state, unable to communicate on any meaningful level or participate in any interactive manner.

Tom's every physical need would be her responsibility for an unknowable number of years.

Monday it would be Ariel's responsibility alone to process results of the tests, evaluations and brain scan, reach conclusions and make that decision. Sitting in the dim room she couldn't even form a prayer. Her very core had been hollowed out … empty.

Before leaving that Friday evening, Ariel whispered into Tom's solitary available ear that it was OK if he wanted to go home; he didn't need to fight any longer. Following the regular prayers including the Confession of Faith, Apostles' Creed, Lord's Prayer and portions of Psalm 23, she silently prayed. If it truly was God's will he not survive, she could and would accept that, asking only that his death be without pain. He had gone through so much. Her only wish was that he have peace. Similar prayer and permission-giving was nothing new. It was the format she had followed consistently throughout his numerous admissions, ER visits and hospitalizations during many of which his survival of a given night was highly uncertain.

She tip-toed ever so carefully around stating any actual prognosis during the evening phone calls that Friday, sticking with the standard: "Tom is receiving excellent care, and there is really nothing new to report." That was absolutely true as it had been consistently since the surgeries, and especially so that evening.

Tom had not regained consciousness or exhibited the slightest hint that could be possible. He remained totally unresponsive; there was no change. Ariel was not going to share with anyone that on Monday the matter of continuing or discontinuing life support would be hers alone to confront. Tom remained comatose, and completely non-reactive to any and all stimuli. Only his physiology functioned, and that strictly with the auxiliary arterial pump, fifteen prescription IV-pumped drugs, tube feeding, hydration, oxygen supply and drains.

Ariel dreaded going home, but knew there was no point in spending any more time sitting on a stiff chair, staring at monitor screens and working on an afghan to keep her mind from going into orbit. Those screens registered no remotely favorable changes. With another prayer for guidance, grace, and God's will for Tom, she softly kissed the tiny spot on his head not covered by tube or tape.

Again assuring him she would be there in the morning, not having any clue if he was cognizant of anything whatever, it truly was time to leave. At previous times when his outcome was in doubt and he had been aware, he had weakly squeezed her hand in response; but now, nothing.

Was it actually a faint flicker she thought she saw in one eyelid, or just wishful thinking? She stood and watched in vain for several minutes; then reluctantly turned and left.

Silent tears fell unheeded, but she held herself together through the drive home, and answering the inevitable phone messages. Finally, calling the cats in for the night, securing the house and pouring a generous portion of bourbon over ice she yielded to wracking sobs. Tom was clearly dying. What was she do to.

The Biblical promise, "Be still, and know that I am God" together with the reassurances given Apostles long ago penetrated her foggy mind, especially, "Lo, I am with you always, even to the end..." She simply had to trust God; there was no other option. There was nothing she or any of the highly-skilled medical personnel could do. Neither she nor any other human was in charge; God was.

Her Saturday morning hospital visit was no more encouraging; Tom remained just as he had been each and every day since the by-pass and arterial pump procedures. After stroking that one exposed ear and lightly kissing his forehead, Ariel went to the office to put things in order there. She fully expected to be gone for at least the following week.

She contacted the East Wenatchee cemetery office to confirm Tom's purchase of two plots in 1980 when Rose had died. A call was also placed to a minister she knew in the area to make tentative arrangements to contact him further regarding the fully-expected need for his services. He had served a church there where she had attended and sung in the choir.

Corporate client files were tagged with appropriate contact and renewal dates; patent and trademark files marked with renewal fee amounts and due dates. She hoped someone would be able to just pick up where she fully expected to leave off, not jeopardizing essential corporate requirements.

Tom's condition had not changed since the by-pass procedure with absolutely no indication of the slightest hint of improvement. She had reluctantly accepted the medical prognosis that he would not survive.

The building was virtually deserted with the only sound being computer and printer noises. Ariel's phone suddenly jangled sharply; hospital identification on the caller id screen.

She forced a deep breath, and out of habit answered with the company and department identification, with "how may we assist you?" attempting to maintain calm and control. Surely, Tom must have died; and her thoughts raced; "keep it together, don't break down. Just get the information, write everything down, stay calm; get a direct call-back number."

The call was from the same nurse Ariel had spoken with just hours before; but, she was so excited her words tumbled all over each other. She could hardly speak. That was unexpected at the very least.

Not only had Tom not died, but was awake and cognizant for the first time in days. He knew she had been there that morning and wanted her to come back. "Wow!! The dreaded Monday morning consultations and decision-making no longer hung threateningly overhead.

Again she made record time getting back to the hospital, having hastily shoved files into whatever relatively secure spots she could find, closing out the computer mid-project and virtually running through corridors. Tom was awake ... everything else faded away. Not allowing herself to even consider those critical remaining questions of neurological damage, prayers of thanksgiving were few actual words, more glad tumultuous fragmented thoughts, all in heart-felt thanks, however ill-spoken. Tom was her rock; the one remaining person in her life and nearby who loved and supported her regardless of her feelings of incompetence and worthlessness.

Her son and daughter Jillian fully supported her and their concern was for both Tom's and her welfare, helping to pass updates to numbers of friends and family members. However, both were adults with their own lives, jobs, concerns, and miles away. Daughter Annie had maintained closer than usual telephone contact over the previous weeks with inquiries as to Tom's health, voicing hopes for his recovery; she also an adult with family, job and a life full of responsibilities.

Tom was sleeping quite as usual when she arrived at the Cardiac Critical Care unit, giving nurses an opportunity to relate the morning's happenings. He had been independently evaluated after his special duty nurse observed one eye opening, briefly. He had responded to stimulation tests, and was able to communicate "yes/no" answers by blinking.

Three additional and totally separate evaluations followed, with no communications between doctors or nurses providing any hint as to the reason for additional attention and evaluation requests. At the last two he had also responded with the slightest pressure on a doctor's finger. All his responses were appropriate; no apparent mental confusion was present.

Ariel sat silently by his bed and waited. Tom opened one eye, and then the other. "Welcome back, Dear" she voiced softly, bending to kiss his forehead and stroke that one free ear. She held his fingers and felt the slightest pressure of his response. This was indeed a miracle.

The question of neurological damage remained, of course, but for now it was more than enough that Tom was cognizant, appropriately responsive and reactive. Nurses gathered, beaming at him and all relishing this unexpected positive. Ariel did not stay long as Tom was exhausted, needed rest more than anything else, and drifted off despite noticeable effort to remain awake. She had so many calls to make, and this time there was good news to relate. The office could wait. She never could actually recall the drive home; phone calls were so happy.

Sunday she spent most of the day with Tom, talking to him even as he frequently slept, sharing best wishes sent by friends and family, and worked on the current afghan while closely watching the ever-present monitor screens. That night she enjoyed the first relaxed restful sleep in weeks.

His cardiac surgeon's response on Monday morning was a sight to behold; as he stood at the foot of Tom's bed, chart in hand. A broad grin spread over the normally brash New Yorker's face. He slowly turned to Ariel and spoke ever so softly, "There he is, the Miracle Boy, resurrected for sure." That he was delighted constituted a major understatement.

Ariel's schedule resumed as before; at the hospital in the wee hours, medical updates, some time with Tom, to work until mid-afternoon, back to the hospital and home by evening. As medications were suspended one-by-one, tape and a few tubes removed, she could actually massage his arms and hands generously with lotion. His skin was so very dry. To the office for the intervening hours and back to the hospital to spend time massaging his arms to help regain a little movement and straighten them as much as possible. Once feeding and oxygen tubes were removed his wrists were freed from restraints and preliminary therapy begun.

Her daily hospital/work/hospital/home pattern continued through the weeks until Tom was able to transfer from hospital intensive care to a local rehabilitation facility. He had made great strides regaining his health once he regained consciousness; tubes were removed and was able to eat actual food. Nurses fed him most meals, with Ariel there for late afternoon snack and dinner, as he was still much too weak to lift a hand. Even a flimsy plastic spoon was too heavy. A major milestone was reached when he was strong enough to hold the two-handled, child's training cup and actually drink by himself.

As he gained strength and ability to speak again, Tom's recalling channel numbers and television schedules accurately together with querying Ariel as to payment of individual household bills, stating due dates and exact amounts to the penny for each, put the neurologist's fears to rest. He asserted that since Tom was not responsible for engineering the next phase of space exploration, his mental status was no longer a concern. Against all odds, Tom had not only survived physically but neurologically as well.

His Neurologist was totally blown away, never having dared even consider the possibility of an outcome remotely this favorable. Tom had defied all neurological case histories, research studies and expectations.

Tom was absolutely determined to regain full mobility and worked diligently toward that goal at the rehab facility. Her weekday schedule remained much the same, bringing his clean clothes, paper, mail and messages before work. Returning in the afternoons, Ariel often found him in the gym working on exercise equipment. Before long he was strong enough to take phone calls from relatives and his pals, which were a great help, and eased Ariel's evening phone time considerably.

After a month in the rehab facility, Tom was fully ambulatory, had demonstrated his ability to get into and out of a sedan, eat meals at the table, and was quite ready to go home. What a change from being comatose, wired for sight and sound and on full life support with only a negative prognosis. He might still be weak, and use his walker out in public; but Tom, psychologically her personal rock, was back and communicative. She had so missed their being able to talk about news items, her work, politics, their neighborhood—just anything and everything.

Out-patient cardio therapy was scheduled, all his belongings loaded into the truck; Tom walked from the wheelchair to his truck. The last hurdle was demonstrating he could get into the vehicle unaided. With one hand on a grab bar, the other on the seat, he launched himself into the passenger seat. Ariel had to blink hard and fast to see through joyous tears as she and Tom waved to the smiling, well-wishing nurses and drove out onto the road home. Once home he admitted he was getting into that truck by means fair or foul, regardless.

Ariel concurred, that she had been ready to bodily hoist him in if required.

Snow, and More Snow

Tom eagerly looked forward to each of his cardio therapy sessions on alternate week days. This not only provided the recommended therapy and health benefits, but provided him opportunity to be out and about, talking with people and socializing a bit. Ariel's concerns were more for his mental and emotional well-being than physical health at this point. She knew he needed the interaction with non-medically-related adults. His deep depression during the time in Idaho was a major concern; he had not made friends there. She did not want that pattern to recur and the therapy schedule was a preventive measure as well as good physical exercise. The only fly in the ointment now was the diarrhea that still lingered following the prolonged tube feeding in the CICU that frequently evidenced intestinal bleeding. While Tom used various exercise routines and worked on assorted pieces of equipment, Ariel took long walks through the area.

She explored new streets and even a few alleys in this older mixed-use neighborhood which included medical offices, apartments and single residences, hospitals and the rehab facility. That had originated as a hospital decades past, but lacked adequate space to meet current requirements for full clinical services.

The location in an interesting and historic part of town evoked the sense that a horse-drawn carriage just might suddenly appear around a corner or emerge from a narrow drive. Some older homes were well maintained with orderly flower gardens and tidy pathways. Others had been turned into multiple unit rental properties; some single and multiple unit structures had suffered neglect; but original design and some quite grand features remained apparent. Gardens fascinated her as well and she appreciated the different styles of casual landscape and more formal planning represented, or not in yards left untended.

Ariel prayed as she walked, both giving thanks for blessings and asking for guidance in caring for Tom during this new phase of his continuing recuperation and in their marriage. It was somewhat problematic trying to determine when Tom needed help, and when he just needed more time and a little space to do things himself. She wanted to do what was right for him, not erring on the side of omission or commission; certainly not wanting him to feel inadequate or put down in any way. She had experienced way too much negativity in her life and truly didn't want Tom to feel he was in any way a burden on her, or anyone else. It was a very thin line to traverse, trying to avoid too much or too little, both of help and restraint.

She had retired from her paralegal work in the corporate legal department working with contracts, patents, trademarks and compliance data the day he had been discharged from rehab … a major adjustment not having an actual office job. She had worked all her life, from picking berries and babysitting at age eight, moving to office environments at 14, with only brief periods of unemployment, until now. School and then work environments had provided positive feedback that for decades had long been withheld in her personal life.

While he lived her Dad did his best to support and encourage her, but had to be ever so careful in voicing anything positive about Ariel, lest Edythe overhear. That would only have boded ill for both father and daughter. Only once did he dare softly whisper in her ear that he loved her. She knew he did from his attempts to soften Edythe's ongoing criticisms and the way he spoke, also well-hidden.

Ariel never once heard any such sentiment expressed by Edythe; only blame, queries and criticism. Her only concern seemed to be that Ariel avoid any statement or behavior that however remotely could cause Edythe any potential possibility of embarrassment, or ever do something the neighbors might 'see'. See what? There had never been any explanation.

Was going to school, church, or even on a teenage date somehow of interest to those neighbors? They had always treated Ariel kindly, with no indication of undue curiosity about her beyond interest in her school activities and recreation. The two sisters lived in the family home, were both well educated and employed; remaining there following their widowed mother's passing. Neither ever married. In the period immediately following WW II, eligible men were in very short supply, which certainly did not enhance their opportunities for social interaction.

As she aged, Edythe's suspicions and paranoia increased. She perceived only dire threat and danger everywhere from numerous unidentified sources. She fretted about the decline of moral standards throughout the country, specifically about 'the youth', claiming she alone could provide a suitable environment for young girls who would otherwise 'go astray'. Ariel learned of one such proposal when a minister contacted her about Edythe's seeking to take young girls into her home, thereby correcting their errant thoughts and ways.

Ariel's response was a resounding 'NO' – not under any circumstances should that occur or even be given a moment's consideration. She had endured Edythe's efforts at 'correct and proper' along with unending suspicion from earliest childhood. She briefly related Edythe's deep suspicion of anything and everything not in compliance with her narrow and small-minded concept of the correct and proper. No more was heard about Edythe's grand plan to rescue all female youth of the universe, single handedly.

Roger had threatened to kill Ariel numerous occasions, or in the alternative have her committed to a mental institution. He lacked ability for the most part, although he had used her long hair to cut off her breathing on occasion; and there was no logical explanation for evidences of tampering with her car. The methods and timing were unknown, but there had been quite clear indications he did dwell on her demise, and for that to appear accidental. If indeed he had tampered with her vehicle, it apparently didn't occur to him it was Ariel who usually transported their children. Perhaps it didn't matter; he could free himself of all the pesky responsibilities.

Those experiences, while utterly terrifying at the time, had provided her with tools to better deal with family law clients years later and various courtroom situations. She had lived through the mental and emotional abuse, some physical as well. She could relate well to clients and genuinely assure them life was worth living; they were worthy individuals and their lot(s) would improve. Several sought her out months and even years later with thanks and hugs, broad smiles on their once-gloomy faces. Ariel cherished those meetings.

She was convinced that no bad, frightening or otherwise horribly negative occurrences in life cannot be of value, perhaps in helping someone else years down the road. That had certainly been her experience.

The first days and even weeks after fleeing Roger and finding refuge in her little apartment, physical weakness and pain had increased, becoming a major concern. Her very bones hurt; stepping up onto a four-inch curb was painful and significant in walking to work. She could not even staple sheets of paper together without pain. Both hands were required to pick up the stapler or slide pages into position. Pulling a hymnal from a pew rack was also a source of major pain and required use of both hands. She was convinced this signaled a serious medical problem, most likely bone cancer at the very least. Without any medical insurance, no consultation or evaluation was made. As her decades-long fears subsided and tension eased with new-found freedom, so did the pain, finally disappearing altogether.

She had made her desperate run for life and freedom with the grand sum of $600 in her pocket, 10-year old Ryan, no job, no current skills and no source of income. It took nearly six weeks to find employment and that carried an agency fee with it. Her tiny stash dwindled. Was Roger correct? that she would starve on her own? No. She was determined to make a go of being single; she would survive, somehow. And survive she did, barely.

Until Tom came into her life, home environments had been consistently negative, from early childhood through the escape and divorce from Roger. During the time of being single, her paralegal employment was of prime importance in keeping a roof over her head and being able to provide for herself and Ryan. She reveled in the freedom, but greatly feared for their financial future.

A tentative sense of confidence and self-worth slowly emerged. Walking miles along irrigation canal paths, and the several blocks to work each day, Ariel repeated over and over, "I am a worthy person; I do deserve to live." Eventually she almost believed it. Singing in the church choir also provided a source of both comfort and confidence along with new acquaintances. Tenor voices tend to be in short supply in small choirs, and she frequently found herself constituting the entirety of that particular vocal section.

Walking to work each morning and back in the evenings, she also concentrated on finding at least one positive element; a friendly dog, pretty cat, a particularly nice flower, quail devouring bugs, bird songs, cloud formations, or sunsets. She held those images dear throughout the days, and evenings. Replacing negative with positive and always finding something for which to give thanks, helped to clear her mind and raise her spirits bit by bit. She also grew stronger physically.

Her long walks now during Tom's cardio rehab sessions strengthened Ariel's resolve to make good in this next chapter in her life as well as Tom's. He looked forward to each hour-long session and made excellent progress building back muscle strength and improving balance. While he probably was not going to fully regain his former physical strength, he continued to make far more progress than physicians and Ariel had ever thought possible.

The intermittent diarrhea that had been present since the tube feeding following by-pass surgery continued, serving to mask more minor bleeds and interfered with Tom's ability to attend some rehab sessions. Various treatments were prescribed however, those were only partially effective; it could not be totally controlled. He was able to cope for the most part and refused to allow that problem to completely control his life—limiting to some degree, but not control.

In late November another serious bleed occurred with the diarrhea and she once again rushed him to E.R. in the late night hours. Ariel provided all the insurance information to the admitting office and he was once more installed in an Intensive Care unit. More tests were done, and finally the various medical professionals admitted his problem just possibly could be lower, not upper, intestinal tract. Another scope was performed and a specific area identified as at least one source of bleeding … in the lower intestinal area. That scoping procedure itself further weakened him despite replenishing blood transfusions.

Surgical procedure to remove that specific portion of the lower intestinal tract was medically recommended; however, Tom was still not strong enough to realistically tolerate another invasive procedure. His triple by-pass procedure had been in mid-September, with the numerous complications including full life support and a month in CICU; this new bleed had occurred the third week of November. The problem needed to be addressed medically. He was again transferred to a tower room, received six units of whole blood and another six of plasma.

He was discharged Thanksgiving Day and home in time for a light dinner of traditional turkey, mashed potatoes and gravy with all trimmings; then off to bed. A light snow fell throughout the afternoon and evening. A portent perhaps?

He was able to attend his cardio rehab sessions again by mid-December. On the 18th more light fluffy snow was falling when they pulled into the rehab parking lot. An hour later, during which Ariel had remained indoors reading, nearly eight inches of heavy wet snow had fallen. Just clearing the truck was a task, and although Tom wanted to help, she insisted he stay inside and warm until she could bring the truck closer to the door. He didn't need snow-removal stress added to his still weak system.

She selected the least trafficked, most level route home possible. Even so, traversing the eleven miles home required over an hour of strictly white-knuckle driving; and Ariel was not one to be the least bit intimidated by winter road conditions. She drove carefully, but not timidly. Traffic was a total chaotic mess with cars, trucks and everything else off roads and in ditches, everywhere. Snow fell steadily for the next several days, piling up new records by the hour. Rehab sessions were cancelled.

There was plenty of food in the house and she didn't actually need to get out on the roads immediately; mail could just wait at the Post Office; somehow the daily paper arrived, and only a little late. Local news reports were basically concerned with the mounting snow depths, traffic snarls and other problems in the area. People dependent on public transportation were of particular concern, as well as elderly and infirm, with various agencies struggling to make their way to known residences. Roofs began collapsing throughout the region; mostly older commercial buildings, but some of more recent construction along with a few residences.

For the first several days of this apparently unending snowfall, Ariel was not much worried about the house roof, due to age and construction. She concentrated on the drive, walks and enough of the patio so the kitties could get outside for their daily inspection duties. Each had a path of routine patrol, checking for evidence of any night-time intrusions by other cats. Deep snow soon curtailed those, but they still wanted to be outdoors a bit.

As inches became feet of snow building up on roofs as well as the ground, and some rather sharp, loud creaks were heard overhead, her apprehension increased. Any need to transport Tom for medical care again, day or night, would not be a simple matter of getting him into the truck and driving there. Roads were increasingly hazardous with strong recommendations by all emergency services and news media to drive only if absolutely necessary.

Police, fire services and towing companies were totally inundated and utterly unable to timely meet demands. If need for a hospital run presented, it would be up to Ariel to get him there safely. Realistically, several hours would elapse before any official aid might be available.

It was a valid, if somewhat remote concern; but much worse if the roof caved. Ariel did not want to chance that with Tom still weak and experiencing both the diarrhea and bleeds. He was anxious enough about the mounting snow level and her spending most of each day shoveling and blowing it just to keep one walkway and drive partially clear. Creaks and snaps overhead increased together with her growing angst. Snow continued falling steadily from leaden skies.

Out came the extension ladder, and with shovel in hand, Ariel climbed to the roof and began clearing it. This was not light fluffy snow, but wet and heavy. If she dared rest for a moment, Tom was at the slider door checking to see if she was still okay. Finally shivering and soaked to the skin she descended, stripped off the wet garments in the garage, wrapped up in a blanket and made some hot tea. That full day and some three hours the next morning were required to lighten the load from the house and garage roofs. She wondered how much progress was actually made as flakes quickly covered what had just been cleared. Snow pushed down onto the driveway took on the appearance of a mountain range. Clearing just one lane of the drive required still more hours with both shovel and snow blower.

Christmas Day found her on the roof once more, removing even more new accumulation. This however, was light, fluffy and beautiful. Afternoon sun shining on the snow-covered houses and roofs, sparkled in all colors of the spectrum was stunningly beautiful. Tom worried she might fall from the roof; however, with several feet accumulation, she assured him the only thing he might need to do was call for a 'dig-out', or wait for spring thaw. Breaking legs or arms was definitely not of major or even minor concern; suffocation possibly.

Eventually the record-breaking snowfall eased, slowed and actually stopped. Throughout the region the digging-out continued, plows eventually prevailed and life returned to normal.

Still More Medical

Tom was scheduled to undergo a follow-up scope procedure in early February to re-evaluate the specific lower tract intestinal problem area identified in November. Alleged clinic policy denied him being treated by the physician of his choice, requiring him to see another with whom he did not feel at all comfortable. His urgent request was not even considered. He was required to be treated by the scheduled doctor despite his requests, preference and prior experience with that individual. Ariel made numerous calls to this clinic administrator spending considerable time and effort attempting to secure the treatment Tom strongly preferred, all to no avail.

Reluctantly the appointment was kept and Tom was whisked away, sedated and both hearing aids removed, Ariel waited anxiously for his return from the procedure; seeming far longer than any such prior.

When he was finally wheeled into the cubicle she learned an endoscopy had also been performed without having been scheduled or even mentioned. Even now, this physician maintained the bleeding originated in the upper digestive tract and was apparently quite determined to prove himself correct. Results of the November scoping procedure were summarily ignored.

Tom's questions and Ariel's concerns as to his sore throat and the severe rectal bleeding were brushed aside by that physician and staff with clearly expressed opinions those were of no consequence or any interest whatsoever. It was quite clear both of them, Ariel in particular, were annoying nuisances.

Tom was not only miserable and bleeding, but emotionally distraught. He had undergone several such previous procedures with only minor discomfort; this had been a quite different experience in every respect, none positive.

Other clinic patients and family members present for procedures that day were provided evaluation questionnaires at discharge; not so Tom or Ariel.

No results were provided beyond an off-hand casual comment that no obvious carcinoma had been identified. For Tom to receive any definitive results from biopsies or diagnostic results of the procedure, he must schedule and appear at the clinic for an office consultation.

No results would be provided to him directly by any means, transmitted by any means, nor shared with his primary care physician. That clinic physician was adamant; no exception would be made despite Tom's worsening state and obvious weakness.

He weakened still further, unable to even leave the house, much less travel several miles by car, ride elevators, walk long corridors and sit in a waiting room until this particular doctor might elect to speak with him. He could barely be out of bed other than to the toilet, at times successfully, but not always. He needed assistance to stand and support to walk even a few feet. No matter how Ariel pleaded, explained and clarified Tom's severely deteriorated condition and inability to attend an office consultation, there was no deviation from that physician's in-office appointment requirement.

Her frustration was over the top; even Tom's primary care physician was unable to extract any information from that clinic doctor despite their years of professional relationship, not to mention his professional responsibility.

Unable to do much of anything, with diarrhea steadily increasing along with bleeding, Tom weakened steadily. By mid-April it was clear Ariel could no longer care for him at home, as she was unable to lift him from the ever-increasing falls. Her prayers for strength, answers, and guidance seemed to go no higher than the ceiling. His doctor understood and arranged for him to be admitted to hospital again.

Just getting him out of the house, into the truck and to the hospital was a major undertaking. He was so weak he could scarcely walk even with her support. She pulled in to the ER entrance, left Tom sitting in the truck, whisked through the entrance, grabbed a wheelchair, managed the transfer without dropping him; placed insurance cards in his hand before wheeling him to the admitting desk. She raced back to correctly park the truck; leaving it in an "ambulance only" lane was truly not an option.

She didn't even want to think about what might be on Tom's and her horizon. He had been through so much, and truthfully so had she. Was there to be more?

Would she really and truthfully be strong enough to deal with whatever loomed in their future? What had she done to inflict this on Tom? Was she at fault? She must be; Tom certainly had not caused his problems.

Was Edythe correct in consistently asserting and reinforcing Ariel's guilt about anything and everything? Roger had continued that pattern, adding threats of death and/or mental institution commitment because of her inadequacies and incompetence. Maybe they were right. What had she done that resulted in Tom's ever-worsening health problems? There had to be some reason, didn't there? It had to be her fault.

Teams of doctors ran test after test attempting to isolate Tom's problems. Diarrhea and bleeding continued, lessening to an almost hopeful degree and promptly increasing again. A nuclear test was performed on a weekend, requiring a specialist be called in to run it and interpret findings; still no clear answers. Finally on a Monday afternoon the latest CT scan showed the lower intestine had actually burst; emergency surgery was required. Outcome was unpredictable; prognosis highly uncertain.

Tom was in too much pain and had received far too many medications to have any actual awareness of what had occurred, or was about to. Ariel could only pray for his safety, freedom from pain and wisdom for all the medical personnel involved. Originally scheduled for 7:00 pm, delayed until 9:00 and then 11:00 pm, he was finally taken into surgery just before midnight. An emergency procedure at another area hospital involving a young patient had resulted in the delay.

Ariel huddled in a darkened waiting room, praying and working on yet another afghan to keep panic subdued to a mere level of high apprehension. Wild stormy winds howled at the dark windows, drenching rain pounded against the glass, much in keeping with her dismal thoughts. What would be the outcome of this procedure, providing he even survived? Was she wrong for signing the consent documents when Tom was unable to?

When consent documents were presented to him, Tom was ranting, raving, calling Ariel every name in the book, peeling paint from the walls with profanities. He shouted accusations of her of trying to kill him and promised to shoot her with her own gun. He was in no condition to consent to anything, much less another surgical procedure offering only minimal chance of any positive outcome. Several possibilities had been discussed, but only the procedure itself would determine his best, truly only, chance of survival. Without intervention he would die within a few hours as infection raged through his body.

Ariel prayed wordlessly, adding rows upon rows to yet another afghan as wild storms raged outside the walls and in her heart. Stone-cold coffee in the urn was undrinkable, even for her.

Shortly after 4:00 am a weary surgeon dropped to the sofa beside her, quietly assuring her Tom had withstood anesthetic and the invasive procedure very well, despite his relatively recent by-pass and all the intervening bleeds.

An iliostomy had been required, involving removal of the entire lower intestine. His abdominal area had been seriously infected; antibiotics were administered before, during the procedure and would continue. Time would tell if the infection could be controlled and/or eliminated. Tom was wearing an ostomy device and would for the remainder of his days. There was no medical reason he should not heal from this procedure to lead a full and completely normal life.

As Ariel processed the considerable quantity of medical information and facts, her mind hovered between despair and relief; the familiar guilt swirling all around. The bright spot was that Tom had survived the procedure with a positive prognosis. He was expected to make a full recovery.

Physical healing proceeded generally according to schedule, except that Tom steadfastly refused to eat adequately, actually barely at all. The 1800 calories per day administered through IV tubes along with hydration were woefully insufficient for his healing and regaining any degree of health. Weight loss had already been extreme, and continued.

He was encouraged by one and all to eat, anything and everything, without any dietary restrictions whatsoever. Surgeon, cardiac specialists, internists, one and all voiced the common instruction, "you simply must eat and there are no restrictions, eat anything wish and everything you like…home cooked, commercially prepared; just eat."

One problem presented itself immediately; Tom simply did not wish to eat anything, at all, and he failed to thrive despite all efforts. Ariel brought home made chicken soup, tomato soup with whole milk, and baked potato soup from his favorite restaurant. Wait staff there slipped notes into the take-out orders wishing him a speedy recovery and that they all missed him, wanted to see him back for steak and baked potato dinners. Friends and family called; his son visited from across the state, Ariel provided personal nursing care throughout each day along with home cooking; all to no avail.

His only wish was to die at home, with his kitties. His room in their home was soon equipped for intensive care at home, lacking only the overhead monitors for tracking all bodily functions. He was transported home in compliance with his oft-repeated wish to die at home, not in hospital.

Ariel was to provide care despite lack of any medical training whatever. His team of doctors predicted a three to five-day life expectancy at home, less if he remained hospitalized. The slim hope was he might agree to eat home-cooked food, in his own home, with a kitty present. Not only a slim hope, it was the only hope.

He was installed in a fully-adjustable hospital style bed, barely aware of his surroundings. Ariel was left completely on her own to cope with flushing IV ports, changing tubing in IV pumps, spiking hydration bags, administering all medications, adjusting oxygen levels, suctioning his throat, administering inhalation therapy, emptying Foley as well as the ostomy bags, changing the bags, and charting vital signs six or more times each day.

She charted each drop of liquid or morsel of food ingested together with output also measured and charted faithfully. Ariel was absolutely certain he would die the first night, especially when she had to change out tubing in the IV pump with no instructions. Reading and re-reading the brief written instructions she was convinced they must have originated in Sanskrit; translated by primitive jungle tribes, not resulting in any recognizable form of Americanized English, primitive or other.

The only thing she thought to be absolutely significant about the tubing procedure was that no air be allowed to enter his blood stream, but not any means of prevention. Years later she learned that was not critical; however, at the time was her utmost fear. Flushing the PICC ports was accomplished with trembling hands. Angels were not visible, but Ariel knew they had guided her hands; and more than made up for her lack of training and skill. Her desperate prayers for help, guidance for her hands in dealing with tubes, syringes and hydration bags, suction and oxygen were poorly formulated through tears streaming down her face, but answered nonetheless. Despite her terror and lack of skills, Tom was still alive and breathing with minimal reliance on oxygen in the morning.

The Hospice nurse finally arrived that afternoon, checked Tom, the room set-up and all the equipment and supplies. Why she had not been at the house the day before as scheduled was somewhat unclear. Apparently there had been miscommunication as to the County in which Tom resided. She pronounced all to be perfectly in order and very well done; Tom's extreme weakness the only problem. Her only instruction was to be sure Tom ate. Good luck with that. And just what did she think doctors had been saying for the past weeks.

Wow. For Ariel to be congratulated and even praised for her efforts was amazing; more amazing was that Tom still lived.

She gave him bed baths at least twice each day, massaging lotions into his paper-dry skin and fixing tiny meals throughout each day trying to temp him into eating something, anything. She changed his bedding and gown at morning bathing, and again as needed in the afternoons and through the nights when ostomy appliances failed. The Hospice aide visited three days a week for bathing, and found Tom clean and skin softened with lotion each time. Multiple loads of laundry were run each day. A registered nurse was available on call for emergencies. Specific liquid prescription medications awaited in the refrigerator to administer through IV if deemed appropriate. And who might determine what might be appropriate? No answer. Those remained, chilled and unused, on the shelf.

Ariel was exhausted; just keeping Tom alive; trying to get even small amounts of food into him was her major focus. Prayers were of thanksgiving for each day he survived, also with pleas for strength and guidance for herself.

The stated three days passed, then five and became seven, nine and ten, to everyone's amazement. Every trick in the book was employed to present nourishing food on attractive tray settings with fresh flowers, windows open to spring breezes – all geared to encouraging Tom to try just one or two more bites. Television was also employed, hoping he could be distracted and perhaps automatically open his mouth for an approaching spoon. Not so.

He did like bite-size bits of vanilla ice cream coated with chocolate, so Ariel made sure they were on hand and quickly available in an event Tom might inadvertently open his mouth. One and sometimes, two, were popped in before he again refused.

Notwithstanding the dire prognosis, Tom survived. Ariel began sleeping in two-hour segments as his health slowly improved, waking instantly to address any changes in breathing, oxygen generation, IV pump beeps, or need to suction his throat. Slowly, bit by bit, a few medical equipment items were eliminated as he gradually improved and his environment began to look a little less like an intensive care unit.

After a month the Hospice care was transferred over to Home Health and therapy begun. Ariel relaxed marginally. Tom had then been bedridden for over three months, and chances of his ever standing, much less ever walking independently were slim at best. Ariel worked with him as well as the therapist, and he made great progress. Her fears and tears began to decrease in very tiny increments. Several people offered assistance, but Tom was dealing with enough, definitely not eager or even willing to have any caregiver but Ariel. She also wanted to preserve whatever dignity remained.

She consistently struggled with guilt that she must have done something to bring all this down on Tom. That made no sense whatever, it just existed. Was it more than slightly ridiculous? Logically, of course but, Ariel had been raised on guilt, and then that was reinforced by Roger for another twenty years. Guilt was familiar and a weirdly comfortable state of being.

Ariel's spirits slowly lifted as Tom finally began to eat, gained strength and participated willingly in physical therapy sessions. Standing and walking were considered extremely remote possibilities, but he was determined and so was she. The first successful transfer from hospital bed to wheelchair was cause for major celebration, bringing a rare smile to Tom's face and hugs from Ariel. She had not dropped him –altogether amazing. Just into a chair after months in bed was a major accomplishment. They worked on the therapy routines, increasing repetitions, strengthening his muscles and re-establishing mobility. Standing with the walker, the first hesitant steps, then more; before long he was out of his room and walking with assistance to the table for meals. After four full months, Tom was ambulatory. More medical equipment, including the IV pump, bags and related items went out the door, followed by the Foley bag. Vital signs were monitored only once a day, and no longer charted. He was definitely improving. It was slow, but they had done it, together.

Peaceful Interlude

With Tom's health improving steadily, Ariel dared relax and resume some of her more normal and usual activities. Floors needed cleaning and waxing, cupboard contents thinned and shelves cleaned, gardens tended, even a bit of painting. Canvases were stacked in the basement waiting, along with scores of frames, all neglected for too long. Tom was able to be up and about each day, taking care of himself for the most part.

2010 was a U.S. Census year. Ariel applied and was hired to do follow-up visits to residences from which no forms had been returned. This was a perfect opportunity … part-time work, with flexible hours, and in their general area. Not only could she get out of the house for a bit and interact with adults in a non-medical environment, but it gave Tom a chance to re-gain some self-confidence. He would be on his own for a few hours each day and out from under her constant watchfulness. It worked beautifully for both; they enjoyed each other's company much more, with independent and separate experiences to share. Both emerged from the gloom of winter and illness, enjoying summer and autumn.

While travel plans had been set aside, short jaunts helped to expand Tom's horizons a bit and his depression eased. Even getting the mail each day and then lattes at the market helped to get him out of the house and conversing with other people. A major plus of having lattes was fun he had chatting with the baristas; they teased and joked with him while Ariel did a little shopping.

Late September and October found Ariel undergoing two invasive surgical procedures, each requiring hospitalization. Tom assured her he was able to take care of himself and that she should take the time to care for herself and not worry about him. Her first procedure corrected an internal blood vessel thrombosis. Sutures failed requiring a second procedure and session of anesthesia in early,

early morning hours following what seemed to her far more than one night's heavy bleeding. Memories of hemorrhaging decades past surfaced bringing old fears to the fore. Requiring the two procedures within thirty hours was hardly surprising given her prior history of suture failures and hemorrhages, but brought back so many dark memories she had hoped were long gone and forever relegated to the past.

She was severely weakened by blood loss, but determined to get home as quickly as possible. If Tom had a serious seizure there was no one available to address that or call for help. Hospital staff was adamant about her having transportation available, but Tom was not driving and there was no one to call for a ride. They did not insist she call a taxi, and by persistence and persuasion Ariel was able to convince a transport aide to release her at the door of a sky-bridge. She needed walk only a short distance to the little truck and drove home the morning of day three … very carefully. The transport aide reluctantly pushed her wheelchair to the hospital exit adjacent to the parking lot, fussed and fretted the whole way, but is all worked beautifully.

No way was Ariel going to reveal the truck was a standard 5-speed – not an automatic transmission vehicle.

A CT scan in September prior to the first procedure had also revealed an ovarian cyst, resulting in Ariel's finally having both ovaries removed just a month following the first procedure. That was something she had wanted for years and provided her with significant peace of mind. After this procedure the surgeon specifically prohibited her driving for ten days; which lasted almost five without any negative effect. She was after all the sole driver, and not about to confine Tom to the house for nearly two weeks.

Tom did very well being alone for those few days and gained considerable self-confidence. He was delighted to have her back home and enjoyed being able to take care of her for a change. She was determined to bounce back as quickly as possible and was out raking leaves and winterizing the outside areas before the first snow which arrived early again.

The winter proved quite similar to the previous, with heavy snowfalls. Ariel again spent hours removing it with both shovel and the blower. Tom didn't worry quite so much about her spending time out in the cold, knowing she rather enjoyed it while he certainly did not. He had also finally accepted that shoveling snow was something he should not try or even think about any more.

There was enough snow that Ariel could snap on her skinny skis and glide off to the neighborhood grocery with her backpack and return with a lovely fresh donut or two for Tom along with whatever food items were actually needed. She relished those short trips in the crisp winter air.

He felt somewhat obligated to consume those bakery treats and actually began gaining a few pounds.

Suburban snow was not at all like hiking in the mountains, which she sorely missed. Days of relative solitude having time to ponder natural wonders, sort out thoughts, contemplate, sketch, and just give over to the physicality of trekking upward trails were likely past. That had been a valuable time of healing when she sorely needed it. So many personal fears had been examined, met and discarded. Those days of hiking mountain trails had enabled her to grow spiritually, heal emotionally and become a far more confident person. Muscles ached and blisters formed, but Edythe's and Roger's negativity shrank. With each trip planned, accomplished, and then highlighted on her topographical map Ariel's sense of worth and value grew, seemingly in direct correlation with decrease of prior years' denigration importance.

Spring was lovely, slowing morphing into summer. Tom was now quite able to be outdoors and enjoy the great weather. His seizure medication cautioned against direct sunlight, but he could enjoy the waterfall and pond in the shade of the large Cleveland Maple. The cats loved having their 'dad' outside where they could doze on his lap. As Ariel gained confidence in herself and her personal value, she relaxed and felt less and less guilty about everything and anything. She continued with sincere effort to eliminate the automatic guilt response to even the slightest concern.

Quite a bit of the automatic guilt response had been lifted with Edythe's passing, only to re-emerge at a slightly lesser degree with Tom's series of medical problems. Those now appeared at least at bay if not fully resolved. The seizure incidents were more manageable and quite well controlled. His primary care physician, neurologist together with assorted specialists and surgeons were amazed and delighted at his survival and progress; largely crediting Ariel, as they had basically given up.

She knew it had been God's will along with Tom's eventual determination, but quietly appreciated the compliments in any event, not instantly succumbing to unspecified guilt and negativity.

They were able to attend both grandsons' high school graduations, join in the family and friends celebrations, even over-nighting in hotels, the first in a city on the West side of the mountains and the second just about two hours from home. Dinners at Tom's favorite steakhouse, visiting with friends, enjoying visits from his cross-state pals were again normal enjoyments once thought gone forever. Life was really quite enjoyable; Ariel looked forward to having many more years with Tom; evenings of just being together. The kitties were totally pleased.

Ryan and his lady friend visited at Christmas, and Jillian and her family came at New Years. They exchanged phone calls with Tom's family members. Snow fell, enough so everything was beautifully covered, but not too much and travel was easy.

Life relaxed into a pleasant routine of daily visits to the Post Office, then lattes at the grocery and normal errands. Tom kept regular appointments with his doctors who made only minor adjustments to medications, and pronouncing him physically and mentally fit far beyond their wildest expectations. He had not driven much following the initial wreck and not at all after his by-pass procedure; which worked very well; he didn't really like driving. Ariel was also probably the worst passenger on the planet, much preferring to be at the wheel.

If all could just continue in this general manner, they could expect several more peaceful years of retirement together. Communication with each other was good, and they enjoyed lively discussions, sharing ideas, not always agreeing, and just being together. Evenings generally found them watching television, a cat in Tom's lap and Ariel working on yet another donation afghan. They weren't exactly living the high life and plans for any additional travel had been put firmly away; however all in all; things were pretty good. Tom was in reasonably good health; Ariel relaxed to a degree she never expected. Tom had survived so many medical crises and Ariel had certainly learned more about general patient care, critical care and life-saving procedures than she ever expected or particularly wanted to.

Once again they dared hope for many years of relative peace and quiet together and were thankful, especially when the potential alternatives were considered.

Her life had taken so many unexpected twists and turns; and now was absolutely nothing like she had imagined, tried to picture, and even tentatively planned it to be years before. Despite past difficulties and turmoil that could easily have resulted in various types of disaster, she was not only content but quite happy. Ariel felt her prayers of desperation on numerous occasions had not only been heard, but answered positively … not perhaps as she originally thought and wished, but according to God's plan for her life. Over the years prayers of thanksgiving preceded those seeking answers to dilemmas.

And then...

Early in 2012 Tom began experiencing ever-increasing pain. More gastro intestinal professionals were consulted for that in addition to the rather mild, but disturbingly ever-present rectal discharge. That had been considered temporary following the iliostomy procedure, however, had never actually ceased. While not in itself painful or of major concern, it continued to be bothersome and required consistent product use which was annoying. Compared to some of his prior problems however, this ranked rather low on the scale.

The increasing pain was a different matter. Various cushioning means were employed with limited degrees of temporary success. His G-I physician prescribed a number of medications at intervals, none of which proved successful. Finally another invasive procedure was deemed the only option, and the surgeon was consulted.

December 20th Tom was once more admitted to hospital; the numerous out-patient tests having been completed. He was absolutely determined this be completed before year-end in light of the expected changes to health insurance coverage.

A completion proctectomy procedure is truly a last resort. The procedure itself went well, his heart had tolerated yet another major invasive surgery, and once more only full recuperation was expected.

He was confused the night of the procedure, loudly ranting at everyone and everything. Ariel was called and returned to the hospital near midnight, managed to calm him by staying at his side throughout that night, and all the next day. Tom truly preferred that Ariel tend to his patient care, particularly cleaning his ostomy appliance and dressing surgical incisions. She had provided his personal nursing care for years, knew what and how to keep him as comfortable as possible. She went home late that evening and enjoyed a night's sleep. The following morning he was quite rational and cooperative.

That day was excellent; Tom ate well, was out of bed and walked; all systems appeared to be functioning well and properly. He was very appropriately tired, drifting off to sleep easily and frequently. He requested minimal pain medication and appeared to be making good progress. She cleaned his ostomy bag, administered his evening medications and tucked him in for the night, promising again to be back early in the morning. All indications were positive for a relatively short and successful recuperation.

That was not to be. This incision steadily seeped that same blood-tinged mucus, neither lessening nor increasing. Kidneys showed stress; mental instability erupted.

Next morning, the 24th, her "good morning, Merry Christmas" greeting evoked a raging tirade accusing her of confining him to wherever it was he was being held against his will – she was just after his money, and he wanted a divorce – immediately (if not sooner). All attempts at calming him failed. His accusations, cursing and demands were even worse than those following his regaining consciousness after the cardio procedure and days on life support. Ariel was utterly devastated.

She knew his outbursts were a result of the anesthetic, antibiotics and assortment of other drugs; however, this was absolutely too much. Assuring him he could certainly have his divorce, truck, house and anything else he wanted – just not today. All offices were closed for Christmas; he would have to wait until the following day. Another barrage of obscenities and accusations was Tom's response; Ariel fled to the corridor, sobbing uncontrollably.

What had she done to him this time? That old familiar mantle of guilt abruptly dropped, permeating her very being. Edythe was correct; so was Roger; she was totally at fault, not worthy of any good whatsoever, and now she had dragged Tom down, again. It was absolutely her fault. Doctors, specialists, surgeons, nurses and hospital staff were all good people, well trained and highly capable. They had all performed professionally with care and concern. Tom was failing. She ... Ariel ... had failed; she alone was to blame.

Tears flowed freely and silently as her mind spun wildly searching for some hope of comforting Tom and giving him some small measure of peace. Finally she heard through her confusion and misery. *"Be still, and know that I am God."*

"I will never leave you nor forsake you." A small measure of calm returned. Those very promises had also surfaced after Tom's iliostomy surgery when his survival was not thought possible. She had been desperate then as well, and God had answered. She was not alone.

Three days later hospital staff made quite clear Tom was medically fit for discharge. It was also clear to everyone Ariel could not manage him at home in his current mental state. Efforts to locate a care center were totally unsuccessful; hospitals were clearing as many beds as possible in anticipation of holiday need. The one available bed within a 50-mile radius was in the farthest section of town from where Ariel and Tom lived; provided the lowest level of care imaginable. With no alternative choices to be had, he was transferred to that facility late afternoon of December 29th, by wheelchair ambulance. Snow fell heavily; roads were slick and traffic badly snarled. Ariel had no idea where the facility was actually located, only an unfamiliar street address. A small dark sign under a snow-covered branch finally identified the site.

Tom was rolled in and placed in a bed. Personnel were cheerful and most pleasant; the facility was well appointed and beautifully decorated. Actual care was quite another matter

No staff bothered with any form of personal patient care for Tom, attention to or even acknowledgment of his still-seeping incision, ostomy appliance, or sufficient blankets for warmth. Ariel raced to a nearby store to purchase long-sleeve shirts and brought bedding from home along with more warm clothing.

Tom seemed to re-establish connection with reality, however, and following the evening meal, definitely did not wish to stay there. He endured a strenuous therapy session and two nights on a hard-surface bed with no padding or adequate room heat.

Qualified physician evaluation of his condition was alleged to be required for discharge; no physician was available. That individual was apparently on vacation, not returning until after New Years Day. Tom could not leave without that evaluation, and Medicare would not pay the bill. He simply was not allowed to leave.

Quietly, but firmly, Ariel stated patient rights under the law; that lacking a Superior Court order to the contrary, Tom could not be held in the facility against his will. He most definitely did not wish to remain.

She then demanded the bill for his two plus days. There was much stuttering and stammering from staff, but a dollar figure was finally produced. Ariel wrote out her check, loaded Tom and his possessions into the truck and they were home in good time to greet the New Year.

He was delighted; there was no more ranting, raving or crabbiness. Had a cold, hard look at a few residents at that care facility triggered his turn-around? That was, and remains, unknown; but he was absolutely pleased to be at home, in his own bed, and kitties hungry for attention. He thanked Ariel over and over for bringing him home and for all the care she continued to give him, day after day, endlessly. Ariel just smiled, stroked his face softly and assured him of her love and desire for him to just rest, please eat, and…heal.

The care facility refused to release Tom's hospital discharge orders, original documents or copies, despite telephone requests, and statutory requirement to provide those to patients. She didn't realistically have the time to go through any lengthy processes; orders were needed for Tom's care right then not later. Ariel pulled forms from her computer, completed and hand-carried those to the hospital to obtain copies of the hospital discharge orders. She had them in hand within minutes, including surgeon notes from the procedure. Those were very revealing; Tom's very life had once more teetered dangerously on the edge, for certain.

Alarmingly, she discovered significant changes had been made to Tom's medication dosages during hospitalization. That information had been kept from both Tom and Ariel; not known until she obtained the full hospital record. The withholding of significant prescription and dosage information undoubtedly constituted malpractice. Ariel did not pursue that however, having quite enough on her plate caring for Tom.

Damage resulting from that facility's actions could not be reversed. Taking legal action would only have consumed more time and caused Tom stress which he did not need at any time, and certainly not then. Also, Ariel knew only too well how much time and money such a malpractice suit would require to pursue.

During January Tom's post-operative condition improved slightly. His primary care physician was not overly pleased about his determination to undergo this last procedure and particularly without any input from her. At his mid-January check-up she sent him for several tests at two different and quite separate locations.

This January was extremely cold, icy conditions prevailed; not especially good for an already weakened patient to be in/out of vehicles and wheelchairs, carted from one facility to another, experiencing long waiting periods and becoming steadily weaker and more weary. All those tests extracted a heavy toll, while providing no new helpful or significantly informative data.

Yet another test procedure a few days later resulted only in additional stress, a long wait period and little if any useful information.

In early February, Tom's appetite waned again; he slept more and more, steadily declining, and losing even more weight. Once again, he did not choose to eat, finally accepting only small portions of milk shakes Ariel made with ice cream, chocolate syrup, whole milk and a powdered nutrition supplement. Valiant efforts met minimal success. Only the barest small amounts were consumed.

Tom continued to weaken; organ failure was again obvious, even to the lay observer. Weight loss was alarming; he was virtually skeletal. He quit taking calls from his good friends, barely rousing for bathing and meal attempts, wanting only to rest with his favorite kitty beside him.

Ariel kept trying valiantly to get some nourishment into him; but, finally had to admit her efforts were in vain. Once again her prayers were that Tom be taken home peacefully and without any more pain.

She took great comfort in recalling Tom's April 2010 quiet declaration, that while just looking out at birds in the yard, he had a significant experience. He shared that in a matter-of-fact manner. "It just came to me, watching those robins; I do believe in God," had been quite simply and softly voiced.

There had been no angel choir, trumpet blasts or rolls of thunder; that calm assurance was quite sufficient.

Late February brought absolute certainty that Tom was dying; there would be no reprieve this time. Jim arrived the wee hours of February 28th, and Tom not only recognized him but was able to speak a bit. Later that morning they had a good, if slightly interrupted conversation. Jim was seated on a low stool at his bedside, and Tom drifted in and out of consciousness. Ariel treated his still-seeping incision, addressed his decreased urinary and ostomy needs, bathed him and attempted to ensure he was warm, gently holding his hands. A few sips of milkshake and a little water were all he consumed. She massaged his arms and legs with lotions, washed his face and neck gently. All clothing was refused with unexpected strength.

Tom seemed to rally somewhat with Jim present, and insisted he would be just fine; Ariel was to pick up the mail, deliver items to the church office, and get out of the house for a while. He was somehow aware she had not done so for several days. Looking at Jim and then Ariel, he again insisted she get back out in public, with old friends, meet new people, live a full life. He was dying; she was not. She was to find someone, or at least allow someone to find her and live fully.

Ariel silently acknowledged shushing him now was futile; he was giving her marching orders. She stroked his cheek softly and kissed him, assured him she loved him and God loved him. He smiled slightly and closed his eyes, breathing lightly and shallowly. Kitty lay quietly at his feet tucked under the sheet.

Jim sat at the bedside, assured Ariel he didn't need anything and would call her immediately should there be any change or if Tom roused and wanted her for anything.

So she gently rubbed his shoulders, stroked his cheek again and kissed him a temporary 'good-bye' with more assurances she loved him and would be back very soon. Reluctantly she drove away. Jim sat by Tom's bed, only leaving briefly for a call to assure his wife he had arrived safely, while moving laundry from washer to dryer. He was not away from Tom's bedside for more than 2 or 3 minutes.

Ariel's cell phone rang as she was returning home. "I think Tom's gone," was all Jim said; with "I'll be right there" her reply.

Prayers of thanksgiving rose immediately and almost automatically. It all seemed so utterly unreal. She had voiced her farewells, assurances that they would be together again, and prayers for his peace and freedom from the anxiety and pain so often in past years, months, weeks, days and even recent hours. Tom's actual passing was almost anti-climactic. Her mind went dull, muscles somehow responded to visuals and she managed the remaining short drive home. Were other hands or angel wings guiding her? There must have been.

She immediately fell into her automatic 'take care of everything' behavioral mode. The ever-present stethoscope and blood pressure monitor only confirmed what she already knew. Years of listening closely for the irregular heartbeat now met only silence; pressure cuff registered 'error'. She telephoned the nurse who had visited earlier that morning to return now, pronounce and set all the wheels in motion.

Tom's wish of years earlier had been granted. He had died peacefully at home, favorite kitty under the covers, sleeping at his feet. Ariel was the widow she had never, ever wished to be.

The Home Health nurse returned, pronounced, notified the cremation entity, and expressed her sympathies. Everything seemed surreal, occurring in a fog. Ariel kissed Tom's still-warm forehead, and tucked the sheet around his shoulders. Kitty had fled, nowhere to be seen.

The crematory representatives arrived, wheeled their gurney down the hallway and positioned the black body-bag alongside Tom on the bed. Ariel pulled away the covers, replaced them with the blue and white afghan that had accompanied him on so many transports to emergency and provided a bit of home during hospitalizations. Even though it could provide no warmth or comfort now, she felt it only right that it be with him, regardless. A final kiss, silent prayer and unheard whispered assurance they would be together again, she relinquished her Tom to the attendants. No tears; those would come later.

She and Jim stood at the door as the gurney with Tom's body was rolled across the broad brick porch she and Tom had built, and was loaded into the waiting transport van. They watched as the vehicle slowly turned at the corner and disappeared. Turning back toward the door, they clung to each other for a bit, hoping to both give and gain a bit of comfort and strength. Ariel had lost her husband, her friend, her love; Jim the only real dad he had ever known.

So, Now What?

Ariel wasn't at all certain what lay ahead for her now. This was another entirely new path – widowhood. It apparently didn't come with any manual or set of instructions.

Her early years had been a wilderness of unidentified fear that lasted well into adulthood. She had always thought it was only in her mind, and due to her own inadequacies; that no cause actually existed. As young children her daughters had spent one night in Edythe's care, endured wild nightmares for weeks, and were unable to identify any cause of fear, just that they were terrified. Ariel had finally realized she had not dreamed the unnamed terror. Edythe was the source. However, despite that omnipresent fear, Edythe's constant disapproval and criticism, Dad had attempted mitigation as best he dared. He had been careful always to avoid showing too much care or support for Ariel lest Edythe determine he had somehow slipped out of her control and seek to have him re-committed to whatever mental institution she might select. That pattern was far too well established by the time laws were changed that would have thwarted her ability to carry out her unspoken, but known threat.

Her marriage to Roger had been a disaster just waiting to explode one way or another; they never really had a chance. Neither had any concept of living in close contact or harmony with other people. Their childhood homes were anything but open, loving or communicative. Both had very dominant maternal figures, with quite submissive fathers. Roger sought total control over Ariel similar to his mother's control of his father and of him.

Ariel was determined to be as opposite Edythe as possible; to be the submissive, compliant wife, not ever challenging her spouse. She put aside expressing any personal wishes or expectations in any way whatever. However, she lacked the basic characteristic ability to accomplish that degree of submission over the long term. Her innate curiosity, intelligence and hunger for learning prevented her from being totally subservient to anyone else's demands.

Roger shared many of the abnormal and negative personality traits of both Edythe, and the controlling characteristics of his own mother. She was quite fond of Ariel, but also demanding in many ways. Both women were strong controlling personalities.

The familiar negativity had developed into what Ariel firmly believed to be absolutely true until she slipped out from under her marriage vows. That brief affair enabled her to trust herself enough to escape, and become not only a better, but more loving person. That she and Tom had found each other, been so good for each other, would never have been possible without it.

Roger demanded his personal freedom to come and go at will, pursuing individual goals outside marriage and home. He expected Ariel to fully support him in anything and everything he wanted. His wishes were to prevail at all times and in all circumstances.

His father was largely submissive; a recovering alcoholic by the time Ariel met him, and a quite sensitive, private person, although that trait was closely guarded. He, and also his father, attempted vainly to counsel Roger regarding relationships, while supporting Ariel and the children whenever possible.

Roger lacked self control, especially with respect to finances, and absolutely no ability to manage money. He even failed in efforts to achieve bankruptcy status due to his refusal to follow court orders.

Only after meeting and marrying Tom did she begin to gain a better understanding of having accepted years of blame and humiliation unreasonably placed by both Edythe and Roger.

Ariel was single for nearly four years before marrying Tom; and only doing so with sincere trepidation, but great hope. He was a rock, and unafraid to show his love for her, open affection, support, companionship and great sharing of plans and dreams. He was proud of her and made that known; he liked taking her out, being seen with her, and wanted her at his side.

They had thoroughly enjoyed each others' company; not always agreeing, but finding common ground with open communication. He had been her strength and much-needed support, allowing Ariel to heal emotionally and gain a degree to self-worth. When his physical health deteriorated, Ariel became the one on whom Tom leaned for support emotionally and physically. Ariel was his advocate, caregiver and spokesperson. Theirs was an absolutely good marriage, lasting thirty-one years, severely altered and cut short only by his health problems. His passing had finally become a given, fully expected, but nonetheless devastating for Ariel. He had been through far too many years of seizure episodes, gastro-intestinal bleeds, heart problems and surgeries, additional critical invasive procedures, and short-term life expectancies. His ultimate death left Ariel devastated, though she would never have wanted him to physically survive longer under existing conditions.

She met each day in her usual manner, always smiling in public, and never mentioning the enormous void in her daily life, always assuring everyone she was doing quite well. Tom had been adamant about her not holing up in the house after he went. His passing had been eminent on many occasions, but following the final procedure in 2012, his attention focused intensely on what he wanted her to do with the rest of her life. His one regret was not providing for her as well financially as he had wanted.

They had planned and hoped for more travel; all cancelled by his health situations. He now wanted her to be able to do that for both of them. Decades of seizure incidents, following by cardio and intestinal conditions had initially prevented his purchase of insurance; with prohibitively high premium costs dashing his hopes when pre-existing health conditions could no longer exclude coverage. Her financial situation could have been better, certainly; however, it could also have been far worse without his efforts on her behalf. Terms of his unplanned medical retirement from the finance industry had ensured full lifetime medical coverage for both. That, in and of itself, had proven an invaluable asset. The corporate life insurance policy was not large, but provided her some financial stability and eased her transition in becoming a single person again.

Tom had also been exceedingly clear that Ariel was not to remain alone the rest of her life; she was to find someone or at the very least allow someone to find her. She was to be a little careful in this matter but definitely to be an active and outgoing person. He wanted her to be in a good relationship with a healthy, pleasant, happy and close companion, if not a spouse. He had clearly repeated that wish for her on numerous occasions, in hospitals to various physicians and nurses, to ministers who made calls on him, and over and over to Ariel. There was no doubt in his mind whatsoever.

Ariel's mind, on the other hand, there was not just doubt, but lack of any desire to even consider such a thing. Tom was her friend and her love. They had shared both responsibilities and enjoyment.

Now she was on her own again and unsure how to build a life for herself in this new situation. She had some church activities and choir played an important part in filling her schedule. One evening a week, and Sunday mornings, there was adult conversation, the joy of singing, and words of inspiration to mull over and consider. That helped a great deal. She also continued the process of clearing out miscellaneous personal and household items that truly just constituted extraneous "stuff". Boxes were filled with household goods, clothing, unopened food containers and all donated to the community food and clothing bank.

The years of care giving, rushing to emergency rooms in the dead of night, intensive care unit vigils, struggles coping with series of medical problems and dealing with barriers to diagnoses had taken their toll. She was physically, spiritually and mentally exhausted. There were mornings she didn't want to do a solitary thing. Getting out of bed was virtually impossible. Making coffee a major hurdle; turning a newspaper page loomed ominously as too much to accomplish. A grapefruit resting on the kitchen counter needed to be cut with the knife beside it and simply put on the adjoining plate. She just sat, too lethargic to even get off the couch and prepare a small breakfast.

Would she ever again have the energy and ability to perform even simple tasks? Much less to walk for miles, ride her bicycle, mow lawns and prune trees?

Ariel contemplated her bare feet and the scars from rocks fallen on, stumbled over, hauled by truck and built into garden edging, porches and water features. Old marks on her legs were reminders of bicycle spills, logs hauled from creeks and lakes for garden projects as well as firewood. Encounters with concrete blocks in building the Barbaria house, retaining walls and patios had left their marks as well. Now just cutting into a piece of fruit was too large a task to accomplish.

She had done considerable masonry work using rock, brick and pavers, mixing concrete or mortar evenings after work and weekends. Stone had been collected from various sites to construct a water fall and pond; now even cleaning that loomed too large a task. Could she even lift a single brick now? That she was physically and emotionally worn down was a given. The struggle to keep Tom alive and at least relatively healthy at times had lasted more that six years; she had been a 24/7 caregiver for much of that time. During the last years even leaving the house to pick up mail, buy groceries and make other necessary purchases required planning worthy of a military operation. Tom's doctors' office appointments filled calendar pages during times he was not hospitalized.

Strength returned in tiny increments and the process of figuring out her future began. She resumed painting a bit, initially completing a canvas that had remained on the easel for nearly five years. It was so long since there had been time to squeeze out color, add medium and actually dip a brush; it felt more than a little strange, but also rather nice.

Writing came next. There was so much swirling in Ariel's heart and head. She needed to put all that down in text, sort it out, and replace the years of Ted's medical ups and downs with calm, logic and reason. She had to get rid of the "what ifs" and "perhaps I should have" doubts, put it all on paper and close that painful chapter of Tom's life and hers. He was without pain and at peace. She should be as well, even as she grudgingly accepted the unwelcome widowhood.

So many maintenance tasks had been put off during Tom's last years, and at last she slowly began to address those. She 'de-mossed' the roof, and checked for any potential problems, firmly nailing down any piece that could possibly be impacted by high winds. Neighbors were aghast to see her on the roof, hammer in hand; but then, she had done that all before, not permitting Tom to climb ladders, ever. His seizures had been totally random, and a roof was certainly the last place he needed to be. But, he had been there to watch out for her, and that had always been a great comfort.

She also had flooring replaced in the kitchen, utility and small bathroom, taking out and repainting mop-boards, which saved costs; the entire house interior looked considerably more current.

Selling this house and moving, somewhere, was much on her mind. It was more square footage than she needed and on an over-sized corner lot with considerable landscaping to maintain. Granted, she had done the digging, planting, pruning, placing of patio blocks and mixing concrete to set the rock borders lining it all. She had also leveled the lawns, maintained them throughout the years and had both stripped, soil added and re-seeded. While she addressed those outdoor tasks, Tom had supported her, prepared meals, vacuumed floors and always had a glass of chilled wine waiting.

Together, she and Tom had built the large front porch. She designed the expansion, chipped out the old concrete, built the forms and hauled rock for fill. Tom opened mortar bags, and kept the mud moist while she set paving brick. He had adjusted over the years to her taking on building projects and managing to complete them, even when he hadn't a clue as to the plan she had. He simply could not visualize at all, but gracefully waited for the project to take form, lending what physical support he could.

The chimney had also been repaired, facing it with basalt. Again Tom had kept the mortar pliable, filling small buckets that she pulled up to set the stones she had gathered, sorted, arranged by size and hauled up to the roof one bucket at a time. That not only preserved the chimney itself, but definitely improved the general appearance of the real property.

The fall of 2012 had been warm late enough to allow for repair of cracks in the driveway. Tom had been able to sit out in the garage for short periods, watch the progress and talk. That had been the final project undertaken. Ariel was glad it was completed when clearing snow that winter and her shovel no longer slammed harshly into raised concrete chunks.

She had no family closer than 135 miles and no real friends. There were many very good acquaintances, yes; but, any true close friends she might call on for support or help? No, not really. There had been little opportunity to form friendships; doing so requires time and attention. Her days and nights had been fully filled with Tom's care for several years, in addition to all house and yard maintenance. With their marriage Tom's friends had become hers, and quite naturally those connections no longer existed in the same manner they had during his lifetime.

Her neighbors were very pleasant and one couple in particular had been helpful far above and beyond during Tom's many hospital stays. They were excellent neighbors and good acquaintances, but not close friends; and much younger with both family and good friends nearby. She simply did not fit in other than in casual settings.

That was not exactly a new situation for Ariel. Edythe had not allowed her to maintain any childhood or school friendships for any significant time, deeming each such person unsuitable for a variety of reasons. Workplace associations, while close for a time, gradually cease as employment areas change, despite the best intentions of all. Roger had not permitted her the freedom of forming friendships in their neighborhoods or even churches.

The one exception had been Helene who took care of the children while Ariel worked, cheerfully ironed baskets of laundry while watching television, and encouraged Ariel's painting. She finally accepted some compensation for childcare and ironing; and Ariel provided her transportation for shopping and appointments. They spent significant time drinking coffee and talking during evening hours as her husband worked swing shift and Roger was rarely present.

He had objected strenuously to their close association, though neither paid him much heed. He was seldom around anyway, preferring to spend off-work hours at the local fire station. Ariel maintained contact with this friend despite relocating; however, she had passed away several years before.

There was plenty to do to occupy Ariel's time; the list of 'things to do' kept growing item by item, despite many being accomplished and crossed off. Writing the lists and crossing out items accomplished helped her stay focused and moving toward unidentified goals.

She truly longed for friendship, good conversation and sharing of experiences and ideas. Tom had been so adamant that she find that very friendship and companionship. But, where? She certainly wasn't going to start hanging out at bars; nor was she going to seek companionship of any sort on the internet. Moving from the area, perhaps to a small town, and just plunging into a completely new environment looked like a real and practical possibility.

Jillian and her long time companion treated Ariel to a community theater production in a town near where they lived, and all enjoyed a very pleasant evening out. That little community had several churches, very limited shopping, but a very active theater group and a few art galleries. She had thoroughly enjoyed the community theater productions in which she had roles during her time while a 'single' in Wenatchee years before.

Possibly she might find some opportunities, acting, working props, or with general production. Housing could be iffy, but surely there must be something both livable and reasonable. Initial inquiries failed to produce much if anything in the way of possibilities.

Ariel checked into available housing in a small college city also with an eye toward completing her bachelor's degree. This town also had an active community theater, numerous art galleries and was very bicycle friendly. Housing costs, however, were completely out of sight, especially in light of any reasonable expectations of selling her house. Preliminary appraisal by a real estate agent only served to confirm the soft resale market at the time; plans to sell were put on hold.

The investment company representative who handled her simple IRA account for years had repeatedly urged her to meet with him for a full review of what funds she did have, and plan for her financial future. There had not been time while Tom's health was her major concern. Now there was. He was able to put together an annuity using her long-term whole life policy, some savings to provide a set amount deposited to her checking account each month.

Amending her IRA and consolidating bits and pieces of other funds produced an additional automatic monthly deposit, which together with the widow's portion from Tom's retirement plan and her social security, provided enough to live on each month. She still had some funds in savings to cover reasonable emergencies that might arise. There would not be the travel she had hoped for, but neither would she be out on the street. Pieces began coming together in creating a new chapter.

The question of new friendships and possible companionship remained wide open.

Details and More Details

Even the death of one's love does eventually evolve into dealing with scores and more of seemingly endless minor details. Arrangements need to be made, friends, relatives and various entities to be apprised of his passing, claims filed, name changes made, funds transferred; and on it goes. Ariel was thankful for the years of working in banking, insurance offices, the courts and law firms, even wholesale and retail marketing. All those experiences were of value in dealing with her new reality.

Helpful as her varied career experiences were, she missed being able to discuss things with Tom most of all. They had not always agreed, but were able to talk about anything and everything, consider various possibilities, and reach decisions. Now there was no discussion, no input from anyone else, no bouncing of ideas off each other and consideration of questions from different aspects. It was an incredibly lonely time with prayers for wisdom and guidance even more than for comfort.

She was grateful Tom had purchased the two burial plots so many years ago; it was one matter she didn't have to deal with. Cremation arrangements had been made years earlier when he had been released from hospital with the three to five-day life expectancy. That was another matter already addressed.

There was, however, the matter of an inurnment service; date and time, notification to friends and family members, someone to conduct the services. Tom had been absolutely adamant about keeping everything simple and not spending even one dime unnecessarily. At least there was no question as to his wishes; those had been quite clear and voiced repeatedly to relatives and frequently to Ariel.

His family now consisted of a very few elderly siblings, Rose's daughters and their families, her son Jim, Susan and their boys; and Ariel's son, daughters, and families. He had no biological children, and none formally adopted. She knew his two long-term close friends would want to attend any services, and neither was in particularly good health. There were old acquaintances from boating and yacht club days as well, but at least they were fairly local.

During March and into April, snow was still falling heavily in the mountains over which most people would need to travel, with the passes closing frequently either for actual avalanches or control. Only her son and Jim were of ages for whom mountain winter travel was not problematic. Elderly relatives and older friends on the coastal side of the Cascades were not particularly good candidates for bad weather driving.

Standing outdoors in stiff winds, perhaps in snow or rain, also did not seem logical or very practical. In addition, Ariel's eldest grandson was studying in Italy, granddaughter and her fiancé were traveling through Europe and Asia; Jillian was also scheduled for a two-week trip to Italy. When could a graveside service be scheduled allowing those interested to attend? When would everyone be back on the continent, weather relatively decent, with the fewest major calendar conflicts? A question begging answer.

Ariel and Jillian finally selected May 18th, avoiding holiday weekends, allowing for planned returns to the U.S., and hopefully avoiding most extremes of weather.

Then Ariel discovered the only clergy person she knew in the area had fully retired and was no longer available. Pastor of her local church had only met Tom once, and that when he was sitting in the truck waiting for her. He didn't know Tom at all, and she truly did not expect him to travel half-way across the state to conduct a brief service at which she would be the only person he knew. She also knew for certain that Tom would consider that a totally unnecessary expenditure, not expecting a minister to provide uncompensated services.

Ariel pondered this question, approaching it from several aspects before deciding to conduct the inurnment service herself. She wrote, edited and re-edited the homily, prepared the memorial folder, ordered and transported the grave marker in marble as similar to Rose's as she could find.

Two quick trips to meet with the cemetery representatives were required, along with payment of obviously inflated fees and set the inurnment schedule.

She also designed and wrote text for the folder. A photo of Tom in his Navy uniform graced the cover, giving his date of birth above the picture, date of his setting foot on his upward path toward peace and answers to his myriad of questions below.

For years he had questioned events both local and global, asking why God allowed them. At last he had reluctantly accepted that we simply have to wait for some answers and don't get all of them here on earth. Ariel smiled to herself recalling the numerous occasions Tom had given up searching and agreed a question had to be added to his every-growing list.

The Apostles' Creed, Psalm 23 and Lord's Prayer were printed on the back; a brief life history and his family information inside. A large white azalea was purchased as the sole floral tribute and given to Tom's step-daughter for her garden.

Tom had been absolutely adamant over several years that no money be, in his terms, *'wasted' on his 'planting'*. "You just drop me in the ground, and go have a drink", was his oft-repeated and clearly stated instruction. Sorry Tom, but it was not going to be done quite that simply and easily.

She included a notation in the folder than any memorial tributes would most appropriately be to his favorite animal shelter or another of an individual's choice. That did happen, contributions were made, and shelters most grateful.

Ariel drafted, edited and re-edited the homily, wanting to reflect Tom's life experiences, military and community service, struggles with health, enjoyment of family and friends, great love of animals and eventual acceptance of God in his life. Could she possibly present this at his graveside? Copies were provided for Jim, Jillian and Ryan in the event she could not manage.

Not one of them expected her to get through even part of it. Conducting the inurnment service, giving a homily, and properly concluding all that? Her role should be that of 'widow', being consoled, not consoling.

However, they underestimated Ariel's core strength in dealing with whatever a situation was at any given time during her entire life, processing information and determining what needed to be accomplished, and her stoic ability to maintain composure under stress. She had faced so much fear, psychological and physical threats, her own and Tom's health crises and desperate decisions over her lifetime, while keeping emotions firmly in check; she would quite simply do this. And indeed, she did.

Difficult to the utmost, Ariel greeted each person upon arrival. Sons, daughters and grandchildren circulated among attendees, made introductions, distributed the folders and minded the guest book. Near the appointed time, she stepped to the front of the group, stood beside Tom's urn, opened her folder and delivered the homily successfully. She felt Tom's arm around her shoulders as he softly whispered, "go on, you're ok, you can do this".

And she did. All joined in the Lords' Prayer at conclusion after which many wonderful memories of Tom were shared. Ariel learned several interesting incidents of his early years she had never before heard. Tears were held in abeyance only by sheer force of will.

Gretchen and her family, with Jim and family, had prepared a splendid buffet which not only fed people physically, but emotionally as more memories were shared over delicious food. Ariel was amazed at the number of persons having made special effort to attend; old friends of Tom's she hadn't seen in decades, and mutual friends. Among them was Richard from many years past, with whom she had worked in Seattle. He and partner James, who had passed away, were wonderfully supportive during her single years in Wenatchee. Both had been so pleased when Tom came into Ariel's life.

It truly was a great send-off for Tom and she felt he would have been quite pleased, even while insisting all that fuss was totally unnecessary; they should all have just gone to a local tavern.

It was not until she settled into her little convertible, adjusted sun glasses, mirrors, secured her seat-belt and actually started down the highway toward home that the weight of this day crashed down on her. She had held it all together, emotions in complete control while greeting friends and family, conducting the brief service, sharing more memories and stories, thanking one and all for their presence and condolences.

She had learned so much more of Tom's earlier years, anecdotes from his childhood and younger years, shared great memories and hugs, made it through the service and reception with composure.

She even spoke briefly with Roger, and thanked him for his attendance, despite complete lack of sincerity. He had asked Ryan if he could attend, and of course Ariel had not objected. Why he wanted to attend was a question, but it was a rather public place after all. Had that been difficult? More so than she wished to admit, even to herself. Toward him she felt nothing but regret over his wasted opportunities and inability to embrace life. He was in poor health, both physically and from all indications, emotionally as well. Any changes following her escape from him did not appear to have been beneficial.

Ariel was exhausted, totally drained, and realized driving nearly three hours home was not a very intelligent idea. The kitties had plenty of food, water and good places to sleep. They weren't speaking to her anyway since Tom's passing, plainly blaming her for his absence.

She opted to accept Jillian's offer and headed there for the late afternoon and night. Driving home in the morning was undoubtedly a far more intelligent idea.

Jillian met her in the drive with a hug and only mild recriminations as to even considering a drive home, unloaded the few items needed, and poured her a stiff drink. They spent some time that evening relaxing in the hot tub before Ariel settled for the night on a comfortable couch with a purring kitty, very thankful she had heeded Jillian's advice about staying.

Her drive home in the morning was uneventful and quite pleasant in soft sunlight and warm breezes. The miles slipped by. Fields were green with new crops, cows munched contentedly in fresh pastures, birds soared overhead; warm sun shone on her shoulders.

Time to move forward, heed Tom's instructions and not hole up in the house with the cats.

All she had to do now was figure out how to do it.

SECTION VII

One Door Closed... Is there Another?...
How Might it Open?

Shortly before Christmas, nearly a year after Tom's passing, Ariel began to more seriously consider possibilities of at least staying for coffee after church services, perhaps becoming acquainted with fellow-congregants. She knew other choir members, but very few others. Her long time habit was to exit immediately after the benediction and rush home to care for Tom. Only a brief stop at the bakery to pick up some sweet roll or treat he might actually eat, and home. It had taken months for her to realize she did not need to hurry any more; it didn't matter one little bit when she got there. There truly was no one in her life to care when, or if, she returned.

Only the kitties were there; with shelter, food and water in addition to several soft beds for napping. Whether she returned promptly or not was of no concern to them or anyone else.

They had not yet forgiven her for taking their dad away and not returning him. There was precious little indication they might ever do so. Both spent most of their days outdoors, sleeping under the lilacs or on pillowed porch chairs. The full food and water dishes and clean litter boxes apparently constituted their only concern. One would occasionally look into the kitchen, but when Ariel opened the slider for entry, kitty immediately turned away, clearly indicating rejection of Ariel. So one Sunday she decided to stay.

She put her donation in the basket, took a coffee and stood off to the side; maintaining a smile, not initiating any conversation. Responding pleasantly when spoken to, but not initiating any conversation, she did not join any table grouping although empty chairs were available. This in itself was difficult, just standing around with people and not hurrying away, but she made herself do it.

After a few Sundays she found an empty chair at a table with a few women, but still simply responded to questions, not initiating a topic. These ladies usually sat together in services, generally in 'widows' row'.

A topic of table conversation one Sunday centered on a subject covered in a book Ariel had found particularly interesting, so she brought it to share the next week; careful to include her card as she did want the book returned.

An empty chair at her table was taken by the tall, quite handsome and impeccably dressed gentleman she had frequently noticed in the congregation. He asked if anyone minded his joining their conversation. Of course not; this was a gathering of widows. He was a most welcome addition to the group.

The general conversation touched on late husbands' military service and Ariel shared that hers had served in the Navy during Korea, and flown in the VP- Neptune aircraft doing aerial surveillance. So had the gentleman seated at her right. She received newsletters from Tom's Naval Air Neptune VP-2 retirees group and for whatever reason not discarded the latest one.

She brought the reunion newsletter for him the following week in the event he might be interested. He had again sought her out for coffee and they enjoyed a very pleasant chat.

Conversation around the tables on Sundays was lively, interesting and covered a wide range of topics, seldom if ever, the sermon. Each week she seemed to be joined by the same gentleman, eventually learning his name was Bradley and a bit of his background. He had been widowed for some three or more years, she for one. Casual chatting came easily in this group setting.

They also found themselves at the same table the evening of an auction raising funds for kids' summer camp. Ariel voluntarily filled the empty "Vanna White" role for the auctioneer when youth group members lost interest. So she walked about the room, holding up and displaying items for better viewing by the attendees while bids were solicited. Quite unexpectedly it was fun, just a bit like working art shows but without the responsibility of selling. She smiled broadly at one and all while walking about the hall with each item. More than a little shy about displaying her own donated painting, she just kept smiling. That time-honored practice of stand up tall and smile was once more in place. Her facial muscles actually ached when she finally finished; they had not been used much in recent months.

When cash donations were solicited, she returned to the table, her coffee cup and snippets of conversation with Bradley and a few others. Somehow they lingered at the table after others left and the crowd slowly dispersed. Successful bidders claimed their items, money was receipted, and the hall began to empty. They walked out to their cars together, still chatting, and wished each other a 'good night'. He did remark on her driving a very sporty vehicle, her little silver Miata.

Would anything further transpire? Ariel had no idea and thought probably not beyond this having been an unexpectedly pleasant evening. She had very nearly stayed home. Going to events alone was simply not much fun. Tom had never been much for social events or community involvement, generally attending church only when she sang solos, had a specific role in a cantata, or was part of a select ensemble. Her regular attendance at church services and singing in choirs were just a normal and regular habit.

Even when she had attended some event alone, Tom was there when she returned, welcoming and interested in her account of the evening. Returning to an empty house at night was not fun; no fear or apprehension, just not fun. Not even the kitties showed slightest concern or awareness, remaining curled up on their outdoor chair cushions. They no longer came into the house or looked to her for anything beyond kitty-crunchies and fresh water. Ariel had taken 'their dad' away and not brought him back home this last time; they no longer spoke to her.

Sunday morning following the youth camping auction again found Ariel sitting with the other widows at a big round table; soon joined by the handsome gentleman she now knew as Bradley. She had noticed him over a few years, sitting toward the front of the sanctuary, generally alone and occasionally with a younger couple. She hadn't known any names, and only located his through photos in the church directory, having forgotten after initial introductions and their pleasant conversation during the camping fundraising auction. She presumed the younger couple to be relatives, and would later learn they were indeed daughter and son-in-law who lived very near her own home.

Again, following the lively, interesting and varied conversation at the table, and departure of the ladies, Brad lingered as had Ariel. He turned toward her, still holding his now-empty cup, and with a somewhat hesitant smile, asked, "Would you ever consider having lunch or dinner with me?" Ariel nearly gasped out loud, but valiantly retained a façade of composure while her mind whirled.

What to say? How to answer?

During her years of being single, separated and finally divorced from Roger, she had consistently used a pre-programmed automatic response to invitations for dinner or drinks. "Oh, thank you so much for asking, it is ever so nice; but, I am involved with someone. I certainly would not wish to hurt his feelings, so I'm really not available; but, it was ever so nice of you to ask."

She had used her big grey cat Chester Arthur IV in maintaining a protective distance from the local men with whom she truly did not want any social contact whatever. In that small city she knew who they were, their backgrounds, and more often than not, their marital status and reputations. Some actually single were looking for cooks, nursing care, housekeepers, a meal ticket, sympathy over emotional baggage from past relationships, one-night-stands; and the married ones a little 'variety' in their lives. "No, but thank you; Chet and I are in a very close relationship." When they had inquired as to his identity and what he was involved with as they hadn't met him in this small city, her reply, "He's rather semi-retired, absolutely loves the outdoors and is really into hunting and climbing," sufficed well.

She had not damaged any fragile egos with her answer, but left open the distinct possibility Chet could be a very large muscular gun-packing logger-type person without actually saying so, or admitting he was a cat.

Tom had quickly seen through that (being himself the pet human of three felines), asked her to lunch, a cruise, wined, dined, solved her critical car problem, and married her. He also readily accepted her son despite Ryan's initial reluctance and formed an excellent relationship with Chet who absolutely adored Tom. A wonderful outcome for both humans and cat.

Okay, that was then, and this is now; a totally different scenario. What, indeed, was she going to answer? Her mind spun and whirled in confusion. Brad was well aware she was widowed and not involved with anyone. The "Chet", in this case a "Sam" ruse, would probably not work, besides, did she actually want it to? She truly didn't know how to answer, but certainly needed to respond in some reasonable and logical manner.

Seemingly from a distance Ariel heard what sounded very much like her voice, "Why, that sounds delightful; thank you for asking. I would very much like to."

What?!? Had she actually said that? What had just happened? Who had put those words in her mouth replacing the automatic refusal; however gentle, kindly meant and carefully worded. Wow, now what.

She gathered her swirling thoughts sufficiently to offer him her card with phone number, and they slowly started for the door, still talking. Brad grinned broadly as they parted company at their cars, and said he looked forward to calling her with his suggestions for dinner. An exact calendar date was also somewhat subject to a local university basketball game.

But this all sounded just like a date, didn't it. Oh my…and just how does one go out on a dinner date? It was nearly thirty-five years since Tom had invited her to their first lunch followed by dinners, a cruise and marriage.

Date and time were set in coordination with the local university basketball game. Ariel spent considerable time deciding what to wear, even fixing her hair more carefully and paying extra attention to make-up.

A small glass of wine helped to minimally calm her jangling nerves before having a stern conversation with herself. "You have observed this man in church for months, actually a few years, and conversed with him over a several weeks sharing a wide variety of ideas and thoughts. You have learned a bit about his military service which was quite like Tom's; his family background, and know him to be intelligent and conversant. Now, just what cause do you have to be so nervous?

You are doing precisely what Tom wanted, and actually ordered you to do. Calm down, and enjoy the evening, already."

OK, that's great advice; all that remains is to implement it, correct?

At precisely the time arranged, Brad's car appeared in her drive; he mounted the steps and crossed the porch. As always, looking like he just stepped out of a fine haberdashery. A quick glance in the oval wall mirror confirmed she had not summarily transformed into a warty-nosed witch or bag lady just as he rang the bell.

With only slightly shaking hand she opened the door. Virtually their first words, almost in unison, "Do you have any idea whatever how nervous I am?" and they both laughed. Brad had not been out with anyone other than his late wife in some sixty-plus years, and for Ariel it had been a mere thirty-five, plus. Sharing that helped ease the mutual awkwardness.

Brad had made reservations at a fine local steakhouse; the same one where Tom and Ariel had been regulars for over a dozen years. Service was always topnotch with excellent menu choices all perfectly prepared. Ariel had been there only once in the past year, having a salad and glass of wine at the bar so she could chat with an employee whose husband had also died. She had made numerous swift trips there during Tom's hospitalizations for his favorite baked potato soup, desperately trying anything and everything to get additional nourishment into him. He had been a favorite of virtually all the staff and they tucked cheery little notes into the bag along with the soup and crackers.

This evening the manager happened to be at the front desk as Brad held the door and entered with Ariel. He immediately grabbed Ariel in his arms, swung her up and around, planting kisses on both cheeks before placing her back on the floor.

Brad just stood there, dumfounded. What on earth was this? Who was this great big young guy who obviously knew Ariel quite well, greeting her so exuberantly?

And who really was this Ariel person, anyway, who seemed so reasonable and dignified at church, and now received this rather unusual and obviously friendly greeting at an excellent restaurant? What had he got himself into?

Back on her feet, Ariel quickly introduced Brad to the manager, who grasped his hand and clapped him heartily on the shoulder with the warmest of greetings. Brad wondered if all patrons here were greeted in like manner, but there really was an explanation.

The beaming manager quickly explained that Tom and Ariel had indeed been regulars for years. He was absolutely delighted to see her again, and especially in the company of a gentleman. He personally escorted them to their table, brought their menus and drinks, continuing to welcome them and express his pleasure. He also explained to Brad that he and his family lived only about three blocks from Ariel upon learning she had not moved.

Dinner was excellent, as expected. They talked and talked, sharing so many details of their lives, and found they really enjoyed each other's company. Their lives had been so very different with the exception of having the same numbers of children, boating, and making several moves for employment purposes.

Both had also been long-term care providers for spouses. Brad was most assuredly not looking for a meal ticket, nursing care, or psychological counseling. Neither was Ariel. Although her economic status would never come remotely near his; it was not a concern for either. Dinner lasted well over two hours by the clock, and mere minutes in their estimation.

Back in Ariel's drive, Brad hurried to open the door for her, again. She was so accustomed to the years of helping Tom into the passenger seat of his truck, loading walker or wheelchair, ensuring his safety belt was secured and then driving, it was very difficult for her to be comfortable as a pampered passenger. She had also carefully resisted the automatic application of a non-existent brake pedal during their short travel. Having a strong hand on her arm, allowing a car door to be opened and closed for her was completely unfamiliar after so many years.

Brad was absolutely and totally, a true gentleman in every way, not just in opening doors. Obviously it was his very nature to care for a lady, not a learned set of manners trotted out for special occasions. Ariel simply had to relax; she was not totally responsible for every aspect of someone else's life any more. Relax, enjoy, it's not only acceptable, but perfectly permissible. Try to put it into practice; not a simple matter.

Brad walked her to the door, of course, and saw it appropriately unlocked and open. They had not stopped talking since he had called for her, and could well have gone on for many more hours.

Ariel thanked him for the totally delightful evening and was highly tempted to ask him in to continue their conversation. Would that be proper? They had not stopped talking all evening, both hungry for adult conversation unrelated to family or medical problems. Tentative plans were in place for attending a theater production the following week.

This was a first date, and she certainly did not want him to think her too forward. So, better to say 'good-night' at the door. She sensed he could possibly feel a similar hesitancy as she thanked him again and expressed how much she had enjoyed dinner, their conversation, and the very pleasant, companionable evening. Brad expressed similar sentiments, and then with a soft shy smile asked if a hug might be possible.

Possible? Absolutely, and as their arms entwined Ariel felt she might possibly just melt into a puddle of total contentment. She hadn't been hugged by a strong healthy man in years; it felt so good; and he an expert. Nearly in unison once more, they said how good it felt to hug and be hugged. Both had missed that and good conversation more than nearly anything else for so very long. They finally said 'good-night' again and she waved from the doorway as he drove away.

So here she was, a little old widow lady, home from a very real dinner date with live theater on the calendar, having enjoyed a marvelously lovely evening and one of the best hugs ever. Never in any wildest imaginings or dream fantasies had she contemplated anything like this to be remotely possible. She had thought that part of her life over, forever.

Another delightful evening soon followed; another delicious dinner, great conversation, and an interesting live theater performance. Upon arriving home this evening she invited him in for a glass of wine and he accepted. They went right on talking and shared more of their lives as they sat on the couch and slowly sipped. Each had been a caregiver and gone through many stressful and turbulent experiences attempting to sustain spouses, provide loving comfort, and quality of life in addition to meeting medical needs.

Brad's late wife had been ill for several years, undergone a series of surgical procedures, endured pain and suffering for several years. He cared for her in their home until dementia developed, advanced, claiming her memory and cognizance. She still recognized Brad as her husband even after she entered a care facility. He was there the greater part of each day providing her personal care, feeding her meals, gently rubbing her feet and holding her hands. She had died peacefully, wrapped in his loving arms.

Ariel had been Tom's long-term caregiver, advocate through countless emergencies, hospitalizations, and 24/7 critical care nurse in their home.

Each had deep understanding and appreciation of what had been needed by their spouses and lovingly given; more than fulfilling each of their 'in sickness and in health' vows.

This conversation had more to do with future plans, dreams, hopes and expectations each held. Brad and his late wife had been married for fifty-six years, and until onset of her dementia enjoyed a classic, loving and excellent relationship, raised their family, and both had good careers.

Ariel had escaped and was finally able to divorce Roger after 23 years. She and Tom had over 31 very good and loving years together, before he had passed away. Tom had always needed someone in his life he could provide and care for, never looking for someone to take care of him. His concerns were always for her welfare, wanting only her happiness. That Ariel had spent years caring for him had been his major concern.

Even in his final weeks, Tom's concerns had been for her, not himself. He desperately strove to remain alive into March just so she would receive the full amount of that month's retirement check. Ariel's struggles were to restore his willingness to eat, recover and regain health.

He truly had not wanted to live after the iliostomy procedure, preferring to die. She despaired when medical experts depleted all known avenues and he was discharged from hospital with a three-to-five day life expectancy, only in compliance with his stated wishes to simply die at home.

At home with no help or instruction, a room full of critical care medical equipment and Tom unwilling to live, Ariel had turned all her desperation over to God, fully realizing Tom's life and hers were not within her control. Long hours after berating him about refusing nourishment, cutting short his own life and that she never wanted to be a widow, Ariel had fallen onto her bed convinced Tom was dying and the last thing she had done was to yell at him. Guilt overwhelmed; tears streamed.

Late the next day Tom had actually asked, ever so softly, if there was any chicken soup left, and if so, he would like some. Any left? Only a caldron-full. Wonder of wonders; eating and gaining strength, he lived another three and a half years, agreeing that God had not quite finished with him. Together they had circumvented that projected outcome to the total amazement of medicos.

Neither Brad nor Ariel was in any way, shape, or form, interested in re-marrying, and they each stated that most definitively. Ariel had worked with far too many legal situations in which a marriage between older persons, each with adult off-spring, horribly complicated eventual estate settlement matters.

She had soon learned there was nothing like the sniff of even a tiny inheritance to evoke the worst possible traits in some potential devisees. No way was she going to put anyone through that. Tom had no natural children and Rose's were all adults, well off and none adopted by Tom. His small estate had simply passed to her under community property statutes and surviving spousal clauses on accounts and investments.

Ariel had three, two daughters and one son. Jillian and Ryan insisted she spend any and all available assets she might ever have on herself and enjoying life. They did not expect or want any inheritance. Annie's potential response remained unknown as the subject had not been raised, and Ariel had precious little in financial assets anyway.

Contact with Annie had been limited at best for a significant time; Ariel responded to any phone calls, mainly on holidays, and conversation was kept light and cheerful. She did not initiate contact after Annie had exploded in a profane diatribe over Ariel's having resolved a virtually untenable situation involving Roger's mother and kitchen cabinet remodeling. Annie had horribly mismanaged and interfered with her grandmother's remodeling project. Ariel was finally successful in correcting the matter and having the work completed. She gathered all available data, contacted the State's Attorney General Office and the matter was quickly resolved. Her paralegal background was a great help in knowing where to go for answers and obtain resolution for her former mother-in-law who was extremely grateful. Annie's response was entirely different.

At her profane outburst, when she briefly halted for breath, Ariel informed her daughter quietly, but clearly that profanities and berating of her own mother was totally unacceptable, and would not be tolerated. She was much loved, but not particularly liked at that point. She was welcome to call at such time she could speak reasonably, but Ariel was not going to listen to any further profane tirades.

With that she had hung up the phone, drawn a deep breath and sat for some time contemplating what had occurred. The ensuing silence lasted over two years before Annie had contacted Ariel, quite pleasantly and kindly inquiring as to Tom's health.

Ariel's relationship with Edythe had never been pleasant, much less that of loving mother and daughter. Guilt was uppermost from earliest memory. Ariel's every word and deed was questioned, examined in minute detail and criticized. Nothing escaped Edythe's scrutiny, and everything Ariel said or did was suspect, initially, to be re-visited sometimes decades later.

Ariel had sought desperately to show her children she truly loved them; taught herself to express her love verbally and in action. Jillian and Ryan responded in what Ariel thought a normal manner. Even as an infant Annie refused to be cuddled, rocked or comforted allowing herself to be held only briefly, struggling to get down. Childhood bruises and scratches could be treated with cleaning, medication and bandages, but very little hugging or kissing; she was quickly off, and away on her own. That somewhat prickly and contrary demeanor consistently discouraged a close relationship. Could she possibly have been mildly autistic? Another question without answer.

Thereafter when Annie telephoned she was very pleasant, polite, and the conversation centered on her family, work and garden; nothing was ever mentioned about the profane tirade. It was as though no time had elapsed over those two years, and there had never been a problem. Ariel remained a bit cautious in conversing with Annie, limiting all subject matter to pleasantries. How she might react over and future property distribution was totally unknown.

Brad and Ariel were in complete agreement on this quite preliminary, but vitally important point of not marrying thus clearing away any possibility of confusion. No matter what, they were not heading toward any legal and/or binding arrangement. They were simply going to enjoy each other's company, have fun and live their lives to the fullest, somewhat reluctantly accepting that at their ages, they probably didn't have a whole lot of time to waste. Their mutual goal was to remain healthy, and live until they died – not sit in rocking chairs dwelling on aches and/or pains.

They talked of attending theater productions, dining at interesting places, bicycling, and he asked if she like to travel. Absolutely, mentioning the Pacific Rim tour and subsequent return to New Zealand and Australia with Tom; plans for Canadian and California trips, thwarted only by his illnesses and exacerbated medical problems.

While physically able and eager to do so, she simply could not afford much travel much beyond visiting Jillian or Ryan. Her hopes for an Alaska cruise had been firmly packed away.

Brad brightened significantly on hearing that a mere lack of finances held Ariel back from 'taking to the road'. He had traveled the globe with his family, worked in Asia establishing an off-shore corporate site, taken numerous cruises to far-flung places, and vacationed in Hawaii for years. He didn't plan to stop traveling as long as he could still place one foot in front of the other under his own power. He had also traveled extensively throughout North America for his business. Pleasure travels had been with family, which was fine and he had thoroughly enjoyed doing that.

Now widowed however, once a destination had been reached he was somewhat left to his own devices as they all trouped off on various activities.

Would she ever consider taking a trip with him? He wanted someone to be with, share and enjoy experiences with him. Would she consider that?

Oh my; would she? Absolutely, she would be delighted beyond words to have such a prospect to consider. That was a new totally unexpected possibility.

His next question was possible potential destinations. Did she have a passport? Yes. Was it current? Yes.

A wide grin was Brad's response.

What was happening? What might the future hold? She had smiled and even laughed more these two evenings alone, than in weeks or months. How had she and Brad managed to connect? Over coffee at church, yes; however, each had attended there for several years without exchanging more that the most casual nods of greeting. Had there been guidance from someone, somewhere? From what source had her unplanned, unscripted acceptance of his initial dinner invitation come?

Tom had virtually issued her marching orders several times over the years, first following his heart surgery, then the gastrointestinal procedure, and especially during his last months. She was to get out and find someone, or at least allow someone to find her; to live life fully with adventure, love and enjoyment—not be alone. She had consistently shushed him with a kiss, encouraged him to please just eat, heal and live. Theirs had been a completely satisfying and loving marriage; she had been utterly disinterested in ever being with anyone else for any reason.

Brad's marriage had been storybook classic, loving and mutually supportive, with a beautiful family, working together, playing together, also cut short by illnesses and death. They had married while he was still in the Navy. She had graduated her nurses training course, and upon his discharge, traveled across the country, started out hunting first jobs, scrimping, saving, and building their lives together. They endured problems, of course, all was not crystal-clear, cherry-blossom, ever-upward sailing, but they worked together in all endeavors. He enjoyed great success in business undertakings and she pursued a nursing career part-time with schedules arranged to accommodate raising their children.

What did the future hold for Brad and Ariel? Only time would reveal that – good, bad or indifferent. Somehow she hesitantly dared suspect it just might be very good. That happiness apple appeared to have quite unexpectedly come round a second time to provide them each another bite.

The old familiar guilt crept into Ariel's mind, creeping through tiny fissures in this newfound bliss. She was not worthy of such splendid opportunities and this kind, caring and delightful companion. Both Edythe and Roger had been quite adamant; she was undeserving of anything good.

She had also learned to lean on Old and New Testament promises of love, care and help; kindness, gentleness, guidance and compassion both in times of trouble and of great joy. Long-carried guilt ever-so-gradually dwindled as she had learned to let God handle things; everything bad in the universe was not her responsibility.

Ariel also reminded herself of Tom's love and delight in her and her survival after escaping Roger, accomplishments in career, music, art and mostly her love, support and caring. His sincere efforts at negating her first forty years had been significant; only tiny niggling doubts remained. Did she truly have any right to accept this opportunity for companionship, happiness and promise now before her? It was a question.

Was there more than a hint of heavenly guidance involved? Quite possibly, with sense of a soft breeze that just might have sprung from angel wings gently guiding and nudging them toward each other. Life itself began to be joyous.

Ariel had encountered so many hurdles during her lifetime, overcoming a highly diverse array of challenges, the last major one as Tom's advocate dealing with medical professionals, providing personal care during his many hospitalizations and 24/7 care at home. In conversations with his longtime friends, he insisted his survival was due to having his very own "Nurse Ratchet" in attendance. She learned that several months after his demise.

With his passing however, both old and new doubts crept in with a vengeance. What had she done, or not done, for or to, Tom? Had she omitted a treatment that could have helped? Had she not either demanded or forbidden a medication/test/treatment that might have changed his outcome? Even strongly worded statements by a number of medical professionals, many specialists, did not entirely suppress those doubts and second-guesses. The old negativity nibbled at her.

And then, Brad came into her life. Was she truly entitled to happiness, joy, or even… love? At her age?

Now well into her seventh decade Ariel was still trying to figure out just what she might expect in whatever number of years remained. She could never claim her life had been dull. Dire and dismal on occasion; a myriad medical problems, her own and Tom's, difficulties, happy and joyous interludes, exciting travel experiences, desperate times and even despair on occasion; but, dull? Never.

Looking back over those decades was at times painful; there had been so many mistakes, things she should have done differently or not done at all. God truly has a perfect will for us, as well as permissive will in granting us free will: to choose His way, or take our own path.

That Roger was a total error in judgment was undeniable; however, three children and four quite wonderful grandchildren were direct results of that choice. Would she ever have wanted to miss their very existence? Of course not.

Had she not escaped a bad marriage and been single, would she ever have met Tom? No, and to miss out there would not have been good in any way for either of them, or for Ryan. She had learned so much about life and her place in a loving relationship; all things she would never have wanted to miss out on, especially how love can truly grow in the most difficult of circumstances. Caring for Tom as his health declined provided valuable lessons in meeting physical and spiritual needs. Tom had found and openly declared his faith in God, passing peacefully in his knowledge of salvation. Ariel learned at last to simply trust more, turn her fears over to God in prayer and trust His will, both for herself and for Tom.

Learning to more fully trust God and His plans had not been all peace, sunshine, soft warm breezes and pretty flowers, but never boring. Life had been, and continued to be, a great adventure. Even in early childhood, she looked forward to what might be next. Even now, she was eager to see what lay ahead for her on earth, secure in knowing her ultimate future was established.

If not widowed, utterly contrary to her wishes, she would never have met Bradley and discovered another arena of wonderful experiences. They each might well have continued separately, at a distance in the familiar church sanctuary, sharing nothing more than polite, casual Sunday morning greetings.

Both widowed, they had been full time caregivers for extended periods, walked through the fires of fear, desperation and great sorrow. Certainly not young physically, they discovered youth of spirit neither had dreamed possible. They found totally unexpected happiness with plans only to spend whatever years remain enjoying each other's company, and sharing that gladness with others…spreading smiles everywhere.

She had strongly urged him to return to the choir, enjoyed for decades before a corporate promotion and transfer to California. When they returned, his wife's health deteriorated with numerous problems severely curtailing their participation in many previously enjoyed activities. He now insisted he was 'too old' and couldn't sing well enough to be part of that group again.

Ariel explained at bit sternly that he definitely was not too old, and his strong voice was needed. He had sung tenor for many years; Ariel's range had been that for decades. Now due to a lack of men singing, she was summarily relegated to baritone/bass. While possible on many numbers, that range was considerably lower than her comfort level, and his participation would benefit her as well as the entire group. And so, they soon sat together in the back (mens') row. Brad adjusted to singing bass, to great delight of the director and the assemblage. They also set about recruiting some 'real' basses and the choir grew quite nicely.

He had planned and fully arranged a family cruise months before beginning to spend time with Ariel. This was a British Isles trip beginning on the Southeast Coast of England, continuing northwesterly and then returning to London. Weather was typically rainy a good deal of the time, as rather expected. Historic sites were visited, including significant golf courses, castles and pubs.

While he was away cruising with his family, Ariel seized upon the opportunity to attack flower beds at his home. Those had been neglected for some time, partially due to his basic disinterest in gardening and also because he truly did not know which were flowers and which weeds. Consequently, they all – flowers and weeds - continued to grow. Lawns were mowed and carefully trimmed; hedges kept under control, but flower beds? Those were a different matter.

She thoroughly enjoyed bringing a bit of order to flower areas, dispatching all manner of weeds, and loosening the soil. A bit of peat moss also helped make things look nicer and retain moisture.

Before long it was time to meet Brad at the local airport, driving his SUV, not her little Miata. That would simply not have room for any suitcases, but nicely sufficient for two people.

Pulling up to the curb, she saw him standing alone with his luggage, shoulders slumped. That just didn't look right. What was wrong? With a big smile she jumped out and hurried to open the back.

Brad didn't say, 'hello – nice to see you' or anything. He wrapped his arms around her in a hug so hard she could scarcely breathe with, "I'm never, ever going anywhere without you." Wow. That what just about the greatest thing Ariel had ever heard.

His trip had been good in many ways and all had enjoyed family time together. It had also been long, and family all younger, going higher and farther on hikes that he cared to. Also, it had rained, rained, and rained – the British Isles after all. He was exhausted and very happy to be back home.

New Journeys?

Now to that question of their travel. Were they compatible enough to drive, fly or cruise somewhere together? Spend time at a chosen location, sightseeing, dining, etc., together, just the two of them, for perhaps two or more weeks? One way to find out –give it a try.

British Columbia was nearby, beautiful mountain scenery, hot springs and tourist attractions…a good place to start and just for a few days. If they could manage a short trip without major personality conflicts, murder or catastrophic problems, who only knew what might present in the future?

After that short jaunt into British Columbia to test potential compatibility, which included exploring an early island settlement, river ferry ride and visit to a beautiful golf course, with indication they just might return and play there. Ariel had yet to purchase clubs, or have any clue what to do with them. They sang harmony to a variety of well-known old songs on cd's, and talked and talked and talked … about everything.

Back home there were more enjoyable evenings of dinners, theater productions, bicycle rides and a variety of community activities in addition to church committees and choir, they were quite soon considered a 'couple' by their families, church members and other acquaintances. They had wonderful times together while each maintaining and also savoring time apart in their separate homes.

Ariel listed her real property for sale, continued the process of sorting, packing and donating 'stuff'. One 'moving sale' netted some needed cash and helped thin out accumulation. Brad willingly helped her conduct the sale also accompanying shoppers somewhat interested in the house.

Quite unexpectedly she found an over 55 gated community still being constructed. Close to shopping, banks, and only two miles from the church. Rent was higher than she would have preferred, however, the 2-bedroom/2-bath unit was good size—about ½ the square footage of the house—included locked garage with shelving, kitchen appliances, and a great walk-in closet off the master bedroom.

Real estate was not at all 'hot' at that particular time and now Ariel was faced with supporting two pieces of real property, her house and the condo on which she had put a deposit. That was not yet finished and ready for occupancy which provided her a little breathing space.

A couple then living in a South Hill lease/option badly-leaking structure discovered Ariel's house and fell madly in love with it. Now this relocation thing became serious. Another Moving Sale" cleared out still more furniture and general accumulation. More donations went to Valley Partners. Brad also provided tremendous help with this sale and shortly after began the process of moving Ariel into her new place. With his golf cart trailer, SUV and her little sports car everything was eventually relocated, to one place or another.

The kitties were provided good opportunity for new and safer homes with new humans. They were taken to the local humane society along with carriers, blankets, dishes, toys, bags of food and generous donations. Staff people assured Ariel these mature, very healthy and attractive kitties would soon find good homes.

Brad liked to spend a couple of weeks in a warm climate during the dark, dank days of a northern February. He preferred luxury resorts featuring a variety of local tour options, pools, beaches, and good choices of restaurants. He also liked warmer weather activities with travel by air, or car. Plans were implemented.

Going places and doing things; keep traveling and experiencing life; an excellent plan, one he had followed for years, and to which Ariel adapted very quickly.

They enjoyed Mexican resorts on the Caribbean, zip-lining on the West coast, cruising Alaskan waters, kayaking on local lakes and rivers, bicycling, water aerobics, live theater, family gatherings and of course, delightful dinners; all that in just a few months.

So, what is next on the agenda of life? One step and one day at a time is all any of us sees. Of one thing we can be certain…it will not be dull.

Life was proving far better in these later years than either had ever considered possible. Neither Brad nor Ariel had ever expected to find anyone with whom to share this time when their lives had seemed to be winding down.

Any 'winding down' did not appear to be looming closely on the horizon. If so, however, the 'winding' was turning out to be one fantastic and wonderfully loving trip.

458